HIGH WATER

HIGH WATER

PETER LING

CENTURY
London Sydney Auckland Johannesburg

Copyright © Peter Ling 1991

First published in Great Britain in 1991 by
Random Century Group
20 Vauxhall Bridge Road, London SW1V 2SA

Random Century Australia (Pty) Ltd
20 Alfred Street, Milsons Point, Sydney, NSW 2061
Australia

Century Hutchinson South Africa (Pty) Ltd
PO Box 337, Bergvlei 2012,
South Africa

Random Century New Zealand Ltd
PO Box 40–086, Glenfield, Auckland 10
New Zealand

The catalogue data record for this book is
available from the British Library

ISBN 0–7126–2144–X

Photoset by Deltatype Ltd, Ellesmere Port, Cheshire
Printed in Great Britain by
Mackays of Chatham PLC, Chatham, Kent

For Sheilah, with her husband's love

* * *

AUTHOR'S NOTE

The docklands of the Isle of Dogs have almost disappeared now – though there are a few small corners left for those who wish to look for them; in order to recreate the background to this story, I had to do a good deal of research, for which I must thank Christopher Lloyd and his staff at the Local History Collection of the Bancroft Library. I am also grateful for memoirs by local authors, such as *My Part of the River* by Grace Foakes (Futura) and *Ben's Limehouse* by Ben Thomas (Ragged School Books). Wherever public events are included, I have tried to be as accurate as possible.

But this is a novel, and I must explain that all the characters, and some places like The Three Jolly Watermen and the Jubilee Wharf, are fictitious; the dockworkers' guild which I have called 'The Brotherhood' is entirely imaginary, and has no connection with any actual organisation.

· —1— ·

Connor O'Dell sat in darkness, and waited; his hands tied behind him, the velvet hood almost choking him.

He could hear the faint murmur of voices behind a closed door, the sound of men engaged in serious discussion – until one voice, raised in sudden anger, exclaimed, 'Let's do it then! Bring him in, and get on with it!'

He knew the speaker – Ebenezer Judge's sharp, metallic tones were unmistakable. But then another voice cut in, not loudly but with such penetrating force that Connor could hear every word.

'There is only one way to go about these matters. We shall not act in haste – we shall follow the Rules exactly.'

A silence, before the low murmuring was resumed. He knew the second voice too. It was Ebenezer's father, the head of the Brotherhood – Marcus Judge.

Connor's worst enemy could not have accused him of cowardice. He feared no man, and was determined – even now, helpless and blindfolded as he was – that he would not give in without a struggle. However, at the sound of Marcus Judge's voice, the hairs on the back of his neck rose like the hackles of a dog.

The only other sound he could hear was a faint, continuous hiss; the noise of the gas-mantles burning in the wall-bracket – but no light filtered through the punishment hood. Other men had worn it before him – terrified men, awaiting the sentence of the Brotherhood; the smell of their sweaty fear was rank in his nostrils, making him want to vomit.

But he still had one chance left. He strained against the cords that chafed his wrists. It was Eb's brother, Joshua Judge, who had tied him up, and Josh had not troubled to knot the cards securely, so they had slipped loose – not much, but enough to give Connor some hope that he might get his hands

1

free. And then, by God, they'd see an Irishman fight. He had already managed to throw off one of the cords, but another still cut into his wrists, and he fought against time, trying to work it loose . . .

But there was no time left. He heard the door open, and then Eb's voice snarled, 'Come in. Take six paces straight ahead, then stop.'

For now, he had no choice but to obey.

The Inner Circle of the Brotherhood met once a month to deal with routine business, unless they were summoned to an extraordinary meeting, when some problem had to be settled without delay. This evening was such an occasion, to deal with an infringement of the Rules.

Connor held himself erect as he walked forward, out of darkness into darkness. He could hear the sound of men breathing, and he sensed them all around him.

Seated at the centre of a semi-circle, Marcus Judge addressed him in a voice as hard and unyielding as stone. 'It has come to our notice that when you signed as a new member of this Brotherhood, you gave a false name. What have you to say?'

Connor replied evenly, 'I did so.'

'Even though you knew this was against the Rules and Regulations of our Guild?'

'Yes.'

What was the point of arguing? He could hardly say: 'If I'd told you I was one of the O'Dell family – an Irish Catholic – would you have accepted me into your black, Bible-thumping Protestant Guild? Not you! You'd have seen me starve to death, sooner than give me a job shifting cargo off the boats.'

In theory, any man was free to apply for work as a docker but in practice, Connor knew that the labour-force was organised by this group of chapel-going, psalm-singing Nonconformists – all the more powerful because they operated in secret.

Like all the other dockers before him, Connor had sworn obedience to the Brotherhood, and taken an oath of silence. Every man accepted was given a brass tally, with his number on it. Each time a ship docked and a gang was needed to unload it, the numbers were drawn from a bag. If your number was called, you could go to work. If not – you went to bed hungry that night.

'Is it true that your name is Connor O'Dell? And that you are of the Roman persuasion?'

'It is true.'

There was a harsh, indrawn breath of anger from the men who surrounded him.

'You are well aware that no Popish idolaters are permitted to join this Guild . . . Empty his pockets.'

Two men moved in close to him, one at either side, and he felt hands digging into his jacket pockets. He knew they would take the tally from him – and something else, even more important. They would take back the 'claw' that had been given to him on the day he joined; no docker could do his job without the claw. It had a wooden handle like a corkscrew; projecting from it was a curved piece of steel, like a crowbar – a crowbar split into two sharp prongs, so it could be driven into the side of a crate, as a tool for leverage and lifting.

Connor heard the chink of metal on wood, as tally and claw were thrown on to the table. Then they fumbled in his trouser pockets, and he recoiled instinctively from the thrusting hands on his thighs. Roughly, they pulled out all the loose coins – silver and copper – that he had about him.

'You came into this Guild with nothing; the money you have made since then was made under false pretences. Now you leave us as you came – a beggar.' Marcus Judge's voice changed, as he rose to his feet. 'Connor O'Dell, you are hereby expelled from this Guild, upon the seventeenth day of October in the Year of Our Lord, nineteen hundred and twelve. You will remain hooded, so that you may not know which man administers your punishment. After that, you will be cast out into darkness, never again to be received within the Brotherhood.'

Connor heard him walk slowly away. At the door, he turned back to say, 'Now I leave you to the mercy of God Almighty.' The door closed.

'Right!' Eb's voice was thick with satisfaction. 'Get him.'

There was a sudden rush of air, and pain seared his back as a stick was brought down with full force across his shoulder-blades. It was lifted for another blow, and Connor knew the blows would be repeated until he fell to his knees and finished up helpless and humiliated at the feet of his enemies.

In a sudden spasm of rage, he tensed his muscles – and the last cord that bound him gave way. His hands were free. A furious shout went up from the men who encircled him, and he tried to tear off the hood, but before he could do so, they fell upon him from all sides, raining blows on every part of his body.

Still unable to see, he fought back with all his strength, using his fists, his feet and his head as weapons. The love of battle was on him now, the pain forgotten. His fist crashed into a man's nose, and he felt a momentary surge of joy as the bone broke under the impact. Connor leapt forward, his head cracking into an unprotected face, his booted foot lashing out. A man screamed and fell back – but there were too many of them. The wooden clubs beat down upon him – a savage blow took him high in the temple. Even as he fell, Connor grabbed a man's jacket, butting him in the mouth . . . and then the darkness closed in upon him.

Out in the darkened streets, Ruth Judge was cycling home after choir-practice at the Emmanuel Chapel.

Friday evenings were the only time she went out by herself. Every Sunday she attended Chapel, morning and evening, accompanied by her father and mother, her brothers, Eb and Josh and their families. During the week, she would sometimes go with her mother to visit Aunt Emily; once a year they went to the Christmas Bazaar and Sale of Work in aid of the Foreign Missionaries – but always in a family group.

Some girls in the choir went to social evenings at the Glee Club, where they would take tea and eat little iced cakes, and get into conversation with young men. Sometimes these conversations ripened into friendships and led to other excursions. Ruth had heard it whispered that certain daring young ladies had even gone to the music-hall shows at the Poplar Hippodrome, in the Whitechapel Road . . . For Marcus Judge's daughter, such an idea was unthinkable.

4

She had never made any close friends when she was at school. Her father had not encouraged her to visit any of the other girls, or meet their families, and she had never been allowed to bring anyone home to tea at the Rope Walk.

Turning the corner into Jubilee Wharf, she met the wind off the river. A sudden gust lifted the brim of her straw boater, threatening to tug it from her head, though it was fastened with a long hat-pin. Taking one hand from the handlebars, she pulled the hat squarely down on to her forehead, and the bicycle wobbled for a moment as she swerved to avoid a pot-hole in the road.

Very soon now she would be home, in time to have a cup of cocoa and one of Mum's shortbreads before she went up to her attic bedroom. Ruth had slept at the top of the house, in the little room with sloping ceilings, for as long as she could remember. On the floor below were two larger bedrooms; in the front room, her parents shared a grand brass bedstead, where all the Judge children had been born.

When Ruth was very young, the back bedroom had been occupied by Josh and Eb, but as the boys grew up, each of them in turn had married and moved out, to start families of their own. Now they both lived in houses belonging to their father, in neighbouring streets not a hundred yards away; houses for which they paid rent like all Marcus Judge's other tenants.

As soon as the back bedroom became vacant, Ruth's mother suggested she might like to take it over, but her father had refused to give his permission. It was useful, he said, to keep a spare bedroom for visitors; sometimes a travelling preacher or foreign missionary at the Chapel had to be put up for the night. This was a very rare event, never happening more than once or twice a year, but the second-best bedroom had been kept in readiness ever since, spotlessly clean – and empty.

In any case, Ruth didn't care. She liked her attic-room and had grown fond of its lopsided ceilings. Above all, she liked the view from her little window, of the mean grey houses huddled together and – at the far end of the Walk – the huge bulk of a sea-going ship, its masts and funnels riding high against the sky, towering over the slate rooftops.

She had never known any life outside the Rope Walk. As

5

soon as Josh and Eb left school, they had followed in Father's footsteps and gone to work at the Wharf – and though such things were never discussed at home, Ruth knew they had joined the Brotherhood; they never wanted to do anything else.

But Ruth had other ambitions.

She had done well at school. At fourteen, she took her examinations and gained such excellent marks, the Head Teacher wanted to put her in for a scholarship to the High School, with the possibility of Teacher Training College afterwards – but her father soon put a stop to that. Teaching was no job for a woman, he said. A woman's place was in the home, helping her mother. If Ruth wanted to earn a little money to pay for her keep, she could work part-time as an assistant in Aunt Emily's grocery shop.

So Ruth's dream of becoming a teacher was shattered. Every morning, she helped Mum to wash up and make the beds, to cook and clean the house and in the afternoons she worked in the shop, slicing bacon and measuring out sultanas . . . Sometimes she saw her life as a dark tunnel – and she longed to escape from it.

She rode on, below the high wall of the dockyard. There were no street-lamps here and she slowed down, relying on the little cone of light thrown before her by the paraffin-lamp at the front of her machine. If she had been cycling at full speed, she might not have noticed the man who lay at the foot of the wall but as she passed by, he rolled over and flung out a hand, and the movement caught her eye.

At first she thought he must be drunk. She had been taught to avoid drunken men at all costs; her father was a fierce teetotaller, and a member of the Rechabite Society, sworn to oppose the demon drink. But in the light of the bicycle-lamp, she saw that the man's hand was shining and crimson, wet with blood . . . At once she dismounted, propping her bicycle against the wall, and ran across to him.

'What's happened? Have you been run over? Are you all right?' she asked.

His head was shadowed by the turned-up collar of his jacket, and she could not see his face.

6

'Do I look as if I'm all right?' he growled scornfully, and she knew by his brogue that he was an Irishman.

'Was it an accident? Were you knocked down by a motor-car?' she persisted.

'I was not . . . I've been in a fight – and if you'll give me a hand to help me on to my feet, I'll be grateful. Only take it slow, mind, because I'm not sure I haven't broken my back.'

She gasped, 'Then I mustn't move you – we did First Aid at school, and it would be very dangerous. Stay where you are, and I'll fetch a doctor.'

'You'll do nothing of the kind!' he snapped. 'Help me up, and stop gabbing!'

Awkwardly, she put her arm under his shoulders, and he lifted his head. In the dim light of the bicycle-lamp, she saw his face. One of his eyes was shut beneath a black and purple swelling, while the other was half-hidden under a mass of congealed blood from a gash across his brow. His black hair was matted with mud and blood. More blood was still trickling from his nose, and when he opened his mouth, his spittle was bloodstained.

'You'd better wait here while I go for help,' she began.

'Don't talk rubbish – I'm going home. Lucky for me you're a fine tall girl. You can give me a helping hand along the way.' He hauled himself up, hanging on to Ruth's arm, then took a step forward. 'Mother of God!' he swore, as the pain stabbed again, and he almost fell.

'You can't walk – you're not strong enough.'

'Strong, is it? I'll have you know I'm the strongest man you ever laid eyes on. I only need a minute to get my second wind, that's all.'

He tried to take another step, with the same result. Clumsily, he pulled Ruth to him, and she thought they would both finish up in the gutter. By now she was shaking all over; he could feel her body quivering against him. He scowled into her face, trying to focus, and asked, 'What's wrong with you? Why are you trembling? Afraid of me, are you?'

'No . . . No – I'm not afraid.'

It was the truth. She was breathless and a little dizzy, and her heart was beating violently – but she was not afraid. Though

7

Ruth had been brought up with two older brothers, she had always kept her distance from them. Since she was a small child, she had never kissed them or embraced them; in all her seventeen years, she had never been as close to any man as she was at this moment. His body was thrusting against her. She could smell an unfamiliar male smell of sweat and beer and tobacco, and she felt his warmth through her clothes – a warmth so intense it seemed to burn her. His swollen, blood-stained mouth was only inches from her lips . . .

At that moment, a boy came round the corner, pushing a barrow. He was not much more than a child. A big cloth cap, passed on from a father or an elder brother, came down over his ears, and his shirt and trousers were ragged and dirty, but he pushed an empty barrow, six feet long.

'Wait – please. Stop a minute!' called Ruth. She left the man leaning against the wall, while she explained to the boy. 'You must help me get him on to your barrow,' she said. 'He's been hurt, we've got to get him home. I don't know where he lives, but—'

'I do!' The boy peered up at the man. 'You're Mr O'Dell, you are – from the Watermen pub.'

'Good lad,' grunted the man, swaying forward. Luckily, he managed to catch the end of the cart, or he would have fallen full-length into the road. 'Get me back to the Watermen, and I'll give you a tanner for your trouble.'

'Right you are, guv'nor!' exclaimed the boy, promptly.

Between them, he and Ruth hoisted Connor O'Dell on to the cart, where he lay on his back, looking up at the stars in the night sky.

'Is it far?' she asked anxiously, wondering what time she would get home, and what her father would have to say when she did so.

'Nah – no more'n half a mile,' said the boy.

Taking a handle each, they dragged the barrow along the road. Ruth had to leave her bicycle where it was, hoping it would still be there when she came back for it.

It turned out to be a long half-mile. Connor O'Dell was no lightweight and they made slow progress trundling along the side of the dock, where a string of coal-barges and a pair of cargo-boats rose and fell lazily on the slip-slopping water.

8

At last they reached the warehouses, and turned the corner past the shops. Most of them were shut by this time but the pie-shop was still open, and a plump woman, setting out steaming saveloys on the counter, gazed at them inquisitively as they passed by.

The boy stopped the cart outside the Three Jolly Watermen. 'Here you are,' he said. 'This is it.'

Ruth looked up at the public-house with a mixture of fascination and alarm. In spite of everything, she could not help smiling.

Connor O'Dell eased himself up, and stumbled on to the pavement, asking, 'What's your name, boy?'

'Joey.'

'Right you are, Joey – here's a tanner for your trouble.' He dug into his trouser-pocket with difficulty, then cursed as he remembered. 'Damnation take it, I've no money on me. I can't pay what I promised you.'

'Go inside and get some from the till,' suggested Joey hopefully.

'And run into my Mam and Da? They'd have a fit if they saw me like this.' He turned to Ruth. 'Here, young woman – can you lend me sixpence?'

Still smiling, she fumbled in her coat pocket, and he demanded: 'What the devil are you grinning at?'

'Nothing.' Ruth could not explain that the Three Jolly Watermen was a private joke: her father, Marcus Judge, and his two brothers Luke and Matthew, had all been watermen in their time, though none of them could have been described as 'jolly'. 'Yes, here you are. Here's sixpence.'

'Thanks! I'll owe it you . . . Take your money, Joey, and be off with you. And mind you keep your mouth shut – I don't want anyone gossiping about me.'

'See this wet, see this dry.' The boy crossed his heart, then drew a finger across his throat as a pledge of secrecy. 'Good night, guv'nor!' Relieved of his burden, he wheeled the empty barrow briskly away, and disappeared round the corner.

'We'd better go in by the side door.' Connor took Ruth's arm again. 'I don't want to be seen, but I'll need a hand up the stairs.'

9

She held back. 'Oh, but I can't go in there!'

He turned and stared at her. 'Why not?'

'I've never been inside a public-house,' she said. 'Girls don't.'

For the first time that evening, his face broke into a crooked grin. 'That's all you know,' he said. 'Don't be so damn stupid –I won't lead you astray. Come on!' Pulling her closer, he took her round the building, then put his shoulder to a side door and they went in.

Ruth found herself in a narrow passage. At one side, an open doorway led behind the bar – there was a blaze of light, a clink of glasses, and a buzz of voices.

'This way – quick!'

Connor dragged her past the doorway. She had a fleeting impression of shining bottles, and a young man who glanced back over his shoulder – then they were climbing a steep, uncarpeted staircase. Fully occupied with her task, Ruth could not pick up her long skirt, and caught her toe in the hem. She stumbled, but recovered herself.

'Don't make a sound,' he whispered.

When they reached the first floor, he steered her into a darkened room then let go of her, pulling down a roller-blind at the window. She heard him cross the floorboards, and a moment later a match sputtered and a gas-mantle flared into yellow brilliance.

There was a bed against the wall – unmade, with sheets and blankets tossed in all directions. He sat at the foot of the bed, and muttered, 'Take no notice of the mess – I won't keep you long. Just help me get my clothes off, will you?'

She stared at him, appalled, backing away to the door. 'No! No, I can't – you mustn't!'

'For God's sake, woman!' His temper flared. 'I'm not going to hurt you but my shoulder's giving me gyp, and I can't get undressed without some help. I don't want blood on the bedclothes. Get me out of my jacket and shirt, then I'll go and get washed, and you can run away home . . . All right?'

She looked into his scarred, battered face, and hoped that she could trust him. Awkwardly, she managed to ease off his jacket, then began to unbutton his shirt. It fell open, revealing

10

his skin, bronzed and shining, and a tangle of black hair on his chest; he wore no undervest. Breathing a little faster, she tried to pull his shirt up, but it was tucked firmly into his trousers. Without a word, he unbuckled his belt and unfastened the top button of his trousers; she had a glimpse of wiry black hair below his waist.

Looking into her eyes, Connor said quietly: 'You're trembling again.'

'No, I'm not,' she lied, and tugged his shirt over his head.

At home, she was used to seeing her brothers half-naked when they washed in the scullery, but now she could not take her eyes from this man's body. Strong and powerful, even his cuts and bruises could not disfigure it. He stared at her for a long moment, unmoving, then said, 'I'll be fine now. Thanks for your help, Miss . . .' He stopped, realising that he did not know her name.

'My name's Ruth,' she said. 'Ruth Judge.' She could not understand the change that came over him then. It was as if a light had gone out; the expression in his eyes became hard, and the corners of his mouth twisted angrily.

'Related to Marcus Judge, I suppose?' He spat out the words. 'And Joshua – and Ebenezer?'

'They're my brothers. Marcus Judge is my father.'

He stood up, seeming to tower above her. 'Get out,' he said. 'You've got what you came for – I hope you're satisfied. Go and tell them you've seen me beaten and helpless – and leave me alone.'

She stared at him, completely bewildered. 'I don't under-stand.'

'I said *get out*!'

He lunged forward and she thought he was going to strike her, but he brushed past her, flinging the door open. As he did so, another man entered the room. Ruth had seen him already – he was the one who had glanced back at them as they entered the house.

'What the devil's going on here?' he asked.

'Nothing's going on. I was in a fight – now I'm off to get cleaned up. And if you breathe a word of this to our Da, I'll cut

11

your tongue out!' Connor strode out of the room, ignoring Ruth completely.

The newcomer, a couple of years younger, turned to her and smiled, a sweet, easy smile. 'You'll have to forgive my brother –he's no manners,' he said. 'My name's Sean – d'you mind telling me what's been happening?'

Ruth tried to explain, but when she got to the end of the story, her voice faltered, '. . . but when I told him my name, he was quite different – as if I'd said something terribly wrong.' Then she stopped, determined not to break down in front of a stranger.

'And what might your name be?' Sean wanted to know. When she told him, he nodded slowly. 'Ah, now I understand. If you don't mind me saying so, you're deathly pale. You look as if you'd better sit down before you fall down.'

He guided her to the bed, and sat down beside her. 'I think my brother's been in a spot of trouble with your menfolk tonight. I could see it coming, but when I tried to warn him he wouldn't listen. Connor's always been the wild man of this family; he'll fly into a rage for no reason at all . . . It's nothing personal, I'm sure of that.'

'I'm still a little confused,' she stammered. 'So much has happened tonight, all at once. Do you live here as well, over the public-house?'

'Of course – our Da's the landlord. It's the family business.' He smiled again, and Ruth decided that he was very different from his brother – his smile so sweet, and his manner so gentle. Connor's eyes were green and hard, like cut emeralds while Sean's were palest blue, fringed with soft black lashes.

'I help out with the bar and the cellar-work. Da and Mam wanted my brother to take up the trade as well, but Con's stubborn as an old mule, and he'd not hear of it. He preferred to try his luck at the Wharf as a docker. That's how he ran up against your family, and that's why they threw him out of the Guild – us being Catholics, and them and their blessed Brotherhood being a nest of Prots – if you'll pardon the expression.'

'That's all right, I'm not offended. We all worship the same God, don't we?' She tried to speak lightly, and then to her

12

embarrassment found that she was crying after all, hot tears of exhaustion and disappointment overwhelming her.

'Don't cry now,' he said, putting his arm round her shoulders. 'You're too pretty a girl to waste time crying, especially over a great ugly lump like Connor. You're worth a dozen of him, so you are. Wait now, while I kiss them old tears away.' Drawing her closer, he kissed her – at first on the cheek, then on her mouth, and then his lips opened upon hers . . .

It was the first time Ruth had been kissed by any man, and she did not know what to do. In that moment, her whole world had changed – in that moment, she knew there was daylight beyond the dark tunnel of her life. Now that she had seen the sun shining, and felt its warmth, she must never lose it.

But it was important not to make any mistake. She needed time to get her breath back – time to think. Sean tried to kiss her again, but she averted her face, saying, 'I'm sorry, I have to go. I should have been home long ago.'

'Well, if you must . . .' His smile was regretful, but very tender. 'I'll see you out.'

As they went out of the bedroom, Ruth could hear sounds of splashing. At the end of the landing, behind a closed door, Connor was cleaning himself up. Sean led the way downstairs, saying, 'I must get back to work myself – they'll be wondering what's become of me.' He opened the side door, adding, 'Just tell me one thing: will I see you again?'

Ruth looked into Sean's eyes, and he smiled at her – and she heard herself saying, 'Yes. Yes, I'd like that.'

'So would I.' Out under the starry sky, he kissed her once more. 'Now you know where to find me, come again – any time.'

She ran all the way back to the spot where she had left her bicycle; it was still there. Riding home to the Rope Walk, she had no idea how she would explain where she had been this evening, or what had made her so late – but she did not care. Above her, the constellations were pricked out in points of light, but she could only see the faces of the two brothers, so alike in their confident, animal strength, yet so very different . . . Connor, the wild man – fierce and exciting, yet so unpredictable, she had been almost frightened of him. And

Sean, whose smile was so warm and understanding . . . she felt safe within the protection of his arms, as if she had known him for ever.

Of course she would see him again. She had no doubt about that.

2

She had no idea what the time was. In the Judge family, only her father was the possessor of a pocket-watch. But when she turned into the Rope Walk Ruth saw that the fanlight over the door of Number 26 was glowing; the gaslight was still burning in the hall.

She dismounted from her bicycle and wheeled it across the pavement, then bumped it up the two steps to the front door. All the other windows were in darkness but she knew that her father would be waiting up, for she was not allowed to have her own latch-key. Bracing herself, she lifted the brass door-knocker and let it fall.

After a moment she heard footsteps tip-tapping along the hall lino, and then her mother opened the door. 'Ruth – what time do you call this? We wondered whatever had become of you!' Louisa Judge's round apple-cheeks were drawn tight, her forehead seamed with anxiety.

'I'm sorry, Mum, I got held up,' Ruth began.

'Tonight of all nights, too. There's been a bit of an accident – Josh had to see the doctor . . .'

Ruth rested her bike against the wall and squeezed by, following her mother along the passage past the door of the front parlour, which they hardly ever used, and into the back room – which was living-room, dining-room and kitchen all combined.

The back room was warm and cosy, with the gas-lamp bright above the kitchen table, but it seemed to be full of people, and Ruth stopped short. Her brother Josh was sitting in her mother's armchair – but he was almost unrecognisable, with a padded bandage bound tightly round his head, covering part of his face. From the little she could see of his expression, he looked sullen and miserable, and his skin was unusually sallow.

'What is it? What's happened?' she asked.

15

Her elder brother Ebenezer squatted on the rag-rug at Josh's feet, and Marcus Judge stood over his two sons. They all turned towards the door, staring at Ruth accusingly.

'You're late,' said her father. 'Where have you been?'

Before she could reply, Eb cut in. 'Josh got into a fight.' His lip curled lightly, hinting at some private satisfaction.

Louisa took up the story. 'Poor Josh was in a bad way – that's why Eb brought him round here instead of letting him go straight home. Well, there was no sense in worrying Mabel, so they asked me to clean him up and do something about his cuts and bruises.'

'I told you, Mum – a hot poultice to draw the swelling out,' began Josh indistinctly, trying to speak without moving his mouth.

'Doctor Wickham says his nose is broken.' Marcus Judge spoke bitterly. 'He wanted us to take the boy to the Infirmary to be looked at, but I said there was no call for that. Now that Wickham has patched him up, he'll do well enough – eh, Joshua?'

'Yes, Father, I dare say,' mumbled Josh.

Ruth said nothing. She guessed that Josh's injury might have been more serious than her father was willing to admit, for it cost half-a-crown to go to Dr Wickham's surgery – and Marcus Judge never spent any money unless it was absolutely unavoidable.

'You'd better take your brother home, Ebenezer,' Marcus continued. 'His wife will be wondering what's become of him.'

'But how did it happen?' Ruth wanted to know. 'What were you fighting about?'

The men looked at one another, and for a moment nobody spoke.

'There was a trouble-maker at our meeting tonight,' said Eb at last. 'He had to be dealt with.'

Immediately, Ruth guessed who the 'trouble-maker' was: the Brotherhood had ganged up on Connor O'Dell tonight, and although they had thrown him out, he had not gone quietly. She felt certain it was Connor O'Dell who had broken her brother's nose – and her heart beat faster, prey to a storm of conflicting emotions.

16

'Ruth, are you feeling all right? You look quite pale,' said her mother. 'Come and sit down. There's still some tea in the pot –I'll fetch another cup.'

'No, Mum, I'm just a bit tired, that's all. I think I'll go straight up to bed.'

She turned to the door, but Marcus Judge summoned her back. He did not raise his voice, but his tone was like a steel blade. '*Wait!*' he said. She stopped, her fingers on the door-handle. 'You haven't told us yet where you have been this evening.'

'I went to choir-practice, Father. I thought you knew that.'

'Choir-practice finishes at eight o'clock, or thereabouts. And it is now – ' Marcus Judge pulled the gun-metal watch from his waistcoat pocket '—ten minutes to ten. What took you so long?'

'I – I got talking to one of the other girls.'

'Which other girl?'

'Nellie Burroughs. You don't know her . . .' Ruth spoke a little too quickly, her words tumbling over one another in her effort to sound casual. 'She's been making some lovely crochet shawls for the Sale of Work – she wanted to show them to me.' So far, Ruth had told nothing but the truth. Nellie had been tiresomely determined that everyone should admire her handiwork.

'You went to this young woman's house?' her father persisted.

'Yes, I – yes, I did.' Now she had abandoned truth, telling a complete and shameless lie. She had never set foot in the Burroughs' house and was not even sure where they lived.

'Don't address me over your shoulder, please,' said Marcus Judge. 'Have the goodness to look me in the face when you speak to me.'

Unwillingly, she turned to face him. At fifty-two years of age, Ruth's father was still a fine figure of a man. Well over six feet tall, he had broad, square shoulders, yet it was not his physique alone that made such a strong impression. It was something in those craggy features, the wide forehead and beetling brows – his square-cut beard, once jet-black but now streaked with silver and above all, in his eyes, which were deep like the waters of Jubilee Wharf, and as cold as ice.

17

'Look at me,' he repeated inexorably. She forced herself to meet his gaze. 'You tell me you spent part of the evening at the house of this young person – Burroughs, did you say?'

'Yes, Father.' She stared back at him. She would not lower her eyes, nor betray the faintest shadow of guilt.

For longer than she could remember, Ruth had been afraid of her father. When she was very young, she had confused him with God: the God of the Old Testament, of wrath and vengeance. She believed that he could read her thoughts and that he knew everything she did, every little naughtiness, every tiny mistake she made at school. She was completely in awe of him. Until that day, three years ago, when the Head Teacher had offered her the scholarship, telling her father that she had the ability to go on to College and make a career as a teacher, and he had forbidden her to take up the place she was offered.

She knew she could never win that battle. Without her father's help, she did not have a hope of realising her ambition – but she had despised him then for his stubborn, stupid bigotry; she had looked him in the eye for the first time without flinching. That was when she realised that he was not God Almighty, and she was no longer afraid of him. Now she looked into his eyes once more. Her gaze locked with his – and Marcus Judge was the first to look away.

'Very well,' he said. 'You had better go to bed.'

She lifted her chin, saying, 'Thank you, Father . . . good night.' Then she kissed her mother and said, 'Good night, Mum. Eb – Josh – I hope you'll soon be feeling better.' And she ran up to the attic-room, two steps at a time.

Undressing quickly, she slipped between the sheets, expecting that sleep would come to her almost at once, for it was true that she was tired after such an exciting evening – but for once sleep proved to be elusive, and she lay awake for a long time, listening to the tug-boats hooting on the river.

Why could she not fall asleep? Was she suffering from a bad conscience, because she had told a lie to her father? Ruth smiled to herself in the darkness. No, of course that wasn't the reason . . . There were two men keeping her awake – two Irishmen – one who had caught her roughly in his arms, and one who had embraced her gently. One who had stormed at her, and one who had kissed her.

When she closed her eyes at last, drifting off into a dream, she dreamed of Sean O'Dell.

When Connor O'Dell awoke next morning it was still dark, but he knew at once what had broken his slumbers – a tattoo like hailstones on his bedroom window. Old Bessie the knocker-up was doing her rounds in the empty streets, blowing dried peas through a pea-shooter at some of the upper windows. It was not much of a job, but Bessie was glad enough to have it. There weren't many ways an old widow-woman could earn a living.

Springing out of bed, Connor crossed the room, calling from the window, 'Thanks, Bessie – I hear you!'

Down below, there was a clatter of footsteps on cobble-stones as she moved off, and he began to pull on his clothes. That was when the splitting headache hit him with the force of a sledgehammer.

'Sweet Jesus!' He staggered slightly, muttering under his breath, 'I must have thrown back a few gallons last night.'

But he had not been drunk last night. Then it all began to come back to him – the meeting of the Brotherhood – the battering from flailing fists and wooden clubs – and hadn't there been a girl, too, later on? Some girl who had helped him to get home? His spirits lifted as he thought of her – a fine, pretty girl, so she was. Sitting on the end of the bed, he fancied he could still detect a trace of her floating in the air – not scent or face-powder, for she was not that sort at all – but her skin had the sweet freshness of a flower, and she had sat next to him, right here at the end of the bed.

Then he remembered who she was. The bile rose in his throat, and his guts twisted into a knot. Ruth Judge . . . the daughter of Marcus Judge. Blindly, he pushed the thought of her from his mind and continued to dress, pushing his feet into his boots. The room was still dark, and he cursed as he found himself trying to squeeze his right foot into his left-hand boot.

So he was no longer a member of the Brotherhood's Guild of dock-workers. He had no brass tally now, and no claw as the

19

tool of his trade. When they called out the numbers at the dock-gates this morning, his would not be included. He had not thought to tell Old Bessie that he wouldn't need a knock-up this morning – or for many another morning, either. Come to think of it, there was no point in getting dressed at all. He might as well have stayed in bed.

Suddenly he threw back his head and said aloud, 'To hell with the whole bloody pack of 'em! I don't give a sparrow's fart for them or their Brotherhood. What's to stop me going to ask for work on my own account? I'm as good a workman today as ever I was yesterday – haven't I as much right to sign on as any other man?'

Ten minutes later, he slipped out of the side door of the pub, and made his way down the narrow street towards Jubilee Wharf. Several men were moving in the same direction, and some of them threw him speculative glances: he guessed that word had got around already about his expulsion from the Guild. Nobody spoke to him, and none of them came too close to him. It was as if he had caught some infectious disease that might prove fatal.

Looking straight ahead, he tried to ignore them all. By the time they reached the dock, the first streaks of dawn were lighting up the sky. Outside the gates the press of men was so thick, he found himself jostled in the crowd.

'Here, watch it!' someone protested, as Connor's elbow jabbed his ribs. 'Who d'you think you—?' The words died on his lips as he saw Connor's face in the grey half-light: a face that still bore the marks of last night's punishment. 'Oh, it's you . . .' he mumbled. 'I'm sorry.'

'Sorry?' Connor challenged him. 'What would you be sorry for?' He knew the man by sight. Shorter by a head than Connor himself, he had a lively humorous face under a mop of dark curling hair.

'Ah, well – you know.' The man shrugged, spreading his hands. 'I heard you'd been in a spot of bother last night . . . and you'd done nothing wrong, had you?'

'According to old man Judge, I'd broken the Thirteenth Commandment: Thou shalt not worship at the wrong Church.'

'Yeah, that's the way I heard it. Lousy rotten luck.'

Connor peered at him more closely. 'Just a minute – how come they let you into their happy band? Name of Kleiber, am I right? You're not one of the chapel-goers. Unless I'm much mistaken, you and your family attend the Synagogue instead.'

'True enough – Israel Kleiber's the name,' the other man gave a crooked grin, 'but there's still hope for us Jews, seemingly. Mr Judge thinks we'll see the light one day – besides, he should be grateful to us. I mean to say, where would his Chapel be without us? If it weren't for Moses, they wouldn't have no Commandments at all!'

At this moment the heavy iron gates clanked open, squeaking on rusty hinges, while somewhere inside the dockyard, the six o'clock whistle blew. The crowd of men surged forward – only to be halted by a familiar voice.

'You will wait there until your number is called!'

At the top of a short flight of steps, Marcus Judge stood in the doorway of the Wharfmaster's Office. Beside him waited Ebenezer, holding a canvas bag. His father continued, 'Last night, two Dutch freighters berthed from Rotterdam, and a Belgian vessel from Antwerp. All three need unloading, ready to return to sea this time tomorrow – even if that means working a double shift. If any man here does not choose to work all day and all night as well, let him go now and leave the job to those who want it.'

He paused, looking round the assembled throng. Nobody moved. 'Very well. Start calling the numbers.'

Ebenezer plunged into the bag and took out a handful of discs, shouting the numbers one by one, as if he were playing a game of lotto. But this was no game. The waiting men knew that their jobs – their wages – their very lives depended on it. Each number would be called once only, and if a man misheard it or lost his chance, he would return home empty-handed and go to bed hungry. Worst of all, his wife and children would go to bed hungry as well.

'Nineteen . . . Fifty-four . . . Thirty-seven . . . One hundred and five . . .' The litany of numbers droned on in Eb's flat, rasping tones, and each time he spoke, a man pushed through the crowd, holding up his brass tally as he slipped in at the gates.

21

Through the window of the office, Connor could see the Wharfmaster talking to a fat man with a face as round and red as a Dutch cheese – the Captain of one of the Rotterdam freighters, he guessed.

Israel Kleiber gave him a sidelong glance, and asked quietly, 'What are you waiting for? According to what they tell me, you're not likely to hear your number called today.'

Connor shrugged. 'I can still work, can't I? I can still do a day's labour for a day's pay, number or no number.'

'One hundred and seventy-four ... Sixty-three ... Thirteen ...'

'Lucky thirteen – that's me!' Suddenly galvanised, Israel Kleiber thrust himself forward, saying, 'So long, matey – good luck!' before he disappeared through the gates.

Ten minutes later, the last number had been called and Eb tucked the empty bag under his arm. A groan went up from those men who had not been chosen. Marcus and Ebenezer ignored them, walking purposefully down the steps and off along the dock-wall, to supervise their work-gang.

Dulled by disappointment, the men dispersed in twos and threes, wandering off home to break the news to their wives and families. 'Nothing again today, old girl.'

Only Connor remained. The gates were still half-open, and he walked in.

Somebody shouted, 'Here, where d'you think you're going?' but Connor turned a deaf ear, mounting the steps briskly.

Inside the office, the Wharfmaster was still deep in conversation with his foreign visitor. 'We'll do our level best to have you fit and ready to sail on the high tide tomorrow, Captain.' He broke off as Connor appeared. 'Well?' he said sharply. 'What do you want?'

'Permission to work, sir.'

The Wharfmaster frowned. 'Has your number been called?'

'No, sir. But that wasn't likely, for I've got no number.'

The frown deepened. 'You're not a member of Mr Judge's Guild?'

'I was, sir, until last night, when they threw me out on account of my religion. They made it clear to me that Roman

Catholics are not welcome in the Brotherhood. In fact, you could say they made the point very forcibly.'

The Master eyed the scars on Connor's face, and took a deep breath. 'I know nothing about that. It's no concern of mine.'

'I'm aware of that, sir, but you're in charge here, I understand – and even if I don't have a tally, I have a strong pair of arms, and I can still make myself useful. That's why I'm reporting to you, sir – to ask for work.'

'What is this? What is the man saying?' asked the Dutchman, perplexed.

Connor turned to him. 'I'm offering to help unload your ship, Captain – if you'll give me permission.'

'No, no – quite out of the question.' Hastily, the Wharfmaster took the Captain's arm, steering him towards the door. 'We can't stay here talking all day. If you'll come with me, Mynheer, I think we shall find breakfast waiting for us in the dining-room.'

Connor moved swiftly, standing between the two men and the open door. 'Give me a fair chance, sir, that's all I ask.'

'I'm sorry, but as you very well know, Mr Judge is the foreman responsible for loading and unloading. This is a matter you must take up with him – it's entirely outside my province. Kindly stand aside and allow us to pass.'

'So you won't help me?' Connor asked.

'I'm afraid I cannot.'

'You're afraid?' Connor looked the man up and down. 'You never said a truer word. I hope you both enjoy your breakfast.' With that, he turned on his heel and walked out.

'But what is the Brotherhood *for*?' Ruth asked her mother. They were upstairs in the front bedroom, on either side of the big double bed, putting on clean sheets and tucking in the corners.

'What is it for?' Louisa looked mystified, as she smoothed out the creases in the bottom sheet. 'You know as well as I do – it's the Dock-workers' Guild, and your father's in charge of it.'

23

They worked as they talked, unfolding the top sheet between them and ballooning it into the air, so it would fall neatly into place. Ruth's sharp eyes spotted a tiny hole, and she pointed it out. 'Father's toe-nails want cutting again – look at that tear.'

'Oh, what a nuisance. Take that off, or he'll put his foot through it, then fetch me another sheet from the bottom drawer, there's a good girl.'

Ruth went to the chest of drawers between the two windows, and found another clean sheet. 'This one looks all right . . . What I don't understand is why they need a Guild for the dockers at all.'

'Well, there's got to be men unloading the cargo-boats, stands to reason.' Louisa shook out the clean sheet and they began again. 'The Wharfmasters don't want to be bothered with such things, so they put your father in charge to keep it all organised. I don't know what the workers would do without him.'

'But sometimes they turn men out of the Brotherhood, don't they?' Ruth persisted, pulling the sheet tight. 'Like last night.'

'What do you know about last night?' Her mother looked up sharply, and Ruth corrected herself.

'I'm only guessing, but I thought perhaps that was why Josh got into a fight. They do turn men out, don't they? I've heard people say so.' In her mind's eye she saw Connor O'Dell as he was when she helped him up from the pavement, his face battered and bloody.

'You shouldn't listen to such talk – it's no business of ours. I leave that kind of thing to the men. It's nothing to do with you and me.'

Now they spread the blankets across the bed, followed by the eiderdown filled with goose-feathers, and a knitted counterpane over the top.

'Yes, but why are some men allowed to join the Guild and not others?'

'Some men can't be trusted. They misbehave themselves – drinking in public-houses, taking the Lord's name in vain, amusing themselves with women . . .' Now Ruth saw a different face: laughing blue eyes ringed with soft black lashes

24

... She *had* to meet Sean again, but however would she manage it? 'Your father won't have good-for-nothings like that working on the docks. There – that's a good job jobbed.' Louisa picked up the sheet with a hole in it, and sighed, 'This old thing's almost worn through. We'll have to get the sewing-machine out and turn it sides to middle.'

With an effort, Ruth wrenched her mind away from Sean O'Dell. 'I don't know why you bother,' she said. 'That won't last five minutes. If I was you I'd cut it up for dusters and buy some new sheets.'

'Certainly not!' Her mother was scandalised. 'Waste not, want not, that's Dad's motto. He never throws anything away that can still be put to use.'

'Yes . . . and doesn't that ever strike you as a bit peculiar? He must be earning good money being foreman and head of the Brotherhood and all that. How many houses has he bought now? *And* he collects rents from all of them every Friday night, so—'

'That reminds me,' Louisa interrupted her. 'He won't be collecting tonight 'cos they're working a double shift, so he won't be home till breakfast-time. He'll have to go round to the tenants tomorrow, instead.'

'That's what I mean! After all these years he still works every day, and through the night as well sometimes, and he won't let anyone else collect the rents for him. Money – that's all he ever thinks about.'

'Don't you ever let me hear you say such a thing! Marcus Judge has been a good father to this family. We've none of us gone short, and you never wanted for anything.'

'I wanted to go to college,' said Ruth.

'We're not going into all *that* again, thank you very much!' Firmly, Louisa changed the subject. 'Now then, let's go downstairs and make a start on the kitchen. You can scrub the scullery while I black-lead the grate.'

'No, Mum, listen! Don't you sometimes wonder—'

Louisa rounded on her daughter. 'No, I don't wonder – and I won't hear a word against your father. He's a very generous man. Look how good he's been to poor Emily since she lost her husband. Every time she's got into difficulties over money matters, Dad's always helped her out, with never a word of reproach.'

Ruth knew it was useless to try and argue – she would only be wasting her breath. All the same, she suspected Aunt Emily might have a different tale to tell.

Thirty-three years ago, when Louisa Skipps married Marcus Judge, her sister Emily had been chief bridesmaid and Marcus' brother Luke had been the best man. After the wedding breakfast, Luke had escorted Emily home; within a few weeks they were 'going steady'. Five years later, they went back to the same Chapel, and the two sisters became sisters-in-law as well.

When Emily was in the family way, Luke decided to give up work on the docks in favour of more regular employment. He found a job in a small grocery shop at the corner of Millwall Road, and was soon promoted to manager. The shop flourished and when the owner decided to retire, he offered Luke the property – lock, stock and good-will. Buying the shop ate up every penny of Luke Judge's savings, and he had to take out a heavy loan to make up the asking price. Within the year, Luke had died, dragged down by a combination of pleurisy, overwork and anxiety – and his widow had struggled ever since to keep the shop going, to make ends meet, and to bring up two small children.

Unfortunately, Emily had never had a head for figures, and time and again her brother-in-law was forced to come to her rescue. Whenever he helped her out, Marcus gave Emily a severe lecture on the folly of her ways, which left her quivering and tearful for several hours afterwards; and whenever he balanced the accounts, he took good care to add another IOU to the mounting total of Emily's debts. By this time, Emily Judge was the owner of the little corner shop in name only for she had not the faintest idea that Marcus had been steadily increasing his hold upon the property, year by year.

'You Dad's always been so very helpful,' she told Ruth that afternoon, while they weighed out brown sugar into blue-paper bags. 'Every time I've got into a little difficulty with the bank, Marcus has always put things straight and I'm truly grateful. Mind you, he's had to be quite stern with me once or twice – but I don't blame him for that. I dare say I deserved it. Like he says, you have to be cruel to be kind.'

In looks, Emily was a blurred copy of Louisa – a little thinner, a little paler, her hair long since faded to white, her complexion dry as tissue-paper – but her smile was unmistakable. The Skipps girls had been famous for their smiles and even now, though Emily's lips trembled and she had to put her hand to her mouth to stop them quivering, Ruth felt a faint glow from the warmth of Aunt Emily's smile.

She smiled back. 'There, that's all done – twenty pounds of sugar in quarter-pound bags. Shall I stack them on the top shelf, next to the biscuits? There's plenty of room up there.'

There were always spaces on the shelves in the corner shop, for Emily often let the perishable stocks run low, afraid to order too much from the wholesaler in case it went stale before it could be sold. The result was that sooner or later, customers who failed to find what they wanted would take their custom elsewhere.

'Are you sure you don't mind? In the ordinary way I'd ask Arnold to do it when he comes home, only he's got to work all through the night – isn't it dreadful? He told me when he came home dinner-time. I felt so sorry for him, but he says there's three foreign boats to be cleared by the first tide tomorrow morning.'

'Yes, Mum said, but they're not expecting Arnold to help with the unloading, surely?'

Arnold was Emily's eldest. A thin, studious boy with spectacles, he had done very well at school and thanks to his Uncle Marcus' recommendation, had gone straight to work in the Dockyard Office, where he had risen to the status of Chief Loading Clerk.

'Oh, no, not unloading – of course not!' Emily sounded quite shocked. 'But every item has to be checked as it comes off the ship into the warehouse, and entered up in the ledger – that's Arnold's responsibility. He'll be worn out by the time he's finished.'

As Ruth went to the back of the shop, to fetch the step-ladder out of the cupboard under the stairs, Emily chattered on.

'You will be careful, won't you? I'm always so afraid you'll fall. Gloria won't use those old steps nowadays – she says they're not safe.'

'Don't worry.' Ruth had noticed that her cousin Gloria was very good at finding reasons to avoid the more strenuous jobs around the shop. 'I think I can manage.'

'Did I hear my name being taken in vain?' Yawning, Gloria strolled down the staircase and joined them. At twenty-four, Ruth's cousin was strikingly beautiful. Her honey-blonde hair was swept up into a fashionable chignon, and her ample curves attracted glances from all the men in the neighbourhood.

'Yes. We were wondering if you'd like to help me put the sugar-bags up on the shelf?' Ruth teased her.

'Sorry, Ruthie – I'm not feeling quite up to the mark.' Gloria put a hand to her forehead. 'Didn't Ma tell you? I've got this dreadful headache again. I've had it ever since I woke up this morning.'

Emily fluttered around her daughter, torn between concern for her health and dismay at her appearance, for Gloria was only wearing a flimsy lace negligée over her camisole and petticoat.

'Gloria, dear, you mustn't come downstairs half-undressed. Suppose a customer was to walk in and see you?'

'It's not very likely, is it? You don't seem to be exactly run off your feet this afternoon. I only came down to make myself a cup of tea – I thought it might shift this awful head.'

'I'll make some tea for you – you go back to bed.' Emily glanced at the shop door apprehensively in case a male customer should walk in. 'Such a pity. I thought you might be feeling brighter after that nice long rest.'

In theory, Gloria was supposed to help her mother in the shop every morning, but more often than not she wasn't feeling 'quite up to the mark'; either she had slept very badly, or she felt a nasty chill coming on, or she was suffering one of her awful heads. Strangely enough, her health generally improved as the day wore on, and she usually managed to get out for a few hours in the evenings. As she told her mother, she needed a little stroll and a breath of air after being cooped up indoors all day.

'Righty-ho, then. Thanks, Ma,' said Gloria, and took herself off to her room once more.

'I'll be up in two ticks, as soon as the kettle boils!' Emily called after her, then bustled into the back kitchen, still talking – half to herself, and half to Ruth at the top of the step-ladder. 'That poor girl, she said she hardly got a wink of sleep all night. You should have seen her first thing – great black rings under her eyes. I was hoping she'd feel strong enough to go down to the market and buy me a pair of kippers because Arnold's going to need something tasty for breakfast by the time he gets home, but there . . .' Emily sighed. 'I can see she's not up to it.'

Ruth's heart leapt, and she almost dropped the last bag of sugar. 'I can go to the market if you like!' she said eagerly. 'We're not very busy – and you can manage on your own for a while, can't you? Do let me go and buy Arnold some kippers, I'd really like to!'

It wasn't much of a market, not like Spitalfields or Billingsgate – just half a dozen stalls and a few costermongers' barrows lined up along the street.

Ruth was out of breath by the time she got there. She had been walking fast, nearly breaking into a run, to finish her errand as quickly as possible. It was soon done; she paid fourpence for a nice pair of kippers and stuffed them into Aunt Emily's straw basket but then, instead of returning to Millwall Road, she went on further, past the warehouses, past the pie-shop, where a delicious smell of fried sausages wafted from the doorway, and round the corner to the Three Jolly Watermen.

She tried the front door, and found it locked. Only then did she remember that public-houses opened in the mornings and the evenings. How silly of her to forget that it would be shut this afternoon! However, she would not let this setback put her off – she knew that the O'Dells lived upstairs and she knew where to find the side entrance.

It all looked so different in broad daylight. Walking down the alley at the side of the house she felt very conspicuous, and hoped no one would recognise her. When she reached the side door she hesitated, uncertain whether or not to try the handle. It was a private house after all, as well as a public one. There was no knocker, so she rapped on the door-panel. Nothing happened. After a while she tried again, more loudly, and was rewarded by the sound of footsteps within. She nerved herself up. Suppose Sean's mother or father opened the door – what could she say?

The door swung open, and Connor O'Dell stood glowering at her. 'Well?' he began, then his face changed. 'Oh, it's yourself,' he said. 'You'd better come in.'

He took her into the narrow passageway, and for a moment she thought he was about to lead her upstairs to his bedroom, and shrank back. Instead, he showed her into the public bar. It was deserted and chilly at this time of day, but still smelled of beer and stale tobacco-smoke.

He indicated the wooden bench that ran round the walls, saying gruffly, 'Won't you sit down? Will you take a sup of something, to keep the cold out?'

She shook her head vigorously. 'No, really. My father doesn't allow – I mean, I don't drink.'

'I wasn't intending to offer you a glass of stout,' he said impatiently, 'but I can manage a pot of tea if you don't mind waiting.'

'No, thank you. I mustn't stay long.' All the same, she sank on to the hard wooden bench while he stood over her, clearing his throat as if he were trying to think what to say.

She was amazed at the difference in him. Last night he had been wild and unpredictable, unsteady on his feet and at the mercy of his injuries – his voice thick, his face bruised and swollen. Today the marks of violence were already fading. His voice was a low rumble and he spoke slowly, choosing his words.

'I think I should give you some apology. I understand you weren't sent by your family to find me – you didn't know what was going on.'

'Of course not! How could I have known? I could see you'd been hurt, that's all.'

'Then I must ask your pardon for the misunderstanding.' He scratched his jaw, adding, 'I wanted to see you, but I'd no notion where to find you. I was hoping you might call in again.'

30

'Were you?' She looked up at him.

He frowned and lifted his gaze, staring at a point on the wall above Ruth's head. 'Yes ... I wanted to repay you,' he muttered.

'I didn't do anything,' she began. 'It was nothing.'

'You lent me some money for the boy with the cart. I owe you sixpence.' He dug into his trouser-pocket, and produced a silver coin.

'Oh, thank you.' She took it, withdrawing her fingers quickly from the warmth of his palm, and slipped it into her purse. 'I hope you don't think – I mean, that wasn't why I called in.'

'Wasn't it?' Now he stared directly into her eyes and it was Ruth's turn to look away. 'Why did you come, then?'

'I – I was hoping I might see your brother,' she replied awkwardly.

'Ah ... of course. Stupid of me.' Slowly he moved away, turning his back on her, and walked to the bar. He thumped the counter with his clenched fist, shouting, 'Sean! Will you come here now? You have a visitor!'

Without waiting for a response, he moved to the door. He did not look at her again, but threw back a few words over his shoulder. 'Thanks for your help. I'm obliged to you.'

Then he was gone, and the room seemed suddenly bigger and emptier. She felt she should say goodbye and rose to her feet, uncertain whether to go after him – but at that moment Sean appeared through a curtained archway behind the counter.

He was not alone. He had his arm round the shoulders of a girl, not much older than Ruth. She was a very pretty girl, with pink cheeks and rose-red lips and long dark hair that fell in ringlets to her shoulders. They had been talking and joking together, and were still laughing – but their laughter died when they saw Ruth standing there.

'Hello!' said Sean, taken aback. 'This is a surprise and no mistake.'

For a split second, Ruth thought she hated him – and she hated herself for being such a fool. Why had she expected Sean to be alone? Why shouldn't such a good-looking man have a girl-friend already?

'I'm sorry if I'm intruding,' she blurted out. 'I shouldn't have come without being asked.'

'Don't be silly – didn't I ask you myself?' Sean caught the look that passed between the two girls. 'Now I'm forgetting my manners. Rosie, this is Miss Ruth Judge, a good friend of mine – and of Connor's too, if he wasn't too pig-headed to realise it. Ruth, this is our baby sister Rosie, Rosie O'Dell.'

The girl smiled and said in a brogue as soft as her brother's, 'I'm very pleased to meet you, Miss Judge. I won't shake hands, for I've just been peeling spuds for tea and if you'll excuse me, I must go back and finish them. I think p'raps I'm the one that's intruding.'

And she disappeared behind the curtain, while Sean lifted the counter flap and came out from the bar. 'I dare say you were wondering who she was,' he said, with a twinkle in his eye.

'Only for a moment,' said Ruth quickly. 'She's very like you – I should have realised . . .'

'Ah, Rosie's a good girl, and all the better for leaving us alone.' Sean took Ruth's hands in his, drawing her closer. 'How long can you stay?'

Once again, the nearness of him overwhelmed her – his warm breath on her cheek, his smiling eyes that seemed to look right into her soul, seeing and understanding every part of her . . .

'I can't stop long,' she whispered. 'I only looked in because I happened to be passing. They'll be expecting me home very soon.'

'Now isn't that the biggest disappointment I ever heard? I thought you were going to keep me company for a while, that a little bird must have told you it's my evening off. I thought maybe we could go out tonight, you and me.'

'Out?' She felt suddenly giddy. 'Out where? What do you mean?'

'Anywhere! A walk by the river – a visit to the music-hall, or the Penny Picture Palace. Are you fond of the cinema?'

'I've never been. My father says it's a wicked place.'

Sean laughed. 'Devil a bit of it! Come with me and see for yourself – we'll have a high old time, I promise. And I'll see you safe home after. Now be a darling and say yes.'

'You don't understand – my father would never allow it.' Then she stopped, realising that her father would be out all night. Her face lit up, radiant with happiness. 'Yes, all right, I'd love to go to the Picture Palace. Why not?'

3

There was a train coming towards them, at full speed.

Ruth caught her breath, gripping Sean's arm. It wasn't like any train she had seen before, not like the old steam train that puffed across the viaduct at Millwall, or the new Underground train she had once been taken on as a special treat at Whitechapel. This one had a slatted skirt in front of the engine – to keep cows off the track, Sean explained – and a bell that swung behind the smokestack; but as it rushed onwards, the engine made no noise, and the swinging bell was silent.

The only sounds were the continuous tick-tick-ticking of the cinema projector, the gasps and murmurs from the audience and the dramatic musical accompaniment from the upright piano at the front of the hall, below the screen.

Now the train was sweeping along from left to right, with pine trees flying past and there, close beside the railway track, was a galloping horse, with a cowboy riding hell-for-leather, racing the locomotive. Suddenly Ruth found herself inside that speeding train, and there in the corner of the compartment was the unhappy heroine, with tears streaming down her face. She was being sent away to Chicago, to marry the wicked man who was blackmailing her father. Ruth found sympathetic tears pricking her own eyes; she couldn't bear to watch the girl suffering so much.

Outside the carriage, the train hurtled on, and the gallant cowboy struggled to overtake it. A huge caption flashed up on the screen: *'Can Bob Reach the Railroad Depot in Time to Save Her?'*

All around, Ruth could hear people reciting the question aloud. Some of them stumbled over the word depot, pronouncing it dee-pott.

'I do wish they wouldn't keep repeating everything,' she whispered. 'It spoils the story.'

'I dare say some of the old folks can't read,' Sean pointed out.

As he leaned closer, his lips brushed her cheek and he tasted the faint tang of salt on her skin. 'Hey, now – what's this?' he asked. 'You're not crying, are you? I thought we'd come here to enjoy ourselves!'

'Oh, yes, I *am* enjoying it. It's wonderful.'

It had been wonderful from the moment she met Sean at the Watermen. Ruth had expected to walk to the cinema, which was a mile and a half away in Poplar High Street, but Sean wouldn't hear of it. They were going there in style, he told her, and he took her on the horse-drawn omnibus that plied between the East India Dock Road and the very tip of the Isle of Dogs.

Luck was on their side because they found a seat on top, right at the front. The bus had no conductor, so the driver opened a trapdoor in the roof and passed up a tin bowl for the fares; the passengers put in their money, then he shut the trapdoor, cracked his whip – and they set off.

From their vantage-point, Ruth and Sean had an uninterrupted view across the Island, with the river curling round them to the east, and the wide sheets of water in the Millwall Docks to the west gleaming in the setting sun. From Manchester Road across to West Ferry Road, the Island seemed to glow in a strange, rosy light. The distant cranes, the masts and funnels of the shipping were all picked out in gold. There was a touch of magic in the air – or was it the touch of Sean's hand upon hers which made it magical?

'Once the sun goes down, it'll turn chilly. There's a mist rolling in off the water,' he told her. 'You snuggle real close now, and we'll both keep cosy and warm.'

Now in the darkness of the cinema, they were closer still, and his breath tickled her ear, making her shiver with delight.

'Seems like I'll have to kiss those tears away again,' he whispered.

His lips explored her cheek, and she turned her face to him. By now the audience were growing noisier in their excitement, calling out advice or warnings to the flickering black-and-white figures upon the screen – but Ruth and Sean were past caring.

One strong hand drew her into a passionate embrace, while the other began stroking her breast. She felt a sense of shock —no man's hand had ever touched her there – but at the same time she knew that this was what her body had been waiting for. His mouth pressed upon hers, and she felt the tip of his tongue parting her lips.

She told herself that she must be sensible. She had been warned by her mother that men were not to be trusted – that they would overpower her and ruin her if she let them. Yet every nerve in her body was aroused, aching to respond to Sean's touch, to enjoy this incredible sensation that she had never known till now.

As soon as she could speak, she protested faintly, 'No, no. We mustn't!'

But he took no notice, and continued to kiss her and caress her and she wanted this moment to go on for ever. Dimly, she was aware of the audience applauding, and then Sean pulled away slightly, saying, 'Better sit up straight – it's the interval.'

The overhead lights were switched on, startlingly bright, and Ruth settled back quickly on the upholstered bench, patting her hair and smoothing her blouse. A swift glance along the neighbouring rows reassured her. Nobody was staring at them – in fact, several other couples were also adjusting their clothes, and one pair were still locked in each other's arms.

Sean seemed to read her thoughts. 'Don't worry,' he said. 'Nobody's looking. Now you know why I said we had to sit near the back. Are you all right?'

'Oh, yes.' She sighed with happiness. 'Only I'm sorry I missed the end of the story. Now we'll never know what happened to that girl.'

'I bet the cowboy rescued her in time – love stories generally have a happy ending.' Sean looked into her eyes and added, 'Do you suppose it'll be the same for you and me?'

She wasn't quite sure what he meant and cut in quickly, 'Is it all over, then? Do we have to go now?'

'Cripes, no! That's just the end of *On the Midnight Trail*. We've still got the rest of the programme to see – there's a thriller called *The Mysterious Beggar* and a comedy, *Professor*

Parks and his Electric Sparks. Haven't you ever seen moving pictures before?'

'Of course I have.' She didn't want to appear ignorant. 'We had a cinema show at our last Sale of Work in aid of the Missionary Fund. It was called *A Peep into the Holy Land.*'

'Is that so?' The laughter-lines appeared round his eyes. 'But I dare say this is a bit different, eh?' His forefinger stroked the palm of her hand and a physical thrill ran through her, making her shiver again. 'What's wrong?' he asked. 'You're not feeling cold?'

'Not at all,' she said. 'I'm fine.'

'What are you smiling at?' he wanted to know.

'I was thinking about *Professor Parks and his Electric Sparks,*' she said.

By now the public bar of the Three Jolly Watermen was fairly crowded, and Connor O'Dell was kept busy pulling pints; he usually took his brother's place when Sean had a night off. From the saloon, a shout of laughter went up and Connor knew that his father had been telling one of his stories again. A moment later, Patrick O'Dell came through the archway into the public.

'Are you needing me to give you a hand?' he enquired.

'Not a bit of it,' said Connor. 'I can manage fine.'

'Evening, Paddy!' A group of men playing darts broke off to greet the landlord.

'Evening, lads – who's winning?'

'Five bob says Mike's going to give Johnny a thrashing. How about it, Paddy? Are you on?'

Patrick winked. 'I am so. Another drop of stout, and Mike won't be able to see the dartboard. Not that I'd dream of permitting gambling on licensed premises, you understand. If the police should happen to look in, keep your money out of sight, for God's sake.'

He moved over to Connor and lowered his voice. 'The first sign of trouble and you call me in – right?'

Connor frowned. 'I told you, I can handle it.'

'That's what I'm afraid of. You've got a black dog on your back tonight, right enough. What's wrong with you at all?'

Connor rinsed out a glass and began to polish it. 'Nothing's wrong.'

'You're not begrudging your brother's evening off, I hope?'

'You know I'm not. I wouldn't be here now, else.'

'I thought maybe you were envying him, going off for six penn'orth of dark with a pretty girl?'

'How many more times? I'm all right, I tell you!' He slammed down the glass, and some of the customers glanced over curiously.

'Steady now . . . I think I can guess what's troubling you. Sean told me you lost your job at the dockyard.'

'And what if I have?'

'Will you listen to me? If you're out of work, I might be able to find you something more regular here. We're pretty busy nowadays – we could do with an extra pair of hands.'

'No, thanks.'

'But if you've nothing else?'

Connor shook his head. 'Don't think me ungrateful, but God preserve me from spending the rest of my days waiting on that gang of drunken loafers.'

Patrick's expression hardened. As they stood face to face, it would have been obvious to a total stranger that they were father and son. They shared the same square jaw-line, the same dogged stubbornness; the thirty-one years separating them had greyed Patrick's hair and worn away some of his youthful vigour – but the same strength of purpose drove them both on.

'It's been a good enough life for me and your Mam,' he said softly. 'I'm sorry if it's not good enough for you, son.'

'I didn't mean it like that, Da. You know the way I am – I have to stand on my own two feet.'

'Yes, I know that.' Briefly, Patrick clapped his son on the shoulder. 'Well, good luck to you. I hope you find whatever it is you're searching for.'

'Don't worry about me, Da. I'll find it soon enough.'

When the last picture faded from the screen, to be replaced by the words *The End*, the pianist thumped out a shortened version of the *National Anthem* and everyone stood to attention. Then the lights went up, and the performance was over.

'Come on, quick now!' Sean took Ruth's arm. 'Let's get out before the rush.'

'It's been a marvellous evening,' said Ruth. 'I don't know when I've enjoyed anything so much.'

'You mean the fillums?' Sean threw her a quizzical look, and she felt herself blushing.

'Of course I did. What did you think I meant?'

'I've no idea at all,' he teased her, pushing open the swing doors into the street.

They walked out into the cold night air – and stopped short. During the ninety minutes they had been indoors, the whole world had changed. The mist they had seen moving in across the Thames had developed into a full-scale fog. A thick blanket had descended upon East London, blotting out everything.

'S'welp me!' exclaimed Sean. 'It's a regular pea-souper.'

The name was appropriate, for the street-lamps showed dimly through the murk, which was thick and yellow as strong split-pea soup, but much less nourishing. It smelled of sulphur, of smoke and soot, and the sour, dank odour of the river itself.

'Try not to breathe too deep,' Sean advised Ruth. 'This stuff can choke you to death. I'm sorry to say we've a long walk ahead of us – there'll be no buses running in this.'

'Oh, dear, I mustn't be late home. Mum will be waiting up.'

'Then let's be on our way, my darling. Best foot forward, and off we go.'

They stepped out as briskly as possible, but made slow progress. Every road they crossed was an exploration into unknown territory. There were no visible landmarks, and between the street-lamps were patches of total gloom where they could only make their way at snail's-pace, following the line of a wall or the edge of a pavement.

'Your family are pretty strict with you, I expect?' Sean asked.

'My father is – Mum's not so bad. Luckily he's out tonight, working a late shift.' Suddenly an awful thought struck Ruth. 'You don't suppose they'll knock off early because of the fog?'

39

'Shouldn't think so. If there's a ship to be unloaded, they'll carry on till the job's done. Time and tide wait for no man, as the saying goes.' As tactfully as possible, he continued, 'Connor tells me your father's a regular tough nut – and you've two brothers as well. Do they take after their dear old Dad?'

'Eb does. He's like Father – a hard man. Josh is more easygoing but he has to do as he's told, for the sake of a quiet life.' She added, as an afterthought: 'I think Josh was mixed up in that fight with your brother last night. At any rate, he came home with his head done up in bandages.'

Sean chuckled. 'Con's always been useful with his hands. Is that the whole family? No more brothers knocking about?'

'No – except my father has a brother. There were three of them originally, Matthew, Marcus and Luke.'

'Matthew, Mark, Luke – whatever happened to John?'

'Grandfather Judge was a very religious man, just like my father. He decided to have four sons and name them after the Evangelists, only it didn't work out like that.'

'Don't tell me Number Four turned out to be a girl?'

'There never was a Number Four. Grandma Judge passed over soon after Luke was born and Grandpa followed her within the year – heartbroken, they said.'

'So that left your Dad and his two brothers. All of them flourishing, I hope?'

'Uncle Luke passed on, oh, more than twenty years ago.'

'And Uncle Matthew?'

Ruth hesitated for a moment before replying, 'Uncle Matt's still alive, but we don't see him very often. He and my father don't get on. He used to work on the docks as well in his young days, but they fell out over something, and Uncle Matt set up in business on his own, as a ship-chandlers.'

'Of course – that's where I've come across the name. *Judge & Son* – it's that old shop down the West Ferry Road.'

'A *very* old shop, practically falling to bits.'

'Who's the son?'

'My cousin Saul. We don't see much of him, either.'

'Family feud, that sort of thing?'

'Not really. They're just not very sociable.' Ruth was

reluctant to talk about them. 'They keep themselves to themselves.'

'But I dare say there must be a Mrs Matthew Judge around somewhere, as well?'

'There was once, but I never knew her. She died in childbirth. Uncle Matt brought the baby up on his own.' The fog seemed to be creeping into Ruth's bones, and she shuddered. Sean put his arm tightly round her waist, and they trudged on in silence.

She thought of Uncle Matt and Cousin Saul, living in that tall, rickety house above the ship-chandlers on Cyclops Wharf. She remembered visiting it once – she could not have been more than six or seven – accompanying her mother, who had felt obliged to take the two men a Christmas parcel of a pudding wrapped in a cloth and half a dozen mince-pies. Uncle Matt had received these gifts without comment, and had not offered them so much as a cup of tea in return. Something about that dark, draughty house had terrified little Ruth. Whenever she heard the phrase 'the valley of the shadow of death', she still thought of it.

Blindly following the wall, they turned a corner and suddenly a huge grey shape loomed up with a banshee cry, hanging over them for a terrifying moment before subsiding to earth again, with a clatter of hooves on cobblestones.

Ruth gave a smothered cry, and Sean caught her in his arms. 'It's all right, there's nothing to be afraid of. Some fool's left a horse and cart by the side of the road, and the poor brute reared up when it saw us. Jesus – you're shaking like a leaf.'

'No, it's nothing really. I'm only feeling the cold.'

'Let me warm you up.' He pulled her to him, and began to smother her with kisses but she could not respond to him now. Standing in the foggy darkness, with a damp brick wall at her back, she felt frozen and clumsy. His hands roamed over her body, unfastening her coat, unbuttoning her blouse, and his cold fingertips uncovered her breasts, stroking and massaging her nipples.

All she could think was: 'A man is making love to me . . . I wish I was enjoying it.'

41

At last he let her go, saying, 'You're not in the mood now, I can tell.'

'I'm sorry. I keep thinking I should go home. We've still got a long way to walk, and it must be very late already.'

'You're right enough – this isn't the time or the place. Will I see you again?'

'Of course.'

'What about Sunday afternoon? We could go for a walk if the weather's cleared up by then.'

'I'd like that.'

They set off once more on the long, slow journey home. When they reached the Watermen she thought he would leave her, but Sean was quite offended at the idea.

'Leave you all on your lonesome on a night like this? I should say not! I'll walk you to your own house, so I will.'

'But if anyone should see us . . .' She looked nervously at the lighted windows along the street. Some of the shops were still open.

'In a thick fog who's going to recognise us?' He waved aside her fears. 'I'm coming with you, and no arguments!'

She finally persuaded him to leave her at the corner of the Rope Walk, afraid her mother might be looking out for her. He kissed her for the last time, and said, 'Sunday, then. I'll be counting the hours till I see you again, my darling girl.'

Then he was gone, and she walked the last ten yards alone. When she tapped at the knocker, her mother threw open the front door almost at once. 'Oh, you poor soul! What a terrible night – you must be perished. Come in and get warm by the fire. Once this fog came down, I knew you'd be late. Did you have a nice evening with your friend Miss Burroughs?'

Ruth took a deep breath. Lying to her father was bad enough; telling lies to her mother was much worse. 'Oh yes, thanks. Nellie's been teaching me to crochet. It was very interesting.'

On Saturday morning the dockers, who had been working continuously for twenty-four hours, finished their long shift at last and returned home, tired and hungry. Most of the men swallowed a hasty breakfast and then fell into their beds.

In Jubilee Street, at the house of Ebenezer Judge, breakfast provoked a crisis. Eb's wife Florence, a mousy little creature, had known from the first that there would be trouble. She put the hot plate of food on the table in front of her husband, and waited.

After one mouthful, he put down his knife and fork. 'What do you call this, then?' he asked.

'Saveloys, dear,' she murmured, twisting her lips into a smile. 'Your favourite.'

'Saveloys? I don't call these saveloys – I call them rubbish. They're like old boot leather, and they've no flavour. What have you done with 'em, eh?'

'I'm afraid they're a bit overcooked, Ebbie, but—'

'Overcooked? That's a joke, that is. What were you dreaming of, spoiling good wholesome food? What's wrong with you, Florrie?'

She moistened her lips and swallowed. 'Well, you see, there was a bit of a misunderstanding, like. I got them saveloys yesterday afternoon from the cook-shop, and brought them home and put them in the oven to keep hot for your tea, like I always do . . .'

'Tea? What are you on about? I wasn't home for tea last night – I was working right through, wasn't I?'

'Yes, dear. Only I didn't know that then, did I? You didn't tell me you was going to be out last night. You never tell me nothing.' Her voice changed to a whimper, and tears welled up in her eyes.

At once Ebenezer lifted his head: a tiger scenting fresh blood. 'Are you complaining about me again?' he asked, and his voice rasped like a knife dragged over a tin plate.

'No, Ebbie, I never—'

Before she could finish the sentence, he hurled the dish of saveloys across the kitchen. It smashed against the oven door and finished up in a dozen pieces on the hearthrug.

Florence gave a little scream and dropped to her knees, picking up the fragments. 'It's not my fault, Ebbie,' she pleaded. 'How was I to know if you never told me?'

'I told the boy I was going to work through – didn't I, Tom?' Ebenezer turned to nine year old Thomas, who had been sitting at the table throughout this exchange, a mute witness.

43

'Yes, Dad,' muttered Thomas sulkily.

'Why didn't you tell your Ma?'

'I must've forgot, Dad.'

'Forgot? I'll give you "forgot", my lad!' Ebenezer stretched out a hand and cuffed the boy round the head. Tom uttered a single yelp of protest, then went on eating a slice of bread and dripping.

'He did tell me, Ebbie,' Florence tried to explain, 'but not till after I'd been waiting. I kept them saveloys hot ever such a long time, and then I said "Dad's late tonight, Tommy", and Tommy said, "Oh, I remember now, Mum, he told me he'd be working all night" – only by then they was overcooked, see?'

'Why didn't you tell me when I came home?' Ebenezer persisted. His first outburst of anger had subsided a little, but he still had to fix the blame on his wife.

'I didn't like to. You get so cross if I waste anything. I thought if I hotted them up again, they'd be all right. So I cooked them this morning and—'

'You stupid woman!' Ebenezer spat out the words. 'No wonder I couldn't get my knife and fork into them. You should've took them back to the shop and complained.'

'But it weren't the shop's fault.'

'Tell 'em they've no right to sell foodstuff what's uneatable! Go on – do as I say – pick up them pieces and take 'em back to the cook-shop and say if they won't give you your money back, you'll have the law on 'em!'

'Oh, I couldn't, Ebbie – really I couldn't.'

She was whimpering again, and her husband crossed the room in two strides, dragging her up on to her feet and glaring at her with withering contempt. 'No . . .' he said at last. 'I don't suppose you could. Now you listen to me, Florrie: I'm going up to bed now to get some sleep. When I wake up, dinner-time, I'll expect to find a square meal on the table – and afterwards I'll take them saveloys back to the shop myself.'

Ebenezer was rather pleased to have a reason to visit the pie-shop. As a rule he would never involve himself in women's work, but now he had a righteous grievance – and the widow who ran the shop was an old acquaintance, with a knowing smile and a plump, provocative figure.

When he walked in later that day, she appeared from the back kitchen, tossing her head and pouting. 'Well, if it ain't Ebenezer! You're quite a stranger, I must say. What can I do for you, dearie?'

'Don't you be saucy with me, Gladys Harker. I've got a serious complaint to make.'

'Oh, yes? And what might that be?'

He put the package on the counter and unwrapped it. The broken scraps of saveloy, smeared with congealed grease, looked very unappetising. 'You sold these to my wife yesterday – and they're not fit to feed to a dog. So I'd be obliged if you'd kindly give us our money back.'

Gladys studied the remains, then shook her head. 'There weren't nothing wrong with them saveloys when I sold 'em. It's not my fault if your missus don't know how to cook.'

'Don't you give me none of your lip. I want satisfaction, see? And I'm going to have it.'

'Satisfaction, eh?' She raised her eyebrows coyly. 'I'm sure I don't know what you mean, Ebenezer.'

'I mean hard cash, woman.'

'Don't you "woman" me. We've known each other ever since we went to the Junior and Mixed Infants together – remember, Ebbie? I thought you and me was old pals.' She looked up at him under her lashes, and Ebenezer felt the stirrings of desire.

'You wouldn't like it if I made a complaint that this shop's selling rubbish, would you now?' He leaned over the counter, his eyes narrowed. 'If our family puts the word round, there'll be a good many people what'll take their custom elsewhere, I reckon.'

For a moment, the only sound was the buzz of a late bluebottle, investigating the pies in the window.

'You're a devil, you are,' said Gladys at last, opening the till. 'All right, then – seeing it's you. There's your bloody money.' She put the coins into his palm slowly, one by one, fumbling with his hand. 'I bet you sometimes wish you'd picked yourself a different woman. You might have found one who'd be a proper wife to you . . .'

He pocketed the money, then caught her wrist, twisting it viciously as the spark of sexual desire flared up within him.

45

'Ow! Let go!' She tried to pull free, but he was too strong for her. 'You're hurting me . . .'

'Don't you ever talk like that about me and mine,' he told her. 'You show some respect for the Judge family – understand?'

When he let her go, she backed away, rubbing her arm. 'You and your precious family,' she said resentfully. 'They're not all plaster saints, not by a long chalk. What about your sister, eh? What about Miss High-and-Mighty Ruth and her new boy-friends? Bringing one of 'em home drunk, then going out on the razzle with his brother. I seen her with me own eyes – two nights running!'

Ebenezer did not act immediately – that wasn't his style. He preferred to think things over and decide how he could turn the situation to his own advantage. Above all, he revelled in the thought that he alone possessed this item of information; it gave him a very satisfactory feeling of power.

Besides, it was important to pick the right moment. Saturday night, Father would be on his rounds, collecting the rents that were due yesterday. Sunday morning, the whole family would attend the Emmanuel Chapel, singing hymns and praying for the wrath of God to descend and smite their enemies . . . but Sunday afternoon would be the ideal opportunity.

On Sunday afternoon the sun shone from a clear blue sky, and Friday night's fog seemed no more than a bad dream. Ruth met Seán as they had arranged, and walked down Manchester Road to take the air in the Island Gardens.

It was a pretty place. Children played on the grass and young mothers wheeled their babies out in go-carts, while courting couples strolled arm in arm among beds of chrysanthemums. The river was spangled with light; there was a slight breeze off the water, but no hint of a winter chill.

Ruth lifted her face to the sunlight and felt its warmth on her skin. She had never been so happy. 'Isn't this lovely?' she said dreamily.

'You get a good view from here,' Seán agreed.

Facing them across the Thames, the south bank of the river

46

seemed very near. The noble white palace of Greenwich, and the rising ground of the Park behind it looked like a picture from a book of fairy-tales.

'So close – you could almost reach out your hand and touch it,' said Ruth.

'We could go over there, if you like,' Sean suggested. 'Shall we walk under the river, through the tunnel?'

Ten years ago there had been a regular ferry service across the water but these days, so many people from Greenwich and Deptford came to work in the Docks that the old ferries couldn't accommodate them all and a tunnel had been built for foot-passengers, sixty feet underground.

'No – I don't like the tunnel. It's creepy,' Ruth said.

'We'd get a bit more privacy over in Greenwich Park,' Sean urged her. 'These gardens are right enough, but they're terribly crowded of a Sunday. There's plenty of room over there, among the trees. We could be on our own . . .'

She knew what he meant, and for a moment was tempted to agree. Her mother's warning had been well-founded. Men were all 'After One Thing' – but they couldn't help it, for God had made them that way. And she had to admit that she too could be easily swept away on the high tide of physical excitement. It was all so new to her, and so much more thrilling than she had ever imagined . . . but not today, not in broad daylight. Not here and now.

'I'm very happy where I am,' she told him.

He looked slightly crestfallen. 'It's only – how can I show you how much I love you, when there's all these people gawping at us?'

'Love?' She picked up the word and treasured it. 'You never said that before.'

'What d'you mean?'

'You never talked about love. *Do* you love me, Sean?'

'Don't you know I do? You're a darling girl and I love you with all my heart. There, I've said it, so now you know.'

For a moment she felt quite dizzy with happiness. 'I love you too,' she whispered. 'Of course I love you, but . . .' Although there was not a cloud in the sky, a shadow crossed her face.

'What's the matter?' he asked.

'It's all so difficult, isn't it? My mother and father would never understand. They'd never agree to – to . . .' She was too shy to put her thought into words.

'Agree to what?'

'Well, to us getting married.' She searched his face, fearing she had said too much. 'I mean, that's what people do when they're in love.'

'Yes.' He looked away, watching a steamer moored up alongside Greenwich Pier. Girls in bright dresses and big hats were chattering and laughing as they disembarked; their voices carried clearly across the water. 'That's what people do . . . But it's true enough – your folks wouldn't approve of me at all.'

A moment later, he seemed to shake off these melancholy reflections. When he turned back to her, his eyes were sparkling. 'What the hell?' he exclaimed. 'There's no need for us to trouble ourselves with all that now. We're young – we've our whole lives ahead of us. There'll be plenty of time to think about marrying and settling down later. Let's enjoy ourselves while we can, eh?'

'You mean, if we're patient and wait for a bit, my parents might come round to the idea later on?'

He hesitated for a second, then dazzled her with his smile. 'That's it exactly!' he agreed. 'That's how it will be. Everything will turn out all right in the end, you'll see.'

All the same, when they left the Gardens, Ruth suggested they go home by different routes. 'Suppose anyone should see us, someone who knows me? It would only stir up trouble.'

He was reluctant to let her go, but finally agreed. Under the domed pavilion that housed the tunnel lift, they kissed goodbye, then went their separate ways.

Fifteen minutes later, as she turned the corner into the Rope Walk, she fell into step with her brother Josh – and thanked her lucky stars that she hadn't allowed Sean to see her home.

'Hello!' she said. 'Are you coming to tea with us?'

'I don't think it's for tea. Young Tommy came round with a message – Eb wants to see me. I don't know what it's about.'

'Eb wants to see you? But why here? Why not go to his house?'

'Tommy said here. Something to do with Father, I suppose; a family gathering.'

As they walked down the street, Ruth glanced at Josh's profile. He had left the bandages off now, but still wore an ugly sticking-plaster.

'How are you feeling?' she asked.

'Oh, it's a bit easier. I dare say I'll live!' he grunted.

When Ruth knocked at the door of Number 26, Ebenezer let them in. He ignored their cheerful greetings; his expression gave nothing away. Marcus sat at the table in his wheelback chair while Louisa was in her armchair by the fireplace, her hands folded in her lap. Neither of them looked up as Ruth and Joshua entered. The kitchen was very silent; the only sound was the tick of the clock on the overmantel. It was ten past five, and Ruth wondered why her mother hadn't laid the tea things.

'Now then,' said Ebenezer. 'We can begin.'

He sat down at the table and motioned his brother to do the same, Ruth made a move towards another empty chair, but Marcus raised his hand, saying, 'You will stand! I have just learned some unpleasant news. Tell me the truth: have you been meeting young men – consorting with them?'

Ruth's blood froze in her veins. Her heart felt like a lead weight. 'Not "young men", Father,' she replied, trying to keep her voice steady. 'Just one young man – and I didn't "consort" with him, whatever that means. He took me to the cinema on Friday night, and this afternoon I went out with him walking in the Island Gardens. I don't think that's so dreadful.'

'You have lied to me, and to your mother,' said Marcus, and each word he spoke was like the tolling of a great bell. 'That is a sin and an abomination before the Lord.'

Louisa looked up for the first time, and Ruth saw she had been crying. 'You told me a story about going to see that girl from the choir.' Her voice faltered, broken with tears. 'How could you do it, Ruth?'

'I'm sorry, Mum.' Now she felt a deep stab of guilt. 'I didn't mean to make you unhappy.'

'You have told falsehoods to your mother and me,' Marcus repeated. 'You should fall upon your knees and seek forgiveness for your sins.'

49

'She's still lying,' Ebenezer cut in sharply. 'It wasn't one man she's been going with – there were two of them.'

Wriggling uncomfortably in his chair, Josh protested: 'Hang on, it's not a crime for her to go out with boys. I mean to say – that's part of growing up. We've all gone courting in our time.'

'Hold your tongue!' Marcus quelled him with a single glance. 'Ebenezer, be so good as to repeat what you told me earlier.'

'Yes, Father.' Ebenezer rubbed his hands together as if he were trying to warm them. 'Ruth met one man on Thursday night, and he was so drunk she had to help get him home. He lives in a public-house. He took her in with him, and she stayed there for some time.'

'If you'll only let me explain,' Ruth began.

'Be silent!' Her father's eyes were lightning-flashes and she remembered her childhood image of him as a vengeful Jehovah. 'You may speak later. Continue, Ebenezer.'

'Thank you. The next night she went out again – not with the same man, but with his brother. By her own admission she allowed him to take her to a place of lewd entertainment. Afterwards they were seen walking home together, and he had his arms around her.'

'That's not a crime!' Joshua tried to intervene once more.

Eb turned on him with a thin smile of triumph. 'Would you like to know who those two brothers were?' he asked. 'Let me tell you – their name's O'Dell . . . two Irish Papists. It was Connor O'Dell she took home on Thursday night, just after he'd cracked your face open!'

Joshua's mouth fell open, but he said no more. Ruth broke the silence that followed.

'May I speak now?' she asked. 'Because I'd like you to know Connor O'Dell was not drunk when I found him lying in the street. He was unable to walk because he had been set on by your gang of hooligans – and if that's the way your Brotherhood carries on you ought to be ashamed of yourselves!'

'The Brotherhood is no concern of yours!' Marcus thundered. 'You will not escape the consequences of your own wickedness by blaming others. You have been a bad, undutiful girl, and you should repent your sins!'

'What sins?' Ruth flung the word back at him. 'I helped a man who had been badly hurt. I met his brother and – and we fell in love. I love Sean O'Dell, and he loves me.'

Ebenezer moved swiftly. The back of his hand struck her across the face as he shouted, 'Whore! You're nothing but a filthy whore!'

Ruth staggered, thrown off-balance by the force of the blow and by the hatred in his voice. At the same moment, Louisa made a move to protect her daughter, but Marcus restrained her.

'You will remain seated, my dear. Let us pray.' Overriding the hubbub, Marcus Judge put his hands together and began to intone: 'May Almighty God in His wisdom pour down the vials of wrath, and make this sinful child repent her wickedness. May He open her eyes to see the error of her ways. May this lost sheep that has gone astray be washed in the redeeming blood, and return to the fold once more. And in the meantime, let her be locked in her room and given bread and water until she comes to her senses . . . Amen.'

4

Ruth was given no supper that night. This, she gathered, was part of her punishment.

When she awoke on Monday morning, she was very hungry. She tried the door of the attic bedroom, but it was still locked. She banged on it, but without much hope. Her father would be downstairs in the kitchen by now, having breakfast. Perhaps, after he had gone to work, Mum would come up and let her out. So she lay on her bed and waited.

There was a chamber-pot in the bedside cupboard, but apart from that she had no toilet facilities. As a rule she was the first person downstairs in the mornings, and always washed in the scullery before Mum came down to make the breakfast.

All the houses in the Rope Walk had outside lavatories in the backyards and not one of them possessed a bathroom. It was Ruth's custom to take her weekly bath on Friday nights, while her father went out collecting rents and her mother visited one of the neighbours. She would bring in the old zinc tub that hung on a nail in the yard, fill it with hot water from the copper in the scullery, and revel in the luxury of a bath in front of the kitchen range, with a clean towel warming on the clothes-horse.

Now she could hear the murmur of voices, two floors below, and she imagined her parents sitting at the kitchen table. She fancied she could smell fried bacon, and felt hungrier than ever. Some time later she heard the slam of the front door – that would be Father going out to work. She sat up. Now, surely, Mum would come to her rescue!

Footsteps climbed the stairs, and the key turned in the lock.

She sprang to her feet, but when the door opened she realised with bitter disappointment that her punishment was not at an end, for her mother was carrying a tray containing a basin of warm water and a hand-towel, a glass of cold water and a plate of bread and margarine.

52

'I'm to stay here, then?' she asked in disbelief.

Louisa Judge would not meet her daughter's eye, but put the tray down on top of the chest of drawers. 'He says you must,' she replied flatly, and went towards the bedside cupboard. 'You'll want the pot emptied, I dare say?'

'I don't want it at all – I'm not a child,' Ruth protested. 'Surely I can go down to the lavvy when I need to?'

'He says not. He's afraid you might run away.'

'I wish I could. He's cruel, that's what he is! He's got no feelings at all.'

Automatically, Louisa turned to face her daughter, defending her husband. 'You're not to speak of him like that. I won't have it, do you hear?' Then the words faltered on her lips as she saw the pain and misery in Ruth's eyes. 'Oh, lovey!' she burst out impulsively. 'I'm so sorry ... but you brought it on yourself, you know you did, telling us those wicked stories and going off gallivanting.'

'I didn't want to lie to you, Mum, but what else could I do? Other girls might be able to tell their Dads they were meeting a young man, and going to the cinema but if I ever tried telling *him* that, what do you suppose he'd have said to me?'

Louisa shook her head, and Ruth answered her own question. 'He'd have said no. He'd probably have given me a leathering with his belt as well.'

'What a thing to say! You know your father never lifts his hand to you – not since you've been grown-up.'

'Then I expect Eb would have done it for him. What's the good of me being grown-up if I can't live my own life?'

'He'll change his mind in his own good time, I'm sure of that. When he's in a better mood I'll try and talk things over with him, quiet-like. I dare say he'll see reason once he calms down. I shall say you're very sorry, and ask him to forgive you.'

'Don't bother!' Ruth walked away to the window, turning her back on her mother. 'It would only be another lie. I don't want his forgiveness – I've done nothing wrong. He says I'm wicked – I say *he's* the one that's being wicked, keeping me locked up like this!'

After a moment, Louisa followed Ruth across the room and

put her arms round her. 'Then perhaps it's up to you to forgive him,' she said softly.

'Oh, Mum.' Ruth turned, burying her face in her mother's shoulder. 'I can't! I'm sorry, I just can't. I don't want any more to do with him. I don't ever want to see him again.'

'Hush now, you mustn't say such dreadful things. Have something to eat – have a drink of water – you'll feel better, by and by. And if you like, I'll bring you up a nice poached egg and a slice of toast for your dinner, how's that?'

Ruth sank on to the bed, looking up at her mother in despair. 'So you're not going to let me out?'

'I can't, you know I can't. Try to be patient like a good girl, and I'll see what I can do. He's not a bad man – he'll come round. Just give him time.'

Tuesday was the day the coal-merchants should have made a delivery at the Watermen. As the morning wore on, Patrick O'Dell kept looking at his watch.

'I've been expecting him an hour since,' he grumbled. 'The cellar's near empty and if we don't have fires lit in all the bars, the customers will want to know the reason why. It's too bad, so it is.'

'Would you like me to go round to the coalyard and find out what's keeping them?' Rosie asked her father. She was busy cleaning the saloon – washing the windows and polishing the top of the counter – and she welcomed the excuse to get out of the pub for half an hour.

'No, I can't spare you.' Patrick called through the archway to his eldest son: 'Connor! Have you a minute?'

Connor appeared, half-dressed in vest and trousers and wiping his face with a towel, he had been shaving in the back kitchen. 'What is it you want?'

'Will you be running a small errand for me, if you've nothing better to do?' his father suggested.

'I'm just smartening myself up to go round to the Royal Victoria Docks, and see what are my chances of signing on there,' Connor replied. 'I have to go further afield to look for work now, that's certain.'

'Now isn't that the lucky chance – the coalyard's right on your way. Drop in and tell 'em we're freezing to death here, waiting for the five-hundredweight they promised me.'

'You'll not catch me in any coalyard – me in my best suit, with a clean shirt and collar,' protested Connor. 'Fat chance I'd have of getting to see the foreman at Connaught Road if I'm black with coal-dust!'

'I'm not asking you to bring the five-hundredweight back in your pocket, you great lummox. All you've to do is call in the office and ask what the devil's happened to our delivery, no more than that.'

'And if you're so anxious over your appearance, you'd best take another peep in the mirror,' added Rosie. 'For you've still got a dab of shaving-soap behind your ear.' She squealed as Connor flicked her with the corner of the towel and went off to finish getting dressed.

As it turned out, he never reached the Royal Victoria Docks. As Patrick had said, the coalyard was on his way, and when Connor walked into the office he found the place in a state of confusion. Before he could open his mouth, the harassed manager began: 'Don't tell me, I know what you're going to say. Your delivery's not arrived – right?'

'My Da said to tell you – the Three Jolly Watermen are waiting on five-hundredweight that should have come first thing this morning.'

'Don't I know it? Watermen, eh?' The manager scribbled a reminder on his notepad and mopped his brow with the other hand, continuing to talk without pausing for breath, as if he might save time by speaking at top speed. 'Do my best for you, but God alone knows when. All at sixes and sevens today – one of my best men off. Terrible accident last night working down the docks – steam-collier from Tyneside, unloading on to the quay. Our chap supervising, coal tumbling down the chute – chap trips and falls – half a ton on top of him before they could stop the machine. Doctors say he may be crippled for life – and now I'm one delivery-man short.'

Connor squared his shoulders. 'Would you be after someone to take his place?' he asked.

The manager looked him up and down. Although the young

Irishman wore a respectable blue serge suit, it looked as if it might burst at the seams if he took a deep breath. His massive forearms, deep chest and broad thighs were straining at the material, and his face was the face of a man who was not afraid of hard work.

'How soon can you start?' he enquired.

When Connor returned to the pub and told the family he had a job as a coalman, Sean shouted with laughter. 'You'll be marked for life, Con! I'm telling you, once the coal-dust gets into your pores, you never get it out again. You can say goodbye to your chances with the girls, they'll not give you a second look!'

Rosie joined in the teasing. 'What girl would give Con a second look anyhow, with the face on him like a prize-fighter?'

'Now that's not fair,' Sean reproved her with a wink. 'Didn't he come home with a young lady only the other night?'

'Will you shut your gob?' growled Connor. 'I never set myself up as a ladies' man. I leave such nonsense to you, boy – and you're welcome to it!'

Someone in the saloon yelled for service. Rosie called back, 'Coming, sir!' and disappeared, giggling.

Sean was about to follow her when Connor stopped him. 'By the by,' he said casually. 'Will you be seeing that young woman again? What was her name – Ruth?'

'I might.' Sean shrugged. 'There's nothing fixed, but she seems to have taken quite a shine to me, so I shouldn't wonder if she might turn up one of these days looking for me.'

He strolled off, whistling. Connor said nothing, unable to decide whether Sean was just spinning a yarn in order to rile him, or whether he was speaking the truth. He thought about Ruth Judge, wondering where she was at this moment and what she was doing. He had been thinking about her a good deal in the past few days.

Dear Mum, I'm not staying here any longer. It's not right, and I won't put up with this sort of treatment. I know you try to do your best for me, but I can't stay under this roof another day – not while Father is living here.

Ruth paused, chewing the end of her pencil as she read through what she had written, then added a few more lines.

Try not to worry. It was bound to happen. I'd have left home sooner or later anyhow. It would have been nice if we could have said goodbye and parted as friends, but he'd never do that. He tried to ruin my life once before, when I left school and I won't let him do it again. If I can't go with his blessing, I'll just have to manage without. I love you, Ruth.

She signed her name and folded the paper in half, writing *For Mum* on the outside, and leaving it on her pillow.

It was the only thing to do. She had to get out of this room – out of this house. If she stayed any longer, Father might find some way to break her spirit, and that must never happen.

By now she had had plenty of time to think about ways of escape. Last night she had lain awake for hours, trying to make plans. She had considered waiting for her mother to open the attic door when she brought up a tray of food – then pushing past her, running downstairs and out into the street. But that would mean more trouble for Mum. Father would certainly blame Louisa if she let her daughter get away. She had to do it by herself.

Some time ago, she had read a story in a tattered copy of *The Boy's Own Paper* which Josh had found in the street and brought home. It was about a man trapped in a cellar, with the door locked. He had an old newspaper, which he spread out on the floor and pushed under the door; he then poked the key out of the keyhole so it fell down on the outside, then drew the newspaper in again under the door, bringing the key with it. It was perfectly simple, but very ingenious.

Ruth had no newspaper; her father never wasted money on such things – but she did have some old exercise-books, relics of school homework. She had already used one blank page to write the note to her mother; now she picked out the wire staples and removed the double centre-pages. Surely that would be big enough?

Kneeling on the wooden boards, she slid the paper under the door then pushed the end of her pencil into the keyhole. She heard a little clatter as the key fell down; so far, so good. Slowly – with great care – she drew the paper in . . . only to discover

57

that the gap under the door was too narrow to let the heavy iron key pass through; and the paper returned without it. She jumped up, clenching her fists in frustration. She had to escape now, while Mum was out shopping – it was her only chance.

There was only one other way out.

Quickly, she stuffed a few of her belongings into her handbag: her purse, containing a few shillings and some coppers – all the money she had in the world – a clean handkerchief, a change of underclothes and a spare pair of stockings. Then she wound a scarf round her head and flung a woollen shawl round her shoulders. She would have liked to take a hat and her outdoor coat but they were downstairs, hanging on the pegs in the hall.

She unfastened the window-catch and pushed up the sash. It did not run smoothly and for a moment she thought it had jammed, but she managed to get it open at last. It was a small, square window but luckily it was not very high off the floor, tucked away under the slanting ceiling, so she was able to squeeze through without much difficulty.

Outside, the slates descended steeply into a narrow gulley behind a low parapet about eighteen inches high. As she stood up, she felt a spasm of vertigo, for there was nothing but that parapet to keep her from tumbling over the edge and down into the street, three storeys below.

It was cold out here, and breezier than she had expected. The wind tore at her shawl, and she clutched it with one hand, keeping her handbag tightly under her arm while trying to steady herself by leaning on the sloping roof-tiles. Putting one foot before the other, she inched along the gulley to the triangular wall that marked the boundary between Number 26 and Number 24.

This was going to be the hardest part. She had to climb up and over the barrier wall, to get on to the roof of the house next door. If only there had been some railing to hang on to . . . What if she slipped and fell? No – she mustn't think about that. Above all, she must not look down over the edge at the horrifying drop to the pavement.

Bunching up her skirt, she got one knee on to the wall, and hauled herself up. The material hampered her; she wished she had taken it off before she began to climb, but that would have been unthinkable. Straining to keep her balance, she managed to get her other knee on to the wall. The wind seemed stronger than ever, as if it were trying to drag her away in a flying tangle of skirt, petticoat, shawl, arms and legs. Desperately, she clung to the sloping roof, then – with an effort – swung herself over and slid down into another gulley.

Panting, she reached the next-door window. When she peered in through the grimy panes, she saw the horrified face of an old lady staring back at her. Ruth knew she would be there, for she looked after a bedridden husband, and the old couple never left their attic-room.

She rapped on the glass, calling: 'Can you let me in, please?'

With shaking hands, the old lady opened the window and Ruth scrambled in, catching her foot on the sill. She finished up on the floor, not knowing whether to laugh or cry.

The old lady helped her to her feet while her husband, lying in bed, lifted his head from the pillows and croaked, 'What is it, Daisy? What's going on? Is it a visitor?'

'It's that Miss Judge, Percy – come to see you.'

'Who?'

'Miss Judge from next door. You remember, I told you about her.'

'What's she want to come in through the window for? Why can't she come up the stairs like everybody else?'

Straightening her scarf and shawl, Ruth tried to speak calmly. 'I wouldn't have come in that way, only I got shut in my bedroom by mistake and I couldn't get out. I'm sorry to have troubled you.'

'What's she say, Daisy?' The old man cupped his ear. 'Has she come from the Charity Fund? Is it going to be soup?'

'I'm sorry – I haven't brought you anything,' Ruth apologised, then turned back to the old lady. 'Tell him I was locked in. Tell him I'm in a hurry. I'll try and come back another time, if I can.' She made her way towards the door, and the two wrinkled faces watched her – sad and uncomprehending.

'Ain't she going to stay and talk to me?' The old man struggled up on one elbow. The effort brought on a fit of coughing, and his wife went to help him.

59

'I'm sorry,' repeated Ruth. 'I can't stop now – I must go.'

The old lady settled her husband against the pillows, but when she turned back she found that the door to the landing was ajar, and that Ruth had gone.

When Ruth walked into the corner shop, Aunt Emily and Gloria were both behind the counter. They looked up in surprise, and Gloria exclaimed, 'You're bright and early, I must say! We haven't had our dinner yet. I s'pose you're trying to make up for not coming in yesterday?'

'No, not really, but I am sorry about that. I couldn't come to work because—'

'Yes, dear, we know. Young Tommy looked in with the message on his way to school. Are you feeling better?' asked Aunt Emily kindly.

'Better? I wasn't ill. What did Tommy say?'

'Oh, then I must've got it wrong. Your father sent him to tell us you weren't able to come to work. I thought you'd got this nasty cold that's going about.'

'No. I've been locked up in my bedroom since Sunday night. I only got out ten minutes ago.'

The two women stared at her, round-eyed. Ruth told them the whole story, concluding, 'So that's why I'm here. Can I stay with you for a little while, until I make some other arrangements?'

Aunt Emily's hands darted to her head, and she tucked some stray wisps of hair back into her bun. She felt sorry for her niece but at the same time she didn't want to get involved in a family quarrel. 'Well ... I don't know, dear. It's rather awkward, isn't it? Us only having the three bedrooms.'

'That's all right. I can sleep on the sofa in your kitchen. I promise I won't get in your way.'

'Oh, no, we can't have that.' Emily turned to her daughter. 'Perhaps we could make up a bed on the floor in your room, Glory? There's that old mattress in the cupboard under the stairs – I'll find some spare blankets.'

'Oh, Ma!' Gloria protested. 'I don't want to share a room – you know I like being on my own.'

'You mustn't be selfish, Glory. If Ruth's got nowhere to stay, we can't turn her out. Besides, I expect it will only be for a few nights, won't it, dear?'

Ruth sighed. 'I don't really know. I hope I can sort things out soon, but . . .'

Gloria had been turning Ruth's story over in her mind, and now she cut in. 'Just a tick – what's the name of the chap you went out with? Do I know him?'

'I shouldn't think so. He's an Irishman – he works at the Watermen public-house.'

'Oh, dear!' gasped Aunt Emily. 'No wonder your father didn't approve – how very unfortunate. What a pity you couldn't have chosen some nice young man with a respectable job – somebody working in an office, perhaps.'

'You mean someone like Cousin Arnold?' said Ruth politely. 'I didn't choose Sean O'Dell. I met him by accident, and then – it just happened, somehow.'

'Sean O'Dell? No, I don't know him.' Despite her initial objections, Gloria was beginning to enjoy the situation. 'All right, let's go and dig out that old mattress. I'll help you carry it upstairs while Mum minds the shop, then you can tell me all about it.'

That evening, Arnold Judge came home from the office and found his mother in the shop, measuring out a pennyworth of jam for a customer. He was about to walk through into the back room, but his mother stopped him. 'Wait a minute, will you, dear? We've got a visitor, and I want to talk to you first.'

She went on with her work. Jam and pickles were sold loose, out of big earthenware jars, and customers had to bring their own basins. First of all Emily weighed the basin, then she ladled plum jam into it, putting an extra weight on the scales. 'There you are, Mrs Harris. One ounce exactly.'

'Ta very much, Mrs Judge.' The customer handed over the penny, took the basin of jam, and went out. The doorbell pinged behind her.

'What's all this about a visitor?' said Arnold.

His mother told him. The young man's pale, thin face soured with disapproval. He took off his steel-rimmed spectacles and polished them on his handkerchief. 'He's not going to like it,' he remarked.

61

'Who, dear?'

'Uncle Marcus. If he wants to punish his daughter, that's his business. We shouldn't interfere.'

'Oh, but Arnie – such a harsh punishment. Your uncle can be rather unkind sometimes.'

'I know that right enough. You should never have got mixed up in it. He won't thank you for taking the girl's part against him.'

'Oh, I'd never do that!' Emily's lip quivered. 'But she's *family*, Arnie. I couldn't turn her out on the streets, could I? She's got nowhere to go.'

'I'm only saying, it's dangerous to cross Marcus Judge. It'll mean trouble in the long run, you mark my words.'

Emily's knees felt as if they had turned to water, and she supported herself against the high stool behind the counter. 'You don't think he'll be cross with me, do you?'

That night, Gloria did not go out for her usual 'breath of air'; instead, she went to bed early so she could have a good old gossip with her cousin.

The two girls undressed quickly. Gloria put on a frilly nightgown and jumped into bed while Ruth, in her petticoat, sat by the dressing-table unpinning her hair. 'Can I borrow your brush?' she asked.

'If you like.' Gloria watched as Ruth brushed her hair with long, steady strokes. Hanging round her shoulders, it gleamed in the candlelight, a rich chestnut brown. 'Tell me some more about Sean.'

'There's nothing else to tell. I've only met him four times altogether. We've only been out twice. Once to the cinema and once to the Gardens – that's all.'

'But that's only the start of it! There's a million things I want to know.' Gloria sat up in bed, hugging her knees. 'What does he look like?'

'Well, he's very good-looking. Dark wavy hair, and dark eyelashes – and bright blue eyes. He's always smiling, or laughing. He makes me feel happy just to look at him.'

Gloria sighed with contentment. 'Sounds lovely. What do you let him do?'

The hairbrush was arrested for a moment. 'Do? I don't understand.'

'Come off it!' Gloria retorted impatiently. 'Do you let him kiss you and cuddle you? I want to know what it's like.'

'Oh, I see.' Ruth went on brushing. 'Yes, he has kissed me, once or twice.'

'Course he has! When he took you to the picture-house, where did you sit? In the back row?'

'Nearly the back row – the last but one.'

'That's what I thought. And did he try anything else? You know – stroking you, feeling you?'

Ruth put down the brush and stood up, pushing back her chair. 'I've done enough for tonight. I'm a bit tired, I think I'd better get some sleep.' She went over to the makeshift bed on the floor, and turned back the covers.

'Are you going to sleep in your petticoat?' Gloria asked.

'I've got to. I didn't bring a nightdress with me – I couldn't get any more in my handbag. I had to leave all my clothes behind.'

'Whatever are you going to do? Do you want me to go round and fetch your things for you?'

'No, thanks all the same. I'll have to go round and see Mum tomorrow and tell her where I am, or else she'll worry. Shall I blow out the candle?'

'All right.'

A moment later the room was in darkness, and Gloria heard Ruth settling down under her blankets.

'I don't know why you wanted to come here,' Gloria said, after a while. 'If I was you, I'd have gone straight to *him* – Sean what's-his-name.'

'I couldn't do that. I told you, I only met him a few times.'

'But he said he loves you – he's the one that ought to be looking after you. Aren't you even going to let him know you've left home?'

'Not yet. If I went to him now, it wouldn't be fair. It'd be like throwing myself at him.'

'What's wrong with that?'

'Don't you see? It's not as if he's got a place of his own – he only has the one room, over his parents' public-house. I can't expect them to take me in. They don't even know me, and whatever would they think? No, I'll just have to manage on my own for a bit, till I get settled. Then I'll tell him.'

63

'You're a funny one and no mistake. If I had a feller like that, you wouldn't see me for dust.' Gloria lay on her back in the darkness, trying to picture the handsome Irishman. 'Tell me some more about him. Did he try to undress you? Did you let him?'

Under the blankets, Ruth turned over, facing the wall. 'I really am tired. I think I'll go to sleep now, if you don't mind.'

'No, listen – I just want to know. How far did he go?'

'Good night, Gloria,' said Ruth firmly.

On Wednesday morning, a coal-cart turned into the Rope Walk, and the driver cracked his whip, calling out: '*Cooooal-oh!*'

Several of the housewives along the street came to their doors. Connor O'Dell climbed down from the cart, delivering a sack of coal here, a bag of coke there, humping the heavy loads on to his shoulders from the back of the cart then lugging them through the hallways and kitchens and emptying them into the backyard coal-bunkers with a noise like thunder, while the women fussed around, warning him not to get any dirty marks on their nice clean wallpaper.

When he got to Number 26, nobody came out, so he knocked at the front door, and waited. 'Mrs Judge?'

Louisa looked at him in surprise. 'That's right.'

'Will you be wanting any coal today?'

'No, we don't. Mr Judge always lets them know when it's time for another delivery.'

'Ah. Right you are, ma'am.'

He hovered, and she looked at him more closely. Under his mask of coal-dust it was hard to distinguish his features, but she said, 'You're new on this round, aren't you?'

'Yes, ma'am. I'll soon get the hang of it, I dare say.' He still seemed reluctant to leave, his great frame filling the doorway, shifting awkwardly from one foot to the other.

Puzzled, Louisa enquired, 'Was there something else?'

'No. That's to say – well, yes, in a manner of speaking . . . If you don't mind me asking, would Miss Ruth Judge be at home? I was wondering if I might have a word with her.'

Louisa's mouth set in a grim line. 'My daughter's not here.'

'Oh, I see. Will she be coming back shortly? I could look in again later.'

'No, she will not. My daughter's gone away for the time being. Not that it's any concern of yours.'

She was about to close the door, but he put out a hand to stop her. 'Could you tell me where I'd find her, perhaps?'

'I could not. She's—' Louisa hesitated for a split second, then: 'She's staying with friends. I can't tell you any more than that. Good morning!'

Defeated, he retired, and the door shut in his face.

Louisa went back to her kitchen, and tried to get on with her task of peeling potatoes but her thoughts kept returning to the young coalman, and his Irish brogue.

Half an hour later, the door-knocker banged again. This time, Ruth herself stood on the doorstep. Relief, anger and love swept over Louisa all at once, and she exclaimed: 'Oh, thank God! You bad girl, I've been so worried . . . Come inside.' She led the way into the back room. 'Wherever have you been? Let me look at you! What a thing to do, climbing out over the roof like that. You might've broken your neck. Still, at least you're all in one piece, though it's more than you deserve!'

Suddenly she threw her arms round Ruth. 'You're safe, that's the main thing. Your father told me you'd be back – he said you'd come to your senses once you—' She broke off, feeling her daughter's body stiffen in her arms.

'Then he was wrong,' said Ruth quietly. 'I haven't come home to stay. I only looked in to pick up my stuff – clothes and books and things.'

Louisa clung to her. 'No, don't say that, you mustn't go. I won't let you!'

Gently but firmly, Ruth broke from her embrace. 'It's no good, Mum. I told you in my letter, I can't live here any longer. I'm staying with Aunt Emily for the time being, and don't try to lock me up 'cos I'll only get out again.'

'Ruth, your father will be so angry.'

'I'm sorry, but I don't care about that. You can tell him you tried to stop me, but I'm a big girl now.' As she went upstairs, she added over her shoulder, 'Oh, I nearly forgot – can I

65

borrow that old carpet-bag to carry my bits and pieces? I'm only taking what belongs to me. I'll let you have the bag back afterwards.'

Her mother knew it was useless to argue, and followed her up the staircase, saying unhappily, 'You can keep the bag, if you want. I'll come and help you pack.'

Up in the attic, folding Ruth's clothes, she suddenly remembered: 'There was a man here a little while ago, asking for you. Irish, by the sound of him.'

Ruth's face lit up. 'Sean O'Dell?'

'He didn't tell me his name. He was a coalman on his rounds, a new chap – I hadn't seen him before. Is he the one who – ?'

The light faded in Ruth's eyes. 'Not, that wasn't Sean – a friend of his, perhaps. I don't know who it could have been.'

Carefully, Louisa went on packing the carpet-bag. 'What are you going to do?' she asked. 'How will you manage?'

'I shall earn my own living, somehow. I'm going to begin all over again,' Ruth told her mother. 'I've got to make up for lost time.'

5

Thursday went by, with no word from Marcus Judge.

Emily began to think that her son must have been wrong for once. It seemed that Marcus had decided to ignore his daughter's change of address. She began to feel rather more cheerful, and by Friday evening she was talking to Ruth about plans for Christmas.

'Exactly two months to go,' she said happily. 'I do so enjoy Christmas, don't you? Of course, we don't make such a fuss about it like we did when Glory and Arnie were little, but it's still a special sort of day, isn't it? I always put up decorations in the shop – we make paper-chains, and get in some holly . . . Glory doesn't bother much about that sort of thing, but this year you'll be able to help me, won't you?'

'I'd be glad to,' said Ruth. 'We never had decorations at home because Father doesn't agree with them.' She was interrupted by a sharp bang at the front door. It was nearly nine o'clock, and the shop was shut. 'Who's that, calling at this time of night?' she asked. Then she saw Emily's face – and knew.

'Talk of the devil . . .' Emily whispered. Realising what she had said, she straightened her lace collar and patted nervously at her back hair. 'Oh no, I didn't mean it like that. I only meant, that'll be your Dad, come for his rent. Fancy me forgetting today's Friday.' She stood up, looking uncertainly at her niece. 'He doesn't usually stop long, but would you rather go upstairs?'

'It's all right,' Ruth told her. 'I'm not afraid of him.'

Emily took the oil-lamp from the sideboard to light her way through the shop. Ruth heard her unbolting the street door. She tried to breathe deeply and evenly, telling herself that she had no reason to be afraid. Marcus couldn't do anything to hurt her now.

'Good evening, Marcus.' Emily's voice was unnaturally high

and thin. 'I'll just get your money – would you like to take it right away? I'm sure you've got plenty of other people to see.'

'I should like to come in, nevertheless.' Ruth's heart beat a little faster at the sound of those deep, familiar tones. 'May I go through?'

She sat quite still, facing the doorway, but when he entered the kitchen he did not even look at her. Taking off his hat and overcoat, he placed them carefully on the back of a chair, then sat at the kitchen table.

'Good evening, Father,' said Ruth.

He gave no sign that he had heard her. Emily, following him into the room, looked apprehensively from one to the other, and suggested, 'Perhaps you'd like a cup of tea, Marcus? Ruth, dear, put the kettle on for your father.'

'I won't take tea, thank you, Emily. Shall we get down to business?' He took out a notebook, and laid it on the chenille cloth. 'Would you please fetch me the shop accounts? I wish to check last month's profit and loss.'

'Oh, but don't you think it would be better to do that some other time, when we're on our own?'

Marcus raised his eyebrows. 'I understood that your son would be working late at the office and I know your daughter generally goes for a walk in the evenings. Perhaps she is still at home?'

'No, they're both out, but since *your* daughter's here, you might like to—'

'I have no daughter,' said Marcus evenly. 'I thought you knew that. The child I raised as my daughter has removed herself from my household. She has cut herself off from the family. Kindly fetch the account book.'

Seeing that Emily appeared to be paralysed, Ruth stood up, saying clearly and firmly, 'I think perhaps I will go up to bed, after all. I'll see you in the morning, Auntie. Good night.' On her way to the staircase, she added, 'Good night, Father.'

Still gazing fixedly at the table in front of him, Marcus repeated in the same level tone, 'The accounts, Emily – if you please.'

Emily's hands were shaking as she put the ledger in front of him, then laid the rent money on top of it – fifteen shilling and sixpence, in silver.

Taking a purse from his coat pocket, Marcus put the coins away, saying, 'I will sign the rent book in a moment. First I wish to examine the state of your business. It's high time we took stock of your situation.'

Slowly, he turned the pages, scanning the entries Emily had made in her spidery writing, the columns of figures, the blots, the crossings-out – until she could not bear the suspense any longer.

'Well, Marcus?' she said at last. 'Is it all right?'

'It is not. I'm sorry to say that the income from the shop is considerably less than the outgoings. You have not balanced the books.'

'Oh, dear. What does that mean, exactly?'

'It means that I shall have to put some of my own money in, to clear your debts,' he said, with a flash of irritation. 'You should understand that by now, surely? It happens often enough.'

'Yes, Marcus.' Her voice shook. 'You – you're very good to me.'

'I have been very good to you, Emily, because you are the widow of my unfortunate brother and I feel some measure of responsibility for you. Over the past twenty years I have paid out large sums of money to keep this business afloat, and I have never put any pressure on you to repay those loans.'

'No, Marcus, I know you haven't.'

'That is because I have always thought of you as a loyal friend, but now it appears that you have decided to ignore your obligations to me and go your own way.'

'Oh, no – I never – I wouldn't . . .' She broke off as his meaning sank home at last. 'You mean, because of Ruth staying here?'

'I mean you are trying to defy me. I am hurt and disappointed.'

'But Marcus, Ruth's my niece! I couldn't turn her away.'

'Don't you understand plain English?' Suddenly Marcus' anger blazed up. 'I told you – I have no daughter, you have no niece! The girl you are sheltering is a stranger whom you have brought in off the streets. If you choose to take her into your home, I can't prevent it – but I warn you I shall not lift a finger

to help you in future.' He paused, breathing hard, then continued more calmly. 'Furthermore, I shall take steps to recover all the money I have lent you since my brother died. I can't tell you the exact total until I have checked my records, but it is a considerable amount.'

Emily's face was white. 'I can't pay you back. I've no money.'

'That's up to you. I have always tried to do right by you, Emily. Now I am asking you to do right by me.'

'How—exactly?' Her voice was only a thread of sound.

'The girl must leave. And the sooner the better.'

Arnold came home at the end of the evening, and found his mother alone in the kitchen, obviously distraught. When she had poured out the whole story, he sighed deeply.

'I won't say "I told you so" – though of course I did – but there's no two ways about it. He's got you in a cleft stick, to coin a phrase.'

'Whatever shall I do?' Emily clutched her son's hand, trying to draw some support, some strength, some warmth from him.

'God knows you can't pay back his money – and you can't afford to make an enemy of the man. You'll have to do what he says. Ruth must find somewhere else to live.'

'She's got no money either – she can't possibly do that.'

'That's her look-out, isn't it? Perhaps she'll learn her lesson from this – she oughtn't to have been so rash in the first place. If you want my advice, I'd say she'd better swallow her pride and go back home.'

'No, Arnold. I shall never do that.' Ruth stood in the open doorway at the foot of the stairs, her shawl thrown over her nightgown.

'I'm sorry to interrupt you but I couldn't get to sleep, and when I heard voices, I came down to see what was happening. My father has asked you to turn me out, has he?'

'Well, yes, but it seems so dreadful,' Emily began.

'Don't worry – I won't embarrass you any more. I see now I shouldn't have come here, it wasn't fair to you.' She turned to Arnold. 'But I won't take your advice, either. My father has disowned me – I can't go home again. Tomorrow, I shall start looking for somewhere to live.'

*

70

Emily came down to breakfast with mauve circles under her eyes, saying, 'I hardly slept a wink. My thoughts were going round and round – I kept wondering whatever you would do.'

Ruth kissed her aunt. 'You mustn't let it upset you. I'll be all right. I'm sure I can find a room to let, somewhere. As long as I go on working for you, half-days, I should be able to manage.'

Emily bit her lip, and looked away.

Ruth frowned. 'Did I say something wrong?'

'I'm sorry, dear – I didn't explain very well, did I? He doesn't want you here at all. Not even in the shop.'

For the first time, Ruth felt a surge of real, cold fear. 'I suppose I should have guessed,' she said at last. Then she lifted her chin. 'Well, I'll just have to find myself another job, won't I? Anyhow, whatever he says, I'm still going to help you out this morning. Gloria asked me to tell you she's got another nasty headache, so she's staying in bed.'

'I thought as much.' Emily sighed. 'I heard her come in ever so late last night – it must have gone twelve. I try to tell her she can't burn the candle at both ends, but she won't listen to me. You're a good girl, Ruth. Whatever will I do without you?'

After breakfast Emily went out to do her Saturday shopping, while Ruth made herself useful slicing bacon and weighing out packets of tea. The weather had taken a turn for the worse. A damp chill in the air hinted that the fog might be returning – there was a haze of moisture everywhere, something between a mist and a drizzle, as if a cloud had settled down on the Isle of Dogs. Through the glass door, Ruth could see dim shapes like moving mushrooms, as people drifted by under umbrellas; it was a raw, cheerless morning. Then she heard a harsh voice raised in song and recognised the singer at once, before she could see him. Gradually the blind beggar came into view along the street, pacing steadily, tapping with his stick, wearing black glasses over sightless eyes. He carried a tin cup, and he was singing:

> *Call round – any old time—*
> *Make yourself at home . . .*
> *Put your feet on the mantelshelf—*
> *Open the cupboard and help yourself . . .*

71

It should have been a cheerful song, but in his hoarse, aggrieved voice it sounded like a dirge, and Ruth found herself unexpectedly close to tears. On a sudden impulse, she fumbled in her purse and ran out into the street, dropping a penny in the tin cup. He touched his battered hat, and wandered away into the mist.

'You shouldn't encourage him,' said someone close behind her.

Startled, she whirled round. A gaunt, weatherbeaten man in his early forties was standing in the doorway of the shop. It was her cousin Saul.

'Oh, I didn't see you there!'

'I was coming round the corner when you run out. I wondered where you was off to in such a rush.'

'I heard him singing. I wanted to give him something.'

They went into the shop together, and Saul Judge continued, 'That's what he relies on – people's good nature. Prob'ly a bloomin' millionaire by now, if truth be told. Prob'ly see as well as you or me, I shouldn't wonder.'

His own eyes were sharp enough, though they were almost invisible, screwed up as if he were forever flinching away from a threatened blow. Not for the first time, Ruth wondered what kind of childhood her cousin must have had, brought up by his father in that lonely house over the ship-chandlers. No doubt he had known more kicks than ha'pence.

He eyed Ruth narrowly, commenting: 'Don't often see you here, mornings. Where's Aunt Em? Where's Gloria?'

'Auntie's out shopping and Gloria's upstairs. She's not feeling very well.'

'But how d'you come to be minding the shop? I thought you only did afternoons.'

'I've been staying here for a few days. I'm not living at home now.'

'Oh, ah. B'lieve I heard something of that. Had a row with your Dad, didn't you? Surprising how the word gets round, here on the Island.' He gave a sudden, unnerving bark of laughter and put down an empty shopping basket. Delving into the pocket of his tattered reefer-jacket, he produced a crumpled scrap of paper.

'My old Dad writ a list – he says as how we need to stock up our larder. Can't make head nor tail of it, can you figure it out?'

Ruth glanced at the scrawled shopping-list. Though Uncle Matt had mastered the rudiments of reading and writing, he had never passed on these skills to his son; not that Saul would ever admit to being illiterate – he always blamed his father's bad handwriting.

'Yes, I think I can.' She began to fill the basket, making conversation as she did so. 'As a matter of fact, I won't be here much longer.'

'Oh? How's that then?'

'My father's trying to take it out on Aunt Emily, so I've got to find somewhere else, and get myself a job as well. The trouble is, there's not much work for girls round here.'

When she had completed the order, she began to tot it up. 'That'll be six shillings and sevenpence altogether, please.'

As Saul fumbled in his pockets again, the door opened and Aunt Emily returned from her own shopping expedition.

'Oh, good morning, Saul. How's your poor father? I expect his joints are playing him up. It's rheumaticky weather.'

'Yeah, that's what he says.' Saul counted out the money laboriously, a piece at a time. 'Four – five – six shillings and sixpence.'

'Sevenpence,' Ruth reminded him.

'Oh, ah – sevenpence.' Reluctantly, Saul produced the extra penny. 'Work in a bank, you oughter.'

'I wish I could, but you need exams for that. No, I'll have to stay a shop assistant, unless . . .' Ruth rang up the money and put it in the till, saying to her aunt, 'Perhaps I should look for something where I could live in? I might try to get a job as a housekeeper.'

Emily moved away, taking off her hat and coat, unwilling to discuss Ruth's situation in front of her nephew. 'We'll talk about it later. Give my regards to your father, Saul.'

He frowned, as if he were wrestling with a complicated problem. 'Would you really do that?' he asked Ruth.

'Do what?'

'Take on as a housekeeper? Living in, like?'

'Yes, why not? If anyone would have me.'

73

'We'd have you,' said Saul, abruptly.

The women stared at him, and he tried to explain. 'Me and the old Dad – we'd take you on. You could come and live with us. How much money would you want?'

Ruth and Emily looked at one another blankly, then Emily said, 'No, it wouldn't do. It's very good of you to offer, Saul, but it's out of the question.'

'What d'you mean? I'm fed up with doing the cooking and shopping and all that. It's what we're needing, a woman about the house.'

'Oh no! A young woman, living with two men? Certainly not!'

'She'd have her own room, like. We got plenty of rooms upstairs an' I could put up a bed for her. What's wrong with that?'

Ruth had been listening to his argument with cool, detached interest, as if they were talking about someone else. Now she said to her aunt, 'I think it's quite a good idea. At least, it's worth thinking about. I'd look after the house – cooking and cleaning and so on – and they'd give me a weekly wage. How much could you afford to pay?'

Saul scratched his head. 'I couldn't rightly say. You'd have to ask the Dad about that.'

'No, Ruth, it's not right.' Emily tried to intervene, but Ruth brushed aside her objections.

'There's nothing wrong with it – it's not as if they were strangers. Why shouldn't I live in my uncle's house?'

Her first instinct had been to agree with Aunt Emily. She remembered her childhood fear, when she visited Uncle Matt's house – the 'valley of the shadow of death' – but that was only a silly fantasy. She was grown-up now, and she didn't believe in bogey-men. What if the house was rather cold and dark? At least she would be making her way, living her own life. Best of all, she could go and meet Sean again as an independent woman, not asking for charity or pity – only offering him her love . . .

'I'll come and see Uncle Matt this afternoon,' she decided. 'Why not?'

*

It would be better, she told herself, than going to strangers – although they were still strangers to her in many ways. She had met Saul occasionally, when he came to buy groceries, but she couldn't say she knew him, and Uncle Matt rarely set foot outside his own front door.

When she entered the shop on Cyclops Wharf, carrying her carpet bag, she hardly recognised her uncle. He had grown so much older – his back was twisted, his shoulders hunched, and his bald pate showed through tufts of long grey hair.

The old man squinted at her, appraising her. 'So you're Ruth, are you?' All the time he spoke he kept nodding, as if he were well satisfied. Gradually she realised that it was a continual tremor he could not control. 'Yes – Saul told me you were a fine strong lass. And you're willing to come and look after our house, are you?'

She looked about her. The shop, at any rate, was unchanged; crammed with shelves and cupboards, each one filled with open cardboard boxes that contained a multitude of objects. Some were the stock-in-trade of any hardware shop – screws, hinges, tools of all kinds – but most of them were unfamiliar to her: items required for use on boats – cleats, stanchions, marlinspikes, coiled ropes of every shape and size, rolls of canvas – along with more specialised items such as a telescope, a sextant, a binnacle and compass . . . The solitary window that gave on to the street was so crammed with merchandise, the daylight could hardly filter through. A ship's lantern hanging from a chain cast a little pool of light around the counter. And everywhere – on the floor, on the shelves, and on all these objects – lay a fine grey dust which rose in clouds as the old man pottered about, touching things, picking them up and putting them down.

'It looks as if you could do with a spring-clean,' suggested Ruth.

'Not here!' Her uncle scowled, immediately defensive. 'I'd not let you touch the shop. You go moving things about in here, I wouldn't know where to find anything . . . Upstairs, in the living-quarters, yes, maybe we could do with a bit of help up there. Come with me, and I'll show you.' Still nodding, he shut the street door and hung up a piece of card that said

75

in scrawled letters: *Back in five minutes*, then led the way upstairs.

Originally the shop had been a warehouse, timber-built, with storage space on four floors, and the old staircase had never been replaced. It had open wooden treads, with rickety newel-posts at intervals and there was no handrail, only a worn rope, black with dirt and grease, sagging between iron rings.

Upstairs, the house was even gloomier. It was just as Ruth remembered it – very dark, and very cold. Now she realised why – the windows were small, and when they were broken, the glass had never been replaced. The window-frames were roughly filled in with slats of wood, and the wind off the river whistled eerily through the cracks.

Many of the upstairs rooms were still used for storage; the sloping floors were weighed down with tea-chests, crates and barrels, all piled high with objects – most of them broken or rusty, and of little use to anyone. In this establishment, nothing was ever thrown away.

On the second landing, Uncle Matt took Ruth into a room which served as kitchen and parlour. The old-fashioned stove under the brick chimney-breast was covered in pots and pans, still containing the remnants of past meals, and there was a stone sink with a dripping cold-water tap, under the window. Faced with this grim spectacle, Ruth's heart nearly failed her. For two pins she would have run downstairs and left the house at once . . . but where else could she go?

At the dilapidated dresser, stacked with chipped crockery, Saul was slicing bread. Seeing the look on Ruth's face, he said, 'We've let it get into a bit of a state, eh? Fact is, I'm not what you'd call a dab hand at housework. That's why we want for you to come and sort things out for us – ain't that right, Dad?'

Uncle Matt continued to nod, and Ruth looked round the room, trying to imagine what it would be like to live in such a place. 'Where should I sleep?' she asked.

By way of reply, Saul opened another door, which she had taken to be a cupboard. Inside, she found a very small room, dimly lit by a grimy window with a cracked pane and containing a wooden chair, an old sea-chest and a narrow iron bedstead.

On the window-sill stood a jam-jar with a single mauve aster in it.

Saul grinned sheepishly. 'I bin trying to cheer the place up for you,' he said.

Ruth guessed where the flower came from; she had seen a bed of mauve asters at the Island Gardens, last Sunday, but it was a kindly thought, and she smiled back at Saul. 'Thank you. That's very nice.'

'You could put your clothes and suchlike in here,' he went on, kicking the wooden chest. 'And I put the sheets and blankets in front of the kitchen stove, so they've bin aired.' Obviously he was anxious to please her. She returned to her uncle, waiting in the kitchen for her verdict.

'How much would you pay me?' she asked.

'Oh, I dunno so much about that,' grumbled the old man, nodding and shaking his head at the same time. 'Wages don't grow on trees! I thought as how you could do the housework in exchange for your bed and board. That'd be fair do's, to my way of thinking.'

'I'm sorry, I couldn't agree to that. I'd have to be paid like any other housekeeper. I should want ten shillings a week.'

Uncle Matt wheezed with laughter, showing yellow, broken teeth. 'Ten shillings? D'you think I'm made of money? I'll give you five.'

'Ten, Dad.' Saul spoke up unexpectedly. 'You know very well it's worth it. I'll make more'n that when I can get out on the river all day, not waste time with cooking and shopping and such. Go on – give her ten bob.'

The old man glowered at his son, and scratched his armpit. 'All right, then,' he said at last. 'Ten bob. Just for a month's trial, mind, to see how you go on. D'you think you'll settle down here, with nobody to talk to but an old codger and a Resurrection Man?'

'What's that?' Ruth looked at Saul for enlightenment. 'I don't understand.'

Saul's face darkened. 'Don't take no notice of the Dad – he's talking rubbish.'

Ruth knew that Saul did not work in the shop with his father. He followed a different trade, plying for hire as a wherryman.

His rowing-boat served as a river-taxicab, picking up passengers and taking them over to the Surrey bank, or out to the big ships at anchor in deep water. But she had never heard him described as a 'Resurrection Man'.

Impatiently, Saul dismissed the phrase. 'It's just a daft nickname I bin give . . . it don't mean nothing.' Then he thrust out his hand, asking, 'Well, then – is it agreed? Have we struck a bargain?'

Ruth still felt uneasy about her uncle, and she knew she had a heavy task ahead if she was ever to make this house fit to live in, but she felt she had an ally in Saul.

'All right,' she said, and shook his outstretched hand. 'I'll do it. I'll move in right away.'

Saturday nights were the busiest time of the week at the Watermen. This was the evening when the local men brought their womenfolk into the pub, spending their pay and having a bit of a knees-up. In the saloon, someone was banging out a popular song on the old upright piano in the corner and some people were already joining in.

> *Strolling along down the Mile End Road*
> *Every Saturday night,*
> *Strolling along down the Mile End Road*
> *That is my delight . . .*

Men and women took up the tune, sitting shoulder to shoulder on the wooden bench that ran round the wall. For the moment, the floor was empty, but soon the dancing would begin.

Although he did not enjoy working in the pub, Connor had agreed to help out tonight. He and Sean had been almost run off their feet in the last half-hour, filling pint mugs, taking them back empty, rinsing them out and filling them again. Now the singsong had started, things were easing off, and they could pause for breath.

Leaning on the bar, Connor said quietly to his brother,

'While I was out on my round the other day, I chanced to go down the Rope Walk – where your young lady comes from.'

'Which young lady might that be?'

'You know damn well which young lady! The Judge family live in Rope Walk, don't they?'

'Ah, you mean Ruth! Now I remember – I believe she does live there.'

'Not any more, she doesn't. Her Mam told me she's left home. Staying with friends, she said.'

'Is that a fact?'

'But I've been asking around since then, and I've kept me ears open . . . According to the neighbours, Ruth Judge had a row with her father and he turned her out of the house – and all on account of you!'

> *Arm in arm with my young man*
> *His name is Billy Morgan,*
> *He's the champion down our way*
> *Playing the tanner mouth-organ!*

The customers roared out the last line, then surged forward into the middle of the room as the pianist went through the tune again in a livelier tempo. The noise of the dancers' steel-tipped boots on the floorboards almost drowned the melody, and Connor had to shout to make himself heard. 'It was you taking the girl out that started all the trouble! I'm telling you, you ought to go looking for her – it's up to you to help her now!'

'How the hell would I find her? She could be anywhere . . . Besides, I hardly know the girl at all. Is it my fault she fell for me handsome looks and me charming manners? If you're so struck on her, maybe you should go looking for her yourself!'

'I would so, only . . .' Connor broke off, frustrated and confused.

'Only you know you don't stand a bloody chance with her, is that what's bothering you?' Sean began to laugh, and suddenly Connor gripped him by his collar, almost lifting him off his feet.

'If you're wanting a thick ear, you're going the right way about it!'

The quarrel flared up so quickly, they had both forgotten where they were. By now several customers were aware of their angry voices and the threat of violence.

'Fight – fight – fight!' they chanted, stamping rhythmically.

The curtain across the archway rattled back, and Patrick O'Dell charged in from the public bar. Sizing up the situation instantly, he dragged the boys apart, rapping out orders. 'Connor – get yourself into the public – I'll take over here. Sean – make yourself useful, there's people waiting to be served . . . And don't let me see you two within ten yards of one another for the rest of the night, d'you hear me?'

When seven days had passed, Ruth looked back over the longest week of her life.

That first Saturday, she had stayed up till ten o'clock talking to her cousin. This week, she went to bed as soon as supper was over. Uncle Matt reminded her that there was still a pile of mending to be done – odd socks with holes in, ragged vests, underpants and shirts – but she told him she was too tired. She would tackle that job tomorrow.

'On the Lord's Day?' His head was bobbing wickedly. 'Whatever would your sainted father have to say?'

'I shall go to Chapel in the morning. What I do after that is my own business,' she replied.

Naturally, she didn't attend the Emmanuel Chapel now as she did not wish to run into the other members of her family. Instead she had discovered the Presbyterian Chapel in West Ferry Road, built for the Scottish shipyard workers. There she felt safe – comfortably anonymous and unknown. It had been one of her few moments of happiness since she had moved to Cyclops Wharf. Time and again in the past week she had regretted her decision. Not that she had lived a life of luxury at the Rope Walk, for she had been brought up in poverty and was used to hard work, but the relentless drudgery and squalor of her new surroundings were beyond anything she had ever known.

The two men were not accustomed to sharing the house with a woman, and it did not occur to them to mend their ways.

Their habits were dity and untidy. They never put anything away, left their clothes lying on the floor wherever they took them off – not that they took their clothes off very often, for they rarely washed – and they bolted their food like animals.

They appeared to enjoy the meals Ruth cooked for them, although they never uttered a word of thanks. Uncle Matt was very stingy with the housekeeping money; he grudged every penny Ruth spent on food, and forced her to make meals with next to nothing – she had to concoct a stew from a pennyworth of bones from the butcher and a handful of bruised vegetables.

She had known from the start that cleaning the house would be a mammoth task. Tackling one room at a time, she did her best to remove layers of dirt and dust that had been accumulating for years, but the work was back-breaking; after one week she ached all over, and her hands were red and raw.

She could never get warm. An ice-cold wind blew through the cracks in the windows: there were no gas-lights, and the candle-flames flickered wildly in the draughts, or guttered out in pools of wax – but she could have endured all this, if it had not been for the cold. It was a cruel, biting cold that lurked round every corner and seeped out of every stick and stone of the old house.

Today had been the beginning of a new month. November stretched ahead, promising still more miserable weather – a winter of fog and frost – and black despair. And tonight she could not sleep at all. She had felt so tired all day, longing to get to bed, certain that sleep would come swiftly and allow her a few hours' reprieve from the daily treadmill. Perhaps she was too tired to sleep. She watched the patterns of light on the ceiling above her bed and listened to the sounds outside her window – the chink of a mooring-chain, the slapping of waves against the stone piers of the wharf, and the mournful mooing of foghorns, down-river.

Then the creaking noises began again.

Every night she heard the creak of the wooden stairs; either Saul or Matthew kept late hours, for she often woke in the night to hear one of them creeping around the house, and saw a faint line of light under her door as someone lit a candle in the kitchen.

81

Tonight they were both up and about; she could hear a murmur of voices, two floors below. Saul had said he would be going out again after supper, plying for hire along the Wharf, but surely he wouldn't find many passengers on a night like this?

Unable to rest, she decided to make herself a cup of tea. Perhaps the men would like some, too. Wrapping herself in a shawl, she went into the kitchen, and lit a candle. Then she made her way downstairs, moving silently, feeling the grain of the wood beneath her bare feet. From the first floor landing, she looked down into the well of the stair. The shutters were up on the shopfront now, but the ship's lantern was alight, and the two men were stooping over a bundle that lay in the middle of the floor.

Matt poked at the roll of wet tarpaulin. A puddle on the boards shone in the light, and as he turned it over, the bundle fell open and something flopped out . . . A navy-blue cuff, with brass buttons – a glimpse of flesh, bluish-white and puffy – a bloated hand.

At the sound of her stifled cry, the two men looked up.

'What are you doing there?' growled Matt.

'He's – dead – isn't he?' Ruth clutched her throat, as if the words were choking her.

'Aye, he's dead right enough. Been in the water a few days, by the weight of him,' said Saul.

Slowly, she descended the stairs. 'You just found him – floating out there, in the river? Are you going to the police?'

'Of course. All part of my job, this is.' Saul straightened up, looking her full in the face. 'I'm sorry you had to find out like this.'

'He fishes 'em out and turns 'em in to the river police – the Water Rats, we calls 'em.' Old Matthew's head jerked convulsively with private glee. 'And them coppers always see him right – they give him a little present for his trouble. That's why folks call him the Resurrection Man. Them as go down under, he fishes 'em up again – d'you see?'

She saw all too clearly. Now she understood why this house had always been a house of death.

——6——

It was an unpleasant shock for Ruth to find that some of her cousin's passengers were no longer alive.

Over the next few days, she tried to put the thought from her mind but she could not forget that pale, misshapen hand, or the pool of river-water creeping across the floor of the shop like a dark stain. Time and again, her thoughts returned to the corpse. What sort of man had he been – young or old – an Englishman, or a foreign sailor? She wondered what he had looked like, then with a shudder rejected the image that came to mind, thankful that she had been spared the sight of a grey face, similarly distorted.

She could not blame Saul for his trade – somebody had to do such things. There had to be undertakers to bury the dead, and there must be someone to drag the bodies from the river – but she wished she had not left her bedroom that night, to stumble upon the secret.

As a consequence, she tried to avoid Saul and his father. She continued to do the housework, to shop and cook and clean, but she retired to her own room as soon as possible every night, and never left it after dark.

One evening, when she was clearing the supper-things from the table and Matthew was going downstairs to potter about in the shop, Saul lingered for a few moments, then said abruptly, 'I'll give you a hand with the dishes.'

Ruth was pouring a kettle of hot water into the stone sink, and she looked at him with surprise. It was the first time he had ever volunteered to help her with the household chores.

'There's no need for that,' she began.

'I want to,' he said, and began to wash the pots and pans. 'I allus used to, afore you come. Bin doing it all me life.'

They worked in silence for a few minutes, then he remarked, 'You ain't happy living here, are you?'

83

'What makes you say that?'

'You're so quiet, these days. When you did come here first, you used to talk to me sometimes – I don't hardly see you lately. You ain't comfortable in this house.

'Oh, well. I suppose that's because it's different from what I was used to. I expect I'll settle down, presently.'

'This ain't much of a place for a young woman,' he said, swilling out a saucepan. 'Dark – cold – not many comforts . . .'

'I'm not complaining,' she told him. 'Only sometimes I find it hard to sleep. The footsteps wake me up in the night and then I lie awake, listening.'

'Footsteps? What footsteps?'

'You, or Uncle Matt, walking up and down the stairs.'

'T'aint me – I don't never walk about here at night,' he said. 'Often as not, I'm kep' out late working on the river.'

'Yes.' Ruth wouldn't look at him, but polished a plate with special care. 'I hadn't forgotten that.'

'So it must be the old Dad, wandering abut. Where do he go to?'

'I don't know, somewhere upstairs. I think I'm sure he tries not to wake me – he always creeps about very quietly.'

'Is that a fact?' Saul frowned, considering this. 'I wonder what the old man's up to?'

He swilled the last of the dirty water away, and it gurgled down the drain. He had not made much impression on the saucepans, Ruth noticed. She would come back and give them a good scouring when he had gone out. She expected him to leave the kitchen now the task was done, but he hovered uncertainly in the doorway; then he made up his mind and came back to her, fumbling in his pocket.

'Here,' he muttered. 'I got a present for you.'

He dropped something on to the table. Ruth went closer to examine it – it was a pretty little crucifix carved in ivory on a metal chain. She picked it up, turning it over in the candlelight.

'It's very nice,' she said. 'Where did you get it?'

'Found it,' he said gruffly. 'Last night.'

He screwed his eyes up tightly, avoiding her gaze, and suddenly the crucifix felt cold as marble in the palm of Ruth's hand. She put it down, saying, 'Thank you, but I can't take it.'

84

'Why not? T'aint no use to me.'

'It belonged to someone you – *found* – didn't it?'

He hunched up one shoulder. 'Maybe . . . but what if it did? She was a goner when I dragged her in – she'd no use for jewellery and suchlike.'

'She?'

'A young woman. Done away with herself, I reckon. You might as well keep it – why not?'

Ruth shook her head, unable to explain her revulsion. 'I'd rather not.' She turned away, then began to wash her hands under the cold tap, saying over her shoulder, 'I'm surprised the police let you keep it. I'd have thought they'd want everything that was found on . . . on the poor creature.'

'How would they know what she'd got on her?' he asked.

For some time she had ben wondering why Saul brought the corpses back to the shop before handing them over to the police. Now, in a flash of intuition, she understood.

'So that's it.' She turned to face him. 'You rob the bodies first, don't you? That's what you were doing, the night I saw you and Uncle Matt downstairs. You were going through the pockets.'

'What of it?' he retorted angrily. 'By the time I find 'em, they've no need of money. Anyhow, they never have much – silver and coppers mostly. Rich folk don't drown as often as poor ones . . . Sometimes there might be a ring on a finger, if I'm lucky.'

'You don't even leave their wedding-rings?'

Saul gave a bark of laughter. 'If I did, the police would soon have 'em off, never you fear! The Dad gives any rings to a pawnbroker what he knows – he makes us a fair price.'

Ruth dried her hands on a ragged towel. 'Please take that cross. Give it to your pawnbroker – do what you like. I don't want to see it again.'

He began to argue. 'There's no call for you to take on so. I ain't doing no harm to no one.' Then he broke off, listening: 'Sssh! What's that?'

The shop was shut, but they both heard sounds from the ground floor, a man's voice, raised in anger. Saul opened the kitchen door; and Ruth heard her father saying: 'I know she's here! Don't try to put me off with falsehoods.'

Drawn as if by a magnet, against her will, she followed Saul out on to the landing. With fear at the pit of her stomach, she looked down into the shop two floors below. Marcus Judge was pointing an accusing finger at his brother, who leaned comfortably on the counter, his head bobbing more animatedly than ever as he retorted, 'Falsehoods? I'm not saying she's here, and I'm not saying she ain't. I'm only telling you to mind your own business!'

Marcus was more than a head taller than his elder brother, but from Ruth's viewpoint he appeared so foreshortened, the two men could have been the same height.

'Don't take that tone with me!' Marcus struggled to control himself. 'The girl is living here and I won't have it, do you understand? Call her down at once.'

'What makes you think you can order me about? You're not my landlord, you know. This is my house!'

'I demand to see my daughter,' Marcus began.

'Your daughter?' Matthew cackled with amusement. 'From what I hear, you've been announcing she's not your daughter no more. You're telling all and sundry you ain't got no daughter now . . . So be off with you, little brother – I'm taking no orders from you!'

Slowly, Marcus Judge drew back, pulling his greatcoat more tightly around him. 'You will regret this,' he said quietly – and each word was sharp and pointed as a dagger.

Then he turned and walked out of the shop. Still wheezing and chuckling, Matthew shut the door after him, and bolted it.

Ruth realised she had been holding her breath; with a deep sigh, she began to breathe again.

The following week, another visitor called at Cyclops Wharf.

Next door to the ship-chandlers was a workshop that made masts or flagpoles, and oars for barges and rowing-boats. The carpenters were kept busy all the year, turning out oars; masts were less often in demand, and when there was one on order, they had to move their trestles and tools into the street to work outdoors, since masts were too long to fit into the workshop.

The carpenters took no measurements, working entirely by

86

eye. First they shaped the tall tree-trunk with long, deft strokes of the adze, then – once it had reached the correct length and diameter – they finished it off with a spokeshave. Chips of raw wood flew out from beneath their blades, falling in drifts on the roadway, and Ruth went out of the shop to collect a sackfull; they would be useful for lighting the fire in the kitchen range. She was sweeping up the wood chips with a battered old broom when she heard her name called.

'Ruth – so there you are!'

The broom fell from her hands, clattering on to the cobblestones, and she whirled round, wide-eyed. Sean O'Dell was walking towards her, with his arms outstretched. She didn't care if the workmen were looking; she ran to him, and fell into his arms.

'Oh, Sean – it's been such a long time!' She could say no more, for he stopped her mouth with kisses. When he let her go, her face was hot and she hid her blushes, diving for the broom.

'Hey, now – what's all this?' He put his fingers under her chin, lifting her face. 'I hoped you'd be pleased to see me.'

'I am, you know I am. It's just – the head's come off the handle of the broom . . .' She dashed the tears from her cheeks, kneeling to pick up the pieces.

Sean laughed. 'Sure, that's no tragedy. I'll mend it for you in a minute, if you've a hammer and a nail.'

'No, it's all right, I can do it myself. You took me by surprise, that's all. It's been so long . . .'

'Much too long,' he agreed. 'At first, I'd no notion where to find you. I heard you'd left home, but I knew no more than that.'

'Who told you?' she wanted to know.

He grinned. 'That no-good brother of mine picked up the news somehow – so then I started asking questions, and kept my ears open – and now I've found you at last, my darling girl.' He took her in his arms again, and she could feel the passion stirring within him.

'We'd better not stay out here,' she whispered, aware now that the carpenters had abandoned their work and were openly staring at them. 'I live next door, over the shop. Do you want to come in? I could make a cup of tea.' Even as she said it, her heart sank. The kitchen on the second floor was no place to entertain guests, and she was not sure how her uncle would look upon her receiving a visitor.

As if he were reading her thoughts, Sean said, 'I heard that you're living with your uncle. Would he be at home now?'

'Yes, he's in the shop. Would you like to meet him?'

'Well, it'd be a great pleasure for sure, but the fact is I can't stay long. I have to get back to the pub. Only now I know where to find you we can meet again, can't we? Will I see you Sunday afternoon, perhaps? We could go to the Gardens if the weather's fine.'

After that, they began meeting regularly, and life became a great deal happier for Ruth. Now she knew that Sean really cared for her – that he had spent weeks trying to find her – everything was perfect.

What she did not know was that Sean had been nagged by his 'no-good brother' again and again until one evening another young lady had broken a date with him to go off with someone else, and Sean suddenly remembered Ruth. He remembered how sweet and sincere and loving she had been, with no tricks to her at all. He remembered how attractive her face and figure were, and he decided he had been a bloody fool to let her slip through his fingers.

There was only one real problem: they had nowhere to go.

Now the winter had set in, strolling in the Gardens on a Sunday afternoon was not so pleasant as before, and when they crossed the river to explore Greenwich Park, the grass was too damp to sit on and it was very muddy under the trees. Sean always had Thursday nights off, but they didn't want to go to the cinema every week. He suggested spending one evening at another pub, the Bunch of Grapes, but somehow Ruth shied away from the thought of meeting the man she loved in a saloon bar.

'I'd invite you back to the shop, but I don't believe Uncle Matthew would like it,' she said awkwardly.

'I don't suppose he would. And I've nowhere to take you at home, except my bedroom and well, me Mam and Da are rather old-fashioned in their ways.'

So Thursday nights were usually spent in the back row of the Picture House – moments of intense sensual passion, mingled with physical discomfort on the cramped benches, and the unpleasant feeling that they might be spied upon by an over-zealous attendant.

Then, just before Christmas, there was a change of plan. Sean said he had to go shopping for the family's Christmas dinner at Smithfield Market, and would Ruth like to go along to keep him company?

They left immediately after tea, travelling by steam-train on the London and Blackwall Railway to the City. It was already dark when they left, and as they rattled over the viaduct at Limehouse, high above the streets, they looked into the lighted upstairs windows of the houses that they passed. Ruth felt as if she were in a dream – upon the threshold of a new life altogether, setting off on a wonderful adventure that would never end. The train journey did not take long, but as Ruth hardly ever travelled beyond the Island, for her it was amazingly exciting and romantic, and she held Sean's hand tightly.

When they reached Smithfield, there were crowds everywhere. The alleys between the stalls were thronged, and Sean had to push through the press of people – yet he made his way so rapidly, Ruth found it hard to keep up with him. He was brisk and businesslike, going from one stall to another, comparing prices and looking for bargains – vegetables, apples and pears, oranges at sixpence a dozen – a box of dates, a box of figs, a string-full of mixed nuts – and a turkey that cost twenty-five shillings. It was the biggest bird Ruth had ever seen; she tried to imagine what Uncle Matt would say if she bought such a turkey out of the housekeeping money.

On the way home in the train, surrounded by bulging shopping bags, Sean put his arm round her waist and said, 'What are you doing on Boxing Day?'

'Nothing, as far as I know. Why?'

'I've got tickets for the pantomime at the Poplar Hippodrome. They're doing *Cinderella* – would you like to come along?' When he saw the look in her eyes, he pulled her closer still, regardless of the other passengers in the carriage.

'Anyone'd think I'd just offered you the Crown Jewels!' he teased her.

'It's better than the Crown Jewels,' she said breathlessly. 'I went to the Tower of London once on a school outing, so I've seen the Crown Jewels already – but I've never been to a theatre!'

The question was – what should she wear? That night, she pulled out her little stock of clothes – one dress for working days, one for Sundays – two blouses, her special shirt with the starched collar – but none of them looked good enough for a night at the theatre. The next day she had to go shopping, and when she called in at the corner grocery she asked Gloria's advice.

'Oh, my, some people have all the luck,' sniffed Gloria. 'But you'll have to smarten yourself up a bit. Men don't like going out with girls who look poor, it makes them feel like failures.'

'But I've got nothing pretty enough to wear!'

'I might be able to find something that'll fit you.' Gloria looked her over critically. 'You're skinnier than me, but I dare say we can pin you up.' She called to her mother in the back room. 'Ma! Come and mind the shop while I take Ruthie up to my room – shan't be two ticks!'

Gloria had a large collection of dresses, and she went through them swiftly, discarding several ('Too grand – don't want to frighten him off . . . No, not that one – you haven't the figure for it') and throwing others on to her unmade bed.

'Here, slip your things off and try on some of these.'

Ruth undressed obediently. Privately, she thought most of Gloria's dresses were too fussy and frilly, but there was one beautiful plum-coloured silk with a tight waist and a full skirt which suited her perfectly.

'That'll do,' agreed Gloria. 'I don't care for it much, myself. It's too plain, and it should have more embroidery round the bust – but I must say it suits you quite well. You'll need a hat and gloves to go with it, though. Hang on, let's see what I've got up here.'

Climbing on a chair, she lifted down some hat-boxes from the top of a cupboard, and produced a very grand confection of fruit and feathers. 'Where's your gentleman-friend taking you?

90

Not the gallery, I hope?' she asked. 'I can't let you borrow this if it's the gallery. They're a vulgar lot up there, and I don't want this to get damaged.'

'I don't know where we're sitting. Sean says he's got,' Ruth pronounced the unfamiliar word carefully, 'complimentary seats – because the O'Dells put up an advertisement for the theatre in their public-house.'

'That's good – they'll be dress-circle then, I shouldn't wonder. You'll look a proper bobby-dazzler in this get-up!'

As Ruth put on her own clothes once more, she asked, 'How do you know what the gallery's like? You've never been to the theatre, have you? Surely Aunt Emily wouldn't allow it.'

Gloria pursed her lips. 'I've been to one or two places Ma doesn't know about . . . you'd be surprised.' She began to put her dresses back on their hangers, adding, 'Boxing Day, you said? Where are you meeting your friend?'

'Six o'clock at the Watermen,' Ruth told her. 'We're going to what he calls the First House – it starts at a quarter to seven.'

'Oh, yes?' Gloria looked thoughtful. 'If you like, I'll come to the pub with you. There's bound to be a good many chaps wandering round the worse for drink, that night. You don't want to go walking on your own.'

'That's very kind, but I don't want to put you to any trouble.'

'It's no trouble at all. You know I'm partial to a breath of air of an evening. You'll be coming here first of all, anyhow, to get into your glad rags. In fact, I might even dress up a bit myself. Don't want you putting me in the shade, do we?'

Christmas Eve and Christmas Day dragged by, horribly slowly. In other years, Ruth had enjoyed Christmas, but it was very different at Cyclops Wharf. Uncle Matt and Cousin Saul did not mark the occasion in any way – they gave no presents and put up no decorations. Ruth did her best to provide a festive dinner, roasting a small chicken and making a few mince-pies, and at the end of the meal Uncle Matthew remarked grudgingly, 'I call that not bad – not bad at all, my girl . . . but how much of the housekeeping money did you have to spend on that lot?'

'Never you mind,' Ruth told him. 'It's cost you nothing. That's my Christmas present to you both.'

91

Her uncle relaxed, and for once he nodded his head with genuine approval. 'Much appreciated, I'm sure – eh, Saul?'

Saul scowled. 'I didn't get you nothing for Christmas,' he said.

'It doesn't matter,' Ruth assured him. 'I don't care about that.' By now she didn't care about anything. She was counting the hours until Christmas Day would be over, and she could go to meet Sean.

On the afternoon of Boxing Day, she and Gloria helped each other to dress, then set out to walk across the Island to the Three Jolly Watermen. It was a chilly evening, damp underfoot, with the street-lamps mirrored in the wet paving-stones, but it was not actually raining.

The two girls both looked very smart, and several passing men gave them inquisitive or admiring glances. Gloria affected not to notice, but she nudged Ruth and said out of the corner of her mouth, 'What would Uncle Marcus and Aunt Louisa say if they could see us now?'

'Oh, don't!' The idea of coming face to face with her parents made Ruth shiver. 'If they ever found out where I'm going, they'd have a fit!'

When they reached the pub, Ruth was going to knock at the side door, but Gloria wouldn't hear of it, and they made a grand entrance in the saloon bar. Ruth was relieved to find that at this early hour the bar was almost empty; two old men in the corner, playing cribbage, did not even look up from their game when the girls walked in.

Sean, wearing a smart brown suit and a wing-collar, was chatting across the bar to his brother, who was in his shirtsleeves, polishing glasses. As usual, he had agreed to lend a hand on Sean's night out. Sean came forward to greet Ruth, smiling politely as she introduced her cousin, but looking slightly anxious. 'Pleased to meet you, I'm sure, though I wasn't expecting . . .'

'Don't worry, I'm not going to intrude on your little outing,' Gloria hastened to explain. 'I promised I'd come with Ruth, so she wouldn't have to walk here all on her ownsome. There are some rough people about nowadays – it's not safe for a girl to go out alone.'

'But you'll have to walk all the way back by yourself,' Sean pointed out.

'Oh, I'm in no hurry about that. I'll just sit and wait a bit, till I've warmed myself through . . . Besides, if I wait long enough, I might run into one of my friends and acquaintances, you never know.'

She looked about her, and her eye fell on Connor behind the bar, watchful and stony-faced. 'Good evening,' she said. 'I don't think I've had the pleasure?'

Sean hastened to do the honours. 'My brother, Connor O'Dell. Ruth's cousin, Miss Gloria Judge.'

'How do you do?' Gloria leaned forward, showing off her bosom to advantage, and gave him her hand.

Connor grunted something, then went on putting clean glasses away on a high shelf. Undaunted, Gloria turned back to Sean. 'Ruthie tells me this is a family business. How many of you are there altogether?'

'Father and mother, Connor and me – and Rosie, our kid sister,' Sean replied. 'The others will be down directly; perhaps you'll meet them.'

Connor glanced up at the clock on the wall, and reminded Sean, 'You'd best be making a move, or you'll miss the start of the show.'

'Ah, maybe you're right. But before we go, can I offer you a little something to keep the cold out, Miss Judge?'

Gloria lowered her eyes demurely. 'I don't as a rule, but since it's a special occasion . . . Just a small port, please.'

'A small port for the young lady, Con. Put it down to me on the slate, will you?' Sean offered Ruth his arm. 'Then we'll be on our way.'

'I hope you both have a jolly time,' Gloria said, with a little wave of the hand. 'I'm sure you will.'

Sean held the door open for Ruth, and escorted her out.

Then there was no sound but the crackle of the coals settling in the grate, the flick of playing-cards, the rattle of the cribbage-pegs – and a thud, as a small glass of port was set before Gloria.

'Oh, thanks very much!' She toasted Connor. 'Cheerio!'

He nodded curtly, and she sipped the drink, running the tip

of her tongue over her lips. 'Delicious! Aren't you going to have one as well, while we talk?'

'I'm not a great talker . . . Excuse me.' Connor moved away to the other end of the bar, where he occupied himself by checking that the bottles were all tightly corked.

'You're what I call the strong silent type.' Gloria was determined to keep the conversation going. 'Not like your brother – he's more the sociable kind, isn't he? Families are funny like that. I mean, to look at us, you'd never think me and Ruthie were cousins, would you?' She preened herself, fluffing out the lace frill that curved around her breasts.

'I would not,' said Connor shortly.

At that moment, Mrs O'Dell appeared from the back kitchen. She was a homely woman shaped like a cottage loaf, with a round face wrinkled by a lifetime of smiles. On seeing Gloria, she stopped smiling.

'And who might you be?' she asked.

Connor introduced them. 'This is Miss Judge, Mam. She only called in for—'

'I thought Sean was taking her to the the-ayter?' Mrs O'Dell inspected the newcomer, but did not offer to shake hands.

'No, Mam, it's Miss Ruth Judge who's gone out with Sean. This is her Cousin Gloria.'

'Is it indeed?' said the landlady, coolly.

'I just walked over with Ruth, to keep her company,' began Gloria.

Mrs O'Dell cut in: 'Then you'll be leaving shortly, no doubt?'

'Oh, I'm in no particular hurry.'

'I don't wish to be inhospitable, Miss Judge, but we have a strict rule in this house. We don't allow female customers unaccompanied.'

'Well, really!' Gloria bridled.

'It's for your own sake, you understand. We get a mixed crowd here – it's not always suitable for single women. So I'd be much obliged if you'd kindly finish your drink and leave the premises.'

Furiously, Gloria drained her glass, slammed it on the counter, and walked out without another word.

'That was a bit thick,' said Connor uncomfortably. 'I told you, Mam – she's first cousin to Sean's friend Ruth.'

'I'm sorry to hear it,' said his mother grimly. 'I know her sort –and they're not welcome here.'

When Ruth got to bed that night, too excited to sleep, she looked back over the most thrilling evening of her life. The theatre had been beyond anything she could have imagined. She had expected songs and dances, and the old familiar tale of *Cinderella* – but she had never dreamed of such a shimmer of light and colour, such fine dresses, such handsome people, or such a fairyland of wonders.

She had laughed at the clowns dressed up as the Ugly Sisters, and applauded Prince Charming when he – or she – waltzed with Cinderella, circling the palace ballroom; and her heart had gone out to poor Cinders, as midnight struck and her fine clothes turned to rags, and she had to go home to her drab, lonely kitchen . . .

But Ruth had not gone home alone. Sean had brought her back to Cyclops Wharf, and there in the dark alley between the old house and the workshop next door, he had taken her in his arms, kissing and caressing her. She had been dizzy with excitement, and her skin trembled at the touch of his hands as he explored her body.

'I wish we had somewhere to go,' he said thickly. 'I love you –love you – love you . . .' Desire and frustration and anger tore him apart until, panting and breathless, he released her, groaning, 'It's no good here. We can't.'

Ruth leaned against the wall, trying to control the great waves of longing that swept through her. 'Some day,' she whispered. 'Some day, I promise.'

Now she lay on her back, remembering, and her body ached for him.

Suddenly she raised her head, hearing the creak of a floorboard outside her door and a soft, cautious footfall on the stair. It could not be Saul, for he would be out on the river all night. It had to be Uncle Matt, prowling round the house again. She pulled the bedclothes over her head, trying to blot out the sound.

Ruth was wrong; Saul was not out on the river. He had returned home half an hour earlier, and was waiting down below in the shop to find the solution to a mystery. Ever since Ruth had told him of his father's nocturnal habits, Saul had been plagued by curiosity. Tonight he had said he would be out till dawn, then returned secretly, determined to find out what was going on. When he heard the stairs creak, he smiled to himself; this was the chance he had been waiting for.

The top floor of the house was one long attic room, and at the furthest end of that room a single candle threw an uncertain, wavering light. Matthew Judge, a ragged greatcoat thrown over his shirt and trousers, was crouching on the floor in front of an open cashbox: the candle-flame threw back golden gleams from the coins inside. Matthew rocked to and fro, crooning like an old pigeon as he counted the money.

'*One hundred and ten . . . twenty . . . forty. One hundred and fifty . . .*'

'I thought as much,' said Saul quietly.

Shocked, the old man scrambled to his feet, scooping up the cashbox and cradling it in his arms. 'What are you doing here? I thought you was working tonight!'

'I know you did – but I come back to keep an eye on you, didn't I? What've you got in there, old man?'

As Saul approached him, his father backed away, and they moved slowly round a battered cabin-trunk that stood in the middle of the floor. The candle-flame leaped convulsively, sending monstrous shadows dancing across the low ceiling.

'Keep away from me, son. This ain't none of your business.'

Saul held out both hands. 'Give it me. I could see it was money – gold coins – hundreds of 'em. You old miser, you bin hoarding it away, ain't you?'

'My nest-egg, Saul, my little nest-egg,' said the old man in a hoarse whisper. 'And it'll all come to you, some day. Just go away now, there's a good boy. Go away and leave me alone.'

'All my life I bin kep' poor, living on scraps and left-overs, on account of you telling me you ain't got no money. Lies, all of it – nothing but a pack of lies! Give me that box, you old devil!'

He lunged forward, and the old man skipped back a pace,

making for the door and wheezing, 'Keep your voice down! You don't want the girl to hear you.'

'*Give me that box!*'

The old man moved swiftly, dodging out on to the landing, but Saul was after him in a flash, making a grab for the box. For a few seconds they struggled together then suddenly Saul let go, and his father staggered back, still clutching his nest-egg. Thrown against one of the newel-posts, he tried to recover his balance . . .

The splintering of wood – the old man's scream of terror – the sickening crash that followed – all these came together in one horrifying crescendo of sound that echoed through the house.

On the second floor, Ruth was torn from sleep, wondering what had happened. Had she really heard that dreadful sound, or was it part of a dream? She lay still, listening, but everything was silent . . . Yet she felt sure she had not imagined it.

She got out of bed and went into the kitchen, where she lit a candle. The sound – whatever it was – had seemed to come from the bottom of the house. Cautiously, she peered down into the stair-well, but could see nothing; there was no lantern alight in the shop tonight.

'Hello?' She forced herself to call out. 'Uncle – Saul – are you there?' There was no reply. The house was very still.

Slowly, she began to go downstairs, pausing every so often to listen, but the silence was unbroken. On the first floor landing, a sudden draught took her by surprise, blowing out the candle. The matches were still upstairs in the kitchen. Oh, why hadn't she thought to bring them with her? But there would be matches on the counter, in the shop. Moving very slowly, she went on down the staircase, clinging to the swaying rope in the darkness. When she reached the last stair, she stepped down, expecting to feel the floorboards beneath her.

Instead, her bare foot met soft, yielding flesh – flesh that was still warm. With a smothered cry, she stumbled forward, banging her knee against the end of the counter. Pain shot through her, but she hardly noticed it as she fumbled for the matchbox, and with shaking hands managed to strike a match. The tiny flame spurted up, throwing just enough light for Ruth to see what was at the foot of the stairs.

97

Uncle Matthew lay on his back, surrounded by hundreds of gold coins, and an empty cashbox. She knew immediately that his neck was broken, for his head was horribly twisted – the mouth gaping, the eyes wide open, the ceaseless nod stilled for ever.

With a spasm of nausea, she realised that she had stepped upon his face.

And at that instant, the match burned her fingers, and she dropped it; it sputtered out, and the darkness overwhelmed her.

7

A week later, the memory of that night was as vivid as ever.

Ruth sat in the kitchen with a cup of tea in front of her, and the tea grew cold as she thought back over all that had happened. She remembered kneeling by her uncle's body, fearfully putting out a hand as if to comfort him, in some way – but she could not bring herself to touch him, knowing there was nothing anyone could do for him, ever again.

As she knelt there, paralysed with horror, Saul came down the stairs. She looked up, gasping, 'I thought you were out!'

'Yeah, I was, but there was no work on the river tonight so I came home and went to bed.' He looked down at the twisted figure on the floorboards. 'He's done for, ain't he?'

'Yes. I heard the crash. It woke me up and I came downstairs . . .' Ruth couldn't go on, and found that she was shivering uncontrollably.

Saul helped her to her feet. 'Don't be afraid – it'll be all right. I heard the noise, too,' he added. 'I was asleep an' all.'

Momentarily puzzled, she said, 'But you're dressed.'

'Oh . . .' He looked uncomfortable and mumbled, 'I got me clothes on real quick, when I heard him fall . . . Look at all that money! I never knew the old Dad had so much saved up.' Ignoring the corpse, he began to pick up the scattered coins, dropping them into the open cashbox. The sound grated on Ruth's overwrought nerves.

'Shouldn't we do something about him?' she asked, her voice shaking. 'Fetch a doctor or the police or something?'

'Police?' Saul's head jerked up quickly. 'No call to bring them into it. It were an accident. He was wanderin' around like he does – like he used to, I mean . . . You know how he was. Must've slipped and fell.'

They both looked up, seeing the sagging rope and the splintered newel-post hanging askew from the top landing.

'An accident,' he repeated. 'I'd best get this money put away before the doctor comes. We don't want strangers knowing our business, do we?'

After that, Ruth's memories were blurred. During the next few hours, the doctor had signed a certificate but insisted on informing the police, since Matthew Judge's death had not been due to natural causes. The Police Inspector had questioned Ruth and Saul, then pronounced himself satisfied that it was a case of accidental death.

The news went round the neighbourhood like wildfire, and early next morning Ruth's father arrived to take charge of things.

'There will have to be a laying-out,' he told his nephew. 'Everything must be done rightly. This shop is hardly a suitable place, so I shall make arrangements with the undertakers to have the remains carried to my own house. Matthew and I may have had our differences of opinion, but ties of blood are stronger than personal disagreements, and the family must honour its dead.'

Saul agreed at once, glad to be relieved of this responsibility. Throughout their discussion, Marcus Judge never mentioned his daughter nor made the slightest reference to her, and Ruth stayed upstairs in the kitchen all the time he was in the house, well out of his way.

The undertaker's men removed the body, which was laid out traditionally in the front parlour at the Rope Walk, surrounded by white lilies, on show to family, friends and neighbours. According to local custom, it remained there for nearly a week, so that no one could accuse the Judges of rushing the burial through with inappropriate haste. During the entire week, the ship-chandlers remained closed.

It was an unhappy time for Ruth. Saul went out every day, plying for hire with his boat as usual, and she was left alone in the old house. She only saw her cousin in the morning and the evening. One day she suggested he should put Uncle Matthew's savings into the bank for safe-keeping, and Saul said he had already done so – but when he told her she needn't bother to clean his room in future, she had a shrewd suspicion that, following his father's example, he had hidden the cash away somewhere, probably under his bed.

100

When she called in at the corner shop to buy groceries, Aunt Emily kissed her, saying, 'What a terrible ordeal for you, dear. Have you been home yet, to pay your respects?'

'No, I haven't. I expect my father will have given orders not to let me in. Anyhow, I saw Uncle Matthew the night it happened – that was enough.'

Aunt Emily shuddered. 'If only you'd never gone to live there, you'd have been spared all this unpleasantness. How soon will you be moving out?'

'I hadn't thought about it. I believe Saul's expecting me to go on looking after the house.'

'Oh, but you mustn't do that!' Emily was horrified. 'Just the two of you – a single girl, and a single man – it wouldn't be right. You must move out as soon as possible.'

Privately, Ruth thought her aunt was making a great deal of fuss about nothing. As long as Saul wanted a housekeeper, and she needed a place to live, what was the harm in that? Then she remembered the talk when she first left home. She didn't want to give people anything more to gossip about.

'Perhaps you're right,' she sighed. 'I'd better look for somewhere else. I suppose I could move into lodgings, and go on working for Saul by the day.'

'You want a furnished room with a nice respectable landlady. A widow would be best – I'll make enquiries.' Another thought occurred to Emily. 'You'll be attending the funeral, of course? Would you like to come with us? Arnie's ordering a cab to go to the cemetery, so there'll be plenty of room.'

'I haven't really thought about that either. I'll let you know.'

Until this morning, she had still been undecided. At breakfast-time, Saul, dressed in a rusty black suit a size too small that had belonged to his father, asked her, 'Shall you be going with me, then?'

'I'd rather not. I don't want to see the family. You'd better go without me.'

'Can't say as I blame you. I've never been struck on funerals, myself, but I s'pose I got to go. It's expected.'

Now, sitting alone in the kitchen with a cup of stone-cold tea in front of her, Ruth suddenly made up her mind. The hearse would soon be leaving the Rope Walk, on its way to the Chapel. Pulling on her hat and coat, she hurried downstairs, and set off along the West Ferry Road. It was a raw, damp morning, and she took an umbrella, holding it well down over her head and hoping she would not be recognised.

When she got there, the hearse had just turned out of the Rope Walk; it was drawn by two shining black horses with black plumes and black velvet saddle-clothes, accompanied by eight 'mutes' – professional mourners, with long black overcoats, and top hats wreathed in black crêpe. Behind the hearse a line of cabs moved at walking-pace, decorated with black ribbons, and after them a straggling crowd of friends and neighbours followed on foot. Nearly everyone was in mourning; the family would be expected to go on wearing black for a full year after the funeral.

Huddled under her umbrella, Ruth joined the tail-end of the procession, falling in beside a pale girl of about her own age with a black shawl over her head. Ruth did not recognise her as a friend of the family, and after a while she broke the silence, asking, 'Were you a neighbour of Mr Judge?'

'No, I didn't really know him myself,' said the girl. Her voice was hoarse, and Ruth could tell that she was not far from tears. 'I don't come from round here – I just come over for the funeral.'

Something in her tone discouraged further questions, and Ruth said no more. When they reached the Emmanuel Chapel, the procession halted, waiting until the coffin was carried in on the shoulders of the eight pall-bearers.

By now the girl was crying openly, her thin body racked with sobs, and Ruth put a hand on her arm. 'He died at once,' she said. 'He can't have suffered any pain.'

The girl lifted her face. Tears and raindrops mingled on her cheeks, as the words were torn from her. 'I'm not crying for him – it's for *her* . . .'

'Her?' Ruth was bewildered. 'Who?'

'My daughter – my little girl. Only a week old, she was. The doctor said as she never had a chance – and now she's gone.'

'I'm afraid you've made a mistake.' Ruth tried to explain. 'This is the funeral of Matthew Judge.'

'I don't care who it is. I ain't got no money for funerals, but I'm not having my little girl thrown into a pauper's grave. I give the undertaker two half-crowns, and he said he'd see me right. He's put my baby in with that old man, so she gets a Christian burial, and nobody's none the wiser. His family won't never know the difference . . .' She broke off, eyeing Ruth with sudden suspicion. 'Here – you're not one of them, are you?'

Ruth hesitated, then said gently, 'No. I'm not one of the family.'

'Course you're not . . . if you was, you'd have been riding in a carriage with the rest of 'em. Promise you won't tell nobody what I said?'

'I promise.'

The mourners were filing into the Chapel by now, and the girl turned away, knowing she had no place there. Glancing back over her shoulder, she asked Ruth, 'Aren't you going in, then?'

'I don't think so. I'll stay here and say a prayer for Mr Judge – and one for your daughter.'

The girl nodded, and walked away down the wet, grey road. The last of the mourners went into the Chapel, and the doors were closed. Ruth stayed on for a few moments, listening to the rain pattering on her umbrella. She thought of her uncle, and the infant who would accompany him to his grave. He had been a difficult, disagreeable old man but he had been kind to her; she was glad he would not be alone on his last journey.

They had tea early that night, and Saul went out as soon as the meal was over. Ruth assumed he was going on the river: it seemed rather extraordinary that he should be working as usual on the day of his father's funeral – but Saul Judge was not an ordinary man.

After she had washed up and tidied the kitchen, she sewed some patches on Saul's working trousers, which had worn through at the knees. By the time she finished, her eyelids were growing heavy, and she began to get ready for bed. She was in her nightgown, boiling a kettle for a hot drink, when she heard the street door bang and the sound of footsteps coming up the stairs. She threw on a shawl, and when Saul walked into the kitchen, she said, 'Hello – you've finished work early. I'm just making myself a cup of cocoa. Would you like some?'

'Cocoa? No bloody cocoa for me,' he replied thickly, and the smell of whisky reached her across the room. 'I've not been working tonight.'

'No. You've been to the Ferry, I suppose?' The Ferry House was the nearest tavern to the Cyclops Wharf. Saul was not a regular customer there, for his father had disapproved of wasting good money on drink, but tonight he was feeling reckless.

'What if I have? It's right and proper after a funeral, ain't it? A wake, that's what it was.' He stumbled towards the table, adding, 'Here . . . I got something for you, girl – little present.' He pulled something from his pocket, and dropped it on the table; it glinted in the candlelight. Ruth went closer and saw that it was a brooch – pinchbeck, set with green beads.

'It's very nice,' she said. 'But I can't take it.'

'Why not?' He frowned, trying to focus on her. 'It weren't took off one of them fished out the water, if that's what you think. I bought this for you with me own money – off of a bloke what I met in the Ferry. He said them's emeralds . . . Go on, put it on! I never give you nothing at Christmas, did I? This is your Christmas present from me.'

'It's very nice,' she repeated, pinning it to her shawl. 'You're very kind.'

'Come and sit down.' Saul slumped into a chair by the stove. 'You'n me's got to have a little talk.'

'Can't it wait till the morning?' She moved towards the door of her bedroom, unwilling to get drawn into a conversation when Saul was drunk.

'No, no – sit down. We got to get things sorted out.'

Reluctantly, she returned to her chair by the table. 'I thought you might be too tired.'

'Tired? I'm not tired! Full of beans, that's what I am!' He chuckled, then continued solemnly, 'But we got to agree what to do 'bout the shop. Now the old Dad's gone, somebody's got to mind the shop. I got my own job, so I can't do it. So I got to thinking – how about you, girl? You won't have so much to do

104

around the house now there's just the two of us, and you got 'sperience of shop-work – dealing with customers and giving change and that. Course, I'd let you have a bit extra on top of your wages, like.'

'No, I'm sorry. I can't do that, Saul. You see, I shan't be here much longer. I've got to find some other lodgings now.'

'Do what?' He stared at her, his eyes and mouth wide open. 'What're you on about?'

'It's not right for me to live here with you – people will talk. So I must go and find somewhere else.'

'Go? You can't go! I won't let you! This is your home – you live here, girl. You live here with *me*!' He tried to emphasise the point by thumping the table, but missed. Dragging himself to his feet, he lurched towards her. 'You're not going away, d'you hear? You can't leave me all alone – I won't let you!'

She stood up, hoping to put an end to the argument, but as she moved towards the door, he grabbed her. 'I want you here – d'you understand? *I want you with me!*'

She struggled, but he was hugging her like a bear. Drunk and unsteady, he was still too strong for her. 'You'll be all right here. You'n me together – we'll have some good times!' With mounting excitement, he began to laugh. 'I told you – I'm full of beans. I'll take care of you, girl, an' you take care of me – right?'

He tried to kiss her. The rank smell of his unwashed body and the fumes of whisky made her feel sick. She gripped his wrists as tightly as she could, trying to hold him off, but he pressed his lips to her face. Feeling his spittle on her cheek, she put up a hand instinctively to wipe it away. As soon as she let go of his wrist, he lunged for her breasts, tearing the thin cotton of her nightgown. The brooch was ripped from her shawl, and fell to the floor.

'Stop – please stop!' she pleaded with him, but he was thrusting himself against her. She felt his fingers, slippery with sweat, groping inside her torn nightgown, fumbling for her nipples, as she was forced back against the table-top, helpless under the weight of his body.

Desperate, she brought her knee up hard into his groin, and heard his indrawn gasp of pain. As he recoiled, momentarily

105

releasing his hold upon her, she seized her chance of escape. Picking up a chair, she held it out like a shield, fending him off; before he could make another move, she ran into the bedroom and slammed the door, then wedged the back of the chair under the handle. He began to bang on the door, shouting and cursing; she prayed that the chair would not give way, and her prayer was answered.

Eventually she heard him move off. A moment later the kitchen door slammed, and she listened to him stumbling up the stairs. Then there was a thud and the creak of springs overhead as he flung himself down on his bed. And then – mercifully – there was silence.

She thought of getting dressed and leaving the house, but where could she go at this time of night? Aunt Emily might take her in for a few hours, in defiance of Father, but she shrank from the thought of her aunt's reaction when she heard what had happened, and the finger-wagging conclusion that Ruth had brought the situation upon herself . . .

In the end she decided that, once asleep, Saul would probably not regain consciousness before morning. She would stay where she was till then. Physically and emotionally exhausted, she fell into a deep sleep as soon as she got into bed. Some hours later she awoke, ready to face her problems.

She packed the carpet-bag quickly, taking everything that belonged to her. Cautiously, she opened the door into the kitchen and listened . . . Saul was still asleep; she could hear him snoring in the room above. She sat at the table and tried to write him a note, then remembered he would not be able to read it. She did not wish her letter to be read aloud by guffawing strangers at the Ferry House inn, so sadly, she put down her pen, leaving her farewell message unwritten. She found the brooch he had given her, lying on the floor; she picked it up and left it on the table.

When she had put on her hat and coat, she took one last look round the room, then went quietly downstairs and out through the shop.

It was still dark in the street, but there were plenty of people out already; men going to work – many of them off to report at

106

the dock gates, hoping to be taken on as casual labour by her father, or foremen like him.

It was over two miles from Cyclops Wharf to the Three Jolly Watermen, for she took the long way round by Cubitt Town, not wishing to run into any of her family. The carpet-bag seemed to get heavier at every step, and she changed it from hand to hand several times before she reached the public-house.

Of course it was shut at this early hour, but someone was up and about, for there were lights on inside. She went round to the side door, hoping Sean was an early riser. If he were still in bed, she would have to sit on the step and wait for him.

Timidly, she knocked at the door. After an agonising delay, she heard a bolt being slid back, and a chain unfastened. The door opened a couple of inches and Rosie O'Dell asked suspiciously, 'Who is it?'

'It's me – Ruth Judge. I don't know if you remember, but we have met.'

'Oh, to be sure.' Rosie let the door swing open. 'What can I do for you?'

'Could I speak to Sean, please?'

'Sean's not up yet.' Seeing Ruth's disappointment, Rosie added, 'But I'll go and give him a shout. Would you like to come inside?' She took Ruth in, bolted the door behind her, and left her sitting in the bar while she ran upstairs.

Ruth heard a muffled knocking, then the creak of a door, and a muttered exchange. After a few moments Rosie reappeared, saying, 'He'll not be long. Will you excuse me while I get on with my work? I have to do the fires and start the breakfast.'

She went out through the bar, and Ruth continued to wait. The minutes dragged by, and she began to wonder if Sean had gone back to sleep, but at last she heard him coming down the stairs. The moment he walked in – hastily dressed in shirt and trousers, his braces dangling, his hair uncombed – her heart went out to him, and she found it hard to speak.

'I'm sorry,' she began. 'Sean – I'm so sorry.'

'Sorry? Dearest girl, what's happened? What's wrong?' He was rubbing the sleep from his eyes. 'What time is it?'

'I don't know, but it's very early. I've no right to come and bother you like this, but I – I've nowhere else to go . . .' And then her voice broke, because he held her in his arms, and she knew she had nothing to be afraid of any more.

'You'd best come up above, where we can talk,' he murmure, stroking her hair. 'But not a word, mind! We don't want to disturb the family.' He took her up to his bedroom, a small back room, sparsely furnished, with an unmade bed and some clothes flung over a chair.

'Forgive the mess – I wasn't expecting visitors at this time of day,' he said with a grin, pulling the bed-covers straight. 'Now will you sit down and tell me what this is all about?'

They sat side by side on the edge of the bed, and she began her story. She told him about Uncle Matt's death, and the miserable week that followed – she told him about the funeral yesterday, and the evening after the funeral. When she came to Saul's drunken return from the pub, she faltered, too embarrassed to go into details, but Sean understood what she was trying to say and his face darkened.

'He's a filthy devil, that cousin of yours – and you're a good, brave girl, and I'm proud of you. You did right to come to me, my darling. Don't fret yourself – I'll look after you now.'

'But what shall I do?' she asked. 'I must find somewhere to live!'

'You've found somewhere,' he told her. 'You're going to live here.'

She tried to argue, but he silenced her with a kiss. 'No more talk,' he said firmly. 'You just sit here and make yourself easy, while I go and have a word with me Mam. It's going to be all right – I promise!'

When the O'Dells assembled for breakfast in the back kitchen, Sean gave them a brief account of Ruth's situation, concluding, 'She's got nowhere to live now – so I said she can stay here. That'll be all right, won't it, Da?'

Patrick O'Dell put down his mug of tea and said, 'Seeing as you already told the young lady, I can hardly say no, can I? Well, I'm proud to know you've such a generous nature.' He winked at his son. 'A more Christian and unselfish act of charity I never heard!'

Rosie giggled, Connor dug into a plate of bacon and egg, apparently deaf to the conversation. Relieved, Sean said, 'That's settled, then. I'll just slip upstairs and tell her.'

As he pushed back his chair, his mother cut in sharply, 'You'll stay where you are! I'll not have that young woman living in this house. I told you, I know her kind.'

They all stared at Mrs O'Dell in astonishment. Even Connor looked up as Sean protested, 'How can you say that, Mam? You never even laid eyes on the girl!'

'I saw her cousin, didn't I, and that's sufficient. She's not wanted here.'

'Wait now – her cousin's a different kettle of fish altogether. At least meet the girl, before you set your face against her.'

'He's right, Mam. I've met her and she's very nice,' Rosie chimed in.

'That's fair enough, Mary,' Patrick told his wife. 'You should see her for yourself before you decide.'

'Of course, you would take her part. Very well – bring her here, and I'll speak with her.'

A few minutes later, Sean brought Ruth into the kitchen and introduced her to his parents.

'Glad to know you,' said Patrick O'Dell, smiling broadly and shaking her by the hand, then she turned to Mrs O'Dell.

'How do you do?' Ruth held out her hand. 'I'm sorry to interrupt your breakfast. I shouldn't have come here like this, but – I hope Sean explained to you . . .'

Mary O'Dell's face softened, and she took the outstretched hand. 'You're very welcome,' she said. 'And you couldn't have come at a better time, for I'm sure you've not had a bite to eat this morning. Rosie, lay another place for Miss Judge, and give her some breakfast while we think what's best to do.'

Then they all began to talk at once – all except Connor, who said nothing and never took his eyes from his plate.

'The trouble is, we've not a spare room or an empty bed in the house,' Mary O'Dell continued. 'I'll have to put on my thinking-cap to decide how we're to make you comfortable.'

'She could move in with me,' said Rosie. 'I've got a good big bed. There's plenty of room for two, if you don't mind sharing. I'll try not to kick!'

So it was arranged, and as soon as breakfast was over, Rosie took Ruth upstairs to unpack her bag and put her clothes away.

Sean thanked his mother. 'Bless you, Mam. I knew you'd not let me down.'

'That was the quickest about-turn I ever did see!' Patrick teased his wife. 'What made you change your mind so sudden?'

'The minute she walked in, I could see I was mistaken. Her and her cousin are different as chalk and cheese, thanks be to God! She's a good girl, and I'll be glad to help her.' As her eldest son got up from the table, she turned to him. 'You've not had much to say for yourself this morning. What do you think of us taking in a lodger?'

Connor shrugged. 'You can leave me out of this – it's none of my business, is it? Anyhow, I'll be late for work. If you want her here, that's up to you.'

At first Ruth wasn't sure how she felt about sharing a room with Rosie. She had not found Gloria very comfortable as a room-mate, and the idea of sharing a bed seemed strange. To her surprise, it was much easier than she expected. That night, when they settled down and Rosie had blown out the bedside candle, Ruth said, 'It's funny, I've just remembered something. When I was little, I used to envy my brothers because they shared a room. I wished I had a sister so I wouldn't be always on my own.'

When Rosie spoke, Ruth could hear that she was smiling. 'Me too! My brothers slept in this bed when I was very young, while I had a tiny room with a cot in it. I used to wish I was twins!'

They stayed awake for a long time. It was very easy, talking in the darkness, and Ruth felt she could have told Rosie anything. Perhaps Rosie felt the same, because after a while she said, 'I call them my brothers but they're not really, you know. Mam and Da aren't my true mother and father, either. They adopted me soon after I was born.'

'I never knew that! Sean said you were his sister.'

'So I am, in every other way. We were brought up together, ever since I was a baby.'

110

'But why?' Ruth tried to be tactful. 'I mean – why didn't your own parents keep you?'

'Oh, it was the usual thing. My mother wasn't married, so she couldn't keep me. It was our Parish Priest arranged the adoption – and I couldn't have wished for a better family.' She touched Ruth's hand lightly. 'And now I've got a sister as well, so that makes it perfect.'

Ruth soon got accustomed to her new home. In exchange for her board and lodging, she helped with the housework, cooking and cleaning. When Patrick suggested she might like to take a turn behind the bar to earn some pocket-money, Ruth shied away from the idea, and Mary O'Dell was quick to reassure her.

'You don't have to if you don't want to. Many a young lady wouldn't feel easy working in a pub, and I don't blame you at all.'

'It's not that . . . but I'd feel awkward if any of the customers knew me. It might be difficult if they were friends of my family.'

'Sure, I understand that. And we've more than enough to keep you busy about the house, my dear, so don't give it another thought.'

At the end of her first week with the O'Dells, Ruth told Sean she had never been so happy. 'Everyone is so kind and friendly, making me feel at home. Everyone except . . .'

She broke off, and Sean completed the sentence. 'Everyone except my brother, you mean.'

'Well, yes. Connor never speaks to me unless he has to. Why does he hate me so much?'

'Don't bother your head about him. Con's a moody devil – always has been. There's no accounting for him . . . I dare say he'll come round, in time.'

But time passed, and Connor kept out of Ruth's way.

The weeks rolled by, and winter turned to spring. The grey fogs lifted and the river sparkled under blue skies, silver in the sunlight. On Sunday mornings, Ruth continued to attend the Presbyterian Chapel while the O'Dells went to mass at St Anthony's, the local Catholic church; when they returned from their devotions, the joint and the roast potatoes were put into the oven, and gradually an appetising aroma filled the kitchen.

111

After lunch, the girls washed up while Patrick O'Dell sat in his favourite armchair with the *East End News* spread on his knees, reading out any headlines that caught his fancy.

'*Man Steals Gold Watch!*' he intoned dramatically. 'Ah, these are terrible times we live in, and no mistake . . . And will you listen to this? Here's a young girl attacked by some villain in broad daylight. You be careful when you go out – the streets aren't safe for women nowadays.'

On this particular afternoon, Mary and Rosie were to go visiting with Ruth. Mary's sister Moira and her husband, Henry Marriner, had invited them to tea, and Ruth understood that this was a special occasion. She had often heard them speak of 'Auntie Moira'. Mary's sister had married well, and lived across the river in a fine house not far from Greenwich Park.

As it was a sunny day, Mrs O'Dell suggested they should walk there and back through the tunnel under the river, to the Marriners' house on the Surrey shore. They left the menfolk behind. Connor had gone off on some mysterious errand of his own, while Sean – who had arranged to take Ruth out for the evening – planned to have a luxurious bath in front of the kitchen fire, then shave and put on a clean shirt and his best suit. Patrick, who had dozed off over his newspaper as usual, went upstairs for an afternoon nap.

'Don't the men ever visit your sister?' Ruth asked Mrs O'Dell, as they walked down to the pedestrian tunnel.

'Oh, they think Moira's a touch too grand since she was married,' explained Mary. 'And she's very house-proud. She wouldn't care to have them clumping about on her carpets with their dirty boots, or throwing themselves into her delicate armchairs and breaking the springs!'

'Besides, she doesn't trust the boys not to come out with one of their terrible jokes in front of Uncle Henry,' added Rosie, with an impish grin. 'He's that strait-laced – if he ever smiled, I'd be fearful it might crack his face!'

'Hush now!' Mary scolded her. 'Take no notice of her, Ruth. Henry Marriner's a very decent, respectable man.'

But Rosie was irrepressible. 'I can remember when I was little, Auntie Moira used to be one of his lady-typists – that's

112

how they met. It's funny to think she used to work for him. Now they're married, he goes to his office every day while she sits at home and never does a hand's turn!'

'Rosie, behave yourself!' Mary tapped her on the wrist. 'You shouldn't speak of your Aunt like that. Though I must admit, Moira did well for herself when she picked Henry out of the lucky-bag!'

This was no more than the truth. The Marriners' house, in a side road leading up to the Park, was the most beautiful house Ruth had ever seen. It had not one garden, but two – a small one in front, and a large one at the back. Inside was a handsome staircase with a curved mahogany hand-rail, and there were thick carpets in every room, set on floorboards stained and polished until they looked like glass. In the drawing room was a pianoforte with candles on it, and a central gasolier that could be raised or lowered from the ceiling. It had a marble fireplace, and a mantelpiece crammed with crystal vases, dried flowers under glass domes, and a gilt clock that chimed every quarter of an hour. The splendour of it all quite took Ruth's breath away.

'How do you do?' she said in a whisper, shaking hands with her hostess.

Moira was a few years younger than her sister, tall and slim and elegantly dressed, with her hair swept up into a tight fringe of curls over her forehead in the style favoured by the old Queen, Alexandra. But she had an attractive smile, and Ruth found her easy to talk to.

'I'm so glad you could come today,' Moira said, in a voice that had only the faintest trace of her original Irish brogue. 'Mr Marriner and I have heard so much about you. Henry, come and shake hands with Miss Judge.'

Henry Marriner was less sociable. Well-built, if a little fleshy, and dressed in a dark, formal suit with a stiff collar almost up to his chin, he bowed over Ruth's hand, and seemed ill-at-ease.

'Ah, Miss Judge. I think I've had the pleasure of meeting your father – Mr Marcus Judge, I believe? I have occasion to visit Jubilee Wharf now and then, in the way of business. He is a very fine man. Please give him my regards when you next see him.'

'I'm afraid I don't see my father,' said Ruth politely. 'Not since I left home.'

'Henry – I did tell you!' Moira reminded her husband reproachfully. 'That's why she's staying with Mary's family now.'

'Oh, ah, quite so. I beg pardon.' His attempt at social intercourse having failed, Mr Marriner withdrew into himself, and took no further part in the conversation.

They sat down to tea, consisting of dainty watercress sandwiches, cut into triangles, followed by doll-sized fairy-cakes. Ruth balanced a cup and saucer, while Mrs Marriner enquired how she was settling into her new home.

'I don't know how we ever managed without her!' Mary exclaimed. 'She's a treasure – in fact, she's taken on so much work about the house, Rosie is able to spend more time helping behind the bar.'

A faint pucker of anxiety wrinkled Moira's brow. 'Is that really wise? Of course, I know the Watermen is very respect-able, but the rougher element can get out of hand. I do think Rosie should look about for some other line of work . . . Why don't you take up shorthand-typing?'

'Oh, we're not all born geniuses like you, Auntie,' Rosie retorted cheerfully. 'I'd soon get fed up, stuck behind a desk all day long.'

'Well, then, you must find something else. They say working in a florist's shop is very interesting.'

'Maybe I could get taken on as one of them mannequins, showing off clothes?' Rosie suggested. 'I've always been keen on dressing up.'

Aunt Moira looked dubious. 'I don't know about that – one hears such tales . . . But I certainly think you should look for a suitable opening, for you don't want to stay behind a bar for the rest of your life, do you?'

Mrs O'Dell did not venture an opinion, but later, when they left the house, she remarked unhappily, 'I know Moira means well, but I do wish she wouldn't be forever running down the licensed victualling trade. It's been very good to me and your father . . . Still, she may be right. Perhaps you should try to better yourself, Rosie, like she did.'

'It wasn't shorthand-typing that bettered Aunt Moira!' sniffed Rosie. 'It was catching Uncle Henry!'

As they approached the entrance to the tunnel on the way home, they passed half a dozen wherries moored up beside Greenwich Pier, with the boatmen waiting for passengers.

'Take you 'cross the river, lady,' began one of the men, then broke off on seeing Ruth. 'Oh, I didn't reckernise you at first.' Embarrassed, he turned away, flushing darkly.

'You go ahead – I'll catch you up,' Ruth told her companions. As they walked on, she said, 'How are you, Saul?'

'I'm right enough,' he muttered, without looking at her. 'And you're all right, too, I dare say?'

'Yes, I am.' Impulsively, Ruth blurted out, 'I'm sorry about – you know, leaving you like that. But I had to.'

'Yeah . . . It were my fault, I know that. Only, I did wish . . . You might have said goodbye.'

He saw another likely customer approaching, and moved away, touching his shabby cloth cap. 'Take you 'cross the water, sir – and your good lady?'

Ruth walked on to join her friends, with a heavy heart.

That evening, she could not put the incident out of her mind. Sean took her for a ride on one of the new motor-omnibuses, which were gradually replacing the old horse-drawn vehicles. They drove north from the river, to Victoria Park; he had seen the announcement of a band concert, and when they alighted from the bus, the music had already begun.

There was a bandstand under the trees. As the sun went down, and long shadows crept over the grass, the gas-lamps went on, one by one. It had been a bright, sunny day, but when evening fell it was too chilly to sit about on chairs. Many of the audience drifted away through the trees, two by two, and Sean and Ruth followed their example.

He stopped when they reached the shrubbery. 'Nobody will see us here,' he said, and began to kiss her.

She wanted to be kissed, she wanted to respond to his urgency, but she could not. After a few moments, he released her.

'What's wrong?' he asked.

'Nothing – I don't know. Perhaps I'm tired; we walked a long

115

way this afternoon,' she said lamely. Then she added, 'On the way home, I met my cousin Saul. You know – the one I told you about.'

'D'you mean to say he had the nerve to speak to you?' Sean's voice hardened. 'I've a good mind to break his bloody neck.'

'It wasn't like that – he was quite polite. But it upset me, somehow. It started me thinking, about my family. I feel a bit sad.'

Sean gripped her fiercely. 'Don't say that! They're not your family – not any more. We're your family now.' He embraced her again and this time, his passion lit a spark within her, and she returned his caresses.

He had spoken carelessly, without thinking – but suddenly the words took on a different meaning for him. Well, why not? He couldn't go on playing around forever. He realised that he would have to settle down some day and become a family man. And he could do a lot worse than Ruth. He found her exciting and attractive – his parents liked her – he felt sure she would make him a good wife . . .

'I'll be your family,' he said, between kisses. 'That is, if you'll have me. I want you so much, my darling. Will you marry me?'

8

'Now let us think of a snowflake,' said Father Riley.

'A snowflake?' Ruth was mystified.

'You've seen pictures of snowflakes under a microscope, haven't you? The lovely patterns they make – the perfect symmetry of them?' The chubby Irish priest peered at her over his spectacles. 'You know what I mean by symmetry?'

'I think so, Father.'

'To be sure you do – you're an intelligent girl. Well, now, this is one of the seven proofs of the existence of God. Could anyone really believe such perfection of design – a snowflake, a flower, a crystal – came about by pure accident? Doesn't that convince you that there's a Mind behind the whole of creation?'

'But Father, I don't have any doubts about the existence of God,' Ruth said. 'I *know* He exists.'

They were sitting in a drab little room with faded green wallpaper and worn linoleum on the floor, furnished with plain, upright chairs and a wooden table, decorated with nothing but a crucifix and a coloured picture of the Sacred Heart of Jesus. It was the parlour of St Anthony's Presbytery, and Ruth was there to take 'instruction', as it was called, in order to be received into the Catholic Church.

When Sean had asked her to marry him, she didn't even stop to think – the answer sprang to her lips. 'Yes, of course I will – oh, yes!'

After that, a great many things happened. They went back to the Watermen, and when the pub had closed for the night, Sean broke the news to the family. The O'Dells were delighted. Patrick slapped his son on the back and congratulated him, Rosie hugged Ruth and said, 'Now we shall really be sisters!' and Mary, with tears in her eyes, concurred, 'It's what I've been praying for. Sean couldn't have a better wife, I'm sure of that.'

Patrick insisted that the news called for a celebration, and opened a bottle of sparkling wine. At that moment Connor, who had been out since dinner-time, walked into the middle of the festive scene.

Patrick pressed a foaming glass into his hand. 'You're just in time to join us in drinking a toast!'

Rosie laughed. 'You haven't told him what's happened – he doesn't know what it's all about!'

'I dare say I can guess,' said Con quietly. He raised his glass. 'Here's to the bride and groom. A long life to you both.' He nodded briefly to Sean, then turned to Ruth. Unsmiling, his eyes met hers above the rim of his glass. He looked away, and threw back the wine at a gulp, saying, 'You'll excuse me if I leave you now. I've to make an early start in the morning.'

When the door shut behind him, Rosie pouted, 'You'd think he could spare five minutes to stay and talk about his brother's wedding!'

'Con's never been much of a one for talking.' Sean gave Ruth a quick, reassuring smile. 'He wished us well, anyhow – what else is there to say?'

But there were a thousand and one things to be discussed. They had to settle where they would live, for although the O'Dells were quite willing to let the young couple begin their married life upstairs above the pub, Sean's single room would not give them much space – and as Mary pointed out, two women sharing a kitchen was a recipe for trouble! Then there was the date of the wedding to be fixed, although it was taken for granted that they should be married at St Anthony's . . . and that presented another problem.

'When I say I prayed you and Sean might be wed, that was only part of my prayer,' Mary told Ruth. 'I don't want you to think I'm prejudiced, but I could never feel entirely happy at the idea of our boy marrying a Protestant. It's not so long since true believers weren't permitted to marry outside the Faith, and even now they've changed the rules to allow mixed marriages . . . Well, what I'm trying to say is – would there be any chance of you crossing over, so to speak? That would make the whole thing perfect.'

Sean put his arm round Ruth, coaxing her. 'I seem to

118

remember you saying the first time we met: "We all worship the same God" – and isn't that the truth? D'you think it would be such a big step for you to take?'

Ruth promised to think it over. At first, the step had seemed very hard and the gulf impossible – a huge leap into total darkness – but when she considered how far she had already travelled since she left home and set out on a new life, she began to see it as part of a natural progression. And now here she was, taking her first lesson from the parish priest.

'I know God exists,' she repeated. 'I don't need proof – He sent Sean to me, when I needed him. He gave me someone to love – someone who loves me.'

A fortnight ago, Father Riley had been a stranger to her, but already he seemed comfortable and familiar. From his accent, he might have been another member of the O'Dell family. Smiling, he took off his glasses, wiping them carefully before replying, 'You must be careful not to confuse your love for Sean with the love of God, my child. They're not the same thing, you know.'

Ruth shook her head. 'Excuse me, Father – but I think they are.'

Two dates were fixed: Ruth was to be baptised and received into the Church on 19 May 1913 and five days later, she and Sean would be married. Time speeded up, and the weeks flew by.

Some wedding-presents began to arrive. Since Sean slept in a single bed, Mr and Mrs O'Dell bought them a splendid double bed – brass-railed, with knobs on all four corners – which caused giggles from Rosie, and blushes from Ruth. Aunt Moira called in to ask what they needed for their new home, but as they had not yet succeeded in finding anywhere else to live, this was hard to say.

'Very well – I'll just have to think of something, and it can come as a surprise,' she said kindly.

When she heard that Ruth was trying to make her own wedding-dress, with Mary's help, she exclaimed: 'There's no need for that! I've a beautiful white garden-party dress I've

119

hardly worn. It only wants taking in a little, and turning up the hem, and it'll fit you like a glove. You're more than welcome to it.'

And then there was the question of the Best Man.

Sean and Connor were washing the front windows of the pub, when Connor had to go back indoors for the chamois-leather. Sean told his brother he was getting absent-minded, and warned him not to forget to bring the ring with him on the great day.

'Me?' Connor frowned. 'What are you talking about?'

'Well, you're to be the Best Man, aren't you?' Sean asked.

'I don't know about that,' muttered Connor uncomfortably. 'You never mentioned it before.'

'Sure, I took it for granted. Who else would I ask?'

'How should I know? One of the saloon bar regulars, maybe?' Connor plied the soapy chamois vigorously over the engraved plate-glass. 'I'm no good at that sort of thing – you'd do better to find someone else.'

When Ruth came out with mugs of tea for the two men, Sean appealed to her. 'This awkward brute's telling me he's no wish to be our Best Man. Will you help me persuade him?'

Ruth looked up at Connor, perched on a step-ladder, and shaded her eyes against the spring sunlight. 'We'd be very sorry if you don't,' she said simply.

'Well, in that case . . .' He climbed down, taking the mug of tea from her. 'All right then, if that's what you want.'

'Don't be bashful!' Sean slapped him on the back. 'There's nothing to it. Mind you, you'll have to make a speech afterwards – and you'll be expected to kiss the bride, so you'd better start practising. Go on now, give her a smacker – you've my full permission!'

Ruth and Connor stood facing one another, not more than a few inches apart, but the distance between them might have been ten miles.

'I'm covered in soapsuds,' Connor said hoarsely, and cleared his throat.

'For pity's sake, give the girl a kiss and be done with it,' his brother teased him. 'Won't you wish her good luck?'

'You know I do.' Connor squared his shoulders, then slowly

120

leaned towards her, touching her cheek with his lips. It was no more than a token gesture, and Ruth felt chilled by his obvious reluctance.

'Thank you,' she said, and went back into the pub.

By now, the news of the forthcoming wedding was an open secret, and word got round the Island very rapidly.

One Friday night, Gloria came into the Watermen with a young stevedore, who had just been paid his week's wages. Sean was serving in the saloon, and Gloria approached him, saying sweetly, 'I hope your mother won't object to me calling in again, seeing as how I've got a gentleman escorting me this time.'

'Good evening to you both,' said Sean, professionally welcoming. 'And what can I get for you, sir?'

The young docker ordered a pint of bitter, and a port-and-lemon for Gloria. As Sean passed the glasses across the bar, she said, 'I did have a special reason for asking my friend to bring me here tonight.' She moved closer, lowering her voice. 'Is it true what I hear – that you and me's going to be related? Or is that just a lot of silly talk? Go on, tell us – I'm dying to know!'

Sean smiled. 'If you mean am I going to marry Ruth? Yes, I'm proud to say I do have that honour.'

'Then we're going to be cousins by marriage!' Gloria exclaimed, digging her companion in the ribs. 'What did I tell you?'

The young man seemed to be tongue-tied, but it wasn't easy to get a word in edgeways once Gloria got into her stride.

'Where's the lucky girl?' she rattled on. 'I do hope she's here – I must see her. We heard the rumour at the shop, but Ma said it couldn't be true. Oh, where's Ruthie? Can I talk to her?'

Ruth had been in the back kitchen, but Gloria's voice carried well and now she pushed back the curtain across the arch, and appeared at Sean's side.

'Hello, Glory. How are you?'

'I'm very well, ta, but how are *you*? Blooming, by the looks of you. Being in love must be a regular tonic. I've never seen you so . . .' Her voice trailed away, as Mary O'Dell followed Ruth into the bar.

121

'Good evening, Miss Judge,' she said coolly. 'This is an unexpected pleasure.'

'I hope you don't mind me popping in – my friend brought me,' Gloria hastened to point out. 'But of course I had to come and say hello, seeing as how we're going to be family. Can I be one of your bridesmaids, Ruthie?'

'My daughter is going to act as Ruth's maid-of-honour, thank you,' said Mary. 'And in any case, I don't suppose your family would allow you to attend the ceremony.'

Seeing Gloria's blank look, Ruth added, 'Mrs O'Dell means because we're getting married at St Anthony's Church. I'm going to become a Catholic.'

Gloria's eyes widened. 'Ooh, I say! Your Dad's not going to like that!'

'It won't concern him,' said Ruth, 'Since he tells everybody I'm not his daughter any more. I've got a new family now.'

Sean put his arm round Ruth's shoulders. 'And we'll do our level best to make her happy.'

'I hope so, I'm sure.' Tossing her head, Gloria turned to her escort. 'I think p'raps we'd better be getting along – I promised Ma I wouldn't be late tonight.'

She could not wait to get home and tell her mother the shattering news – that Ruth's break from her family was to be final and irrevocable. Marcus Judge's daughter was about to become a Roman.

The following morning, Gloria's mother put on her bonnet and went round to the Rope Walk. She found Louisa on her hands and knees, wearing a rough sacking apron and scrubbing the front step – for this was Saturday, and Louisa Judge always whitened the front step on a Saturday morning.

'Morning, Em.' After one brief glance, Louisa went on with her work.

'Lou, dear, I've got to talk to you,' Emily began breathlessly.

'That sounds like trouble,' said Louisa, taking a closer look at her sister. 'Why, you're all of a tremble. Whatever's the matter?'

'It's something Gloria told me last night.' Emily swallowed, anxious to tell Louisa the dreadful news, yet almost afraid to put it into words. 'She was going for a walk with one of her friends, and while they were out, she happened to run into poor Ruth.'

'Did she now?' Louisa's tone was noncommittal. Ruth's name was no longer mentioned at Number 26, Rope Walk. 'How was that?'

'From what Glory said, I think they must've bumped into each other in the street. It was a mercy, really, 'cos if they hadn't met, we might never have known till it was too late.'

'Till what was too late?' asked Louisa, applying the block of whitening, and rubbing it in with a wet cloth.

'I'm just coming to that.' Emily looked nervously over her shoulder, in case of eavesdroppers. 'The thing is – Ruth invited Glory and her friend to go in with her – into that place where she's living.' She lowered her voice. 'That public-house.'

This produced a reaction, at least. Slowly, Louisa stood up, dropped the cloth and scrubbing-brush into the bucket of water, and said, 'I think you'd better come inside.'

They went into the kitchen, and as soon as Emily had taken off her bonnet and sat down, Louisa said, 'Right then! Suppose you begin at the beginning.'

So Emily told her as much as she knew, or as much as she could remember of her daughter's highly-coloured version of the conversation.

'The wedding's to be the last Saturday in May, at the Roman church in Manchester Road. And before that – oh, Louie dear, I don't know how to tell you this – Ruth's going to be "received" – that's what they call it.'

'Received? What's that supposed to mean?'

'She's going to join their church. She's going to become a Roman Catholic.'

For several moments, Louisa said nothing. Her hands had been folded in her lap, and now she began to rub them – slowly at first, then more briskly, as if she were very cold.

'I see,' she said at last. 'So it's come to that, then.'

'But what are you going to do about it?' asked Emily.

'Have some sense, Em, for goodness sake! If that's what the

123

girl's decided, there's nothing anyone can do, is there? Still, I suppose I ought to be grateful to you for letting me know.'

'Well, I had to tell you, didn't I? But it wasn't only you I was thinking of. It struck me right away – I said to myself, "Whatever's Marcus going to say?" I mean, he's been rather peculiar since Ruth left home, if you'll forgive me for saying so. And just lately, he's been ever so silent – not like himself – hardly talking at all. Well, that's how it struck me, anyhow.'

'Yes, you're right.' Louisa sighed. 'He's been very quiet with me as well.'

'P'raps it would be better for you not to say anything – about Ruth, I mean,' Emily suggested. 'P'raps it will be easier all round if he doesn't know.'

Louisa stopped rubbing her hands. Standing up, she walked across to the flaky looking-glass that hung beside the dresser, staring at her reflection as if she had never seen it before – as if it were the face of a stranger that stared back at her.

'I don't think I'll need to tell him,' she said at last, in a voice not much more than a whisper. 'I believe this is why he's been so quiet, just lately. I think he already knows.'

When Marcus Judge came home at midday, he ate his dinner in silence as if he were alone. Louisa had expected some small comment on the suet-and-bacon roll she had made and eventually, she asked him point-blank if it wasn't to his liking.

He looked up irritably, his train of thought having been broken. 'What's that? The meal – oh, yes, there's nothing wrong with it. Why do you ask?'

'You were so quiet, I thought perhaps you weren't enjoying it. Once upon a time, this used to be one of your favourites. I remember you saying you loved bacon pudding.'

'I'm quite sure I never said that. We do not love food, Louisa,' he reproved her. 'We may love people – certain people – and we must love our Almighty Father, but we do not love food.'

When he had finished the last morsel, he said, 'I have to go out this afternoon. I can't tell you what time I shall be coming home.' He had to preside over a special meeting of the Brotherhood. The Inner Circle had been summoned in an emergency to deal with a flagrant breach of their Rules.

124

Within the Guild Office at Thames Wharf, nine men sat in a semi-circle. Although it was a bright, sunny afternoon, the blinds had been drawn over the windows to prevent any inquisitive outsider from spying upon them. In the murky half-light that filtered through the green oiled-cloth blinds, the twelve faces floated, pale and glimmering, like fish in an aquarium.

At the centre of the half-circle, Marcus Judge sat with his arms folded across his chest, and his head bowed – the biggest fish of all. He might have been asleep, for he scarcely moved a muscle, and his eyes were fixed upon the table in front of him.

On his right, his eldest son gave a report on the situation, reading from notes that he had prepared. 'It is with deep regret I have to announce certain irregularities in the work of our Brotherhood during the past week,' he said. 'Over the last few days, the Clerk in charge of Lading, Mr Arnold Judge, has brought to our attention two instances of cargo found to be damaged or otherwise faulty after unloading . . . One crate of oranges, off the steamship *Jose Columbo* which arrived from Barcelona on Wednesday, had a hole smashed in the side, and consequently the total weight of oranges contained in that crate was several pounds light. The following day, a side of smoked ham was missing from the cold-store cargo aboard the *SS King Olaf*, out of Bergen.'

'Could have been a mistake in the Company's listing, perhaps?' said his brother Josh.

'A mistake? And the missing oranges the day before – that was another accident, I suppose? An unfortunate coincidence? No, Joshua, let's not turn a blind eye to the obvious conclusion. One of our men, working on those ships, is a thief. That man must be caught. He must be stopped, and he must be punished.' With a faint smirk of satisfaction, Ebenezer looked round the assembly. 'I take it we are all in agreement?'

A mutter of approval went up from the table.

'Very well,' he said. 'The names of all men working on those two ships will be compared. Any man found to have worked on both shifts will be watched closely from now on – and I expect you all to report any suspicious findings at our next meeting.'

Then he turned to his father. 'Is that in accordance with

125

your wishes, Mr Chairman? Do we have your permission to take all necessary steps to bring the culprit to justice?'

Without raising his eyes, Marcus Judge said in a flat, metallic tone, 'Theft must never go unpunished. One man's crime is a shame and a reproach to all. If our members cannot be trusted, the Wharfmasters will not employ us and the Brotherhood itself will be at risk. That is why offenders must suffer a severe punishment. I leave that in your hands, gentlemen.' Then, in an attempt to wind up the meeting, he asked, 'Do we have any further business to discuss?'

'No, sir, not today,' began Ebenezer, but his brother, sitting beside him, spoke up.

'There is something else. You know what we were talking about last week – the wedding at St Anthony's Church?'

Ebenezer threw Josh an angry, sidelong look. 'There's no need to bring that up now. It's a family matter.'

'It's not only family,' Josh argued. 'If it weren't for some of our members in the Brotherhood we mightn't have heard about it, but I can tell you now, arrangements have been made. You can take it from me, my friends, there's going to be some surprises at my sister's wedding. I've fixed up with some of our best lads, and they've promised to—'

'Will you hold your tongue?' Marcus' anger was all the more shocking because he did not even raise his voice. Without looking at Joshua, he flung the words out with stinging contempt. 'Are you so stupid that you cannot understand what you are told? The girl is *not your sister*, therefore the wedding is of no interest to you or me. It is not to be mentioned again.'

'Yes, but listen, Father,' Joshua stammered slightly, trying to defend himself. 'It's like you said – that wedding's a shame and a reproach to us all! That's why I thought you'd be pleased to hear that there ain't going to be no wedding! We'll soon show 'em they can't spit in our faces and get away with it. If they try to go against the Brotherhood, they're going to learn their lesson!'

Marcus looked up from the table at last, fixing his two sons with a level stare as cold and hard as marble. 'You must do whatever you think best,' he said finally. 'It is a matter for each man to settle with his own conscience – but you will not tell me,

126

for I have no wish to be kept informed. I hereby call this meeting to order. All members will now stand for our closing prayer.'

Obediently, the men shuffled to their feet and joined in the ritual responses, as Marcus Judge addressed himself to Almighty God, calling upon Him to let their enterprises flourish, and to send down His terrible wrath upon their enemies. When the last Amen had been said, they all filed out of the room, and the meeting was over.

'Stand up straight, dear, so I can make sure the hem doesn't dip at the back.'

Mary O'Dell was on her knees in the girls' bedroom, putting the finishing touches to the wedding-dress. Moira had been quite right – it had not needed much alteration.

'There now!' she said, with satisfaction. 'It might have been made for you.'

Ruth caught a crooked glimpse of herself in the tilted dressing-table mirror. 'It's perfect,' she said, and as Rosie entered the room, she twirled, showing off the long white dress. 'Well – how do I look?'

'Fine,' said Rosie quickly. 'Only you've to come downstairs. There's someone called to see you – a woman. She's below, in the kitchen.'

Ruth stared at her. 'Who is it?'

'I don't know. She wouldn't tell me her name and I didn't get a proper look at her, for she's a black veil over her face. What'll I say to her?'

Ruth's heart leapt – and yet she hardly dared to hope . . . 'I'll come down right away,' she said.

'Aren't you going to change out of your dress?' Mary asked.

'No. If I keep her waiting, she might change her mind.' Holding up the long white skirt, Ruth ran downstairs and into the back kitchen, where a woman in black was sitting at the table. 'Hello, Mum,' she said.

Louisa rose from her chair, and put back her veil. 'Well, Ruth,' she said. 'So here you are.' She did not open her arms to her daughter, but stood quite still, studying her from a distance. 'The girl said you were trying on a dress,' she added politely. 'I hope I didn't call at an awkward time?'

'Oh, no. It's for my wedding, Mum. It was given me by Sean's Aunt Moira.'

It all seemed unreal and artificial. They were speaking to each other like strangers, and Ruth even heard herself saying, 'Can I get you a cup of tea?'

'No, thank you, I'm not stopping.' After a pause, Louisa continued, 'That dress suits you. I'm glad I've seen you wearing it.'

Ruth blurted out: 'I wish you'd come to the wedding.'

'You know I can't. I shouldn't be here now – I just hope nobody saw me coming in.' She took a deep breath, then began again. 'I suppose it's true, what Emily said about you going over to the Romans?'

'Yes, Mum. I'm sorry if you and Father are unhappy about it, but . . .'

'Leave Marcus out of this. He won't speak of it – not even to me – but he knows, of course. You can't keep a thing like that secret. Why d'you have to do it, Ruth?'

'I don't know how to explain. It just sort of – happened.'

'These Irish people – they talked you round, I suppose?'

'No, not really. It's something that happened inside me. I could feel the pull of it, stronger and stronger. It was . . .' She hesitated, struggling with such a complicated idea. 'At first it was like a bell chiming in my head. Whenever I heard anything about the Catholics, I heard the bell ringing – and every time it seemed a bit louder and a bit nearer, so then I knew it was ringing for me. In the end, there was no doubt about it at all. It's the right thing for me, I know that.'

'I see.' Louisa sighed. 'Well, as long as that's what you want. I won't say any more.' She took a step towards her, and as if that were the signal she was waiting for, Ruth moved forward, her arms outstretched.

They stood in the middle of the kitchen, holding one another. Ruth felt the soft warmth of her mother's face against her cheek, and breathed in her sweet, familiar smell, and her eyes pricked with tears.

'Silly girl,' Louisa scolded her gently. 'Why'd you have to go upsetting everyone like this? When I came round here this morning, I didn't rightly know what I'd say to you. Try and talk you out of it, perhaps – I hadn't thought it out properly. But I knew I had to see you . . .'

The door opened, and Mrs O'Dell looked in, a little embarrassed. 'You'll excuse me for interrupting, but the brewery men are here with the delivery, and Sean's got to come through to get into the cellar, so . . .'

'That's all right!' Ruth pulled out a handkerchief and dabbed at her eyes, smiling through tears. 'Come in, let me introduce you. This is Sean's mother, Mrs O'Dell. Mrs O'Dell – meet my Mum.'

'Very pleased to make your acquaintance, Mrs Judge.' The two women shook hands. 'Ruth, have you not given your mother a cup of tea? And there's some fresh soda-bread in the larder.'

'Thank you, Mrs O'Dell, but I can't stop,' said Louisa. 'I only looked in, in passing, for a word with my daughter.'

They were interrupted again by voices from the doorway, where Rosie was arguing with her brother. 'You mustn't go in there!'

'I tell you, I've got to . . .'

Sean pushed past her and entered the room. Red-faced, in waistcoat and shirtsleeves, he wiped his palms on the seat of his trousers, saying, 'Glad to meet you, Mrs Judge.' He shook her hand enthusiastically. 'Does this mean you'll be coming to the wedding?'

'I'm afraid I can't.' Louisa looked at Sean for a long moment. His smile was infectious, and she could not help smiling back at him. 'But I'm glad to have this chance of meeting you. I hope you'll look after my girl.'

'Certainly I shall,' he said stoutly. 'You can rely on that, ma'am.'

'Thank you. I wish you both well – and you have my blessing.' She held Ruth a moment longer, saying, 'I shan't come here again. And I'd sooner you didn't say anything to anyone else about me being here today. You know how people talk.'

They said goodbyes all round, and then she was gone. As the

129

side door closed behind her, Sean exclaimed, 'I must go down and open up the cellar-flaps – the men will be waiting.' He took a last look at Ruth, grinning. 'So that's the famous dress? Very handsome, I must say.'

'I did try to stop him,' grumbled Rosie. 'It's terrible bad luck, seeing the dress before your wedding.'

'Bad luck?' Sean laughed, and kissed Ruth once more. 'I don't think we need worry about that, do you?'

In the midst of so much excitement, one event was set apart. On the Monday before the wedding, Ruth was received into the Catholic Church. The one thing she had been dreading was her First Confession, but Father Riley made that very easy for her. Mr and Mrs O'Dell stood as her sponsors, and she was baptised by Father Riley, with the sign of the Cross upon her forehead. Sean and Rosie were the only other people present in the empty, echoing church; it was a quiet and simple ceremony.

Ruth had expected Connor to be there too, but of course someone had to stay and mind the pub.

When they got back to the Watermen, Connor was nowhere to be seen; only the young potboy was on duty, sweeping out the public bar.

'Mr Connor said as how he had to go,' said the boy, wiping his nose with the back of his hand. 'He left a letter – he said you'd understand.'

The letter was addressed to his parents. In a few words, Connor wrote to say that he was fed up with his job at the coalyard, and had given in his notice. He had prospects of work elsewhere, and was moving up north. When things were settled, he would get in touch again.

There was a postscript, addressed to Sean and Ruth. *Sorry to let you down. Good luck to you both on the great day.*

'Cripes! Isn't that just like him?' Sean exclaimed, torn between anger and amusement. 'Sure, I knew he was fed up with working that old coal-cart, but I'd no notion he'd run out on us like this. He might have warned me – now I'll have to find another Best Man in a hurry.'

*

On Friday evening, Connor sat in the public bar of the Ring o' Bells at Poplar and asked himself, 'What in God's name am I doing here at all?'

He had been drinking too much; he knew that. He had started to hit the bottle as soon as he left London, four days ago.

'Well, I needed to lift my spirits a bit, didn't I? Going off to new places, meeting new people – that's understandable,' he told himself, but in his heart he knew that was not the real reason.

Although he had put away a good many pints, he never lost control of his drinking for he had seen too many of his mates go down that slippery slope. But from the moment he arrived at Doncaster racecourse, with an introduction to a sportsman named Solly Gold, life seemed to revolve around beer-tents and four-ale bars. For a day or two, Connor was never quite sober – and in his present frame of mind, that suited him pretty well.

He and Solly took a liking to one another. Solly explained that he was a travelling showman, touring round the country, dividing his time between the races and the fairgrounds, and he was in need of a chap with muscle to join his gang of 'carney-men'.

Carney-men – the slang term for the men on the carnival circuit – were a tough bunch; they had to be, for they worked long hours in every kind of weather, putting up and pulling down the tents, loading and unloading the wagons, fighting off rival mobs, and putting their backs into every job they were given.

Connor spent two days and nights with Solly's team, learning the ropes, and was then informed that he would not be needed again until Sunday, when the travelling show would be moving on to Sheffield.

Suddenly, unexpectedly, Connor found himself with time on his hands, three whole days with nothing to do, and a little money left in his pockets. That was when he fell in with a lorry-driver on his way down from Bradford, carrying a load of

131

woollen cloth to London. They had a few drinks, and – without really knowing when he took the decision – Connor found himself travelling south again.

Now here he was, in Poplar, not quite sure why he had come back.

Last Monday, he couldn't wait to get away – so what had drawn him here, on the eve of his brother's wedding? Could it have been a touch of guilt, perhaps?

He cursed himself for being a fool. 'Right, now – you didn't want to stand up as the Best Man when they went to the altar, so you took yourself out of the way. Nothing wrong in that – Sean will have found someone to take your place by now. But might it be the decent thing to look in on them some time tomorrow, just to wish them well?'

Pondering this, he raised his glass, and found it empty. Perhaps if he had one more, it might help him make up his mind. Shouldering his way through the crowded bar, he went up to the counter. Beside him, a flimsy partition separated the public bar from the snug; and as he stood waiting to be served, a voice in Connor's ear sounded vaguely familiar . . .

'Believe me, there'll be no wedding tomorrow. The Brotherhood will make damn sure of that!'

'How can they stop it?' another man wanted to know.

'Nobody crosses the Judge family, you know that as well as I do,' the first voice replied. 'Ruth Judge may think she's got away from them, but she'll find out different. When she goes to church tomorrow morning, she'll be in for a big surprise.'

He would have said more, but at that moment a fist came down on the table with a thump that set the beer-mugs rattling.

'Myself, I don't like surprises,' said Connor. 'That's why you're going to tell me what this is all about.'

Israel Kleiber looked up at the man towering above him, and the taste of fear soured the beer in his belly, but he forced a smile.

'Hello, stranger!' he began. 'I haven't seen you around these parts for a while.'

'I've been away.' Connor sat down beside him, pinning him against the wall. 'And I'd like to catch up on all the news. What's been going on?'

132

Izzy turned to his friends, stammering an introduction. 'This is Connor O'Dell. He used to work with me, at the Wharf.'

The other men at the table were already on their feet, muttering excuses and remembering pressing engagements elsewhere. Izzy would have been glad to follow them, but Connor held his arm in a steely grip.

'I fancy you were discussing a certain wedding tomorrow?' he said. 'I'm naturally interested in anything that concerns my family – so just keep right on talking.'

Helplessly, Izzy had to tell him everything he knew. He hastened to explain that he would not be personally involved, for only the biggest and heaviest members of the Brotherhood dockers had been recruited for duty tomorrow morning. Around midday, when the ceremony at St Anthony's was due to begin, a dozen picked men would leave Jubilee Wharf, armed with crowbars and pickaxe-handles, on their way to invade the church and put a stop to the ceremony. Their plan was to take Sean by force, drag him back to the dock, and chuck him into the water, to sink or swim.

'. . . and that's all I know,' Izzy concluded miserably.

'More than enough,' said Connor pleasantly, and let him go. 'Thanks for telling me. But if you'd allow me to give you a word of advice – in future, you want to be careful of that mouth of yours, my friend. Some day it could get you into trouble.'

When he walked out of the pub, the night air cleared his head. Ice-cold sober, he was already making some plans of his own. Before the night was over, he would be calling upon a few old friends.

It had been a hectic week for Ruth, and Saturday arrived so quickly, she felt quite dizzy. If only she could have had a moment to stand still, to catch her breath, to stop and think . . . but there was no time at all.

When she looked back on it, the 'great day' was a kaleidoscopic pattern of light and colour – of people and places – of excitement and terror and joy.

She remembered dressing in the bedroom, with Rosie

helping to arrange her hair, fitting the headband of orange-blossom and the white lace veil which had been worn by Mary O'Dell on her own wedding-day, then folded carefully and packed away in mothballs ever since.

She remembered Mary kissing her before they left the house, welcoming her into the family; she remembered walking into the crowded church on Patrick's arm, and the blur of faces turning to look at her.

To her surprise, she wasn't nervous. She felt dreamlike, and curiously detached. The sensation of unreality continued, even when she heard a commotion going on somewhere outside the church – a distant noise of men shouting angrily – then the sound of running feet, and whistles blowing – but the heavy doors remained closed. Father Riley raised his voice slightly as he announced the next hymn, and the choir sang more loudly than before.

Some time later, the doors opened, and half a dozen men slipped in at the back, taking their places among the congregation. Their wives looked at them askance when they saw the state they were in, for their clothes were dishevelled and they were all very much the worse for wear, but no one was looking at them, for at that moment Sean placed the ring on Ruth's finger, and they were man and wife.

When they left the church, there was no sign of any disturbance, only a pair of police-constables at the street corner, smiling sheepishly as the happy couple emerged in a shower of confetti.

The saloon bar had been cleared for the wedding breakfast and a long trestle table set up, garnished with cold meats and salad, together with a great many wine glasses and pint mugs. The substitute Best Man was one of the Watermen regulars. His speech was rather too long, with jokes that were either incomprehensible or improper, and he got Ruth's name wrong – but the guests applauded him warmly, and the bride and groom cut the cake.

After the toasts had been drunk, the table was whisked away and the floor cleared for dancing. The pub pianist thumped out a selection of favourite tunes, and Sean led Ruth out for the

134

first waltz. He was a little unsteady on his feet, and kept laughing for no reason at all.

Ruth noticed that several people were behaving oddly. She caught some conspiratorial exchanges between Mary O'Dell and Aunt Moira, and Rosie insisted on taking her upstairs, to change out of her wedding-dress.

'I thought you might like to wear your blue art-silk,' Rosie said, taking it from its hanger. 'That'll do nicely for your going-away dress.'

'But I'm not going anywhere,' Ruth objected.

'Just you wait and see!' Rosie giggled. 'Come along – I'll do your hair again when you're ready. It's funny to think that when you come back, you won't be sleeping in this room any more.'

'When I come back from where?' Ruth wanted to know, but Rosie shook her head and refused to say another word.

The mystery was solved when they went downstairs. Aunt Moira was saying to Sean, 'Henry sends his apologies. He couldn't get away today – you know how busy he is. Of course we're going to give you some furniture when you move into your new home, wherever that may be, but in the meantime we'd like you to have a little extra wedding-present.' She produced an envelope addressed to *Mr and Mrs Sean O'Dell*, and the sight of her new name put the finishing touch to Ruth's feeling of unreality.

Inside the envelope was a pair of return railway-tickets, and a sheet of printed notepaper, headed: *Marine Drive Hotel, Southend-on-Sea*, confirming that a double room had been reserved for Mr and Mrs Sean O'Dell for the night of 24 May.

'The hotel manager's one of Henry's business acquaintances,' Moira explained. 'We often stay there ourselves. I can highly recommend it.'

Ruth had not expected a honeymoon, for she knew the O'Dells had spent a lot of money on the wedding breakfast and Sean couldn't afford to take much time off from the pub – so she was quite overwhelmed.

In the train to Southend, she held hands with Sean, murmuring, 'I still can't believe it. Wasn't it kind of Mr and Mrs Marriner?'

'I dare say, though it wouldn't have hurt them to stand us a whole weekend, instead of one night,' retorted Sean. 'Still, it's better than nothing.'

'I think your family have been wonderful,' she said. 'Compared to mine, at any rate.'

Sean gave her a wry smile. 'Not all my family were on their best behaviour this day,' he said. 'D'you know what I was told, by a couple of my old pals? It seems that no-good brother of mine hasn't gone up north at all. He's still hanging around the district, large as life, getting into trouble as per usual!'

Ruth stared at him. 'I don't believe it. Connor's in London?'

'So I'm told. He was spotted just after midday, staggering along the road with a bloody nose and a black eye. Maybe he meant to come and see us off, but apparently he'd drink taken, so he ended up in a fight. Good old Con – he'll never change.'

'I think that's disgusting.' Ruth turned her head away, looking out of the window, watching the flat Essex fields whizzing by. 'Don't tell me any more, I don't want anything to spoil our special day.'

'It won't.' Sean put his arm round her waist, squeezing her tightly. 'We've got better things to think about – haven't we?'

Feeling reckless, they took a cab from Southend station. Their hotel was an ornate building, covered with stucco decorations and not unlike their wedding-cake – cupids and columns and swags of flowers and fruit made of white plaster – and their bedroom looked out over the sea.

Ruth stood at the open window, drawing back the lace curtains to get a better view. In the early evening sunlight, the long pier stretched out across the estuary, golden against the blue. 'It's the most beautiful place I ever saw,' she said happily.

Sean wasn't listening; he was telling the pageboy who had carried up the luggage to bring a bottle of champagne and two glasses, as soon as possible.

'Do you think we should?' asked Ruth, when the boy had gone. 'I mean, we've had plenty to drink already with all those toasts.'

'You can't have too much champagne,' Sean told her firmly. 'Besides, Moira and Henry are footing the bill – expense no object!' Suddenly he began to laugh again. 'Will you look at this?' he said, and flicked a switch on the wall. Of course, such a very grand hotel was bound to have electricity, but it was the first time either of them had ever used the electric light, and Sean was as delighted as a child, switching it on and off.

When they went down to supper, the other guests all looked very smart. Ruth felt they were staring at her as if they knew that she did not belong in these elegant surroundings, and she buried herself behind the menu. Afterwards, she could not remember what she had chosen. She only picked at her food, and left her wine almost untouched, so Sean finished it for her. She was glad when the meal was over, and they could go up to their room.

The bedroom wash-basin was discreetly hidden behind a folding screen, and while Sean performed his ablutions, Ruth slipped into her nightdress. She was sitting up in bed, under the pink-shaded electric light, when Sean reappeared, self-conscious in a nightshirt.

'Bloody silly thing,' he grumbled. 'I never wear one at home, but Mam made me promise. She says no gentleman would sleep without a nightshirt on his wedding night.'

He pulled back the bedclothes and tumbled in beside Ruth. She had got used to sleeping with Rosie, but to share a bed with a man was a different matter and she shivered in anticipation.

'Are you feeling cold? Never mind.' He put his arms round her. 'I'll soon warm you up, my darling.'

He began to kiss her, and she smelled the alcohol on his breath. His speech was a little slurred, and she realised that he was half-drunk. His fingers fumbled with the ribbons of her nightdress. He began to undress her, and to fondle her breasts – she remembered Saul, but put that thought out of her mind. As she returned Sean's kisses, his embraces become more violent.

Suddenly he exclaimed, 'For God's sake – I'm no bloody gentleman!' and pulled off his nightshirt, tugging it over his head.

It was the first time Ruth had seen him naked. She was half fascinated, half frightened. Although he had explored her body, she knew very little about his. Timidly, she began to caress him, but he pushed her hand away.

'That's all right,' he said, breathing faster. 'You lie still and

137

leave it to me – I'll do everything.' He reached for the electric switch, and turned the light off, then rolled over on top of her – and again the memory of Saul returned to her.

In the darkness, Sean did not say any more. He was panting now, like an animal, and she gasped as a searing pain stabbed her again and again. Tense and rigid, she lay helpless beneath him, biting her lip to keep herself from crying aloud.

She tried to ignore the pain, and think of something else – to remember everything that had happened during the day – but it was no good. In despair, she found herself reciting the prayer she had been taught:

> *Hail Mary, full of grace*
> *Blessed art thou amongst women.*

She let the words run through her mind like beads through her fingers, waiting for the pain to end.

> *Holy Mary, Mother of God, pray for us sinners,*
> *Now – and in the hour of our death.*

9

'Mind the brass knobs!' exclaimed Patrick O'Dell as the new bedstead, in three separate sections, was lowered down the staircase.

The newly-weds had had a stroke of luck; on their return from the one-night honeymoon, a customer in the saloon bar had told them of a little flat which had just fallen vacant, only ten minutes walk away, in Meadow Lane. It sounded attractive, and they went round to look at it the following morning. The name was sadly misleading, for Meadow Lane was not much more than an alleyway squeezed between two grey rows of identical houses. If there had ever been any meadows there, they had disappeared a long time ago.

Still, the first-floor flat was clean and fairly dry, and the rent was reasonable: seven shillings and sixpence a week, for two rooms and a kitchen the size of a shoe-box, with a cold-water sink and a gas-stove. Naturally, there was no bathroom, and the lavatory was downstairs, outside in the backyard, shared with the ground-floor tenants.

Sean and Ruth looked around. It happened to be a fine morning, and a tiny patch of sunlight fell upon the bedroom wall, lighting up the blue wallpaper, which had faded sprigs of roses on it. Outside the cramped window, a pigeon perched on the sill, fluffing out its feathers and prospecting for crumbs – and Ruth's spirits lifted.

'I like it,' she said.

'Fair enough!' One place was very much like another to Sean. 'Right, then – we'll take it.'

The entrance to Meadow Lane was though an archway at either end. They were too narrow to allow wheeled traffic to pass, so moving day became a problem; each piece of furniture had to be lifted down from the hand-cart and manhandled under the arch, over the cobblestones, and up the stairs. Not that they had much in the way of furniture. The pair embarked upon married life with nothing but the bare necessities – a table, two chairs, three wooden boxes that did duty as a chest of drawers, a kitchen dresser (which had been their 'proper' wedding present from Mr and Mrs Marriner) and of course the brass bedstead.

'Mind how you go!' Patrick warned them again, as Sean and the potboy carried the frame downstairs and out to the waiting cart.

'Yes, we don't want to do any damage to our bed, do we?' Sean grinned, and winked meaningly at Ruth.

She smiled back politely. For the first two weeks, Sean's life had revolved round that double bed; they had 'had some fun', as he called it, almost every night. It had never again been as painful for Ruth as upon their first night and gradually, as she got used to Sean's clumsy assaults upon her body, she learned to relax, and found herself responding to him – if not with pleasure, at least with some brief satisfaction. But this was not how she had imagined the act of love would be; it was never romantic, or thrilling, as their frustrated attempts at lovemaking had seemed to her sometimes, when they were engaged.

Now the marriage had been consummated, and it had become her duty.

By the third week, Sean's interest was flagging a little, and they 'had some fun' less often. Soon, Ruth thought, they would establish a regular pattern – once a week, perhaps, on Saturday nights or after a party. From now on, this was what married life would be like.

Sean set up the bed-frame in their new home, and left Ruth to add the mattress and pillows, the sheets and blankets. The sun was not shining today, but there were two pigeons on the bedroom window-sill this time, preening and cooing hopefully.

'You'll have to wait till I get some food in,' she told them. 'Then I'll put out some crumbs.'

She wondered if the two birds were male and female and she thought of other pigeons or seagulls she had seen on walls or rooftops, in the act of mating, one suddenly descending upon the other in a momentary flurry of wings – then, seconds later, the birds would part and fly away. Since that was how it happened in the natural world, what right had she to expect anything more?

As soon as the furniture was all in place, she went out to the shops and came back with a supply of groceries. When she asked Sean for some housekeeping money, he grumbled and emptied his pockets on to the kitchen table. 'I can see married life is going to come expensive,' he muttered ruefully.

When they were living above the pub, they had been provided with regular meals, and Ruth's help with the housework had paid for her keep. Now she had her own home to look after, the bills for rent, food and fuel would make a big hole in Sean's weekly wages.

'You'll have to find yourself a job,' he told Ruth. 'Part-time, at any rate. You've got to do your bit, to keep the money coming in.'

She knew he was right. Most young married women who had not yet started a family went out to work, though this seemed strange to Ruth, since her own mother had never done so. Marcus Judge would have considered it as a reflection upon his status as the breadwinner and head of the household, if Louisa had been forced to go out to work – and Ebenezer agreed with his father, declaring that a woman's place was in the home. His mousy little wife Florence had never been out to work, even before their son Tommy was born.

On the other hand, Joshua's Mabel had been a laundress when he met her, and she carried on at the laundry until their first baby came along; and of course Aunt Emily and Gloria were still working at the corner shop.

Ruth wished she could have gone back to join them, for she had another, more personal reason for wanting a job. After the first few days in the new flat, she found time hanging heavy on her hands. It wasn't too bad during the day, for Sean generally came home for his afternoon break, so she had someone to talk to, and her mornings were taken up with the shopping, cooking and cleaning. But Sean was also on duty at the pub each evening, and the hours between five and eleven-thirty were long and very lonely. If she could just go out to work in the

141

mornings, she would be able to get her housework done in the evenings, and that would be a way of passing the time.

The only question was, what kind of work could Ruth hope to find? Jobs for women were few and far between on the Island.

For the sake of a little company, she often dropped in at the Watermen herself after tea, and sat in the back room chatting to Mrs O'Dell.

One evening, Rosie looked in from the public bar and interrupted them, saying, 'Hey, listen now. You know you've been talking of going out to work, Ruth? And Aunt Moira's forever pestering me to look for something, too? Well, there's a feller in tonight who says there could be an opening for both of us. Will you come through and talk to him?'

So Ruth followed her into the public, and Rosie introduced her to a cheerful young man with dark curly hair and a wicked monkey grin. 'This is Mr Israel Kleiber. My sister-in-law, Ruth.'

As they shook hands, Israel said, 'We haven't met, but I know your family already. I work at the dockyard, along with your brothers.'

'I'm afraid I don't see my family very often nowadays,' said Ruth. 'Since I got married, we've rather drifted apart.'

'Yeah, I know about that too,' he shrugged this off quickly, 'but that's beside the point. Is it right you two young ladies are looking for employment?'

'Quite right.'

'Now there's a coincidence! My mother and father are looking for extra help. They run a little tailoring business in Poplar, and they're doing pretty well – so well, in fact, they've more orders than they know what to do with. So I was wondering – can either of you handle a sewing-machine?'

The girls exchanged glances, nodding. 'Yes, both of us can.' Rosie often helped her mother when she was dressmaking, and Louisa had taught Ruth to use their old treadle Singer, to patch a sheet or let down a hem, when she was quite a little girl.

'Isn't that just fine?' Israel beamed at them both. 'Then why not come around tomorrow, so I can introduce you?'

At closing-time, when the last customers had gone and Sean

142

was locking the doors, Ruth told him about Israel Kleiber's suggestion and he seemed to be quite keen on the idea.

'Why not?' he said. 'They're decent enough people, by all accounts. Jewish, of course, but they can't help that – and Izzy Kleiber's been a good friend to you and me already. He's the chap who tipped us off, when those hooligans were after breaking up the wedding.'

'The one who was a friend of Connor?'

'The very man! That's how they met, when Connor was still working on Jubilee Wharf.'

The following day, when the girls visited the little workshop to be introduced to the rest of the Kleiber family, Ruth thought she sensed a slight feeling of embarrassment.

Israel had an older brother called Ernest; taller and thinner than the mercurial Izzy, he seemed to be rather ill-at-ease when he met Ruth.

'We are acquainted with your brothers Ebenezer and Joshua,' he said, choosing his words carefully. 'And of course we sometimes work for your father, Mr Judge.'

'Of course,' Ruth repeated, shaking hands. 'In that case, you probably see more of them than I do.'

Ernest twisted a smile, but said no more. As soon as he could decently escape, he made his way across to the other side of the room, where he began talking to Rosie in low tones.

However, if Ernest had an awkward manner, his parents easily made up for his shyness. Aaron and Miriam Kleiber were a delightful couple in their middle forties, though they looked older, for both were prematurely grey. Aaron was the shorter of the two and rather stooped, with a sad, lined face, but Ruth could see a flash of Israel's humour in his dark eyes. Miriam stood upright. Quiet and reflective, it was easy to see that Ernest took after his mother, yet she too had a wonderfully warm, generous smile.

'We are very pleased to meet you, Miss Judge,' she said. 'We have heard so much about you.'

'And Izzy is telling us you may be interested in coming to work here?' Aaron ran his hand through his untidy grey locks. 'We are crying out for a little help – isn't that the truth, Mama?'

They both had strong European accents, which Ruth could

not identify, but they were so friendly, she felt at ease with them very quickly. They met in the Kleibers' parlour, and were taken through the house. A large, extra room had been built on at the back; it was not much of a workshop, with a skylight in the roof that let in piercing draughts, but after her stay at Cyclops Wharf, Ruth had become accustomed to icy blasts and anyway, the summer weather would soon be here.

There were four work-benches, and four sewing-machines. Along one wall, coats, suits and tailored dresses hung from a rail, while other unfinished garments were piled in baskets beside the benches. At the far end of the room stood an old-fashioned steam-press.

'This is the kind of work we are doing,' explained Aaron, picking up a jacket with one lapel stitched and one not yet begun. 'Take it – feel it. We are using nothing but the finest materials, you understand.'

'And very fine workmanship,' said Ruth, tracing the seams with the tip of her finger.

'Thank you, Miss Judge. You are very kind,' said Miriam, bowing her head. 'We are trying to keep up the old traditions.'

'I don't know if I could ever do good enough sewing. I've never tried anything like this,' began Rosie, honestly. 'Nothing but dressmaking at home, with Mam – never anything like this kind of work.'

'We can teach you, isn't that right, Mama?' Aaron patted Rosie's shoulder. 'If you are willing to learn, we can teach.'

They discussed wages, and it was agreed that to begin with Ruth should work half-days only, but Rosie would work a full day, from the start.

Back in the parlour, Miriam Kleiber brought out some thimble-sized glasses with gold rims, and poured plum brandy for everyone. It was strong and sweet. The girls sipped cautiously, then decided they liked it.

'To our new agreement – may we work together in harmony,' said Aaron, and they drank a toast to that.

Afterward, the two brothers insisted on escorting the girls back to the Island. Israel walked ahead with Ruth on his arm, while Ernest and Rosie followed at a slower pace.

'I noticed there were four benches in the workshop. I

144

suppose your mother and father both use the sewing-machines?'

'Papa does, not Mama. She's busy in the house, mostly. You wait till you taste her cooking! Of course, she does help out sometimes, when they have a rush job on. Papa leaves the finest sewing to her – embroidery – that sort of thing.'

'So who sits at the other bench? Do you help out as well?'

He roared with laughter. 'Can you picture me with a needle and thread? That's not my style at all. No, there's a young lady called Vogel – Sarah Vogel.' He hesitated, as if wondering whether to say any more, then added confidentially, 'Me and Sarah's been walking out for six months now. We're going steady, as you might say.'

'Oh, that's very nice. I look forward to meeting her when I start work. Is your brother going steady, as well?'

Izzy shook his head. 'Ernest's more the quiet type. Photography's his hobby – his camera's his pride and joy. He keeps himself to himself.'

Ruth looked over her shoulder. A hundred yards behind them, Ernest and Rosie were deep in conversation. 'Well, he seems happy enough now at any rate, though I must admit when I first met him, I thought he was a little shy.'

'If he was a bit reserved with you, that's on account of who you were, not who you are.' After this enigmatic statement, Izzy cocked an eyebrow at Ruth. Seeing that she did not understand him, he went on, 'You're one of the O'Dells now –and that's fine. But you used to be one of the Judge family, and we have to mind our manners with anyone by that name!'

'I see.' Ruth considered this. 'You mean, you still work for my father and he might not be best pleased if he heard your parents had given me a job?'

'Something like that,' he agreed, then laughed again. 'Quite honestly, between you and me, I don't give a monkey-nut what people think of me, but Ernest is on the cautious side.'

'Of course, now I remember!' Ruth exclaimed. 'Sean told me, it was you that tipped him off about my brothers, when they tried to—'

'Ssh!' In spite of his confident assertion, Izzy glanced round quickly, relieved to find nobody was within earshot. 'I wouldn't talk about that, if I were you. Least said, soonest mended.'

'All right to come in?' A week later, Israel was knocking on his brother's bedroom door.

'Yes, you can come in. I've finished the developing now.'

Izzy found Ernest sitting on his bed, surrounded by the component parts of a big, old-fashioned camera which he had just taken to pieces. He protested, 'What are you doing? You said you'd be ready half an hour ago!'

'Is it so late?' Ernest peered at his watch. 'I hadn't realised. When I checked these negatives, I found they all had little white marks on them. Specks of dust must have got inside the camera, so that meant taking it all to pieces and cleaning it thoroughly. I'm afraid I lost track of the time – you'd better go without me.'

'You and your damned camera!' Izzy threw up his hands in despair. 'I told you, we have to be there sharp on eight o'clock –both of us! Don't you realise how important this is? Get a move on, will you?'

'Look, to be perfectly honest, I don't much fancy going out tonight. My stomach's playing up again – I must have eaten my tea too quickly. You can explain that I'm not feeling so good, can't you?'

Izzy groaned. 'My God, you can be so stupid sometimes. Tonight could make all the difference to us. If we do a good job for them, we might even get elected to the Inner Circle. Once you're that high in the Brotherhood, you're made for life.'

'Yes, but I don't know . . . What is it we have to do, exactly?'

'I can't tell you the details. All I know is, they asked us to go back for some late work – special rates, they said. They'll explain when we get there. For goodness sake will you stop arguing, and hurry up?'

Ernest and Israel had been enlisted as dock-labourers in the Brotherhood more than two years ago and had earned a precarious living ever since, dependent upon the lucky numbers Ebenezer drew from the tally-bag each day.

'Will we need to take our tallys and our claws?' asked Ernest.

'No, it's not a cargo job, it's private work.'

Israel would not tell his brother all he knew – or guessed – about tonight's activities, for fear of putting him off. He had caught a whisper about the 'punishment squad' and knew it had to do with the recent thefts at Thames Wharf. But he also knew it was essential to fall in with anything the Judge family wanted.

They hurried through the twilit streets and Ernest asked, 'Where are we going? The Guild Office?'

'Not tonight. Number Three Warehouse, they said.'

'But that's not been used for cargo since they found rats in it.'

'I tell you, this isn't a cargo job. Don't waste time asking questions – save your breath.'

Number Three Warehouse was one of the oldest on the docks. Inside it were some disused crates at one end, but otherwise the building was empty, and the lines of iron pillars supporting the high beamed roof gave it the appearance of some deserted cathedral. Beneath the eaves, the walls were broken by two rows of small windows, but the light outside was fading fast, and the warehouse was almost dark. A single lamp was alight, hanging on a chain from the roof. Ernest saw the pattern of shadows cast by pillars and beams and, even at this moment of urgency, found himself noting that the alternate bars of light and shadow would make a splendid photograph.

'Come *on*!' Izzy tugged at his arm.

In the corner, a row of crates had been piled on top of one another as a temporary partition, and he could hear a low murmur of voices. Behind the crates, a dozen men stood facing them: Ebenezer and Joshua Judge were at the heart of the group.

'You're late,' Ebenezer accused them.

'Couldn't help it, Mr Judge. My brother was took ill – touch of food-poisoning, most like,' Izzy improvised rapidly. 'But he's fine now, aren't you, Ernest?'

Ernest nodded unhappily, adding, 'Sorry about that, Mr Judge.'

'Very well, we can't waste any more time. Stand here, and don't ask questions. Say nothing – just do as the others do.'

147

They shuffled in to join the group. Silence fell, then Joshua asked, 'Are you ready, Eb?'

'Ready,' said Ebenezer. 'Carry on.'

Joshua's footsteps set up echoes under the lofty roof, as he walked across to a side room which had been used as an office. The room was unlit, and when Joshua disappeared into darkness they heard him say, 'Take twenty paces straight ahead, then stop.'

When Joshua returned, he was following a second man, who stumbled forward unwillingly, counting each pace under his breath. As they moved into the circle of lamplight, Israel saw that the man was wearing a shirt and trousers, his head muffled by a black hood and his hands tied behind his back.

Then Joshua said, 'Stop there.'

Obeying, the hooded man began to whine, 'Look, it's all a mistake, see? I ain't done nothing!'

'Silence!' Ebenezer's voice was a whiplash. 'You may speak when I give you leave to do so, not before. Your name is Arthur Herbert Bailey?'

'Yes, but . . .'

'Arthur Herbert Bailey, you are charged with the crime of stealing from the cargoes passing through this Wharf, upon three separate occasions.'

'I never! I only . . .'

The prosecution continued relentlessly. 'Firstly, from the steamship *Jose Colombo*, a quantity of oranges estimated at five pounds in weight. Second, from the steamship *King Olaf*, one side of smoked ham. Third and lastly, from the steamship *Tropic Sun*, a length of fine Indian silk. When you were caught and questioned, the same silk was found wrapped around your body, beneath your shirt. Do you deny this?'

'I can explain! I was only taking it home to show the missus, see, meaning to bring it back next day.'

'Don't lie to me. You know that under the Rules and Regulations of our Guild, any theft has to be punished with the utmost severity?'

After a moment, the man said brokenly, 'Yes, sir.'

'Have you anything to say in your own defence?'

'Our kid ain't bin well. We got doctor's bills to pay, see . . .'

'Poverty is no excuse. You will remain hooded, so that you may not know the men who administer your punishment – and may God Almighty have mercy upon you.' There was no mistaking the thrill of excitement behind his words as Ebenezer concluded, 'Let the sentence be carried out.'

He signalled to the men, and as they moved forward, Israel noticed that they all carried thick wooden clubs. Ebenezer pushed a club into his hands and gave Ernest another, indicating that they must follow their workmates. The gang took up their positions in a circle round the victim, who dropped to his knees as if his legs had given way beneath him.

Joshua struck the first blow, and the others followed suit, beating the helpless man. Within seconds he was spreadeagled on the floor, his face in the dust, and as the rain of blows fell he began screaming – high-pitched screams of pain and terror.

They were all shouting now, and their shouts were punctuated by the hammering of wood on flesh – but those shrill screams rose above all other sounds. Israel forced himself to join the attack, trying not to imagine the suffering of the man at their feet, but suddenly he saw his brother's face – drained of all colour, set in a mask of horror.

Ernest stood paralysed, unable to use the weapon he had been given – unable to move. Ebenezer shoved him violently forward, urging, 'Go on – give it to him! Make the thief take his medicine!'

Ernest tried to obey but as he lifted the club, another upraised arm knocked it from his hand. It flew up, striking the overhead light and setting it swinging. A rocking see-saw of light and shade followed – and in spasmodic flashes of brilliance he saw blood soaking through the man's shirt. Heaving, he doubled up, vomiting again and again.

Later, on their way home, Izzy took his brother into the Watermen for a nip of brandy. Behind the bar, Rosie looked very concerned.

'You're white as a sheet!' she told Ernest. 'Whatever is the matter?'

'Nothing – he's been a bit sick, that's all. Must've been something he ate,' Izzy told her, steering Ernest on to one of the bench seats and giving him the brandy. 'Get that down you, then you'll feel a lot better.'

149

Under cover of the background chatter, he added quietly, 'Good job I already told 'em you'd got food-poisoning. Better they think you were ill, rather than you'd lost your nerve.'

'I *was* ill.' Ernest closed his eyes, feeling the brandy's warmth stealing over him. 'And I had lost my nerve, if that's what you call it. But more than anything, I was revolted . . . Like animals, all of them – even you.'

'Bailey was asking for it,' Izzy retorted. 'He'd got it coming to him. Now for God's sake, will you shut up about it? If anyone was to hear you, they'd throw us out of the Brotherhood.'

'The Brotherhood.' Ernest shook his head, as if he were trying to wipe out the images imprinted on his brain. 'They call themselves Brothers . . . I call them barbarians.'

One Saturday afternoon at the end of July, Ruth was in her little kitchen making a rabbit pie for the next day's dinner, when Aunt Moira arrived unexpectedly.

'All alone?' she said, walking into the flat. 'I thought I'd find my nephew here as well. It's after closing-time.'

'I'm sorry. Sean's working on this afternoon – they're stocktaking. Did you want him for something special, or can I help?'

'I wanted to see both of you. To be quite honest, I've been dying to have a peep at your new home!'

'There's not much to see, but you're very welcome. Come and sit down, while I put the kettle on.'

'You're sure it's not inconvenient?' Mrs Marriner settled herself, looking round the little room. 'I must say it's all very neat. Simple, of course, but there's nothing wrong with that.'

Over the tea-cups, she asked, 'How do you find your new life, then?'

'You mean the tailoring work? Well, it is quite hard – and we're under a glass roof, so on a hot day it's like being in an oven, but I'm only doing mornings. The afternoons are the worst. And the Kleibers are ever so kind. Of course, Rosie's there all day – *and* she helps out in the bar when she gets home. I don't know how she has the energy.'

'Oh, dear.' Moira sighed. 'I do wish she'd found a real

career for herself. She's such a bright girl – if she put her mind to it, she could go a long way.'

She broke off, realising she had been less than tactful. 'So could you, of course – but that's not quite the same, is it? You're married. You don't have to worry about the future.'

'No, I don't, do I?' Ruth tried to smile. 'Are you ready for some more tea?'

'Thanks.' Aunt Moira passed her cup, then said, 'Actually, when I asked how you were getting on, I really meant – how are you enjoying married life?'

Ruth did not answer immediately, but occupied herself with teapot and milk jug. When the second cups had been poured, she continued, 'I'm sorry, you were saying? Oh, yes – married life. It's very nice, really.'

Moira looked at her sharply. 'You say that as if you weren't quite sure. Perhaps it's not turned out the way you expected?'

'Nothing ever turns out quite how you expect, does it?' countered Ruth.

'Perhaps not.' Moira stirred her tea, never taking her eyes from Ruth's face. 'But Sean's a good man, I'm sure. He'll make you a good husband.'

'Yes, he's a good man. But . . .' Ruth hesitated.

'Ah, there's always a "but", isn't there?' laughed Aunt Moira. "I think I can guess – men change, as soon as they've tied the marriage-knot. They begin to take you for granted, don't they?'

'Perhaps that's it. Or perhaps I was just being stupid. I thought it would be like the stories – happy ever after – but being married isn't as romantic as being engaged.'

'You never said a truer word. But then men are never as romantic as we'd like them to be. Henry Marriner's just the same. Sometimes I wish I still worked in his office – I'm sure he took more notice of me when I was his secretary than ever he does now I'm stuck away in Greenwich, waiting for him to come home at night.'

She looked past Ruth, past the faded wallpaper and the little window, on to the chimney-tops opposite and the cloudy skies beyond. 'That's why it's important for a girl to have a career of her own. I wish I could make Rosie see that.'

151

Ruth said, 'You're very fond of her, aren't you?'

'Oh, yes,' said Moira dreamily. 'Very fond.'

'Is that because she's a girl? Oh, I'm sure you're fond of your nephews too, but I notice you don't talk about them in the same way.'

Moira's gaze returned to the little room, and she smiled at Ruth – but her eyes were still soft and unfocused, her thoughts far away. 'She isn't my niece,' she said, very quietly.

'I know, she told me herself. She was adopted.' Then Ruth stopped short, suddenly guessing the truth.

'I don't mind you knowing,' said Moira. 'She was born some time before Henry and I got married. I was a working girl – I couldn't look after a baby, and then, thank God, Mary offered to take her and bring her up as her own.'

'And Rosie still doesn't know?'

'Not yet. Perhaps one day . . . when the time is right.'

Very moved, Ruth could find nothing to say. Instead, she reached over and took Moira's hand.

'Thank you, my dear. I know you'll keep this to yourself.'

'Of course I will.' Then a question came into Ruth's mind. 'But – excuse me, I've no right to ask, – but I don't quite understand. Afterwards, I mean after you got married, why didn't you take the baby back and bring her up yourself? Surely Mr Marriner must have wanted to?'

'He never knew about it. That's why you must never say anything. He still doesn't know.'

'You never told him?' Ruth stared at her, incredulous.

'When I found out I was pregnant, if I'd told him he would have been very angry – he's such a respectable man. And he's not a Catholic, either. He would probably have insisted on me getting rid of the baby. You do see, don't you? I could never have risked that.'

·—10—·

'We're going to be married in October,' Sarah Vogel announced one Monday morning in late August, 1913.

Ruth and Rosie looked up from their work, and they both started talking at once.

'Sarah – what a surprise! When's it going to be?'

'I don't know the date yet. Izzy's taking me to the Synagogue to fix up everything with the Rabbi . . . but yesterday evening he said: "If we go on waiting till we're rich, we could wait forever". So now it's settled – we get married in October.'

The two girls left their work-benches and embraced her. Since they had started work at the Kleibers', they had been getting to know Sarah Vogel – slowly, for she was naturally quiet and shy and did not often talk about herself, and anyway Aaron Kleiber did not encourage unnecessary conversation in the workshop.

'If you are talking, you are not thinking about sewing,' he would say. 'And the sewing must come first!' But sometimes Aaron had to go into the house to deal with a customer, and then the three girls would relax for a few moments and exchange the latest gossip. Today he had gone further afield, to visit the cloth-merchants in Spitalfields, so they could talk as much as they liked.

'I'm so glad!' Rosie kissed Sarah again. 'There's just one thing wrong with it – very soon I'll be the only unmarried woman working here and I can see I'm going to finish up as an old maid at this rate.'

'Not you!' laughed Sarah. 'Some handsome gentleman will come and carry you off one of these days.'

Ruth was delighted. 'It's lovely to see you so happy – and only the other day you said you were afraid Izzy had changed his mind! But now you see you must have been dreaming.'

'I wasn't dreaming.' Sarah looked thoughtful. 'These last

153

few weeks he's had something on his mind, I'm sure. Every time I asked him what was wrong he told me it was nothing, but I knew that wasn't true. I began to think he was growing tired of me, then last night he announced we had to get married right away! Men are so strange – you never know what they are thinking.'

'Where are you going to live?' Rosie asked. 'Here, with his family?'

'No, there's not enough room. Besides, I couldn't leave my grandfather. Who else is there to look after him?'

When the Kleibers arrived in England, they had brought the Vogels with them. At that time Sarah was not much more than a child and Mr Vogel was too old and infirm to work. The Kleibers had found them a place to live, and the little girl had cared for her grandfather, cooking and cleaning and making a home for them both. When the Kleibers set up their workshop, they offered Sarah a job so she could support the old man.

'Izzy says he will come to live with us. It's nothing very grand, but I'll try to make him comfortable.' Suddenly an idea occurred to Sarah. 'I don't suppose you'd both like to come round one evening after work? You've never met my grand-father – he doesn't see many visitors, and it would be a change for him.'

'We'd love to, wouldn't we Ruth?' said Rosie immediately.

'Well, yes, but I have to go home each night to give Sean his tea,' Ruth bgan.

'Let him make his own tea!' retorted Rosie. 'He's big enough and ugly enough!'

'I suppose I could leave him some bread and cheese, or something – but I'd have to ask him first.'

'I do hope he says yes.' Sarah's dark eyes sparkled. 'I should be most grateful if you can come, because I have a favour to ask. Mrs Kleiber says she'll let me have one of her dresses for the wedding day, but it's going to need alterations. If you could help me to pin it up . . .'

'Of course we will,' Ruth assured her. 'I had to do the same thing when Sean's Aunt Moira gave me a dress for my wedding. That needed—,' She broke off as the door of the workshop opened.

154

Mrs Kleiber said majestically, 'What is all this chatter I am hearing? Is it a public holiday, that the machines are not working?'

Hastily, Ruth and Rosie sat at their work-benches, and Sarah apologised. 'I'm very sorry, Mrs Kleiber. I was just telling them about the dress you promised me. They're going to help me to alter it.'

'All in good time, Sarah. Today you must work. What would Mr Kleiber say if he saw you all idle when you should be busy?'

'You won't tell him, will you?' pleaded Rosie.

'If he comes back and finds your work not finished, he will certainly want to know why.' Then Mrs Kleiber's expression softened. 'But if you make up for lost time, perhaps he will never need to know.'

That evening, Ruth told Sean about Sarah's invitation, asking if she might go out to supper on Thursday without him.

'If you want,' he said, in an off-hand manner. 'But you needn't trouble about bread and cheese for me, I'll get a bite to eat at the pub. Mam won't let her little boy starve!'

'She'll think I'm not feeding you properly,' said Ruth. 'Look – I'll stay at home, if you'd rather. Rosie can go on her own to help with the wedding-dress.'

'Not a bit of it. You go out with your girl-friends.' Sean grinned. 'Come to think of it, I might take Thursday as my night off. They say there's a good show at the Hippodrome this week. I'll get one or two of my mates to come along and keep me company – we'll have a boys' night out as well!'

'Oh.' Ruth was beginning to wish she'd never mentioned it in the first place. 'Wouldn't you like me to come to the Hippodrome with you? I haven't been there since the pantomine.'

'It's not exactly your style – you wouldn't care for it. They've got Marie Lloyd topping the bill this week, and by all accounts she's a bit saucy. I'd sooner go without you, and spare your blushes!'

When Ruth and Rosie arrived at the Vogels' flat, Sarah introduced them to her grandfather. A patriarchal figure with a long white beard and a bald head, he sat in the corner by the stove, one rug across his lap and another round his shoulders.

'How do you do?' said Ruth.

His hand felt as frail and dry as a withered leaf. Smiling, he kissed the back of her hand, but said nothing.

'You must excuse him for not talking; he cannot speak any English,' said Sarah. 'But he is very happy to welcome you to our home.' She spoke a few words of explanation in rapid German to the old gentleman, and he nodded and smiled at the girls again.

As Sarah had warned them, the flat was not very grand. It was bigger than the one in Meadow Lane and was on the ground floor – for old Mr Vogel could not have negotiated a staircase – but it was very dark, overshadowed by tall buildings on either side, and in need of repair.

'Izzy says he will redecorate it when we are married,' Sarah told them. 'It will look more cheerful then.'

They sat down to a supper of pickled herring and black bread which tasted sour and unfamiliar to the girls, although they insisted that they had enjoyed it very much. When the meal had been cleared away, Sarah took them into her bedroom and tried on the half-finished dress.

As Ruth knelt at her feet, putting in a line of pins, Sarah remarked: 'It's as well that Grandfather can't speak English. He would be so disappointed if he knew we were in London – he thinks this is New York City.'

The girls stared at her, and she explained with a wry smile, 'When we left Frankfurt, it cost Mr Kleiber and my grand-father very much money to pay for our fares. We had sold our furniture, taken out everything we had left in the bank, for we were living in the Jewish quarter, you understand, and times were very hard for us. One day Mr Kleiber met a man who told him that he could make his fortune in America in the garment industry. He offered to arrange everything – the tickets, the passports and so on and so on . . . First there was a long journey in a train, all the way to Hamburg – and then we had to wait for the boat that would take us to the United States. At last the man put us on the boat, and we sailed – and the sea was very rough, and Grandfather was very sick. When we reached

156

London, he did not even know where we had come to; he was too ill to understand it all.'

'But if you were going to America – why did the boat come to London?' Ruth asked.

'The man told Mr Kleiber we had to come here to change on to a bigger ship. He said we must wait one or two days – I don't really remember very well, as I was quite young then, but after we came ashore Mr Kleiber soon found out that the man had tricked him. There was no ship to take us to America. We were in London – with nowhere to go – and no money. It was a terrible time for all of us and that is why my grandfather still believes this is New York. Mr Kleiber could not bring himself to tell him the truth. But now we have settled in London it does not matter, for as you can see he is quite contented here.'

'So your story had a happy ending anyway,' said Rosie, adding to Ruth, 'just like you and Sean.'

'Just like me and Sean,' repeated Ruth, putting in the last of the pins. 'Now then – stand up straight, Sarah, and turn round so we can see how it looks.'

A little self-conscious, Sarah obeyed. 'Is it all right?'

'You look lovely,' said Rosie. 'Pretty as a picture.'

'Oh, I hope so. Ernest's promised to take a photograph of Izzy and me on the wedding-day, so I'll have to look my best for that.' She looked critically in the mirror above the mantelpiece, tugging at the embroidery round her neck. 'You don't think it needs a piece of muslin up to my throat, perhaps? I'm so thin – you can see my bones sticking out.'

'There's lots of fashionable ladies would give their right arms to have a slim figure like yours,' Rosie told her firmly. 'By the by – talking of Ernest, I haven't had sight or sound of him these past few weeks. They must be keeping him busy at the dockyard.'

'I don't think he's been going to work very often lately,' said Sarah, carefully taking off the wedding-dress. 'He spends most of his time up in his room, experimenting with his photography. In fact, I was wondering whether he and Izzy might be catching this summer influenza. They've both been so silent, not like themselves at all.'

'Well, it can't have been anything serious,' said Rosie. 'At

157

any rate, Izzy's feeling well enough to make plans for his wedding! Just you tell Ernest when you see him that it's high time he stopped feeling sorry for himself and came down to the workshop to pass the time of day!'

When they came out of the bedroom, Ruth asked what the time was. 'I don't want to be late. I'd like to get home before Sean so I can put the kettle on ready to make him a hot drink.'

Rosie giggled. 'He won't want any hot drink tonight – and he won't get back till after closing-time, you can bet your boots on that! I know that brother of mine. When he comes out of the theatre he'll go straight into the Ring o' Bells with his boozing pals, and stay there till chucking-out time.'

'Do you really think so?' Ruth sighed. 'Well, we ought to be on our way all the same.'

They said goodbye to old Mr Vogel, who nodded and smiled once more, bowing over their hands, then they departed, telling Sarah that they'd see her at the workshop tomorrow bright and early.

It was a long walk back to the Island, but the Vogels' flat was only just off Poplar High Street and Rosie suggested, 'If we wait on the corner, we could catch the last bus going down to Millwall.'

Suddenly Ruth made up her mind. 'We're only five minutes walk from the Hippodrome so why don't we go and see if we can find Sean at that public-house? It'll be nice if we can all go home together.'

'I wouldn't bother him now, if I were you,' Rosie tried to dissuade her. 'They get a rough crowd at the Ring o' Bells. Better leave him to have a drink with his mates – he won't thank us for barging in.'

'You go back on your own then if you'd rather,' said Ruth. 'I wouldn't feel happy going home and leaving Sean there – especially if he drinks more than is good for him.'

The girls were still arguing when they reached the public-house. 'I'll just look in and see if he's there,' said Ruth. 'You wait here – I won't be two ticks. After all, he's a married man now and you never know, he might have decided to go straight home.' She left Rosie on the pavement, and pushed the engraved-glass panel in the swing door.

But Sean had not decided to go straight home. He was sitting at a table in the corner with a couple of men whom Ruth recognised vaguely from the Watermen. They were red-faced and shining with sweat, guffawing noisily . . . and they had three women with them.

Clearly, the landlord of the Ring o' Bells did not have the same high standards as the landlady of the Three Jolly Watermen; one glance at those women and Mrs O'Dell would have requested them to leave the premises.

The youngest of them, who had brightly hennaed hair tied up with green ribbons, was sitting on Sean's lap screaming with laughter because he was tickling her.

Ruth turned round and walked straight out again. 'You were quite right,' she told Rosie. 'He's there – but he's not ready to come home.'

'Did he see you?'

'No, he didn't.'

'Getting drunk with some of the boys, was he?' asked Rosie sympathetically. 'Oh, well, better leave him to it. After all, to be fair, he wasn't expecting you to come and look for him, was he?'

'No, he certainly wasn't,' said Ruth. 'Come on – let's go.'

On the way home, she said very little; her mouth felt stiff, her face set in an expressionless mask. She did not dare to say much, afraid that if she talked at all, she might break down and cry. Even after they parted, and Rosie went into the Watermen by the side door, Ruth did not break down. She went home to Meadow Lane and upstairs to the flat – and still that rigid mask remained fixed in place.

Slowly and methodically, she fetched an extra blanket and made up a bed of cushions on the living-room floor. Then she went into the bedroom, and shut the door. Remembering her cousin Saul, she wedged a chair-back under the handle. Then she undressed, climbed into bed, and lay awake for a long time –waiting.

It was nearly two hours later when she heard him shambling up the stairs. The flat door was thrown open, and he called out: 'I'm back!'

Then she heard him say, 'What the devil?' and knew he had

seen the makeshift bed on the floor. The bedroom door rattled, and he swore violently when he couldn't open it.

'What the hell are you playing at?' he shouted, in a gurgling voice that sounded as if his tongue were too big for his mouth.

'I went to meet you at that pub near the theatre,' she told him slowly and distinctly. 'I went in and saw you there, with that woman on your lap. If that's what you want – you'd better go back to her.'

There was a long silence, and then he mumbled, 'Thanks . . . If that's your addi – attitude – I bloody well will.' The slam of the door, when he left, made the windows rattle.

Then, at last, the rigid mask cracked and fell apart and Ruth began to cry.

It was very late when she finally fell asleep, and when Ruth awoke next morning she was horrified to find she had overslept. She washed and dressed as quickly as possible, and was still putting her hair up into a bun when a knock at the door made her jump.

She froze – but of course it couldn't be Sean, unless he'd lost his key . . . With her hair half-done, she opened the door and found Connor O'Dell outside.

'Oh, it's you,' she heard herself saying stupidly. 'You're back, then?'

'Just for a while,' he said. 'Can I come in?'

'Of course.'

He strode into the room, and she followed him – puzzled and confused. He had been away for months, and she felt there had been some change in him during that time, though she could not decide what it was.

Connor looked round the room, and his eye fell on the cushions and the blanket, still lying on the floor. Quickly, she scooped them up in her arms, saying, 'I'm sorry it's so untidy. The truth is, I overslept. I'd offer you a cup of tea, but I'll be late for work if I don't go soon.'

'I don't need any tea.' He stood at the window, looking down into the yard.

'If it's Sean you want, he's out,' she said.

'I know that. It's why I'm here,' he told her. He had his back to her, and she could sense that he was embarrassed.

'What do you mean?' she asked.

'I got back to London last night, and went straight to the Watermen . . . I'll be staying at home for a few weeks now, off and on.' He spaced his words carefully, as if they were stepping-stones. 'Anyhow, I was in bed last night when I heard Sean come in. I knew from the sound of him on the stairs he'd taken a drop too many, so I went in to his old room and we talked.'

'So that's where he went.' Ruth sighed with relief. 'Thank God. I thought perhaps he – well, I don't really know what I thought.'

'He told me you and him had a bit of an argument,' Connor said. 'That's why I'm here. I'm not taking his side, mind – he'd no right to walk out on you the way he did, but maybe you shouldn't be too hard on him.'

'Hard on him?'

He turned, indicating the blanket and cushions bundled in her arms. 'It's not surprising he flew off the handle after you turned him out of his bed, is it?'

Ruth felt herself blushing, and tried to cover her humiliation by putting down the bundle and starting to fold the blanket. 'Is that what he told you? And did he tell you why we were arguing?'

'Because he'd come home footless. Because you saw him in some pub, with a few of his cronies. He said you don't admire his choice of friends.'

'I've never criticised his friends!' The blanket fell from her hands. 'Only, I drew the line at the one with dyed hair who was sitting on his lap, laughing . . .'

'*What?* Do you mean to say—?' Connor took a step towards her. 'He never told me that.'

'Didn't he?' She put a hand to her face, dashing away the tears as they welled up. 'Of course, he was drunk – perhaps he didn't know what he was doing, or perhaps I should have been more forgiving. I couldn't think very clearly last night.'

'I'm not blaming you,' he said simply.

Ruth looked up. His green eyes were fixed on her with such

a depth of understanding that she felt she could have poured out everything to him – her unhappiness, her disappointment, her sense of failure. Now she realised what it was that had changed; she had never been aware of such kindness from him.

But she could not burden Connor with her troubles. Automatically, she continued to put up her hair, repeating, 'I'll be late for work. Oh, I wish I knew what to do about Sean. Should I go to the Watermen later, and try to talk to him?'

'No.' He moved to the door, holding it open for her. 'You get off to your work. I'm going back to the pub; I'll talk to him.'

She never found out what the two brothers said to one another that day but when she got home at the end of the afternoon, Sean was waiting for her. 'I have to tell you,' he mumbled, as if he were repeating a lesson he had learned by heart, 'I'm sorry about last night.'

'I'm sorry too,' she said. 'Perhaps I was hasty. It just took me by surprise, that's all.'

He continued to scowl at the floor. 'Connor says he talked to you this morning and you told him about that girl at the Ring o' Bells . . . There was no need for you to mention that, was there?'

'I thought he already knew about her – I thought you'd told him.'

'Why would I do that? She didn't mean anything to me. There's always girls like that, hanging around . . .' Clumsily, he pulled a small box of chocolates from his coat pocket. 'Here – these are for you. Sort of a peace-offering.' He held out the chocolates. 'Will you forgive me? Kiss and make up, like?'

Taking the box from him, she tried to smile. 'All right, then.'

At once he grabbed her, thrusting his tongue between her lips. His mouth still tasted of stale beer, but she forced herself not to pull away from him.

'Thank you for the chocolates,' she said, when she could speak. 'That was a nice thought.'

'Glad you like them.' Relieved to have had won her round so easily, he took the lid off the box and popped one into his mouth. 'Con said flowers, but I settled for chocs so we can both enjoy 'em, eh?'

While Ruth was getting their tea ready, she asked, 'Did

162

Connor say why he's come back to London? I suppose that job of his must have fallen through.'

'Not a bit of it. He's been travelling all over – he's working with some feller who goes about with a travelling fair, he tells me. And now they've moved down to this part of the country, they'll be working their way round London. Con's glad to be back. He can sleep in his own bed some nights – it's more comfortable than living in digs, and a lot cheaper.'

'But what does he do at the fairground?'

'He works at one of them boxing-booths. They're setting up at Poplar Recreation Ground next week so maybe we should go and see for ourselves when I have me night off.'

Ruth didn't see Connor again until the following Friday, when Sean took her to the Fair. It had been another long hot day, but when the sun went down the air was pleasantly cool. They sauntered arm-in-arm along the alleys between the tents, enjoying the spectacle all around them.

'Isn't it amazing?' Ruth began. 'It reminds me of—'

Sean looked at her enquiringly. 'It reminds you of what?'

'Oh, nothing. I don't know what I was going to say. It can't have been anything important.' This was a lie. She had been about to say, 'It reminds me of the transformation scene in the Christmas pantomime' – but she had caught herself in time. She did not wish to remind Sean of the Poplar Hippodrome, or anything to do with it.

The recreation ground had certainly undergone a transformation. As a rule, it was a rather dull piece of ground with patches of grass like threadbare carpet, scuffed by too many feet. Tonight, however, it was a fairyland of light and colour, with flags flying, painted horses whirling about on the merry-go-round, swing-boats and a helter-skelter, coconut-shies and ice-cream carts. Steam-organs blared out popular tunes, while barkers stood on soap-boxes yelling themselves hoarse.

'Walk up, walk up, ladies and gen'lemen. Come and see the Fat Lady – the Pig-Face Boy – the Human Spider!'

Sean was in a good mood. He bought ice-cream from one of

the hokey-pokey men, and repeated the old rhyme, 'Hokey-pokey, penny a lump, the more you eat, the more you jump!'

They wandered along, flowing with the slow-moving crowd, licking their ice-creams from squares of paper.

'Enjoying yourself?' he asked.

'Oh, yes – it's like a holiday,' answered Ruth. It *was* a little holiday from the drab realities of everyday life. She felt easy and contented in Sean's company again and her night of misery, only a week ago, now seemed far away and almost unimportant.

Then Sean pointed to a placard over a marquee. '*Solomon Gold's Champion Prize-fighters*,' he read. 'This is it.'

No doubt the man at the entrance was Mr Gold in person. Dressed in a check suit and a yellow bowler, he puffed at his cigar, shouting between eruptions of smoke: 'Only a few places left! The big fight's just about to commence – get your tickets here, ladies and gents!'

Sean bought two fourpenny tickets, and they ducked under the tent-flap. It was very warm inside the marquee. The hot air had been trapped under the canvas all day and there was a strong smell of trampled grass, human bodies, sawdust and liniment. In the middle, a boxing-ring had been erected, surrounded by an expectant crowd seated on benches. A buzz of excitement arose when Mr Gold dropped the tent-flap, took off his hat and his jacket, and climbed into the ring. He raised his hand for silence.

'To open our display of the pugilistic art we present a demonstration bout between two champions of the boxing world!' he bellowed. 'On my left – Duggie McGraw, from Bonnie Scotland. On my right – Connor O'Dell, from the Emerald Isle!'

Ruth gasped, as the two fighters entered the ring. McGraw wore a faded tartan dressing-gown. He acknowledged the applause, then slipped off the gown, tossing it to his second, who was placing a stool and a bucket in his corner. But Ruth only had eyes for Connor; he had no dressing-gown, but wore a plain white towel over his shoulders, and emerald-green trunks. He gave the towel to his second, who checked the lacing of his boxing-gloves.

164

It felt very strange to Ruth. They were sitting near the back and there were many tall men in front of them, so her view was obstructed, yet she felt extraordinarily close to Connor. Stripped to the waist, he waited for the signal to begin the fight. She saw the strong, broad outline of his torso, and remembered the night she first met him – and how she had helped him to undress . . . For a moment, everything else was blotted out. She forgot the noisy crowd, and Sean at her side, yelling: 'Go it, Con!' She was alone with Connor, upstairs in his bedroom, above the pub . .

Then a bell rang, and the fight began.

It wasn't really a fight, as Solomon Gold had said. This was a demonstration bout – two experienced fighters showing off their skill. Ruth knew nothing about boxing and could not recognise the finer points of their performance but she had a hazy idea that one of them had to knock the other down – and she hoped Connor would not be the loser.

There was little chance of that. Connor's three months on the road had taught him a lot. McGraw was more or less a match for him in age, weight and height but hopelessly outclassed in technique.

Ruth winced whenever the Scot landed a punch, and above the roar of the crowd she heard the sound of a gloved fist striking Connor's body – but that didn't happen often. McGraw seemed to be losing confidence. His attacks grew wilder and Connor parried his blows without difficulty. When the fight came to an end, the verdict was never in any doubt. Connor's gloved hand was hoisted high in the air, and Mr Gold yelled: 'The winner!'

Then there was a short interval while the two fighters disappeared, and Mr Gold took the stage again, announcing that this evening's champion, Mr Connor O'Dell, would now throw down the gauntlet to the young men of Poplar. 'O'Dell is willing to take on any man strong enough to challenge him. The fight will continue until one man is unable to toe the line!'

'What does that mean?' Ruth asked Sean.

'D'you see that white stripe painted on the grass?' There was a streak of whitewash across the middle of the ring, almost obliterated already by the boxers' feet. 'When a feller is

165

knocked down, he has to get back on his feet in sixty seconds, with his toes up to that line,' Sean explained.

Meanwhile, Mr Gold had pulled out a bulging wallet. 'To anyone here present who can stand up to the Irishman for ten minutes, I will personally pay the sum of five pounds! Well, gen'lemen – what do I hear? Are there any sportsmen amongst you? Who's going to be the Pride of Poplar?'

A buzz of discussion broke out, and after a few moments, a challenger emerged from the crowd.

'Demonstrations are nothing,' Sean said in Ruth's ear. 'Them other two know each other too well – I dare say they practice the whole thing beforehand, but this is different. This will be the real thing.'

'You mean, Connor might get hurt?'

'That's how he earns his money!' Sean laughed. 'Solly Gold pays him to take his punishment!'

Ruth did not share his amusement. The local fighter was a great bear of a man, half a head taller than Connor and with a longer reach. He entered the ring, stripping off his coat and waistcoat then, after a muttered exchange with Mr Gold, took off his shirt as well. One of the ring-attendants brought him a pair of gloves and helped him put them on.

Ruth felt a wave of fear mounting within her, and she clutched Sean's arm. 'I don't think I want to stop and watch this—' she began, but her words were drowned by the shout that went up as Connor reappeared; it was too late to make her escape.

Glancing round the sea of faces, she realised that there were very few respectable women present. The ones who clustered round the ringside were gaudy creatures, screeching with excitement and clutching the men beside them. Ruth wished more than ever that she had stayed at home.

Although the challenger had the advantage of height and weight, Connor was able to evade his lumbering onslaught by dodging and weaving, and getting in lightning blows before his opponent could see them coming. Occasionally he managed to get under Connor's guard and then Ruth averted her face, unable to watch. She heard a few heavy blows strike home and flinched every time, as if she herself stood in the ring under

166

those flaring gas-lamps, receiving the shocks of pain upon her own body.

Connor kept up a series of short-arm jabs at close quarters, and his adversary lowered his head, charging in like a bull at a gate and butting him full in the face. Ruth felt sick as she saw blood trickle down Connor's upper lip, flecking his chest with beads of crimson.

Throughout the fight, a caller kept chanting the time that remained, and when he reached the final minute, he began to tick off the seconds, while the crowd joined in. 'Thirty-nine – thirty-eight – thirty-seven . . .'

Connor knew his job; when only twenty seconds were left, he brought the fight to a swift conclusion. Countering the man's roundhouse swings with a series of straight rights, he threw in a sudden left-hook, throwing him forward, and followed it up with a swift, downward chop behind the jaw that sent the man sprawling . . . He did not attempt to get up on his feet and toe the line, so he was counted out; perhaps he felt he had done enough for the honour of Poplar.

In case local pride might have been wounded, Mr Gold let them into a secret when he announced the winner. 'Poplar gains the victory anyhow!' he shouted. 'Because although Connor O'Dell is an Irishman through and through, him and his family live right here in East London – he's one of your own lads!' A cheer went up. Connor was acclaimed once more, and the entertainment was over.

When the crowd streamed out of the tent, Ruth was surprised to find that night had fallen – but the fairyland glittered more brightly than ever. The tents were brilliant with naphtha flares and incandescent gas-jets, and a rainbow of colours twinkled under a sky of stars.

'How did you like your first boxing-match?' Sean asked.

'I didn't. I never want to see another,' she replied. 'I'll know better next time.'

'Still, you must admit Con put on a good show,' said Sean proudly. 'Now it's over, I'll go round to see if he's ready to come home. I told him we'd meet up. You wait here now till I get back, all right?'

'Can't I come with you?' Ruth didn't like the idea of being

left alone in the bustling fairground. A good many men carried bottles of beer, and had been having frequent swigs throughout the evening.

'I can't take you with me,' Sean pointed out. 'He's got to clean himself up and change his clothes, but don't worry – I'll be as quick as I can.'

When he had gone, she waited for what seemed an eternity. At first the home-going crowds kept jostling her, so she moved aside to a quieter spot between two of the tents. Then, gradually, the press of people thinned out, and one by one the attractions dimmed their lights and began to pack up for the night. She saw the Fat Lady, no longer in tights and spangles but looking quite unremarkable, like any other plump, middle-aged housewife going home with her husband. But there was still no sign of the O'Dell brothers . . .

'Perhaps they came back when I moved, so I missed them somehow,' thought Ruth. 'Perhaps they're walking round the Fair now, looking for me.'

Soon the recreation ground would be locked up for the night. She began to walk up and down the alleyways, searching for a familiar face but finding none. At the end of the long alleys were groves of trees and she could see loving couples entwined among the shadows, enjoying a few minutes of privacy before they were turned out. For a moment, she thought she recognised Sean – and a stab of pain pierced her heart as she heard a girl's bawdy laughter and saw a glimpse of red hair and green ribbons – but they vanished into the darkness, and she told herself that she was imagining things. Walking on blindly, she turned a corner and collided with a burly figure. Even before he spoke she knew it was Connor.

'Sorry,' he began, then exclaimed: 'Ruth! Where were you, for God's sake? I've been hunting everywhere!'

'I waited for ages – I thought I'd lost you. Where's Sean? Isn't he with you?'

'I haven't seen him. It's like looking for needles in haystacks, finding anyone here. Have you tried the Refreshment Tent? That's where he'll be.' He began to steer her in that direction, asking, 'What did you think of the boxing-match?'

She did not want to hurt his feelings, and replied evasively, 'It was very interesting.'

He glanced at her more closely. 'Not your style of thing, eh? I told Sean he shouldn't bring you, but he was dead set on it.'

'Do I hear my name being taken in vain?' A little breathless, Sean came running after them. They all began to laugh at the absurdity of losing each other in such a small area, happy to have found one another at last. Linking arms, they headed for the gates, and the homeward journey.

Afterwards, as she was getting ready for bed, Ruth wondered how Sean could have missed Connor. Surely if he had gone to the back of the boxing-booth, he would have found him there?

Then Sean came into the bedroom and seeing her half-undressed took Ruth in his arms. When they kissed, she smelled patchouli on his cheek – a cheap perfume, another woman's perfume – and knew she had not been imagining things. She did not say anything. He would only have denied it – and what was the point of starting another quarrel? When they got into bed, she rolled over, facing the wall, telling him she was very tired after such a long day.

The weekend came and went, and she still said nothing. The longer she left it, the more impossible it seemed to reopen the subject . . . but the thought of that other woman was never out of her head, and suspicion and resentment curdled within her. If she could have talked to someone else about it, that might have helped – but there was no one she could turn to.

The following week, she looked at the calendar and realised that Friday would be her mother's birthday – her first birthday since Ruth had left home – and she had a sudden longing to see her mother again.

'Why not?' she thought. 'Why can't I go and wish my Mum happy returns?'

Suddenly she remembered that it would be simple. Father always went out on Friday nights collecting his rents, so Mum would be on her own. She imagined how her mother's face would light up when she walked in – the joyful reunion. She even toyed with the idea of confessing her problem over Sean, and asking her advice . . .

On Friday afternoon when she left the workshop, Ruth called in at a greengrocers on the way home and paid sixpence for a potted geranium with flowers of vivid, pillar-box red. When Sean saw it at tea-time, he grumbled about her wasting money on such luxuries, but she remained silent. There had been a lot of silences in the little Meadow Lane flat, lately.

After tea, she set out for the Rope Walk. She did not know quite what she expected to find there: common-sense, if only she could summon up enough courage to confide in her mother – sympathy, perhaps – love, certainly.

The moment her mother opened the front door, Ruth heard Gloria's voice coming from the kitchen. How stupid she had been, not to guess that her mother might have visitors on her birthday. 'I thought you'd be on your own,' she said. 'Happy birthday, Mum.'

'It's only Gloria and Emily,' said her mother under her breath, and took a quick look at the houses opposite to see if any of the lace curtains were twitching. 'You'll come in, won't you?'

They embraced in the narrow hallway, and the potted geranium got a little squashed, but Louisa didn't care. She carried it proudly into the kitchen, saying, 'I've got another present – isn't it lovely? And look who's here!'

Aunt Emily and Gloria exclaimed with surprise and delight, and they all kissed each other. Louisa, who had not long cleared away the tea-things, insisted on putting on the kettle and making a fresh pot.

'I'm going to keep your geranium here on the kitchen window-sill,' she said. 'If I put it in the front parlour, I'd never see it . . . Oh, it's good to have you home again, even for a little while.' Then she looked guiltily at Emily and Gloria. 'You won't mention you've seen Ruth here, will you? I wouldn't want it to get about. You know what I mean.'

'We won't breathe a word,' said Gloria. 'Well, Ruthie, you're quite a stranger. How are you keeping?'

'I'm very well, thanks.'

'And your dear husband?' Aunt Emily lowered her voice conspiratorially. 'I haven't actually met him, of course, but Gloria says he's a charming man. I hope he's in good health?'

170

'Yes, he's very healthy,' said Ruth firmly. 'We both are.'

'That's nice,' said Gloria, stirring a generous spoonful of sugar into her tea. 'But then Sean takes a lot of exercise, doesn't he? Always on the go.' Something in her tone made Ruth look up, and she found Gloria giving her a meaningful smile.

'I don't see how he can take much exercise, working in a public-house,' Louisa objected.

'Oh, but he gets away sometimes, doesn't he, Ruth?' continued Gloria, jabbing each word in like a hat-pin. 'From what I hear, he's getting about quite a lot these days.'

Ruth changed the subject. 'Lovely currant cake, Mum,' she said. 'Nobody makes it like you do.' But as she swallowed a morsel of cake, she thought it would choke her. So it was no longer a private problem: Sean's escapades were common knowledge. As soon as she could, she made her excuses and went home, sick at heart.

At the end of the evening, Marcus Judge returned home and asked, 'I hope you had an enjoyable tea-party?'

'Yes, thank you. Emily and Gloria brought me a present – a pot of strawberry jam.'

'I suppose she took it out of the shop.' Marcus frowned. 'If she did – I hope she remembered to enter it in the accounts.' His eye fell on the pot of geraniums, which made a joyous splash of colour on the window-sill. 'Did they bring you the flowers as well?' he asked.

Louisa struggled with her conscience. It would have been so easy to say yes, but . . . she swallowed hard, then replied, 'No, Marcus. I had another visitor – unexpectedly. She brought them.'

'Oh? And who was that?'

She hesitated, briefly. Sometimes Louisa concealed things from Marcus, if she thought they might upset him, or cause trouble for someone else, but in thirty-four years of marriage she had never told her husband a deliberate lie. At last she said, 'Ruth.'

There was another, longer pause. Then Marcus picked up

the geraniums without a word, and went out of the back door into the yard. Through the window, Louisa saw him open the dustbin, drop the pot of flowers inside and replace the lid. When he returned to the kitchen, he took his Bible down from the dresser, and began to read.

The geraniums were never mentioned again.

·—11—·

As good practising Catholics, Rosie and Ruth were not able to attend the wedding of Sarah and Israel Kleiber, but they clubbed together to buy them a lace tablecloth and sent it with their love and best wishes.

The next time they saw Sarah, she thanked them profusely. 'Our table looks so fine now, and Izzy and I want you to come and see it. We would be very pleased if you could have supper with us one evening next week.'

They settled upon the following Wednesday. When they arrived at the flat Izzy welcomed them, apologising that he had not yet had time to start on the redecoration, but he was full of plans.

'There's a lot to be done,' he explained. 'We're going to have new wallpaper, and I shall repaint the doors and the window-frames. That will brighten the place up a bit.'

'It seems different already,' said Rosie. 'It feels happier somehow.'

Sarah and Izzy looked at one another, and smiled.

'Yes, we are very happy here.' Izzy put his arm round Sarah. 'It's like a new world for both of us.'

Love shone from their faces, and Ruth felt a pang of envy. Had she and Sean ever felt like that? Perhaps they had – for a little while – but it seemed so long ago, she could scarcely remember it.

The newly-weds had been given a dinner-service by Mr and Mrs Kleiber, and the plates gleamed under the lights of a traditional branched candlestick; the lace tablecloth provided a fitting background. Old Mr Vogel rose from his place of honour at the head of the table to pronounce a blessing. Although the guests could not understand his words, their meaning was unmistakable – and the supper was delicious. Ruth remembered the pickled herring and black bread at their last visit. Clearly, Sarah was going to great lengths to please her husband.

When the meal was over, Mr Vogel gave thanks for the food they had shared, and Sarah began to clear the table when suddenly there was a loud hammering at the front door.

'I'll see who it is,' said Izzy, going out of the room. They heard voices in the passage and a moment later he returned, looking uncomfortable, and ushering in Ebenezer Judge. 'Mr Judge wants a word with me – on a matter of business,' he said.

Ebenezer glanced condescendingly round the table but his face changed when he saw Ruth there.

'Good evening, Eb,' she said calmly.

He did not return her greeting, but turned away from her, addressing Izzy. 'I understand congratulations are in order. You're a married man now, they tell me?'

'Yes, Mr Judge. This is my wife, Sarah.'

Eb took Sarah's hand briefly, before continuing, 'I'm sorry to interrupt your meal, but this is extremely important. I have to speak to you privately.'

'That's all right, we've finished eating,' said Izzy, growing more ill at ease.

'Shall we take the dishes out to the kitchen?' Sarah suggested. 'Then you won't be disturbed.'

'We'll help with the washing-up,' offered Rosie.

They began to collect up the plates and cutlery, and as Ruth passed her brother on the way out of the room, she said, 'I'll see you later, perhaps?'

Again, Eb ignored her. When the girls had gone, he frowned towards the old man who remained seated at the head of the table and said to Izzy: 'I told you I want to speak to you privately with no outsiders.'

'This is Mr Vogel, my wife's grandfather. He doesn't speak any English.'

Hearing his name, the old man struggled to his feet once more, holding out his hand, but Eb merely nodded impatiently, saying, 'Well, in that case, I suppose he might as well stay.' He pulled out the chair at the opposite end of the table and sat down. 'I'm here on behalf of the Brotherhood. We are very concerned about your brother Ernest. He has not been turning

174

up to report for work for some time now, and we want to know what's wrong.'

'No, Ernest's not been too well. You know he had that go of food-poisoning.'

'That was months ago. He's not still being sick, is he?'

'No, Mr Judge, but he's never really been right since then. He doesn't feel up to any heavy work, on account of it.'

'Are you quite certain that's the only reason?'

Izzy traced the pattern of the lace cloth with one finger, unwilling to meet Ebenezer's accusing stare. 'I'm sure it is, but he's getting better every day. He'll soon be reporting for duty again, don't you worry.' He remembered the endless arguments he had had with Ernest. After the night of the punishment squad, Ernest had refused to do any more work for the Brotherhood – he said he would rather starve . . . but Izzy could hardly tell that to Ebenezer.

'Hmm . . . It's particularly disturbing because the Brotherhood had been very pleased with your record, both of you. We encourage close relatives to work together; we believe in keeping it a family business. And we shouldn't like to think that any member of our family might be disloyal enough to go and work elsewhere.'

'Oh, he's not done that, Mr Judge. I promise you, he's hardly been out of the house.'

'Really? Well, we look to you to bring him back to us as soon as possible. It would be very regrettable if your brother went astray, and began talking to strangers about Guild matters – confidential matters.' He slapped Izzy on the back in a gesture that was meant to be friendly. 'We have high hopes of you, lad, so don't let us down. I expect to see your brother reporting for work as usual in a day or two.'

Awkwardly, Izzy stammered, 'I can't promise that, Mr Judge. I mean, what Ernest does is his own business. I'm not my brother's keeper, as the saying goes.'

Ebenezer's smile faded, and he stood up. 'It's hardly suitable for a man of your race to quote Holy Scripture to me, Kleiber . . . I advise you to think on what I've said – think it over very carefully.'

He walked to the door. Israel, feeling he had gone too far,

tried to put things right by calling out to Sarah, 'Mr Judge is just going, dear! Will you come and say good-night?'

'Don't trouble yourself,' said Ebenezer coldly. 'I know my way out.'

But Sarah was already coming down the hall with the other girls. 'Must you go so soon? Can I offer you a cup of coffee?'

'Nothing, thank you.'

As they stood packed together in the narrow hallway, Eb addressed Ruth for the first time. 'I'm told you called to visit the Rope Walk the other week. Please don't do it again – you're not welcome there.'

'That's for Mum to say, isn't it?' began Ruth, but he cut in.

'Father doesn't like it – and neither do I.' He looked at her with contempt. 'I expect you must be feeling lonely for your own people these days, with nobody but the Israelites for company.' Then he walked out of the house without another word.

Slowly, they returned to the sitting-room. After a moment Ruth broke the silence. 'I apologise for my brother. I'm ashamed of him.'

'You have no need to apologise,' said Sarah quickly. She turned to her grandfather, who was muttering to himself, and they exchanged a few words in German, which she translated for their benefit. 'My grandfather could not understand what Mr Judge was saying, but he tells me that he is not a good man . . . We should not trust him.'

It was a very unhappy time for Ruth. She tried to console herself with the friendship of the Kleibers and the O'Dells – but she could not. There had been a grain of truth in Ebenezer's parting words, spiteful as they were: she *did* feel estranged from her own people.

It would have been very different if she had been happy in her marriage, but these days Ruth and Sean were further apart than ever. They never quarrelled now but talked to each other easily enough, about trivial, everyday topics like the price of bread, or the long hot summer, or the tear in Sean's second-best jacket that needed mending . . . And she had never felt so utterly alone in her whole life.

176

She examined her conscience, asking herself if she were partly to blame. Since the visit to the fairground, they had not made love at all. Once she had rejected him, he seemed to accept that she no longer welcomed his attentions, and left her alone. Was he finding another love, perhaps, somewhere else?

Her feeling for Sean had gone through so many changes since their wedding night. Repelled by his selfish love-making, she had retreated into a kind of limbo – a grey, unemotional desert. She and her husband were two strangers now, sharing a home, with nothing but the roof above their heads to keep them together. Sometimes she wondered what Sean's attitude was towards the situation.

Although he approached it by a different route, Sean had reached a similar conclusion. It had never occurred to him that as a virgin, Ruth would need a gentle introduction to the marriage-bed, and when she did not return his ardour but merely suffered it, stiff and unresponsive, he decided she was a cold fish and that he had made a bad choice of a bride. It was a pity, but it did not particularly bother him; he was a good-looking chap, and he'd never had any trouble in finding his fun when he wanted it. The girls at the Ring o' Bells were far more lively and entertaining; their only trouble was that they didn't believe in giving something for nothing. They were forever pestering a feller for 'little presents' – a drink or a smoke at first, but later on they would ask for sums of money. You could never go with them but you'd be shelling out for this, that or the other . . . Rejected by his wife, and unable to afford the women of the town, he looked for amusement in another direction.

Rosie still took her turns of duty at the Watermen four or five nights a week, very often working side by side with Sean in the public bar. He enjoyed teasing her, tickling her ribs as she reached up to take down a clean glass from the shelf, or pinching her bottom as she stooped to shift a crate of empty bottles under the counter.

'Leave off, will you?' she would exclaim indignantly, slapping his hand, but he was delighted by this new sport.

One evening, as she was passing two brimming tankards across the bar, he took advantage of her helplessness to slip behind her and pull her to him, squeezing her waist. Taken off-guard, she shrieked and dropped the tankards, splashing them both with beer.

The customers in the public – all of them men – thought this was highly comical, and roared with laughter. They laughed even louder when Sean offered to help her mop herself up, running a dishcloth over her body, dabbing at her breasts and buttocks.

'If you don't stop that, I'll tell our Mam!' she threatened, almost weeping with vexation.

'Ah, it's nothing but a bit of fun. What's wrong with you? You never used to mind a bit of teasing in the old days.'

'That's not teasing, it's horrible!' she exclaimed, rushing upstairs to change her dress, with the bawdy laughter ringing in her ears.

After that, he wouldn't let her alone. When she objected, he told her she was a prim little kill-joy with no sense of humour. When she complained to their parents that he was tormenting her, Patrick only chuckled while Mary scolded Sean mildly, telling him to leave the girl in peace – but neither of them saw how he ran his hands over Rosie's body, and she was too embarrassed to tell them the details.

She decided that he might behave himself if his wife were on the premises, and suggested to Ruth that she should come round to the pub in the evenings now and then – without telling her why. Ruth, needing companionship, fell in with the plan and began to spend almost every night at the Watermen, but she did not enjoy the noise and the smoke-laden atmosphere of the bars, preferring to sit with her mother-in-law in the back room – so she never saw Sean when he was up to his tricks.

As the weeks went by Rosie grew desperate, exasperated by Sean's continual assaults and a little frightened by his persistence, which was now far beyond a joke. Her only ally was Connor, who rounded on his brother and told him to mind his manners when he caught him pestering Rosie in front of a crowded bar-room. But most of the time Connor was away, taking on all comers at fairgrounds on Mitcham Common, Shepherds Bush or Hampstead Heath.

Rosie tried asking Sean to stop persecuting her, but he pretended not to understand why she was so upset. 'You know damn well it's only a game we're playing – just to make the fellers laugh. It's not like I was doing anything serious,' he protested. But one evening, when Ruth was not at the pub and Connor was spending a few nights at home, things did become serious.

It had been a long day at the Kleibers' workshop and Rosie went up to her bedroom to change into the dress she kept for working in the bar. Stripped down to her shift, she stood before the wash-stand, sponging her arms and legs with warm water – when the door flew open and Sean walked in without knocking.

'So there you are!' he exclaimed. 'Look what I've got for you, me darling. This chap came in, dinner-time – one of them commercials – and I talked him into giving me a sample bottle of scent. Ashes of Roses, it's called. Here, take a sniff of this.'

He uncorked the bottle and held it out. She put her nose to it and smiled, hoping to get rid of him quickly. 'Yes – thank you, it's very nice. Leave it on the chest of drawers, will you? I'll put some on later.'

He took no notice. Grinning, he ran his eyes appraisingly over the curves of her body. The setting sun, beyond the window, was shining through her petticoat, making it almost transparent.

'Seems like I called in at the right moment,' he said softly. 'Let's put a drop behind your ears, eh?'

He dabbed some perfume on her. It was very cold, and she edged away. 'Leave me be, Sean, and get out of here. I'm not dressed.'

'Sure I can see that with my own eyes! In fact I can see a whole lot I've never seen before. You need a little sprinkle here and there.' He shook some more scent on to his finger-tips and began to touch her bare shoulders. As she put up her hands to push him away, he reached for her breasts. She struggled free, and smacked his face as hard as she could. 'You little devil!' he said, dropping the scent-bottle.

Pushing past him, she ran out on to the landing, not knowing where she would go – then she saw that the door of Connor's room was open, and Connor himself was standing by his bed, pulling on a clean shirt. Rushing in, she threw herself into his arms, saying: 'Don't let him get me!'

Realising what had happened, Connor growled, 'Don't worry, I'll soon settle his hash!'

But she would not let him go. 'No – don't leave me! Please stay.' He hesitated, then kicked the bedroom door shut, letting her cry on his shoulder. Lifting her tear-stained face to him, she whispered, 'Sean's been so horrible. It's a blessing you were here.'

Their lips were so close, the first kiss was inevitable. He felt the softness of her body, almost naked in his arms. 'Yes . . ' he said. 'I'm here.'

Later that night, when the pub had closed and the two brothers were clearing up in the bar, Connor took the opportunity for a private word.

'About Rosie,' he said.

'What about her?'

'She tells me you've been playing games with her.'

'Has she been belly-aching to you? What's wrong with her at all?' Sean looked a little shamefaced, wondering just how much she had said. 'Sure, it was only a bit of slap and tickle. Ask any of the lads, they'll tell you – not a bit of harm in it.'

'That's not the way it seemed to her,' said Connor. 'Do I have to remind you again that you're a married man?'

'Jesus, anyone'd think you were some old nun! I tell you, it was nothing but a joke for God's sake!'

'Is that so? Well, the joke's over. I told Rosie if she needs someone to take care of her, she can count on me. If I catch you mauling her about again, I'll break your bloody neck – and that'll be no joke at all.'

After that night, life was different for Rosie.

She was not in love with Connor, for she had known him too long and as far back as she could remember, he had been a brother to her – but she needed his strength and protection, the warm certainty of his presence. Gradually they fell into the habit of going out together. Two or three times, he took her with him to the boxing-matches, when the booth was set up at a fairground conveniently close to the Island – Victoria Park, or Hackney Marshes. Unlike Ruth, Rosie enjoyed watching the

180

bouts, gloring in his triumphs, thrilled that her own dear Connor was a hero.

Most people at the Watermen knew that Rosie had been adopted, so there was no surprise at this change in their relationship. Only Ruth, when she became aware of these new developments, felt uneasy – but she said nothing. What could she have said? After all, there was no reason why Connor and Rosie should not walk out together. Although Mary and Moira were sisters, there was no law against marriage between cousins, was there? Ruth tried to be glad for Rosie's sake, as she and Connor were obviously happy – and yet, for some reason she could not explain to herself, the thought of their happiness disturbed her.

She was not alone in that.

On the fifth of November, Connor had a free evening and he offered to take Rosie across to Greenwich Park, to see the bonfire and the fireworks. By a coincidence, Aunt Moira arrived at the pub just before they set out. It was soon after opening-time and the saloon bar was empty except for Rosie, who was preening herself in front of a mirror engraved with an advertisement for mineral-water.

'You're looking very smart, and no mistake!' exclaimed Moira. 'Where are you going in all your finery?'

'To the fireworks at Greenwich,' answered Rosie, with her eyes shining. 'We're just off.'

'Sooner you than me,' said Moira. 'That's why I came to see your mother. Henry's had to go to some business dinner in the City and I can't face being alone in the house with those dreadful bangs going on all night, making me jump out of my skin. So I decided to come here instead. There's one good thing about this pub – once it fills up, the noise in here will drown the fireworks!' She looked round the empty bar, adding, 'You're not going there all by yourself, surely?'

'No, of course not.' Rosie put on her hat, skewering it in place with two long pins. 'I'm being taken by my gentleman-friend!'

'Are you now?' Moira smiled. 'And where's the lucky man? I hope he's not going to keep you waiting.'

'No fear of that – he's upstairs,' giggled Rosie. 'He'll be down directly.'

'What do you mean? Oh, Patrick's taking you, is he?'

At that moment, Connor came in, shrugging into his coat. 'Are you ready, young lady?' He threw a smile at Moira. 'Hello there! Are you off to Greenwich as well? Maybe we can all go together.'

'Not me. I've only this minute arrived, and I wouldn't stand out in the cold watching rockets and roman candles if you paid me.'

He turned to Rosie. 'We thought we'd give it a try, didn't we? Are you sure you'll be warm enough? It's a cold night out there.'

'Don't you see I'm wearing your present?' Rosie knotted a pink woollen muffler under her chin, showing it off to her aunt. 'Con gave me this – wasn't it sweet of him? He says it suits me, 'cos it's rose-coloured!' She stretched up to him on tiptoe, snatching a kiss. 'Anyhow if it turns chilly, you can cuddle me till I warm up.' She linked her arm through his, concluding, 'Come on. We don't want to miss them lighting the bonfire.'

Aunt Moira watched them leave, but she was no longer smiling. When she went through to the back kitchen, she found Ruth and Mary winding wool. Ruth had the skein stretched between her hands, see-sawing to and fro, while Mary wound it into a ball. In his favourite corner, Patrick leaned across to put a log on the fire, and they all looked up to welcome the newcomer.

'Is it yourself? Come in – take off your things, and be cosy,' began Mary. 'Excuse me not getting up till I finish this. If you'd like to make a pot of tea, you know where everything is.'

Moira shook her head. 'No, but thanks all the same. I just saw Rosie going out with Connor. Her gentleman-friend, she calls him.'

'Oh, they're thick as thieves lately, the pair of them,' laughed Mary. 'It does you good to see them.'

'How long has that been going on?' asked Moira. 'And why in heaven's name didn't you tell me?'

'Don't look so anxious – I don't suppose it's serious!' said Mary. 'The fact is, I'm glad for both of them. Rosie needs a man to look after her, and Con's been on his own too long.'

'You shouldn't encourage them,' retorted Moira sharply.

182

'It's like putting a spark to tinder. Before you know where you are . . .' She broke off unhappily. 'Well, you know what I mean. It could turn serious.'

'Would it be so terrible if it did?' asked Patrick. 'She's a darling girl and he's a good feller at heart, for all his wild ways. Maybe it's what he needs, a girl like Rosie to sweeten him a little.'

'He's been a different man since they started going out together,' Mary agreed. 'I can't remember when I saw him so cheerful.' She appealed to Ruth, 'Can you?'

Ruth let the last strand of wool slip from her fingers. 'No, I can't,' she said. 'There – that's done.'

'Thank you, my dear.' Mary finished the ball and put it in her work-basket. 'Anyway, if they enjoy each other's company, what's wrong with that?'

'Of course it's wrong – terribly wrong!' Moira clasped her hands, staring at her wedding-ring. 'Them being related, I mean. Being cousins.'

Patrick and Mary looked taken aback, and shot warning glances at Ruth.

'It's all right,' said Moira. 'Ruth knows – I told her myself.'

'Well, then . . .' Mary relaxed a little. 'I don't understand why you're so agitated. There's nothing to stop cousins getting married, if it should ever come to that.'

'That's exactly why you should put a stop to it. The children of first cousins are liable to be weak and sickly – the blood runs thin.'

'Old wives' tales, most like!' snorted Mary scornfully. 'Besides, Connor's off on his travels again tomorrow and there's no knowing when they'll see each other next.'

'But when he comes back, it could all begin again,' Moira persisted.

'What's wrong with you at all?' exploded Patrick. 'I never heard such a fuss about nothing! They've only gone to the Bonfire Night, for pity's sake!'

As they came back from the firework party, walking through the pedestrian tunnel, Connor and Rosie met Aunt Moira again, on her way home.

Rosie greeted her, still bubbling with excitement. 'You

missed a real treat tonight. It was splendid, wasn't it, Con? And at the end there was a huge set-piece – portraits of King George and Queen Mary, with their initials – you should have seen it . . .' Then she faltered into silence. Moira was staring at them, looking from one to the other with an expression of absolute despair. She said nothing, but hurried on – walking very fast, as if she were trying to escape.

'What's come over her?' Connor asked. 'She looked like she'd seen a ghost.'

'Put your arms round me, Con,' said Rosie urgently. 'Hold me tight . . . I'm scared.'

On Sundays, the O'Dells always had their midday meal very late, after the pub shut at three o'clock. Sean and Ruth had an open invitation to join them for a family dinner, and Ruth always arrived in time to help lay the table.

Patrick was serving in the saloon and Sean in the public, and they were both shouting, 'Drink up, gents! Hurry up, please – it's time!' when Aunt Moira walked into the saloon bar.

Patrick frowned when he saw her. His sister-in-law looked very pale – perhaps she had come out in a hurry, for she was dressed carelessly and wore no powder or rouge. 'What's wrong?' he asked, seeing the look in her eye.

'I can't explain now,' she said quickly. 'I wanted to talk to you, but it's impossible. That's why I've written you a letter.' She thrust an envelope into his hand. 'Put this somewhere safe – don't lose it, whatever you do – and read it when you're alone.'

'I don't understand.'

'Please do as I say. I can't stop now, for Henry will be wondering what's become of me. I couldn't tell him where I was going.' Then she went out, as suddenly and mysteriously as she had arrived.

Patrick looked doubtfully at the envelope, turning it over in his hands. The last drinkers were just leaving, and he called through to Sean, 'I'm going into the back. Lock up for me, would you?'

He went into the kitchen, and found Ruth putting the

finishing touches to the table. 'Will you be a good girl,' he said, 'and give Sean a hand locking up? By the time you're done, I dare say dinner will be ready.'

As soon as she was out of the way, he called his wife in from the scullery. She came at once, wiping her hands on a tea-towel. 'What is it now?' she asked. 'I'm just about to dish up.'

'That can wait,' he said, and gave her the envelope. 'Moira was here a minute ago. She looked terrible – she'd a face on her like the crack of doom.'

'What? Why didn't you bring her in? What did she want?'

'She wouldn't stop. She just gave me that letter – she says it's important. God knows what's the matter with her, but I thought we'd better read it straight away.'

They sat down. Mary opened the envelope, and began to read aloud.

'Dear Patrick, It is very hard for me to have to write this, but I must do so. I have to tell you something that I'd hoped to carry as a secret to my grave. When I saw Connor and Rosie together, I knew I had no choice.'

'What the hell is she on about now?' Patrick interrupted. 'Why is she kicking up such a fuss about—'

Mary silenced him. 'Wait. Hear what she has to say.' She read on.

'I'm sure you will remember the time when Mary – ' She stopped, with a catch in her voice, as she read her own name and her eyes raced ahead down the page.

'Well? What's it all about?' he asked impatiently. 'Tell me!'

But Mary O'Dell did not reply. She finished reading the letter, then folded it carefully and put it on the table, among the knives and forks. Without looking at her husband, she rose and walked out – out of the room and up the stairs.

Completely bewildered, Patrick picked up the letter, and was still staring at it when Ruth and Sean came in.

'All locked up, Da,' said Sean briskly. 'By Christ, I'm hungry enough to eat a horse, and its rider as well . . .' He stopped, staring at his father. 'What's happened? Where's Mam?'

'She went upstairs.' Patrick held out the letter. 'She was just reading a letter from your Aunt Moira then she walked out, sudden like. Would you mind just glancing through it for me? I

185

can't quite make it out. Moira's writing's not of the best – and I've had some trouble with my eyesight these last few days . . .'

Sean gave a sudden snort of laughter. 'You old chancer!' he said. 'I do believe you've been fooling us all these years – making up bits out of the newspapers and pretending you can read them, when all the time—'

'I can so read!' Patrick drew himself up. 'Well, the big black letters, anyhow. It's the little joined-up writing that foxes me. That's why your mother tells me what they say, after the postman's been . . .' He looked at the doorway, and the staircase beyond. 'I don't know what's got into her at all. If you wouldn't mind, son?'

Sean began to read aloud, from the beginning.

'Dear Patrick, It is very hard for me to have to write this, but I must do so. I have to tell you something that I'd hoped to carry as a secret to my grave. When I saw Connor and Rosie together, I knew I had no choice.

'I'm sure you will remember the time when Mary was taken ill and had to go in to hospital, before Sean arrived. I know we said we would never speak again about what happened that night, but I have never been able to forget it. Afterwards, when I found out that I was pregnant, I let you and Mary believe that Henry was responsible –but that was not true. And when Mary generously offered to adopt my baby, it seemed somehow right that you should bring her up as your own . . .'

Sean broke off, and looked up at his father as if he had never seen him before, then asked, 'Do you really want me to read this?'

'No!' Ruth broke in, agonised, but Patrick bowed his head.

'You'd better finish it.' He spoke without any expression whatever, his voice utterly lifeless. 'I have to hear it all.'

After a moment, Sean continued, haltingly.

'. . . bring her up as your own, because Rosie is your daughter, and half-sister to Sean – and to Connor. That is why they must be stopped at once, before it is too late. God forgive me for what I have done . . . Moira.'

For a long time there was no sound in the back kitchen, and nobody moved.

Then, slowly, Patrick O'Dell lifted himself out of his chair, holding on to the table. His face was waxen, and he shuffled across the room like a very old man.

'I think I'll just go up and see how Mary is.' He forced the words out with an effort, then set off up the stairs.

'Dear God,' said Sean in a whisper. 'If only Mam hadn't read it first. What can we do? What can any of us do?'

Suddenly Ruth's head jerked up. 'Something's burning!' She sniffed the air, fiercely. 'Oh, no – the dinner!' Rushing into the scullery, she flung open the oven door. Wisps of blue-grey smoke curled out, and she grabbed a dishcloth, snatching the roasting-pan.

At the same moment, Rosie came into the kitchen, saying to Sean, 'Do you realise what time it is? Are we having dinner today, or are we not?' Then she reacted as Ruth had done to the burnt meat. 'Will you smell that? What's Mam dreaming of? Where is she, anyhow?'

Ruth appeared in the doorway, carrying the scorched leg of lamb. 'Your mother's upstairs – and your father's gone to talk to her,' she began awkwardly. 'Something happened that . . . Well, it's upset them both.'

'What are you talking about?' Rosie turned to Sean. 'I don't understand. What's wrong?'

Sean found that he was sweating, and pulled out a handkerchief, mopping his face. 'Moira wrote a letter,' he mumbled. 'See here – you'd better read it for yourself.' He flicked it across the table. Wondering, Rosie picked it up.

'No, don't. You mustn't!' Ruth tried to intervene, but by the time she could set down the roasting-pan, it was too late. As Rosie began to read, the colour drained from her cheeks, and she sank into a chair. Ruth turned angrily on her husband: 'That's a terrible thing to do. How could you?'

'There's no sense trying to hush it up,' he said, fidgeting with the cutlery. 'She's got to be told, hasn't she?'

'Yes, but not like *that* . . .' Seeing Rosie's lips were blood-less, and that the tears were running down her cheeks, Ruth dropped to her knees, trying to comfort her. 'I'm so sorry – so very sorry.'

'No, please. Just leave me alone.'

Rosie looked as if she might faint, and Sean stood up, feeling he should be doing something. 'Will I fetch you a drop of brandy? Are you all right?'

Rosie looked up at him blindly. 'I don't know. I don't know anything, any more.' She shook her head. 'I don't know who I am.'

Upstairs in the big bedroom, Patrick tried to think of something to say to his wife. Mary sat at the foot of the big old-fashioned bed, her back to him; he stared round the room, seeking inspiration. They had shared this room for so many years – he knew every stick of furniture, every flower and leaf in the patterned wallpaper, every crack in the ceiling-plaster – and yet, in a moment, it had all changed, and he felt like a stranger.

'It was such a long time ago,' he said at last.

She did not react in any way. She did not speak, or turn her head.

'Like Moira said – it was when you were in hospital. Connor was about a year old – eighteen months, maybe. I couldn't do my job in the pub and look after a baby as well, so Moira had to move in – well, it was you suggested it. And she was a big help, with the housework and the cooking and all. But I was – lonely. One night I'd a few drinks inside me, and on my way up to bed I – I stopped at Moira's room to say goodnight, and she kissed me. I can't remember how it happened after that, but it was just the once, I swear to God – never again. Next day we both felt ashamed, and we said we'd never speak of it again. A few weeks after, you came out of the hospital and Moira went back to her own place – back to her office, and back to Henry Marriner.'

Still Mary said nothing. He moved a little closer. 'I didn't

188

meet her after that for – oh, six months or more. Next time I saw her, you were sitting in this room with her, and she'd been crying – then you told me she was going to have Marriner's child, and that we should adopt it when it was born, 'cos he must never know . . . I often thought he must be a bloody fool, for all he's such a clever feller – for he never even noticed she was in the family way. I suppose the big heavy skirts you all wore in them days helped to hide it. So then she told him she was suffering from anaemia or some such rubbish, and that she was under doctor's orders to take a short holiday by the seaside, to build up her strength – and she went down to Bournemouth, to have the baby there. And I suppose I must've been as big a fool as Henry Marriner, for it never crossed my mind for one minute that I might be the father of that child. Never – until this very day.'

He was standing beside her now but her head was averted, and he could not see her face.

'So now you know everything,' he said. 'I didn't love her that night, when I went with her – and I don't love her now. It was you – always you, and nobody else.' Tentatively, he put his hand upon her shoulder.

She shied away instantly, moving further along the bed. Speaking for the first time, in a low voice that was heavy with bitterness, she said, 'Don't touch me. Don't ever touch me again.'

The day dragged on – unbearable, unending. There was no Sunday dinner: the food was spoiled, and anyway no one felt like eating.

When Patrick came downstairs, he found the two girls washing up the pots and pans in silence. Rosie had stopped crying now; her face was set and expressionless.

He looked round the kitchen, screwing up his eyes as if he found it hard to focus. 'Where's Sean?' he asked.

'He went out for a walk by the river,' answered Ruth. 'He said he wanted a breath of air before it gets dark.'

'Ah, yes – I see.' Patrick threw a surreptitious glance at Rosie, then addressed Ruth again. 'Why don't you go out to join him? He might be glad of your company.'

'Well,' Ruth turned uncertainly to Rosie. 'I'm not sure.'

'Give me that dish-cloth. I'll finish the drying-up,' he told her. 'And it'll give me and Rosie the chance for a bit of a talk.'

Rosie turned away. 'I don't feel like talking.'

'There's things that need saying.' Patrick took the cloth from Ruth's hands. 'D'you mind? I'd be very grateful.'

'Rosie?' Ruth looked questioningly at her sister-in-law. 'What do you think?'

'Do what you like. Go out if you want – I don't care either way.'

'All right then, I'll go. I don't suppose we'll be out long – the sun's going down already.'

Left alone together, Patrick dabbed at the crockery while Rosie finished the washing-up without looking at him. At last she emptied the dirty water down the sink, and walked out of the scullery. At once Patrick followed her into the kitchen.

'I don't know how to begin,' he said huskily, and cleared his throat. 'There's so much to say, it's hard to know where to start.'

'There's nothing to say.' Rosie fed the fire with some more coal. 'It's too late for talking.'

'But I want to try and put things right – if you'll help me.'

'How can you put it right? What's done is done. It happened years ago – nothing can change that.'

'Of course it was wrong of me, I knew that all along, and I'd give anything not to have hurt your mother like this, but—'

'I suppose you're talking of your wife?' Rosie turned to him at last, contempt in every line of her face. 'She's not my mother, or had you forgotten?'

Patrick winced. 'Don't say that – she's been a mother to you all these years.'

'You needn't remind me of that. I remember hearing the neighbours whispering, "Isn't it good of the O'Dells, bringing up that child as if she were their own" . . . It must have struck you as very comical.'

'How can you say that? I didn't know, did I? Till this very day, I swear to God I never knew.'

'But *she* knew, didn't she, my real mother? The mother who gave me away to be brought up by my real father. What a joke that was . . .'

190

'Rosie, listen to me, please.' He came towards her, holding out his arms. 'Is it such a terrible thing? I brought you up as my own daughter, I treated you as my own. Does it make such a difference, now it turns out to be the truth?'

'Of course it makes a difference!' Rosie spat the words out. 'You cheated your wife – you had a bit of fun with another woman – a woman who couldn't wait to get rid of her own child. Now I find out my mother and my father were a pair of cheats and liars, do you expect me to fall into your arms and say: "Daddy, dear, I love you. I forgive you"?'

Patrick's arms dropped helplessly to his sides. If he had ever dared to hope for her forgiveness, he knew now it was out of reach.

'I love you,' he whispered, so quietly she could hardly distinguish the words. 'And my love will never change.'

Her words were almost as quiet as his, but they were as clear and hard as ice. 'Mine did,' she said – and left the room.

On Monday morning, Rosie went to the workshop as usual. Ruth saw her sitting at her bench, and asked quietly, 'How are you feeling now? What happened after I left – did you manage to sort things out?'

Rosie would not meet her eye, frowning over a piece of cotton that had got tangled up in the needle of her sewing-machine. 'Nothing happened. It can never be sorted out . . . and I can't stand it much longer.'

Then Aaron Kleiber came into the workshop, and Ruth had to go back to her own bench.

During the morning, they were all unusually quiet. Sarah was wrapped up in her own private dream of happiness, and Rosie never looked up from her work. Mr Kleiber was very gratified by their unaccustomed silence. It could not last: in the middle of the morning, when Miriam Kleiber came in with cups of coffee for the workers, Rosie had reached breaking-point. Much to Mrs Kleiber's surprise, she refused coffee, shaking her head.

'But you are often telling me you enjoy my coffee,' began

Mrs Kleiber. 'And you need warming up, I think. Your face looks quite pinched with cold. Come, have some to please me.'

Rosie's self-control snapped, and she exclaimed: *'I tell you I don't want any – leave me alone!'* They all stared at her, and she immediately burst into tears.

'Rosie's not feeling very well today,' Ruth began.

'My dear girl, what is the matter?' asked Miriam, as Aaron left his own work to join them.

'I've a bad headache,' Rosie gasped, between sobs.

'There, there, don't cry.' Aaron fussed over her helplessly. 'We will take Rosie into the house, Mama – you must lend her your smelling-salts. I will come with you, in case we need to fetch a doctor. Poor thing, poor thing.'

He shepherded them out of the workshop, telling Ruth and Sarah to carry on sewing until he returned.

In the parlour, Rosie could not stop crying, and they became even more concerned.

'Is it a bad pain? Show me where it hurts. Perhaps you are straining your eyes,' suggested Miriam, massaging the girl's temples.

'It's nothing like that,' gulped Rosie. 'I'm just so unhappy.'

Up in his room, Ernest heard the sound of her grief and came downstairs to investigate. As he entered the parlour, Rosie was trying to explain. 'Something very bad happened at home. Something to do with my family. My father did something wrong, and now my mother won't speak to him. And in a way, it's all because of me.'

'How can it be because of you?'

'I can't tell you that. But I can't go on like this – I can't stay with them any longer. It will be better if I move out of the house.'

'It can't be so bad, surely,' Miriam tried to calm her.

'It's as bad as it can be, and I'm only making things worse by staying there. Do you know anywhere I could go? Is there anyone round here who might take me?'

'There's no need for that,' said Ernest. 'You can stay here.'

His father gazed at him in astonishment. 'Here? In this house?'

'Why not? Since Izzy moved out, we've a spare room. Why

192

shouldn't Rosie move in? I'll go and fetch her luggage presently.'

Aaron flung up his hands to heaven. 'So many changes – everything happening so quick. You don't even ask the girl if it's what she wants!'

But Rosie's tears had stopped. She sat looking at Ernest with an expression of wonder, a new light in her eyes. 'Could I? Wouldn't you mind? Mrs Kleiber – what do you think?'

Miriam nodded to her husband. 'I think it is a good idea. If you could be happy here, then we are happy to welcome you. Isn't that right, Papa?'

'If you say so, Mama,' sighed Aaron. 'I must get back to the workshop. Send Rosie in when she is feeling better.'

Rosie tried to smile. 'I think I am feeling a little better already.'

When Aaron returned to his sewing-machine, he told the other girls what had been decided. Ruth stood up. 'Excuse me, Mr Kleiber, but Rosie's very mixed up at present and she doesn't know what to do for the best. Will you let me talk to her? I'll be as quick as I can.'

When she entered the parlour she found Ernest sitting on the horsehair sofa beside Rosie. Mrs Kleiber was nowhere to be seen.

'If it's Mama you're looking for, she's gone to make up a bed for Rosie,' Ernest told her. 'She'll be down in a few minutes.'

'That's all right.' Ruth drew up a chair, facing the girl. 'I know you're feeling muddled and miserable now, but don't decide anything just yet. Wait till things are better, and then—'

'How can things ever be better? It's happened, and nothing can change that,' said Rosie. 'I suddenly realised I've got to get out of that place. It's the only thing to do.'

'Try to be patient. Don't do anything you might be sorry for later on – don't make the same mistake I did.'

'Mistake—?' Rosie stared at her. 'But it wasn't a mistake, you know it wasn't! You felt the same way I do and that's why you walked out of your parents' house, when it all went wrong. That's why you came to live at the pub . . . I'm only following your example.'

'I'm asking you to take some time to think things over,' said

193

Ruth. 'If you decide now while you're upset, you might do the wrong thing.'

'She's doing the right thing, the best possible thing.' Ernest put his hand upon Rosie's. 'We want her to come and live here with us.'

At the end of the afternoon, Ruth went back to the Watermen and found Patrick in the back kitchen with Sean; he seemed to have aged ten years overnight. They looked up, startled to see Ruth when they expected Rosie.

'Where's the girl?' Patrick asked.

'She's going to stay with the Kleibers for the moment.' Ruth tried to break the news as gently as possible. 'She thinks it will be better, until things sort themselves out. I've come to pack up her belongings. Ernest Kleiber will come round later on to collect them.'

Patrick's face crumpled up. He shook his head, as if pleading to be spared this new blow.

'Just for a while, eh?' Sean tried to console his father.

'I hope so,' said Ruth. 'I must tell Mrs O'Dell – where is she?'

'In the bedroom. She's been up there all day,' Sean replied. 'Listen – I'm glad you're here – I've something to ask you. D'you think you could stay and help out in the saloon this evening?'

'Work behind the bar, do you mean?' Ruth was dismayed. 'But I don't know the first thing about it!'

'I could teach you. Only if Rosie's not going to work here of an evening and with Da not feeling up to the mark either, I can't run the place all on my own.'

'Well, if you want me to, I'll try,' she said doubtfully.

'That's my girl! Sure, we'll have to look out for someone to take Rosie's place, but till we find the right girl—'

'How can you say that?' asked Patrick, and began to rock to and fro, tormented by a grief too deep for tears. 'How can anyone take her place?'

Ruth went upstairs and tapped softly on the bedroom door. 'Who is it?' asked Mary O'Dell.

'Me, Ruth,' said Ruth, and was told to go in.

Mary was fully dressed, lying on her bed and staring up at

194

the ceiling. 'I'm glad it's you,' she said. 'Come and sit by me. I don't want to see anyone else . . . not even the girl.'

Ruth pulled up a small wicker chair and sat close by the bed, saying, 'I came to tell you – Rosie's decided to stay at the Kleibers' house for a while. They're good people. They'll look after her, I'm sure.'

'I see . . . Perhaps it's for the best.'

'And it means I shall still see her every day. If you want to talk to her at any time, I can take you there.'

'Perhaps I should see her. It's hard to know what I should do . . . I have no quarrel with Rosie – she's done nothing wrong.'

The wicker chair creaked as Ruth shifted her position, uncomfortable in her role as peace-maker. 'And after all – it happened so long ago,' she began.

Mrs O'Dell's voice cut in harshly. 'Don't say that! It's what *he* said . . . and it *wasn't* so long ago. For me it happened yesterday, don't you understand that?'

Ruth realised she had been tactless, and tried to change the subject. 'Have you had anything to eat today?'

'No. They offered, but I didn't want anything.'

'You mustn't starve yourself – let me make you something. A slice of dripping toast, perhaps – you'd like that, wouldn't you?'

'I don't want anything to eat.'

'A cup of tea, then?'

'Perhaps that would be nice.' Mary swung her legs to the floor. 'But I'll do it myself. Don't be offended, will you, only it never tastes the same if somebody else makes it.'

She passed the dressing-table mirror, and winced away from her own reflection. 'Dear God, I look a sight. Ah, what does it matter what I look like?'

They went out on to the landing and were about to descend the stairs when a woman's voice rang out, and Mary gripped Ruth's arm. The voice was so agonised, it stopped them dead. *Jesus Christ – no, not that! Tell me it's not true!'*

Then there came the mutter of male voices, as Sean and Patrick spoke together, trying to explain the situation to Moira.

Mary O'Dell released her hold on Ruth, and took a step back. 'I'll not go down there,' she said. 'You'd better make that cup of tea after all, and bring it up to me. And you can take a message for me, if you will.'

Ruth found Moira sitting at the kitchen table, wild-eyed, holding her hands over her mouth as if she would stifle the cry of anguish that had been torn from her. 'I never knew . . .' she kept saying, over and over again. 'I never knew you couldn't read. How was I to know that? You never told me – I never knew Mary read your letters for you. God help us, *I never knew*!'

She looked up at Ruth desperately, asking in a rush of words, 'You've seen her? What did she say? Can I go up and talk to her? I must try to make her understand.'

'She won't talk to you,' said Ruth sorrowfully. 'I have to give you a message from her. She says she never wants to see you again.'

For Ruth, there was only one saving grace about the long evening that followed. She could never remember working so hard. Already tired after an exhausting day, she had to try and learn the bar-trade in the space of a few hours. Sean gave her a brief lesson in serving drinks, in washing and drying glasses, in working the till and giving change – in refusing any orders 'on the slate' – in consulting the list of prices when she was in doubt – in dragging heavy crates of bottles from under the counter – and in the skills required to pull a pint of beer that had just the correct amount of froth to give it a lively head, but never so much that a customer could complain of being given short measure.

'If you need any help, I'll be right next door in the public,' Sean concluded. 'Or Da will be through in the back room . . . but I'm sure you'll manage fine. Good luck!'

From the instant the doors opened, Ruth never had a moment to stop and think until closing-time. It seemed like a lifetime before she could go home to Meadow Lane with Sean, and they fell into bed around midnight.

'What a day.' She lay upon her back, feeling every muscle in her body protesting. 'I hope you find a new barmaid soon – I can't go on doing that job much longer.'

'It's a devil till you get used to it. You're a darling girl, and I couldn't have got through the evening without you. Thank God I married you.'

196

Humbly, he kissed her on the cheek, and she gave a faint smile. 'That's some consolation, then. I may not be up to much as a wife, but I make a useful barmaid!'

'You know I didn't mean it like that. You're the best wife a chap could wish for – and I don't deserve you.'

They lay side by side for a long while, too tired to move, overwhelmed by the tide of unhappiness that had washed over them in the last day and a half. At last Sean spoke. 'Isn't it terrible to think . . .' Trying to hammer out a complex thought, he stopped, and began again. 'It makes me feel very strange when I think of Da and Aunt Moira, all those years ago.'

'Don't think of it,' said Ruth gently. 'Better put it right out of your mind.'

'You don't understand.' He struggled to make himself clear. 'What I mean is, one act of mortal sin, twenty-odd years ago, and now there's five wretched souls in torment because of what happened that night. It makes you think, doesn't it?'

'Five people?' Ruth started to count. 'Your mother and father – Aunt Moira – Rosie herself – that's four.'

'There's Connor,' he reminded her. 'Of course, Con doesn't know yet – but it's going to hit him hard when he finds out.'

'I suppose so . . . poor Connor.'

She moved closer to her husband, and he put his arms round her. 'Am I forgiven?' he whispered.

She turned her head, kissing him upon the mouth. Perhaps, after all, there was not much to forgive.

It was a long time since they had made love, and in the shadow of the family tragedy, they came together in a different way. He was not as selfish or demanding as before, and she tried to respond to him with tenderness.

'Thank God,' he said at last, drowsily content and repeated, 'Thank God I married you.'

He was asleep within minutes, but Ruth lay awake for a long time.

November went out in thick fog, and the dark days were punctuated by the sad mooing of ships' hooters on the river.

197

The only glimmer of light for Ruth was that Mr O'Dell took on a new barmaid, so she was able to give up her evening job in the saloon. But time seemed to stand still; the family remained locked within the prison of their unhappiness, seeing no way out of it.

When December came in, it brought no relief. Other people were looking forward to the approach of Christmas; decorations went up in pubs and shop windows and there was a general air of cheerful anticipation. Tinselled cards were bought and posted, and children began to dream of Santa Claus, but within the Watermen there was no release from winter's gloom.

Just before Christmas, Connor came home from his fairground tours after several weeks away. He was immediately aware of the change in the atmosphere. He entered the house by the side door and went straight to the back kitchen, where his father sat in his usual chair by the fireside. Connor chucked his coat and bag into the corner, and went over to embrace the old man. Patrick looked up at him with empty, hopeless eyes, then turned away, staring into the heart of the fire as if to find some warmth or comfort in the glowing coals.

'What's wrong?' demanded Connor. 'Are you not well? Where's Mam?'

'Upstairs. She's mostly upstairs, these days.'

Before Connor could question him further, Sean came in quickly from the public bar. 'Is it yourself, then? I thought I heard you.' He took his brother's arm. 'Come away while I talk to you.'

It was early in the evening and the public was empty, so they were undisturbed. As well as he could, Sean blurted out the facts of Rosie's parentage. When he had finished, Connor sank on to one of the benches, trying to make some sense of these revelations. His first words were, 'Where's Rosie now? I must see her.'

'She's not here. The poor kid couldn't stand the strain another minute, and I can't say I blame her. She's living with the Kleibers now – you know, the people she works for. They took her in.'

'Where do they live? Can I go and talk to her?'

'She won't thank you. Seemingly she's trying to forget about the lot of us; but you'd best talk to Ruth about her. Ruth still sees her every day at the workshop.'

'Will I find Ruth at home now?'

'She's above, with our Mam. She comes round most evenings to keep her company.' As Connor stood up, Sean added, 'Be careful what you say. Talking to Mam is like playing with fire – the least little thing will make her flare up. I've spoken out of turn meself, more than once.'

Connor nodded. 'Thanks for the warning, but I have to see her.'

He went up to his parents' bedroom and tapped at the door. Ruth's voice said, 'Come in.'

The room seemed very different. For one thing, there was no sign of his father's presence at all – no pair of boots beside the grate, no old jacket over the back of a chair, no tie rolled up on the dressing-table. And his mother was different, too. In her nightgown, a crocheted shawl around her, she sat up in bed with her rosary in her hands. Her eyes were closed, and her lips moved as she repeated the 'Hail Mary' under her breath.

Ruth, sitting nearby in the wicker chair, looked up at the newcomer – and her face broke into a smile. 'Connor – we weren't expecting you!'

At the sound of his name, Mary opened her eyes, letting the rosary fall upon the eiderdown. She held out both hands for her son. 'Come here this minute.' Then she enfolded him in her arms, scolding him softly. 'Why didn't you tell us you were coming home? I'd have been up and dressed if I'd known.'

'It's good to see you, Mam.' He looked into her eyes, seeing the pain she was living with, and kissed her again. 'How are you feeling now?'

'I'm not ill,' she told him. 'I'm all right in myself – it's just . . .' She could not bring herself to tell him what was wrong, but kept stroking his hair.

Cautiously, he said, 'It's all right, Mam – I know about it. Sean told me.'

'That's good.' She sighed with relief. 'I don't like to talk of it – I try not to think of it. There's no need to say anything, son. Just let me hold you for a while – we won't say another word.'

They remained silent for some time, and then she exclaimed, 'Aren't I the selfish old woman? Have you had anything to eat? I must get up to make your supper!'

'Stay where you are, I'll do it.' Ruth got up, asking Connor, 'Will bacon and eggs be all right?'

'They'll be grand. I'll go down and have a bite to eat, Mam, then I'll come back to sit with you.'

In the scullery, he watched Ruth as she moved between the larder and the stove, preparing his supper. 'How long has she been like this?' he asked, keeping his voice down so that Patrick, in the adjoining kitchen, should not hear him.

'Ever since the day she found out. Your father sleeps in Rosie's old room now; they hardly speak to each other.'

'In the name of Jesus what's to become of them? They're killing themselves by inches. And they've been so close all their lives.' Connor clenched his fist. 'How about Rosie? How is she taking it?'

'It was terrible for her at first, but she's through the worst of it now, I think. Mr and Mrs Kleiber are so good to her – and their son's been very kind.'

'She's young – she'll get over it. It's Mam and Da I'm worried about.'

'It'll do them good to have you at home.' Ruth slipped two eggs into the sizzling pan. 'How long will you be staying?'

'Till New Year at least. Solly Gold's setting up in a Christmas Fair on Woolwich Common – I can get over easy enough from here.' He sniffed appreciatively. 'That smells good.'

'It's almost ready. Go in and talk to your father – try and cheer him up if you can. I'll bring it through to you in a minute.'

'Thanks, Ruth, I'm really grateful.'

'Don't be silly. Bacon and egg is no trouble.'

He turned in the doorway, giving her one of his rare smiles. 'I meant – thanks for being here. Thanks for helping to keep us together.'

Later in the evening he went to give Sean a helping hand. By nine o'clock the bars were crowded, and they were kept busy. Each time the street door swung open, more customers came in. Some of them were carrying holly and mistletoe from the

200

street market while others were laden with Christmas fare – a box of crackers, a bottle of rum, a plucked turkey.

Among the newcomers, Sean recognised an unexpected face. 'Father Riley! We don't often see you in here – what can I get you?'

'Nothing, thanks, I won't be stopping,' said the parish priest. 'But if you'll allow me, I'm hoping to take up a collection for the orphans.' He carried a wooden box with a slit in the lid, explaining that it was in aid of the Christmas treat at the orphanage.

'Sure, you couldn't have a better cause!' Sean dug into his pocket, and dropped a few coins in the box. 'Come on, Con – you can stump up a bob or two, can't you? And I hope you'll take a drop to keep the cold out, Father – on the house? Da will never forgive us if we let you go without a drink inside you.'

'That's very good of you.' The old priest looked around. 'I don't see Mr O'Dell anywhere. Would he be in the other bar?'

'No, Father.' Sean glanced at Connor. 'He's in the back room. The fact is, he's not feeling too good.'

'I'm sorry – is it the influenza? There's a lot of it going about.'

'No, Father, it's not that.' Connor poured him a tot of Irish whiskey, and decided to take a chance. 'Would you do us a favour, perhaps? Could you go and have a word with him? He's very low in his mind, and a talk to you might do him a power of good.'

'If you think it will help, I'll be glad to.'

Connor lifted the bar-flap, and Father Riley went through to the back kitchen.

The two old Irishmen talked to one another for almost fifteen minutes, and eventually the priest suggested that they should go upstairs and see Mary O'Dell together. Patrick looked very apprehensive, but finally allowed himself to be persuaded.

When they entered the bedroom, Ruth said to her mother-in-law, 'You have visitors to see you; I'll leave you to talk.' She offered Father Riley the wicker chair, and made herself scarce.

'I'll talk with you, Father, willingly, but not with him,' said Mary, refusing even to look at her husband.

201

'Now don't be hasty, Mary. I want the three of us to have a chat. Pat's told me what the trouble is, and now we have to discuss it.'

'I don't wish to talk about it,' she began.

'Of course you don't, but I think you should.' Father Riley turned to Patrick, who was looking very uncomfortable, standing by the fireplace and shifting from one foot to the other. 'Just tell me one thing, Pat. After you'd committed that mortal sin, did you go to Confession and make a good Act of Contrition?'

'I did, Father. Not to you, for you were new to the parish in them days, but I took myself to old Father Kincaid, who was still alive then, God rest him.'

'Very well.' The priest turned to Mary. 'You see, my child – God has forgiven him. Why can't you?'

After a short pause, Mary said unhappily, 'It's no good, I can't do it. I'm sorry, Father – I just can't.'

Father Riley sighed. Taking off his spectacles, he began to polish them. 'You must go on trying, my dear. When you say your prayers this night, ask Our Blessed Lady, Help of Christians, to soften your heart a little. That's all it needs – a little prayer, and a little compassion.'

He talked to them both for some time, asking after Rosie, and giving them his blessing before he departed. Downstairs, Connor had gone round the bars on behalf of the orphanage, and by the time the priest left the house, his collection-box was a good deal heavier.

Wednesday was Christmas Eve, so Ruth and Sean decided to move back into his old room at the pub for a few nights, even though it meant sharing a narrow bed. Since it seemed that Ruth would be doing all the cooking over the holiday, it was more sensible for them to sleep on the premises.

There was to be a midnight mass at St Anthony's, and Sean and Ruth had asked Connor to go along with them. As soon as the last revellers left the pub at eleven o'clock, they cleared up quickly and got ready to leave.

Ruth invited Patrick to come to church as well, but he shook his head. 'I don't feel up to it. I'll go in the morning, p'raps. Anyhow, I don't like to leave Mary on her own upstairs.'

202

'I'm not upstairs,' said Mary O'Dell. She walked into the room with her hat and coat on. 'Do you think I'd let the midnight mass go by?' she asked.

They looked from her to Patrick.

'Well?' Ruth asked him. 'Will you change your mind now?'

'I'm not sure . . .' Patrick gave his wife a questioning glance, uncertain what he should do.

Without looking at him, Mary held out her arm. Slowly, he rose from his chair and walked across the room, taking the outstretched hand. Then she turned her head, looking him up and down.

'You'd best put on your thick coat,' she said. 'You could catch your death out there. Well, move yourself, for pity's sake – we don't want to be late, do we?'

Hand in hand, they went out together, and the others followed.

·——13——·

Should auld acquaintance be forgot,
And never brought to mind . . .

At one minute past midnight, the saloon bar was rocking with noise as the customers joined in the chorus, linking arms to welcome the New Year. Outside, the bells of the East End churches pealed, and all the ships on the river added to the din, with sirens and hooters.

'A Happy New Year, my darling.' Sean flung his arms round Ruth and kissed her.

She had been helping out as an extra barmaid tonight, since they were so busy. Everyone was pressed into service – even Mary O'Dell stood beside her husband, smiling and pulling pints.

'God bless this house, and all here!' roared Patrick. 'May 1914 be a peaceful and prosperous year for each and every one of us.'

Across the room, Ruth saw Connor looking at her, raising his glass in salute; she smiled back at him. Certainly, the old year had been miserable enough, but it had ended happily – and one good thing had come out of it. She and her brother-in-law had reached a new and friendly understanding.

Only one thing cast a shadow over tonight's celebrations. She had hoped to see the Kleibers here, joining in the party, but despite Ernest's best endeavours Rosie had jibbed at the last minute, refusing to come back to visit her family. So Ernest had stayed behind as well; they were seeing the New Year in with his parents instead.

Ruth had expected Izzy and Sarah to be here, too, but Izzy had turned up by himself, very late and apologising for his wife's absence. 'Sarah's feeling a bit tired. She decided she'd sooner be at home to keep her Grandad company.'

He didn't seem particularly disappointed, Ruth noticed. In fact, he appeared to be unusually cheerful – his hair was dishevelled and his face was bright pink. She suspected he had called in at several pubs on the way from Poplar, to get into the festive spirit.

> *We'll take a cup of kindness yet,*
> *For the sake of auld lang syne . . .*

On another bench, not far from Izzy, Gloria Judge sang in a shrill soprano, perched upon a man's knee; like Izzy, she had taken rather too many cups of kindness tonight. Her fashionable, upswept hair had begun to tumble down on one side, and her mouth showed traces of lipstick, carelessly applied. Respectable young women did not wear lipstick, and Ruth had been afraid that Mary O'Dell would request her cousin to leave, but on such a special occasion Mary had turned a blind eye, ignoring the girl's behaviour.

Gloria had arrived shortly before midnight with a group of gentlemen friends. Ruth was not sure which of them had brought her, since she seemed to embrace them all indiscriminately, sitting first on one lap and then on another.

As Ruth watched, Gloria got up unsteadily, shrieking to her companions above the tumult, 'Don't go 'way – I'm coming right back. Got to go to the you-know-what!'

She pushed through the crowd, looking confused, and Ruth showed her the way to the ladies' lavatory. Outside the bar, the passage was cooler and a little less noisy.

'Thanks, Ruthie, you're a pal,' said Gloria. 'Can't hear yourself think in there.'

'Won't Aunt Emily be getting frantic by this time?' asked Ruth. 'Did you tell her you wouldn't be home till after midnight?'

'Oh, I don't have to bother with that sort of thing now.' Gloria laughed – and belched – and put her hand over her mouth. 'Oops! Pardon me, I'm sure. Didn't you know? I'm not living over the shop any more.'

Ruth stared at her. 'You mean you've left home?'

'Course I have. Well, don't look so shocked – why shouldn't

205

I? I couldn't go on being tied to Ma's apron-strings for ever. Anyhow, you're a fine one to talk – you were the first to move out. And somebody told me that girl Rosie, the one who was here, has packed her traps and left home as well. Is that right?'

'Well, yes. Rosie's staying with friends, but she had personal reasons for leaving.'

'Don't we all!' Gloria began to giggle again. 'Ooh, stop it, don't make me laugh – I got to go before I wet myself. See you later, dearie.'

'But Gloria,' Ruth called after her as she disappeared, 'where are you living now?'

Gloria's voice floated back as the door swung to. 'Like your little Rosie – I'm staying with friends.' Then the door slammed, like a slap in the face, and Ruth blinked.

She could imagine what a blow it must have been to Aunt Emily with Glory, the apple of her eye, packing up and leaving home. She must be heartbroken, but the others would be more angry than unhappy. Glory's brother Arnold would be deeply offended, and the other men in the family would be furious.

With a twinge of guilt, she realised that Gloria's barbed remark had some truth in it. Perhaps she *had* set a bad example when she left the Rope Walk. Perhaps, if she had not done so, Rosie might have stayed at the pub, and been reconciled with her parents. Perhaps Glory might still be living above the corner shop . . . But it was no good standing out in the draughty passage feeling guilty; she had to get back behind the bar, to help with the rush of customers.

It was noisier than ever in the saloon. Izzy had scrambled up on to one of the tables, waving an empty glass and demanding to be served.

'Gimme a bottle of champagne!' he shouted hoarsely. 'Lots of bubbly – that's what I want – lots and lots of bubbly . . .'

'Get down off there before you break your neck,' Mary O'Dell told him. 'You don't want to go wasting money on champagne – nasty, indigestible stuff!'

'Got to have bubbly,' Izzy repeated stubbornly. 'This is a celebration!'

Patrick came to his wife's assistance. 'Come on down now, sir, if you please! I know you're celebrating – we're all celebrating – but you don't need any more to drink. You've had quite enough.'

'You don't understand. I've got something special to celebrate – just me. Me and my beautiful wife. Sorry she couldn't be here tonight . . .' He allowed himself to be helped down from the table, staggering slightly, and almost falling on top of Ruth. He peered at her closely. 'Sorry, Ruth – it is Ruth, isn't it? Yes, I thought so. Let you into a little secret. You know why Sarah wouldn't come out tonight? She's got to take things easy now. She's only a slip of a girl, see – nothing to her at all, a breath of wind could blow her away . . . So we've got to take good care of little Sarah – 'cos she's going to have a baby . . .'

'Izzy, I'm so happy for you!' Ruth hugged him. 'When is it going to be?'

'Oh, not till the summer. I only found out myself this morning, but now you see why we've got to have bubbly – wet the baby's head and all that. Go and get me a bottle, there's a good girl. You must have a drink with me – you and your husband – and everybody!' He swayed again, clutching at a passing customer to steady himself. 'You too!' he announced. 'Have a drink on me, eh?'

'Drink with you?' The stranger looked at him with hatred. 'Listen, mate, if you was on fire I wouldn't even piss on you . . . Let go of me, you bastard!'

Immediately, Sean moved in, grabbing the man. 'Less of that! We won't have that sort of talk with ladies present!'

Connor appeared from nowhere, taking Ruth's arm, and saying, 'You'd best get into the back room. There could be trouble. Don't argue, just take Mam with you and go!'

Ruth tried to obey, but the sight of Izzy's face arrested her. He was staring at the man, with his mouth sagging – and his eyes were haunted. 'It's you . . .' he said. 'Arthur Bailey – I didn't know you at first.'

'Look different, do I?' The man lurched forward, about to hit him, but Sean hung on tightly. 'Yes – I dare say. Last time you saw me, I was covered in blood, eh? Bloodied and half-dead on the floor, after you'd done with me.'

Ruth stared at them as if she were mesmerised, but Connor

207

stepped in front of her, guiding her firmly towards his mother. 'Out of here, the both of you. It's no place for you.'

Mary took Ruth's arm, and they retired to the kitchen. 'Put the kettle on, there's a good girl.'

'I don't want a cup of tea,' Ruth began.

'No more do I, but if there's fighting they'll need cleaning up and bandaging after, and we'll be wanting plenty of hot water.'

In the saloon, Israel Kleiber stood helpless – a man whose world had collapsed around him. Just a moment ago he had been crowing with pride and delight, rejoicing in his good fortune, but now he looked like a lost child.

'You were there – you were one of 'em!' Arthur Bailey spat out the words. 'You and your lousy Brotherhood. Oh, yes, they blindfolded me so I couldn't see, but you and your brother Ernest was amongst 'em. He started vomiting, and I heard you call out to him – I knew your voice . . .'

By now everyone else had stopped talking. Every man present was staring at Izzy – isolated, and shaking as if he had a fever.

'I didn't want to do it,' he said. 'They made me – Ernest and me. We never wanted to be mixed up in anything like that, you must believe me. They're evil, the whole lot of 'em. They made me do it!'

'Shut your row!' Connor took charge of the situation. 'It's time you were getting off home.' He held Izzy in a grip of iron, propelling him towards the door. Men stood back to clear a path for them as Connor escorted him out into the darkness and the pouring rain.

'Now make yourself scarce,' he said quietly. 'You've been talking too much again, and that's not healthy. Go home and go to bed. With any luck, that pack of drunks won't remember much about it when they wake up. Will you be all right now? Can you find your way?'

'I'll be all right.' Izzy was still shivering. 'I was only trying to explain.'

'Say nothing. If you want a word of advice, don't go in for heavy drinking, neither. Drinking and secrets don't mix – and you've not the head for it. Now be off with you.'

Connor watched him stumble away up the wet street, his

head down against the driving rain, then he went back into the pub and began the long, slow process of persuading the revellers that they had homes to go to.

When the last customer had gone, he went into the kitchen and found Ruth on her own. Mary and Patrick had already gone upstairs, and Sean was doing the rounds and locking up.

'What was all that about?' Ruth wanted to know. 'What was that man Bailey saying to Izzy Kleiber?'

'Oh, I think there's been some trouble among the dockers.' Connor tried to shrug it off. 'If they'd been sober, they'd have kept their traps shut.'

'From what I heard, Bailey had been set on by a gang like you were, the night I met you. That's what happened to you, wasn't it?'

'Look, I don't know anything about Bailey. I must go up to my bed, I'm dropping with sleep.' He tried to get away, but she would not let him go so easily.

'Because Izzy works for the Brotherhood, I know. I was there one night when Eb came round to see him – on business, he said. It's my family that's behind all this cruelty, all this fear.'

Connor put his hands on Ruth's shoulders, looking her full in the face. 'Don't ask any questions, just keep out of it,' he said. 'You've made a new life here, a life that's nothing to do with the Judge family – and I'm glad for you.'

'Yes, but—'

'But me no buts.' Still holding her, he added gently, 'I'll say goodnight to you now. If I don't see you again, I wish you well for the New Year.'

'You say that as if . . .' She looked into his eyes. 'Are you going away?'

'First thing in the morning. I don't know how long I'll be gone, though I dare say I'll turn up some time, like the bad penny I am.' Then he released her, adding, 'I'm glad you and Sean are all right now. He's a lucky man.'

The following morning, Ernest was up in his room when Izzy arrived.

'Careful where you tread – I've been turning out some of

these old plates,' Ernest admonished. 'I'm trying to sort through them, to chuck out the duds and pack up the rest.'

Izzy stayed where he was, just inside the room, and closed the door cautiously behind him. There were glass photographic plates everywhere – on the chairs and the table, spread about on the bed and stacked in untidy piles on the floor.

'Looks like a junk-shop,' he said.

'Think so? A shop, maybe, but I don't know about junk.' Ernest smiled to himself. 'It's funny you should say so, because—'

'Never mind about that – I have to talk to you,' Izzy interrupted him. 'I just got back from the Wharf.'

'Oh, yes? I guessed you must have been turned off, or you wouldn't be home this time of the morning. No work today, I suppose?'

'That's just where you're wrong. There was plenty of work, more than they could handle, 'cos half the Guild didn't turn up at tally-time. Still sleeping off their thick heads from last night, most of 'em.'

Ernest raised an eyebrow. 'And how's *your* head feeling this morning? You're looking a bit red-eyed.'

'Leave off, I'm all right,' snapped Izzy. 'Listen, will you? There was work for every man there – everybody except me. Ebenezer Judge called out all the numbers except mine: my number wasn't even in the bag. When I put my hand up, he just looked straight through me like I was made of glass.'

'You mean he left you out deliberately?' Ernest frowned. 'What had you been doing to upset him? Was it on account of me?'

'I don't know. I think it might be something to do with last night.' Rather shamefaced, Izzy told his brother about the confrontation with Arthur Bailey, and his own drunken outburst against the Brotherhood.

'I see now, I was stupid. The place was packed – the customers all stopped talking, and listened. There must have been some bloke from the Guild there, I reckon. Somebody must have carried the tale back to Mr Judge. They'll have it in for me now, and no mistake.'

210

'Come and sit down, you look terrible.' Ernest cleared an armful of glass plates off a chair. 'Don't worry so much – this is the best thing that could have happened.'

'What are you saying? Don't you see, I broke their precious oath! I talked about Guild matters to outsiders. They'll never have me back again. I'll never be allowed to work for the Brotherhood now!'

'I'm glad to hear it. You should have stopped working for them long ago – you're well out of it.'

'Yes, but they won't let me off that easy. They'll make me go through the whole bloody ritual – blindfolded, beaten up, kicked out, all that.' His voice broke. 'You know what they're like.'

'That's why you mustn't go back. Do like I did – leave the Guild. Have no more to do with it.'

'That's easy to say, but I got the family to think of. I told you, there's a baby on the way. I got to earn a living!'

'That will be all right. You can come and work with me instead.'

'With you?' Izzy stared at him. 'What are you talking about?'

'I've been making plans. All this time, you thought I was just messing about with my camera, taking photos for my own amusement, but I've been planning how to set myself up in business. I'm going to open a shop, Izzy, selling cameras and plates and rolls of film, with a dark-room where I can do developing and printing.'

'But nobody round here wants to buy cameras.'

'That's what you think! It's the latest thing, haven't you heard? Ever since those little box-cameras came on the market, thousands of people have started taking up photography as a hobby. But that's not all – I'm going to turn part of the shop into a studio, where I can take portraits and family groups, on commission – and that's where you come in.'

'Now I know you're crazy. I'm no good at taking pictures.'

'Will you listen? I'll take the pictures and do the processing, while you can look after the shop and serve the customers. I'm telling you, we'll make a fortune!' Ernest went on to explain that he had already started looking for suitable premises; there was a shop to let in Cubitt Town, somewhere off the East Ferry Road.

'I'm going down there this afternoon, to meet the landlord and find out how much he's asking. Why don't you come with me? I've arranged to be there at five o'clock.'

Izzy still looked dubious. 'I don't know so much . . . it seems risky to me. You could lose your shirt by the time you've done the place up and laid out money on stock. Films and cameras don't come cheap . . . Anyhow, I can't do five o'clock – Sarah will be expecting me for tea.'

'For goodness sake! Get there as soon as you can. Make it six o'clock – I'll hang on till you arrive. I'd like you to see the place with me, so we can decide what needs to be done.' He threw a playful punch at his brother, a gesture that took them back to the old days when they were boys. 'Don't you see it's Fate, you falling out with the Judge family just at this particular moment? Believe me, this is going to be the making of us!'

Izzy was not convinced, but he agreed to meet his brother in Cubitt Town at six o'clock.

It was ten minutes to six when he alighted from the omnibus, near the Island Gardens. He remembered how he and Sarah had come here on summer evenings when they were engaged, walking under the trees and smelling the flowers. Now the trees were bare, and wind and rain were lashing the empty flower-beds.

Although the street lamps were reflected in the puddles, they gave very little light. Looking back, Izzy thought he could see somebody following him . . . The omnibus had been almost empty, but there were two men sitting at the back, wearing oil-skins, with sou'westers pulled down over their ears – and they got off when he did. He listened for their footsteps, but all sounds were drowned by the continual drumming of the raindrops and the gush of water along the gutters.

He set off to look for the address Ernest had given him – Silmour Street, off East Ferry Road – but it wasn't easy to read the street-names in the dark. Taking a wrong turning, he found himself in a blind alley, and had to retrace his steps. When he reached the main road, he felt a sudden stab of fear. The men were there, walking towards him, but now there were more of them – four men, moving at a steady pace – and he thought of Connor O'Dell's words . . . *You've been talking too*

212

much – that's not healthy'. Could the Brotherhood really be out looking for him?

Surely it must be a coincidence. After all, how could they have known he would be coming here tonight? He hadn't told anyone, except . . . Then he remembered: he had told Sarah, while they were shopping in the market this afternoon. Anyone in that crowd might have overheard him; anyone could have passed on the message.

Instinctively, he quickened his pace – and still the men came after him. He took to his heels and began to run – away from them, away from Cubitt Town – past the Island Gardens, into the shelter of the first building he reached: a round, glass-domed pavilion, above the staircase that led down to the pedestrian tunnel.

Gasping, he raced down the steps, hearing the noise of his feet echo and re-echo round the spiral staircase. Surely they couldn't catch him now? He only had to keep going until he was through the tunnel, under the river and out the other side, on the south bank . . . They would never find him there.

When he reached the foot of the stairs, he paused for a second, trying to catch his breath and listening for sounds of pursuit – but he could hear nothing except the pounding of his heart and the steady drip-drip-drip of water.

The tunnel was lined with white tiles, lit at intervals by gas-lamps; moisture ran down the walls, shining in the lamplight, and puddles on the floor threw strange patterns of light back to the curved roof: strips of brightness separated by deep shadow. There was nobody in sight, and he sighed with relief – but he could not risk turning back. They might still be waiting for him, up at ground-level; he must go on. He had only covered half a dozen yards when he heard a low whistle ahead of him – and pulled up short, frozen with fear.

Was it a trick of the light, or were those shadows moving, further down the tunnel? Panting, he watched as figures emerged from the patches of darkness, silhouetted against the light – and then he heard an answering whistle behind him, and looked over his shoulder.

The four men were there, still advancing – men behind him,

men in front of him – and his fear turned to panic, knotting his bowels, as he realised that he was trapped.

Ernest waited at the empty shop in Silmour Street until half-past seven; then the landlord looked at his watch and said, 'My missus will be sending out search-parties for me!'

'Yes, I'm sorry. I was sure my brother would be here,' Ernest apologised.

'I can't hang about all night. You've seen all there is to see – d'you think it's what you're looking for?'

Ernest took one last look round the empty shop as the landlord crossed the room to extinguish the gaslights in the wall-brackets, one by one.

'I think it will do very well. I'm only sorry my brother couldn't have seen it too.'

'As long as you're satisfied, that's the main thing. Oh, there is just one little matter we have to settle.' He turned out the last of the lamps. His face was a ghostly blur in the light from the dirty shop-window as he continued, 'It's a question of a deposit . . . I'll be requiring six months' rental in advance.'

Ernest's heart sank: this was an unexpected setback. If only Izzy had been with him. Izzy was a better businessman – he would have known how to handle this problem, but it seemed that Izzy had taken so little interest in the plan, he could not even be bothered to come and inspect the premises.

'I'll have to think about that,' he said.

A little more than a mile away, Israel Kleiber screamed for help – but there was no one to come to his rescue. Jubilee Wharf was deserted at this time of night; the big ships were moored far out in the middle of the river, and there was no one on duty at the wharf but Fred, the nightwatchman. Old Fred had been a member of the Brotherhood in his time, until he grew too old and infirm to do the work, and then they had fixed him up with this undemanding job.

When Joshua told Fred they had some private business to attend to and slipped a coin into his hand, the old man retired to his shed and asked no questions.

214

Nobody but the punishment squad heard Izzy's cries, but Joshua said, 'Better stop his mouth, to be on the safe side.'

They tore the black velvet hood from his face, and forced open his mouth, stuffing a handful of cotton-waste between his jaws.

For the first time, Izzy saw what they intended and terror unmanned him. If he could have spoken, he would have pleaded for mercy – begged, grovelled, promised them anything, if only they would spare him this punishment . . . the worst punishment in the Brotherhood's rule-book.

His legs were tied tightly so he could not kick or struggle as they lowered him over the outer wall of the dock, where the stones were green and slimy, lapped by the oily waters of the river. As he hung there, they fastened his wrists to a pair of iron rings set into the stones, and Joshua pronounced the sentence upon the traitor.

'For the Judas who turns against his Brothers – the man who betrays us by revealing the innermost secrets of our Guild – the punishment shall be as follows . . . Such a man shall be exposed to wind and weather, suspended between the high and low tidemarks, from night until morning – so that he may take time to consider his wickedness, and repent.'

As the tide rose, the icy waters would creep up, slowly covering him, until they reached his chin – and then any vessel that passed in the darkness would set up a wash, breaking over his head at high tide, leaving him submerged for a few moments, choking and half-drowning him.

When the ropes had been made fast, the punishment squad went off and left him there, and Izzy heard some of the men laughing as they walked away.

Long before dawn, Sarah came round to the Kleibers' house, banging on the front door.

Ernest came downstairs, and found his mother trying to calm the girl.

'Ernest will know where he is,' she said. 'Ernest – where is your brother?'

Ernest stared at the two women, bewildered. 'I haven't seen him. What do you mean? Isn't he at home?'

Sarah spoke so rapidly, her words tumbled over one another. 'I thought he was with you. When he left last night, after tea, he told me he was coming to meet you, to look at an empty shop, he said. When he didn't come home, I was a little worried, but I knew you had business to discuss. I thought you must have sat up talking till very late, so he decided to sleep here instead. But this morning I woke up early and I was very frightened. I couldn't go back to sleep, I had to make sure . . .'

Slowly, Ernest shook his head. 'I haven't seen him. I waited at the shop, like we arranged. In fact, I waited there for an hour and a half, but he never turned up.'

Sarah held on to the back of a chair, clutching it for support. 'Where is he?' she asked. 'What has happened to him? Where is my husband?'

It was still dark on Thames Wharf when Joshua and Ebenezer came to find their victim after his ordeal. Eb held a lantern, looking on as Josh leaned over the edge of the wall, reaching down to release the prisoner.

'He's not moving,' said Josh. 'He must have passed out . . . He'll be heavy to lift – you'll have to give me a hand.'

They thought he was unconscious, until they got him up on to the wet stones. When they rolled him over on to his back, the water spewed out of his lungs – and they saw that his eyes were wide and staring, his face a mask of horror.

The continual winter rains had swollen the river, throwing out their calculations; last night, the tide had been almost a foot higher than the seasonal average . . . and Israel Kleiber was dead.

'How much longer?' asked Joshua.

'Not long now,' said Ebenezer.

'Suppose he doesn't turn up?' Josh was getting desperate. 'Suppose he lets us down?'

'He'll be here. It's going to be all right . . . Pull yourself together.'

'If anything goes wrong, it'll be the finish of the Brother-hood, you know that, don't you? It's going to be the finish of everything.'

'Quiet!' Eb's head jerked up. 'Listen – there's somebody now.'

It was Friday evening, some twelve hours since the two brothers had taken Israel Kleiber's body from the river, and they stood waiting in the Number Three Warehouse at Thames Wharf.

A heavy door swung open, its rusty hinges screaming, then old Fred the nightwatchman called out, 'Are you there, sir?'

'Yes, Fred,' replied Eb. 'Send him in.'

'Do you want me to hang on, and let him out when you've done?'

'No need for that, we'll see to everything. Go back to your shed.'

'Very good, sir. In you go, then.'

These last words were addressed to the man at his shoulder, who now walked slowly into the warehouse. The door creaked shut behind him, and he moved into the dim circle of lamplight.

'Well, Saul, so you got my message,' said Ebenezer.

Saul Judge looked suspiciously at his cousins. Since his father had fallen out with Marcus Judge, there had been no love lost between the two branches of the family.

'Your lad Tommy come round dinner-time,' he mumbled.

'Told me you'd got some second-hand goods to be disposed of. I was to bring the hand-cart, he said.'

'Quite right,' said Eb, with a thin smile. 'A little job that needs to be done, and we prefer to keep it in the family.'

'What is it then? Old iron? You can't get much of a price for scrap-metal these days,' Saul began.

'Just come here, will you?' Ebenezer led Saul round the stack of empty crates. Josh followed, saying nothing.

An old tarpaulin lay on the ground, and Saul knew at once that this was no scrap-metal job. When Eb uncovered the face of the drowned man, Josh made a small, inarticulate noise and looked away. Saul expressed no emotion whatever, but asked in a matter-of-fact tone, 'Who was it?'

'There's no need for you to trouble yourself with details. He was a member of our Guild; we found him this morning – he must have fallen in the river last night, in the dark. It's a sad lesson to us all. Most likely he'd been led astray by the demon drink, and took a wrong turn in the darkness.'

Saul stooped, uncovering the body and examining it with a practised eye, then he straightened up, saying, 'His hands have been tied. You can see the weals left on his wrists where he was roped up, clear as daylight. That weren't no accident.'

Eb and Josh exchanged glances, and Josh exclaimed angrily, 'I told you it's not going to work!'

'Shut up, you fool!' Eb turned to Saul, and continued smoothly, 'That's the very reason why we didn't send for the police, as we would have done in other circumstances. I'm sure death was an unfortunate accident, but we shouldn't care to have the police coming round asking questions. So we thought it might be more satisfactory if you were to find the body somewhere else away from here – down-river, anywhere . . .'

'They'll still ask questions when they see them marks on the wrists. There'll be enquiries made. They'll want to know where he worked, everything about him . . .'

'Perhaps if you were to delay finding the body for a while, until the marks have gone, that might be more convenient all round.'

'Maybe so.' Saul scratched his jaw. 'I got a tank back at Cyclops Wharf – I s'pose I could leave him in river-water for a

218

couple of weeks. There wouldn't be no marks on him by that time.'

'Good, good.' Ebenezer rubbed his hands and smiled at his brother. 'You see, Josh? I told you Saul wouldn't let us down.'

But Saul was not smiling. 'What's it worth to you?' he asked suddenly. 'How much?'

Ebenezer's expression changed. 'I don't understand you, Saul. I thought you'd be grateful, as we're putting a bit of business your way. I've no doubt that when you hand the corpse over to the authorities, they'll pay you the usual rates.'

'Oh, no.' Now Saul's face broke into a cunning grin. 'That's not good enough, nowhere near. If you're wanting me to hide evidence from the law, I'm taking a risk, ain't I? You'll have to see me right, if I'm to do a thing like that.'

'I don't know what you mean!'

Eb tried to bluster his way through, but Saul simply laughed at him. 'Come on, now. You wouldn't fancy being took up on a murder charge, would you?'

'Murder?' Josh broke in, his voice rising dangerously. 'It wasn't murder, it was an accident.'

'Manslaughter, then. Look, I don't want to know about it – what you bin up to is your business, and none of mine. But if you want my help, it's going to cost you. That's why I'm asking – how much?'

'We'll see you right,' said Ebenezer in a low voice. 'Just go and fetch your hand-cart, and get that thing out of here.'

'Wait a minute!' Saul knelt down, and began to run his hands over the sodden garments. 'There's nothing in the pockets, nothing on him at all.'

'Of course not – I emptied the pockets,' said Eb impatiently. 'We don't want them to find anything that might lead back to us.'

'Don't be stupid – if they see he's been cleaned out, they'll know it was foul play, won't they? Either that, or they'll say I done it! You put back everything that was on him, or the deal's off.'

Reluctantly, Eb produced the few items Izzy Kleiber had been carrying: a couple of banknotes, a handful of coins, some keys – and the tools of his trade, the tally and the claw.

'But then they'll know he belongs to the Brotherhood!' Josh protested.

'They'll know that anyhow, soon as they put a name to him. And that won't take long, 'cos he'll be reported missing already, like as not. Go on now – put it all back, so I can cover him up and put him on the cart. Then I'll be on my way.'

In fact Ernest had reported his brother's disappearance early that morning, and all day the Kleiber family had been waiting for news – but they waited in vain. Sarah was beside herself with anxiety, and they did their best to calm her, telling her they felt certain that her husband would turn up very soon, that there must be some perfectly reasonable explanation for his absence. But as the hours stretched into days, it became impossible to keep up any pretence of optimism. A fortnight later, the news came through at last.

Ruth and Rosie had come round to spend the evening with Sarah. Since Izzy's disappearance, life had been unbearably lonely for her with no one but her old grandfather for company, and the girls spent as much time as they could with her, trying to find ways of cheering her up.

Tonight, Ruth had brought along an old copy of *The Young Ladies' Companion*, which somebody had left behind in the Watermen, and they did their best to entertain Sarah by discussing the latest fashions. However, as the pictures were all of elegant society beauties wearing incredibly expensive creations, Sarah soon became restless and put it aside.

That was when they heard a knock at the door. Sarah went to answer it, and came back looking very pale, followed by her brother-in-law and a uniformed Sergeant of Police.

Ernest said, 'Good evening,' to the visitors, shook hands with old Mr Vogel, then introduced Sergeant Tonks, explaining to Sarah: 'The Sergeant called at our house half an hour ago, to see my parents and to give us some news. He was hoping to find you there too, so I said I'd better come round here with him. I wanted to be present when . . .' Helplessly, he shook his head, leaving the sentence unfinished.

Sarah looked at him for a long moment, then at the Police Sergeant. 'Izzy's dead, isn't he?' she asked.

Sergeant Tonks said gruffly, 'I'm sorry to be the one to tell you, madam. Your husband's body was recovered today, from the river.'

Sarah stood quite still, shutting her eyes. Her lips moved silently, then she said in a whisper, 'Thank you. It is what I have been waiting to hear. I knew it from the beginning – that he was dead. Thank you for telling me.'

Then she remembered her grandfather, and went to him, holding the old man's hands and repeating the news in his own language. Gently, he drew her to him, and embraced her, without a word.

Rosie broke the silence. 'But how? Why did it take so long? Where had he been all this time?'

The Sergeant cleared his throat, unwilling to add any further grief to the bereaved girl, and answered unhappily, 'According to the police surgeon, death must have taken place soon after the gentleman went missing about two weeks ago. There will have to be an inquest, of course, but the verdict's plain enough – it'll be brought in as accidental death. Dark night, bad weather – the gentleman must have lost his footing and slipped into the water. These things do happen some-times, more's the pity.'

By now Sarah had begun to weep, and Rosie went to her at once. 'Come and lie down. I'll make you a hot drink and sit with you till you go to sleep . . . You need to get some rest.'

'How should I rest?' Sarah asked brokenly.

'You must. You've got to build your strength up for the baby.'

'Izzy's baby – yes, I must think of our baby.'

She allowed herself to be led from the room. When she had gone, Ruth asked quietly, 'How can you be so certain it was an accident?'

Ernest looked at her sharply, as if she were reading his mind, and the Sergeant said, 'What makes you ask that?'

'The night before Mr Kleiber vanished, I heard him having a quarrel with another man. It happened in the pub where my husband works – the Watermen. It looked as if they might come to blows.'

'Ah, yes, madam – you'll be thinking of Arthur Bailey. We've had several accounts of that already, but at the end of the New

Year's party, Bailey went on the rampage and was took into custody, charged with being drunk and disorderly. He did seven days in the cells, madam, so there's no possibility he could have been mixed up in Mr Kleiber's death. You don't know if he had any other enemies, I suppose? Nobody who might have had a grudge against him?'

'None that I'm aware of,' Ruth replied truthfully.

'But he—' Ernest burst out, then he saw Ruth looking at him and stopped.

The Sergeant encouraged him to go on. 'Yes, sir?'

'Nothing. It wasn't important.' Ernest fell silent once more, and turned away.

In the dark days that followed, his time was so fully occupied he had no spare moments to grieve for his brother, still less to try and find some proof of the Brotherhood's involvement in Izzy's death. Ernest did his best to console his parents and to help his widowed sister-in-law in every way he could, and he tried to exorcise the shadow of the Brotherhood, which remained at the back of his mind as a continual reproach, and a living nightmare . . . After all, he had no shred of evidence, no possible reason to accuse the Judge family of any crime – nothing except the memory of his brother's anxiety, and the fear in his eyes the last time he saw him alive.

The inquest was a mere formality, as the Sergeant had predicted, then the body was laid to rest, the family mourned Israel's passing and the matter seemed to be at an end.

Ernest retired to his room, and became a recluse once more.

It was Rosie who helped him return to life. One evening, about a week after the funeral, she tapped at his bedroom door with a tray of sandwiches and some hot coffee.

'You can't go on like this, you know. You'll only make yourself ill and that's not going to help anybody. Even Sarah's trying to think of the future now, for the sake of the baby.' She cleared a space on the table to set down the tray, and discovered that his camera, books and papers and his rolls of film were all thick with dust.

'What future?' asked Ernest bitterly. 'The last time I talked to Izzy, I told him we'd got a wonderful future ahead of us. That was a bit of a joke, wasn't it?'

He went on and told her about his dream of opening a photographic shop and studio – how it had seemed to be about to come true, if Izzy had given up his job on the docks to go into partnership with him, but now it was quite impossible.

'I had to tell the landlord I wasn't interested after all. I haven't got a partner, I haven't got enough capital. I've got nothing but a lot of stupid plans which are never going to happen.'

'You could make them happen, if you want to,' she told him. As she spoke, she began automatically tidying up the table, using the corner of her apron as a duster. 'Has that landlord found another tenant yet?'

'I don't know, but anyway it's out of the question. He wanted six months rent in advance.'

'Find out if the shop is still to let. You could raise the money somehow. Borrow it, ask your father, or go and talk to a bank manager.'

'And start off up to my ears in debt? Besides, I can't run the shop and take pictures at the same time. I had to have Izzy to help me.'

'I could help you.'

She was rubbing the dust off his camera, when he yelled at her, *'Don't do that!'*

Startled, she almost dropped it and defended herself hotly. 'Don't you shout at me! You made me jump.'

'I beg your pardon, but you must never rub the lens with a cloth, especially not with your apron. One speck of grit on that lens could ruin it.'

'I was only trying to help,' she said with dignity. 'In case you hadn't noticed, I was just offering to come and work at your shop. I mean, if you want me to.'

He stared at her. 'Do you mean it? Are you serious?'

'I think I might enjoy it. It sounds like a good idea – and I think I'd like to work with you.' She smiled at him. 'Is that serious enough?'

'And now, ladies and gen'lemen, this evening's champion, Mr Connor O'Dell, is willing to take on all comers. Is there any man here present with the guts to stand up to Mr O'Dell for ten minutes?'

Connor stood in the doorway leading to the dressing-rooms as Solly Gold ran through the same old patter; he wasn't really listening – he knew it by heart. While he waited, he studied the crowd around the ring. The hall wasn't much more than half-full, but that was better than nothing.

It was also a great deal better than working under canvas at this time of year. The cold wet weather had continued all through February, and now March was coming in like a lion, with roaring north-easterly winds. Connor was glad not to be touring the fairground booths in this weather. The period between Christmas and Easter was a barren one for outdoor showmen and Solly preferred to cut his losses, promoting indoor fight programmes in suburban London and small towns around the Home Counties.

He would book a hall in advance, and plaster the town with posters, bringing in a small team of fighters for so-called Championship contests, which were not very different from the demonstration bouts he staged during the rest of the year. And he still used the old 'Challenge to all comers' as the highlight of the night's entertainment.

This week, they were on the outer fringe of the metropolis, at a public hall in South Norwood. Connor ran his eye along the rows of seats. They had a real mixed bag in tonight – a strong contingent of workmen in cloth caps and mufflers in the cheap seats, a fair number of office-workers in dark suits with stiff white collars – even a sprinkling of well-dressed men and women at the ringside. He was surprised to see that a few of them were in evening dress; the men in white ties, the women in shimmering evening-gowns, bare-shouldered or wearing fur stoles to protect them from the icy draughts.

Finding the manager of the hall standing beside him, Connor said, 'Got a few of the gentry in tonight, by the looks of it. Must be plenty of money round these parts.'

'They're not locals,' grunted the manager. 'We get a few of that sort down from the top of the hill – Beulah Spa they call it up there – big houses in private grounds, a couple of hotels – that's where the nobs come from.'

'God save us, will you look at that now?' exclaimed Connor. 'One of 'em's getting into the ring!'

There was a stir of excitement in the hall as a man in evening dress ducked under the ropes. A buzz of speculation broke out, for the well-dressed stranger was a black man, and negroes were an uncommon sight in the South London suburbs.

His teeth gleamed when he smiled, and Connor saw a flash of gold. Whoever he was, he was not taking up Solly's challenge for the sake of the prize-money, that was for sure.

Without a word, the negro began to take off his jacket, his white tie and waistcoat, then he took out his pearl studs and cufflinks. When he peeled off his shirt, the crowd gasped. Stripped to the waist, he was revealed as a titan – his massive shoulders shining, his blue-black skin taut over tightly-packed muscle. Connor could tell at a glance that this man was going to be a serious challenge.

He watched him put on the gloves, quickly and easily as if he had been doing it for years. He appeared to be in his middle thirties, which might give Connor, at twenty-four, some slight advantage, but he knew that he would still have his work cut out to beat this man.

Now he was whispering something to Solly, and a moment later the promoter made an announcement. 'Challenging Connor O'Dell tonight, we have a visitor from the United States of America. I ask you to give a warm welcome to Mr John Doe from Galveston, Texas!'

The fighters pressed their gloves in the ritual salute, and the bell rang. The Texan was still smiling when the fight began, and he continued to smile as Connor moved in, offering a series of quick, exploratory jabs. The Texan swayed to his left, then sent a thundering right cross towards Connor's chin. Connor saw it at the last possible moment, ducking his head to take the punch on the temple and trying to roll with the blow. The black fighter followed up with a straight left that cannoned from Connor's skull.

The Irishman backed away, his gaze locked to the Texan's face with its maddening gold-toothed grin. The man's foot-work was smooth and confident, the speed of his hands unbelievable, and his strength prodigious. More than that, he

225

had hit Connor with a right-hand blow in the opening seconds of the fight – an insult of the worst kind. The right hand was used mostly to defend the chin. In sending that right-cross, the Texan was saying: 'I don't fear you . . . you're nothing.'

Anger flared in Connor and he moved in, fists raised, shoulders swaying. The Texan smiled, stepping in to meet him, hitting Connor hard with a straight left, but this time Connor was ready. Ducking under the blow, he sent a wicked left-hook that hammered into the black man's cheek, staggering him.

He straightened up and backed away, and he was still smiling – but now his eyes had a cold, hard glitter, and Connor saw that he was angry. The edge of fear sharpened the Irishman's mind. This man, whoever he was, was something special.

There was no time to consider that. The Texan moved in, fists flashing out in a blur, thudding into Connor's face and body – under his defence, over his defence, through his defence. For Connor it was like fighting three men at once, but he took it all, replying with sharp hooks to the body. The Texan pushed him away, trying to keep the fight at long range, and landed an uppercut that drove Connor back several paces, but did not follow up his advantage. Connor took a deep breath and stepped in – to be met with a powerful blow to the heart and a left that spun him to the canvas.

The Texan's smile broadened slightly, but when Connor shook his head like a dog emerging from a pond and got on to his feet again, the spectators went wild. Now the challenger's smile was underlined with real hatred.

This was no exhibition match; it had become a fight to the finish, and they both knew it. The chanting of the timekeeper was drowned in the deafening roar of the crowd. Connor was determined to give as good as he got, and for a few minutes the two men slugged it out, shoulder to shoulder, evenly matched.

It could not last. The Texan was ruthless, utterly determined to master this impertinent nobody, and he took his chance when it came: a mighty uppercut lifted Connor off his feet.

Dazed, he sprawled across the canvas, summoning up all his

reserves of strength and will-power in order to carry on the fight. As he pulled himself up to his feet once more, he saw to his amazement that the Texan was already pulling off his gloves, about to leave the ring . . . And yet Connor had not been counted out – there were still a couple of minutes on the clock.

He tried to protest, but the challenger looked at him with contempt, saying, 'Don't bother me, son. I reckon you've taken enough punishment for one night . . . I quit.'

Now the cheers were mingled with boos, and arguments broke out all round the hall, some of them erupting into sudden fist-fights. In vain, Solly Gold called for silence, trying to make himself heard. 'Mr John Doe having retired from the contest, I have no alternative but to declare Mr Connor O'Dell the winner and undisputed champion!'

Nobody was listening. Ignoring the uproar, the American continued to get dressed and a few moments later, surrounded by his friends, he walked out of the hall. One young lady in a white fox-fur flung her arms round his neck and kissed him as they departed.

In the cramped, smelly dressing-room, Connor turned angrily on Solly. 'How could he do a thing like that? How can any man walk away from a fight? Who the hell is this John Doe anyhow?'

Looking him over, Solly remarked dryly, 'You can thank your lucky stars he threw in the towel before you got yourself killed. John Doe is only the name he uses when he's on holiday. That was Jack Johnson – he's on a trip round Europe. Funny way to amuse himself, going round picking up fights on the road, but if that's what takes his fancy . . .'

Standing at the wash-basin, Connor stared at Solly. 'Jack Johnson – the World Heavyweight Champion?'

'Bloody right! He's been World Champion six years now – nobody can knock him off his perch. I suppose it must give him some satisfaction, keeping his hand in like this.'

Connor looked at himself in the cracked mirror above the basin. He had a cut on his temple, a split lip, and a swelling round one eye which was already discoloured. Jack Johnson had left his mark on him, right enough, but he had stood up to a

227

top-class fighter, and he had not been defeated. Eyeing his reflection, he remembered those cold, cruel eyes – that empty smile. Was that what happened if you stayed in this game? Would he himself turn into a fighting-machine one day?

'Ah, the hell with it,' he said at last, and plunged his head into a basin of cold water.

The new barmaid at the Watermen was called Kathleen Simes; she had carroty ringlets and big breasts, and Ruth disliked her intensely.

Soon after she had been taken on at the end of November, Sean told his father that he'd picked a winner this time. The girl was hard-working and she made herself popular with the customers, laughing and joking with the men but keeping them in their place and never permitting them to step out of line.

Sean often came home to Meadow Lane, still chuckling over some pert retort Kathleen had made to a cheeky young devil who tried to get familiar. 'Oh, she's a caution and no mistake, our Kathie!' he used to say.

Ruth began to get very tired of hearing him sing the praises of 'our Kathie', but after a month or two he stopped doing so – which was worse. In the weeks that followed, he never mentioned her at all, and when Ruth asked after Miss Simes, he stared at her as if he were scouring his memory for anyone by that name. With elaborate lack of interest, he replied, 'Oh, yes, Kathie Simes. I hardly ever see her these days. Well, you know how it is when you're working in different bars.'

Ruth's heart sank, and her suspicions were confirmed when she found a long copper-coloured hair on the collar of her husband's jacket and a smear of rouge on his handkerchief. Sean was up to his tricks again. Well, some men were like that, apparently. Perhaps Sean was incurably faithless, unable to resist any passing temptation. Perhaps he had a fatal weakness for girls with red hair . . . or perhaps, Ruth thought, she herself was not sufficiently attractive to satisfy her husband.

In any case, it seemed there was nothing to be done about it. She tried not to brood upon the situation, but kept away from the pub as much as possible, devoting herself instead to Sarah, who needed her help. With just four months to go until the baby was due, Sarah was feeling very tired, looking forward with dread to her confinement, and saying she did not know how she would survive it without her husband.

Ruth did all she could to instil some confidence in her. One sunny April evening, she persuaded her to come out for a stroll but they had not gone far before the unaccustomed heaviness Sarah was carrying became an intolerable burden.

'Can we sit down for a while?' she pleaded. 'My ankles are hurting.'

As it happened, they were within a stone's-throw of the Watermen and Ruth took her inside, going through the side door and avoiding the saloon bar. She introduced Sarah to Mary O'Dell, who made a great fuss of her and gave them cups of strong tea and slices of 'brack' – thick slabs of Irish fruit-bread, with lashings of butter.

Mary knew of Sarah's tragic loss, and skirted tactfully round the subject, telling tales of her own pregnancies and how the first time she had been brought to bed, it had gone so easily she could hardly believe it. 'Just like shelling peas, the doctor told me!' she said, which made Sarah laugh.

They were interrupted by Kathie Simes, who bustled in from the saloon, glanced at Sarah, threw a patronising 'Hello' at Ruth and addressed Mrs O'Dell. 'There's a gentleman in the bar asking for your son – your other son, I mean, Connor. I told him he's not here, but he says he soon will be. What shall I say to him?'

Mary looked perplexed. 'You'd better bring the gentleman in. Why would anyone think to find Con here? He's not been home since the New Year.'

Kathie fetched the gentleman, who appeared rather sur-prised to be greeted by a roomful of females, and then went back to her customers. The visitor was a middle-aged man, smartly dressed and very well-groomed, with pomade on his hair and expensive rings on his fingers. He wore a silk cravat with a stick-pin in it, and carried a gold-topped ebony cane and a top-hat.

'Mrs O'Dell? Allow me to introduce myself,' he said in a strong American accent. 'The name's Cassidy – Leopold

229

Cassidy, from Pennsylvania. I'm very glad to make your acquaintance, ma'am. How do you do.'

They shook hands, and Mary introduced the girls. 'My daughter-in-law, Mrs Ruth O'Dell, and a friend of ours, Mrs Kleiber.'

'Charmed, ladies. I apologise for breaking in on your family circle, but I was expecting your boy to be here. I had a letter from him saying he'd be arriving some time today, and asking me to meet him. We have a matter of business to discuss.'

'Well, I'm very sorry but he's not here, and to tell you the truth I'm not expecting him. But that's Connor all over – he never lets me know when he'll be coming home, does he, Ruth?'

Mr Cassidy turned to Ruth. 'Mrs O'Dell – would I be right in assuming you are Connor's wife? Perhaps you know what time he'll be arriving?'

Ruth explained that she was married to Connor's brother Sean, and that she had no knowledge of his whereabouts.

'I beg your pardon . . . I guess he's on his way right now. Don't let me interrupt you. I'll wait in the bar-room until he—'

Before he could say any more, they heard Connor's voice outside. 'Where is he? In the back-kitchen? What in God's name is he doing there?' Then Connor burst in. 'Mr Cassidy! Sorry to keep you waiting – I had to travel up from Kent, and the train was stuck in a tunnel. Excuse me a minute longer, while I say hello to my family.'

He hugged his mother, then kissed Ruth on the cheek and shook hands with Sarah. Returning to Mr Cassidy, he continued, 'As long as I was on the move with Solly Gold, it was a problem to know where I'd meet you. In the end I decided to wait till I had a few weeks' break so I could see you here, at home.'

'That's OK by me,' said Mr Cassidy, 'but do you have some place we could go and talk privately? I don't want to intrude upon these good ladies any longer.'

'I suppose we could go upstairs,' began Connor, doubtfully.

'Not at all!' said Mary quickly, trying to remember what state Connor's bedroom was in. 'You must make yourselves comfortable here. We can move into the saloon, can't we, Ruth?'

In the end, the party broke up, for Sarah said that it was high time she went home, and Ruth insisted on accompanying her.

'Will I see you later?' Connor asked, as Ruth was about to leave.

'Well, yes. I'll come back at the end of the evening, when Sean finishes work,' she told him. 'I'll see you then.'

She walked home with Sarah, talking of this and that, but thinking all the time of Connor. How well he had looked, how full of life and energy . . . Suddenly, she was feeling cheerful. Now that Connor was to spend some time at the Watermen, Sean would stop pursuing Kathie, and behave himself.

By the time she got back to the pub it was nearly eleven, and she found Connor sitting in the kitchen with his mother and father. They were looking very happy, and Connor pulled out a chair for her.

'I've had a bit of good news,' he said. 'Wait till you hear!' Quickly, he told her about the evening at South Norwood a month ago, when he had been matched with the World Heavyweight Champion.

'It makes me feel ill to think of it,' Mary shuddered.

'Will you hold your peace, woman?' demanded Patrick. 'Let the boy tell his story.'

Connor went on to explain that Jack Johnson's manager, Leopold Cassidy, was in the party on that occasion. 'They came over for a holiday, but now Mr Cassidy's decided to stay on for a while. He wrote me a letter, care of the Public Hall where he'd seen me fight, so it took a while to catch up with me. He wanted to meet me, for he had a proposition to put to me. Well, tonight we got together at last, and – what do you think?'

'Con won't have to go traipsing round those old fairgrounds any longer,' Mary broke in, until Patrick silenced her with a look.

'That's the truth,' grinned Connor. 'He tells me he manages a whole crowd of boxers in America – his stable, he calls 'em! –but he's looking for talent over here as well. He's got a gymnasium up in Liverpool, training some promising lads, and he wants to take me on. How about that?'

Patrick roared with laughter at Ruth's amazement. 'They don't waste any time, them Yankees. He'd a contract in his pocket, ready for the boy to sign! Mind, he's not really American, with a name like Cassidy. When I asked him, he told me his folks came from the Old Country, so he's one of our own flesh and blood, as you might say.'

'I'm very glad for you, Connor,' said Ruth, when she could get a word in. 'But you don't mean you'll be going to Liverpool?'

'Indeed I shall! I was thinking I'd take a few weeks holiday at home, but now I'm off on a train tomorrow morning. He'd even got me a railway ticket!'

'Tomorrow morning?' As Ruth repeated the words, Sean came in from the bar with Kathie Simes.

'What's the almighty excitement?' he wanted to know. 'Visitors popping in and out, everyone talking nineteen to the dozen! Kathie wants to be let in on the secret, don't you, my girl?'

She slapped his hand playfully, 'You're awful, you are, making out I'm inquisitive!'

'Sit down and you shall hear,' said Connor. 'Sean – you'd best fetch a round of drinks. We've got something to celebrate, isn't that right, Ruth?'

Ruth made herself smile back at him. 'Quite right,' she said.

It was a long hot summer, and a lonely one for Ruth. Sean spent more time than ever at the pub, never coming home until long after closing-time. By then, Ruth was usually asleep and although she half-roused when he climbed into bed beside her, he never attempted to touch her but rolled over and was soon snoring heavily.

In her loneliness, she turned to Sarah and spent almost every evening in the cool, dark sitting-room – dark, for Izzy had not lived long enough to carry out his promise of repapering and repainting it in brighter colours. Old Mr Vogel smiled and nodded, cat-napping in his chair, while Ruth read aloud from the newspaper. They did not buy daily papers, but Ruth often picked one up when she went shopping, since old papers were used to wrap the meat and vegetables.

One evening at the beginning of July, she came upon an unusual item from *Our Foreign Correspondent*.

232

'Listen to this,' she said. 'Somebody's been shot – the Archduke Franz Ferdinand, heir to the Emperor of Austria.' She crossed herself. 'May his soul rest in peace.'

'I never heard of him.' Sarah repeated the name to her grandfather, but it meant nothing to him. 'Where did it happen? In Vienna?'

'No, somewhere called Sarajevo. Where's that?'

'I never heard of that, either.' Sarah shifted impatiently. 'Isn't there anything more cheerful in the paper?'

As the weeks passed, Sarah was losing all interest in the outside world. Nothing mattered to her now but the child she carried – the number of times it kicked, the change in her balance when it moved into a new position – and she counted the days until the end of July, when it was due to arrive.

July came and went, and Sarah began to feel frightened again. Had something gone terribly wrong? Ruth reassured her – everyone knew first babies were notoriously unpunctual.

On the first Monday in August, Sarah announced suddenly, 'I think it will be tomorrow. I don't know why, but I have a feeling tomorrow will be a very important day.'

Next morning, when Ruth called in on her way to work, Sarah told her proudly that the pains had already begun. Ruth sent for the midwife, then went to the Kleibers, explaining that she could not come to work today as she had promised to stay with Sarah.

Throughout a long, difficult labour, Sarah was brave and patient; during the last stages, she held Ruth's hand and did not let go until it was over. Ruth had never seen a child being born and watched, marvelling, as the midwife cut the cord, lifted up the tiny baby and said, 'Well done, Mrs Kleiber, you have a fine boy.'

Sarah held out her arms to take her son, and her face was radiant. 'Izzy would be so proud of you,' she whispered.

Ruth's joy was coloured with a touch of envy. She could not help wondering – if she were ever to be blessed with a child, would Sean settle down and change his ways? Might he become a good husband and father in time?

Sarah smiled up at her, her eyes shining. 'I told you this would be a special day.'

233

Half an hour later, Ruth went round to the Kleibers to announce that they had a grandson. Of course the old couple were delighted, yet there seemed to be an underlying sadness in their smiles. Their happiness was a little muted, a little tentative.

Then Aaron broke the news that was spreading through the streets like wildfire, and told Ruth that it had been an important day for everyone . . . For this was Tuesday, the fourth of August – and Great Britain had declared war on Germany.

·——15——·

'It's been a bad week for business, the worst since we started.'

On Friday evenings, Ernest always did the accounts; after the shop closed, Rosie drew the blinds and they entered up the books together before going back to the Kleibers' house.

Thanks to Rosie's support and enthusiasm, the photographic shop in Silmour Street had opened in the spring. Ernest borrowed the extra capital from his father, and was paying him back a small amount each week. He did not like owing money to his father, but it was better than being in debt to the bank.

Aaron Kleiber had encouraged his son to set up in business for himself, so when Rosie told him she wanted to give up her job at the workshop and help Ernest, he could hardly stand in her way.

Business in Silmour Street had been slow at first, but Rosie told Ernest that this was only to be expected – it was bound to take time for word to get round. The summer heatwave helped a lot. It was the ideal weather for taking snaps, and the craze for photography was spreading rapidly. At last the shop began to show a small but regular profit – and then the war broke out, and people had other things than snapshots to think about.

'It's not fair!' declared Rosie crossly. 'Why should the shop lose money just because the Germans have marched into Belgium? I'm sick and tired of hearing about "gallant little Belgium". If their army had stood up to the Kaiser instead of running away, we'd never have got into this mess! What's it got to do with us anyhow?'

'It seems that the Germans are planning to move into France next, and the Kaiser might have his eye on England as well,' Ernest told her. 'After all, it's only a short step across the Channel.'

'What nonsense! It's just a lot of fuss about nothing.' Rosie tossed her head. 'They say it'll all be over by Christmas.'

235

But not everyone felt so confident.

Ruth went to the local Post Office every day, to read the Official Bulletins that were put up in the window, but they did not tell her much.

Official War News

German plan of invading France seriously delayed by resistance at Liège, and intervention of French cavalry . . . Various minor Belgian and French successes reported . . . No British casualties.

So it *was* true that the British Expeditionary Force had been sent across to France, and that young men from Britain were out there now, facing the enemy . . . Ruth could not settle down on her own that evening at Meadow Lane, and decided to pay a visit to the Watermen, hoping to have Mary O'Dell's company.

When she arrived, she found Mary in the back kitchen listening to Kathie Simes who was full of the latest gossip.

'They say there's Russian soldiers been sent over from a place called Archangel, and when they landed in Scotland, they sent them down here in special trains, travelling all through the night with the lights out . . . My cousin's got a friend whose auntie lives right next to the railway line, and she saw them through the carriage windows, lit up by the glow of their pipes and cigarettes – great big men with black beards, she said!'

'Is that a fact?' Mary asked, round-eyed.

'You shouldn't listen to rumours,' Ruth broke in. 'You'd go mad if you believed every tale you heard.'

'Rumours? I suppose it's a rumour they caught six German spies trying to poison the water in Chingford Reservoir?' exclaimed Kathie indignantly. 'They didn't waste time arresting them, neither. They lined them up against a wall and shot the lot of 'em double-quick – and good riddance, says I!'

As Mary crossed herself, Sean came in looking for Kathie.

'Come on, my love, let's be having you.' He broke off, discomfited to find his wife there. 'Hello, my darling girl,' he said quickly. 'Come to keep Mam company? That's nice. I

236

can't stop and chat meself – we've a crowd in the saloon. Will you get a move on, Kathie?'

Kathie rose with a heavy sigh. 'Duty calls . . .'

'It does indeed.' About to leave, Sean turned to Ruth. 'Which reminds me, I just heard from a customer. D'you know who was one of the first to put his name down at the Recruiting Centre? Your brother Joshua!'

'Josh?' Ruth could hardly believe her ears. 'But he's got a wife and two little boys at home! He wouldn't want to volunteer for the Army.'

'Seemingly he couldn't wait! Sees himself as a hero, I shouldn't wonder,' Sean teased her.

'Now that's what I call a brave man!' Kathie told Sean. 'You ought to follow his example, and join up to do your bit.'

'Sure, I'd go like a shot if I was free and unattached.' Sean looked suitably solemn. 'But I can't leave my darling wife, can I? Besides, I've my job here at the pub. I may not be one of them heroes, but I'm doing my bit by staying put.'

The British Government had refused to bring in National Conscription, saying that the Army had no need of men who were pressed into service – although they certainly put a lot of time and trouble into the drive to recruit volunteers.

Public meetings were organised as swiftly as possible. That Sunday afternoon, a big marquee was set up in the recreation ground at Poplar, open to all and sundry. Sean and Ruth went along out of curiosity; they arrived in good time, but found the tent was almost full, and only just managed to squeeze into vacant places on the end of a bench.

The wooden benches, the heat under the canvas, the smell of crushed grass and sweating bodies reminded Ruth inescapably of Connor's appearance in the boxing-ring. There was something, too, in the tone of the speeches from the platform that recalled Solly Gold's challenge to all comers, and his appeal to 'Any man of courage here present . . .'

An elderly Staff Officer, immaculate in khaki, smoothed his white moustaches and passed on a personal message from Lord Kitchener: 'Five hundred thousand men will be needed altogether – the first hundred thousand are needed at once!' he said. 'Lord Kitchener invites every man between the ages of nineteen and thirty-five to enlist. But this is not the standard Army enlistment; as a rule, a man has to sign on for twelve years – all we ask now is that he should enlist for the duration of the war. As soon as the war is won, the new recruits will be free to return to their wives and families.'

Looking around her, Ruth saw a good many men were whispering to the women beside them. She noticed Ebenezer and Florrie – pale and trembling, as he muttered in her ear. A private soldier in a peaked cap beckoned to Eb – and Ruth realised with a shock that it was Joshua, unfamiliar in his new uniform. Eb left his place and went up to talk to his brother then, as the crowd broke into enthusiastic applause, they both walked across to the Recruiting Sergeant, who sat behind a trestle table, and Eb signed his name, while poor Florrie burst into tears.

It seemed unnecessary for Eb to enlist. Ruth knew he was already thirty-four years old – a year or two more, and he would have been too old to qualify. Why couldn't he stay peacefully at home with Flo and little Tommy?

As if spurred on by his gallant example, Aunt Emily's son Arnold took off his glasses and followed his cousins, giving his name to the Sergeant; now more and more young men were coming forward, fired by patriotic fervour.

Ruth tried to imagine how Aunt Emily would feel when Arnold went home and told her what he had done. She had already lost her beloved Glory – how could Arnie desert his mother now, leaving her on her own?

She saw two more faces that she knew. At the far side of the tent, Ernest Kleiber was standing up. At his side, Rosie seemed to be arguing with him, putting a hand on his arm as if she would restrain him – but he shook his head, determined to do his duty by his adopted country, and joined the queue of men in front of the Recruiting Sergeant.

Ruth turned to Sean, wondering what was going through his mind, and he smiled at her wistfully. 'I'd give my right arm to be with those lads,' he said, under cover of the continuing applause. 'But what's the use? I can't leave Da and Mam to run the pub without me. At their age, it'd kill them in six months.'

That evening, Louisa Judge arrived at the corner grocery shop, and found her sister in floods of tears.

'Oh, Louie, thank goodness you're here!' Emily sobbed. 'You've got to help me. Something dreadful's happened – I can't – I can't bear it . . .'

'I know.' Louisa patted her hand. 'I know all about it. Arnold came and told me you were upset, so I put my bonnet on and came round straight away.'

'Upset? Of course I'm upset – it's the most terrible thing that ever happened!' wailed Emily. 'Going off like that, joining the Army, leaving me all alone. How could he do such a thing?'

'Yes, dear, I know it's very hard for you but try not to give way. You should be proud – after all, the boy's only doing his duty. Eb and Josh have volunteered as well, you know.'

'Yes, but what about *me*?' Emily sniffed, fumbling for her handkerchief. 'I can't live here all on my own – it's not safe. There's German spies out there walking the streets. I could be murdered in my bed.'

'Don't talk so silly, Emmie – nobody's going to murder you. Besides, there's no need for you to be on your own. You can find someone to come and stay with you, I'm sure.' A bright idea struck her. 'This might be the right moment to ask Gloria to come back. You never know, she might be glad to come home again by now.'

Emily blew her nose, then wiped her eyes. 'I'm afraid that's not possible,' she said resentfully. 'Glory's gone off with those friends of hers and she's not living round these parts now. I don't even have an address for her any more.'

'Well, then, you must advertise for a lodger. Some nice girl to come and take one of the rooms.'

'I don't want a lodger! I want my own family. I want Glory – I want Arnie . . .' And her tears began again.

Louisa sighed. 'I think we both need a nice cup of tea. Shall I put the kettle on?'

The kettle was singing on the hob, and Louisa was just measuring two spoonfuls of tea into the pot when the door opened again and Arnold walked in, accompanied by a young lady.

'Better put out two more cups, Auntie Lou,' he said. 'This is

Miss Maudie Hopper. Maudie – my auntie, Mrs Louisa Judge, and this is my mother.'

The girl came forward to shake hands. She was not exactly pretty, but she had big eyes, and fair hair in a schoolgirl plait over one shoulder – and she was very nervous.

The two older ladies looked at her in amazement, and then Louisa said, 'I think Miss Hopper and I have met already, at last year's Christmas Bazaar. You are in the choir at Chapel, aren't you, dear?'

'Yes, I am.' The girl spoke very shyly. 'That's where I met Arnold.'

'At choir-practice?' Emily turned to her son. 'You never told me you'd met a young lady!'

'It all happened rather quickly, Mother. And, since I've joined up, things will have to move quicker still.'

'I don't understand.'

'Tonight I asked Maudie if she'd be my wife, and she said yes. We're going to be married as soon as we can get the licence, before they send me overseas.'

Emily fell back into her chair, quite speechless, as he continued cheerfully, 'I know you'll be pleased, once you get used to the idea. After all, you keep saying you don't want to be left on your own, and now you won't be.'

'What do you mean?' croaked Emily.

'We shan't have time to find anywhere else to live, so Maudie can move into my room. You'll be company for each other while I'm away, won't you?'

Tactfully, Louisa had omitted to say that she had seen Maudie Hooper on several occasions – whenever she visited the Minister of the Emmanuel Chapel in fact, since Maudie was employed by the Reverend Mr Evans, and lived in as a maid-of-all-work. Having no family, she had been brought up in an orphanage, where Mr and Mrs Evans had found her and taken her into service.

It was small wonder that the girl had little to say for herself. The Evanses had not been unkind to her, but they had kept her in her place. To be suddenly plucked from that situation and transported into a new life was like the prospect of going to heaven for someone like Maudie Hooper.

She was seventeen years old and very young for her age, while Arnold was a young man of twenty-eight. She was a little overawed, but he told her that she was in love with him, and she felt sure that he must be right.

The wedding arrangements were soon made. Arnold invited all the members of the Judge family, and included Ruth in the invitation.

'I realise that your religious persuasion will not allow you to attend the ceremony,' he told her pompously, 'but there is to be a small reception at the Reverend Evans' house afterwards – nothing elaborate, since that would hardly be appropriate, in war-time . . . and I should very much like you to be there.'

'That's very kind of you, but I'm not sure—,' Ruth began, but he had only paused for breath.

'I should be particularly pleased, since my sister won't be present. Unfortunately we can't get in touch with her and even if we could, I don't suppose she'd turn up. Gloria and I are not very close these days. But if you and – Sean, is it – would like to join us?'

'It might be difficult,' Ruth pointed out. 'My father has made his feelings very plain and I shouldn't want to create any unpleasantness at your wedding.'

'I've already told Uncle Marcus that I wish to invite you,' said Arnold firmly. 'I said that as my cousin you have every right to be there.'

'And what did he say to that?'

'Well, nothing really. To be quite honest, he ignored my remarks completely, and changed the subject. I got the impression that he may not be there himself.'

'In that case, thank you for the invitation. We'll be glad to come.'

After the wedding ceremony, Ruth and Sean arrived at the Minister's house in their Sunday best. As Arnold had said, it was not a very grand reception – just ham sandwiches and little sponge cakes with pink icing, and cups of tea.

Sean muttered out of the side of his mouth, 'Where's the beer?' and Ruth reminded him that the members of the Ebenezer Chapel were teetotallers.

'A wedding with no booze? Why the hell didn't you say that before?' grumbled Sean. 'I'm off!'

'You can't leave! It would look very rude.'

'Who said anything about leaving? I'm just going out to have a fag, and get some fresh air.' Sulkily, he took refuge in the little back garden and later Ruth glimpsed him through the window, flirting with one of the young ladies from the Chapel choir.

Joshua and Ebenezer arrived together, both in khaki; by now they were undergoing basic training at Warley Barracks in Essex, but they had been granted weekend leave to attend the wedding. When they came face to face with Ruth, they greeted her sheepishly and seemed anxious to move on as soon as possible.

Ruth asked mischievously, 'Did Father give you your orders before he allowed you to come? "Don't be too friendly towards Ruth" – was that it?'

Josh scratched his head, unwilling to meet her gaze, but Eb replied coldly, 'Of course not. But since you turned your back on the family, I don't think we have much to say to one another, do you?'

'Probably not,' said Ruth pleasantly, 'except I'm glad to have seen you both. It gives me a chance to wish you good luck.'

'Thanks, Ruth.' Suddenly, surprisingly, Josh kissed her on the cheek, then backed away, afraid he might have gone too far. ''Scuse me, I got to go and find Mabel and the boys.'

'Yes, of course. I think I'd better look for my husband too.'

Ruth made her way through the crowded room and into the garden, which consisted of a parched lawn, a tangle of shrubbery and a little summerhouse. She looked round for Sean, but he was not to be seen; neither was the lady chorister. She went across to the summer-house and peeped inside, wanting to know the worst, yet dreading what she might find.

Sean was not there, but a grey-haired lady sat alone on a garden chair.

'Hello, Ruth,' said Louisa Judge.

'*Mum!*' Ruth stared at her. 'I didn't know you were here. I looked for you indoors, then I thought you must have stayed at home with Father.'

'He wanted me to, but I said it wouldn't be right if neither of us came to the wedding. I shan't stop long.'

'How are you?' Ruth took her mother's hands, searching her face. She seemed older, with more grey in her hair than she remembered.

'I'm quite well, thanks. How about you?'

'Oh, I'm fine . . . I just saw Josh and Eb – they look very smart in their uniforms, don't they?'

'This dreadful war.' Louisa bent her head. 'I won't sleep easy till it's over and they're home, safe and sound.'

Ruth pulled up another chair and sat beside her. 'They seemed a bit embarrassed when they saw me. What had Father been saying to them?'

Without looking up, her mother said quietly, 'It hurt your father very badly when you went away. He's never got over it. You mustn't be unkind – he loves you very much.'

'Oh, Mum, you know that's not true! He never loved me – he doesn't know what love means. He's a hard man, and he's tried to bring the boys up to be just like him.'

'Don't say that.' Louisa shrank away. 'I won't let you.'

'I'm sorry, I've got to be honest with you.' Suddenly the words came bursting out, all the things she had wanted to say since she was a child – the questions she longed to ask. 'Tell me the truth. When you look back at the way he treated us all, how could you bear it? How could you put up with a man like that?'

Slowly, Louisa lifted her head and faced her daughter. 'I love him,' she said. 'He's my husband, and I love him. He's your father, and you should love him, too. Every night of my life, I pray you'll come to understand him.'

'I'll never understand him. And I don't understand you, either. Just because he's your husband, that doesn't mean you've got to agree with everything he says and does. How can you love a man with no love in him?'

'I'll always love him – I must. That's what marriage means.' Louisa looked into Ruth's eyes. 'You must know that, for you love your husband, don't you?'

They stared at each other for a long moment; and this time it was Ruth who looked away.

'Not all the time,' she said.

In Liverpool, Leopold Cassidy flicked the ash from his cigar. 'Nice footwork, boy,' he told Connor appraisingly. 'Keep going like this and I tell you, you're going right to the top. You just need one little thing, that's all.'

Connor stepped out of the gymnasium showers, water streaming over his head and shoulders in trickles of silver. 'What's that?' he asked.

'The killer instinct,' said Cassidy, throwing him a towel.

Connor caught it, laughing. 'Maybe I'll surprise you yet,' he said.

'I kid you not.' Cassidy eyed Connor as he rubbed himself dry. 'You've got the physique for it – you've got the skill. What you don't have right now is that little extra something. You gotta be determined to win at all costs, even if it means leaving the other guy in pieces. That's what I'm still waiting to see.'

Connor began to dry his hair. 'Some day, perhaps.'

'Some day ain't enough. I want to see you toughen up right now. I want to see some action tomorrow – I mean *real* action – OK?'

'Sorry, Mr Cassidy, but I won't be here tomorrow.'

The promoter looked at him in silence for a moment, then asked, 'And what the hell is that supposed to mean?'

'I was going to tell you, but I waited till the other fellers weren't around. I'm joining the Army – you have to let me go.'

Cassidy flung his cigar-stub on to the stone floor, grinding it under his heel. 'You can't do this to me! I got a contract.'

'There's another kind of fight going on right now, and I have to get into it. You never know – maybe they'll knock some of that killer instinct into me, by the time I come back!'

'Don't be a damn fool. I've got plans for you . . .' He put his arm round Connor's shoulders, feeling the damp skin and packed muscle tensing under his hand. 'I know you mean well, boy, but I'm not letting you throw away your career. Forget about England – you could have the world at your feet. I'm planning to take you back to the States with me – I've got it all mapped out. Johnson could have one more year on top, maybe

244

two, but after that he'll be finished – and you're the guy who could finish him. I'll put you in a few small contests, inter-state championships, and build you up gradually. By the time you're ready, Johnson will be on the skids. Think of it, son – the next Heavyweight Champion of the World. What d'you say to that?'

Connor moved away, shrugging off Cassidy's hand. This, too, was a fight – and one that he had to win.

'No, thanks,' he said. 'I signed on at the Recruiting Office this morning. They're sending me off to barracks tomorrow, to join the 21st Lancers.'

By the end of August, the Germans had overrun Belgium, and were moving into France. Within a week, the first great battle of the war had begun, at the River Marne. Over a front line extending for two hundred miles, the first trenches were being dug, while French and British troops struggled to hold off the enemy.

'I'm afraid you were wrong,' Ernest told Rosie, as another satisfied customer left the photographic shop. 'It will not be all over by Christmas.'

'What makes you say that?' she asked.

Outside, an Army lorry rattled along the street, packed with young soldiers who cheered and waved, holding up a home-made placard which bore the words *Berlin First Stop!*

'Haven't you heard the latest news?' said Ernest. 'The Marne was a disaster. Now the armies face one another across the Aisne . . . Germany is determined to win at all costs, and France and Great Britain cannot afford to lose.'

'Well, I refuse to take such a gloomy view,' Rosie sighed. 'Anyhow, you've got to admit it's been good for business.'

This was true enough; one unexpected result of the recruiting drive was a sudden rush of work. Ernest was kept busy as young men in ill-fitting uniforms came in to have their photographs taken – souvenirs they could leave behind when they went off to war.

Ernest winced. Rosie's words had touched a raw nerve. 'Do you think that makes me feel any better?' he asked bitterly.

'For heaven's sake, you must stop blaming yourself. It's not your fault the Medical Board turned you down.'

Ernest had been quick to volunteer, but his rejection had been even quicker. The doctor who examined him put a tape-measure round his chest; although Ernest had taken the deepest possible breath, he only measured thirty-three inches, and thirty-four was the statutory minimum. Immediately, he offered to buy a pair of dumb-bells and take exercises to increase his dimensions. The doctor then listened to his chest through a stethoscope and said that he had a congenital weakness of the lungs: he must be rejected for military service.

When the shop door opened again, Rosie said, 'Another customer! I told you, trade's picking up nicely.'

But the newcomer had not come to be photographed. She was a thin, middle-aged lady, carrying a wicker basket – and she looked frightened. From the basket, she took a selection of lace mats, shawls and handkerchiefs, spreading them over the shop counter. She spoke no English, but Ernest knew a little elementary French, and she produced a few words of German.

Completely in the dark, Rosie asked: 'Who is she? What does she want?'

'She is a Belgian refugee from Bruges,' said Ernest. 'She has no money, but she brought over some lace which she made herself and hopes to try and support herself by selling it.'

He explained that he himself had no use for lacework, but suggested she should go to his parents' workshop in Poplar. He wrote down the address for her. As he was doing this, they heard voices shouting out in the street, and through the shop windows they saw a little group of men and women, pointing and cat-calling. The unhappy refugee turned white, and began to speak very rapidly. Ernest told Rosie she was being followed by a crowd who suspected her of being an enemy spy.

'She's afraid they will attack her,' he said. 'Pull down the window-blinds, please, then we can let her out through the alleyway.'

Rosie obeyed, and he took the woman into the back of the shop, opening a door into the alley and telling her which way to go.

'Poor creature,' he said, when he came back. 'She looks half-starved – she must be quite desperate.'

They were startled by a sudden crash of glass. Rosie moved

towards the blinds, but he gripped her arm: 'Careful! They're throwing stones.'

One window had been shattered, and a moment later the other one exploded in a shower of glass.

'But we must fetch a policeman!' gasped Rosie. 'We can't let them get away with that. I'm going to give them a piece of my mind!'

He held on to her firmly. 'You mustn't go out, you might be hurt. They know I have a German name and I suppose they think I am harbouring a spy. Be patient – if we do nothing, they will eventually go away.'

They waited for some time, and it seemed that he was right, for there were no further developments. Cautiously, Ernest lifted the corner of the blind – the street was deserted.

Rosie helped him to sweep up the glass and clear the stock from the window-display; in the studio, Ernest found some plywood screens which he used as ornamental backgrounds, and did his best to board up the broken windows.

'I must stay here tonight,' he said. 'They might come back after dark and try to break in. I shall make up a bed in one of the store-rooms upstairs; you can explain to my parents.'

'All right, I'll tell them – but then I'll bring back some extra blankets and pillows,' Rosie said stoutly. 'I'm not leaving you here on your own this night – God only knows what might happen. They won't try anything if there's two of us here.'

He turned and looked at her, about to protest, but she put her finger on his lips.

'No arguments,' she said. 'I'm staying here tonight, and that's an end to it.'

When she returned at twilight, she brought some food with her and they made themselves a picnic in the studio, sitting on a rustic bench in front of a painted backcloth. Afterwards, they went upstairs, where they made up shakedown beds on the floor, in each of the two store-rooms.

Ernest said, 'Good night,' and shut his door, then he got undressed and slipped between the blankets. He was very tired, but for some reason he could not settle down.

After about twenty minutes, he heard the door open, and the sound of bare feet crossing the floor – then Rosie's voice said softly, 'I can't get to sleep on my own in there. I'm scared of the dark.'

He put out his hand and touched soft, smooth skin, and he realised that she was naked. 'But – are you sure – don't you think—?' he began.

Again, she stopped his mouth, this time with a kiss. After that he said no more, but drew her down beside him.

'I'm staying here tonight,' she repeated in a whisper. 'And that's an end to it.'

It was not the end. It was only the beginning.

On Saturday nights the Watermen was always full of customers, so Patrick and Mary worked together in the saloon, while Sean and Kathie Simes looked after the public.

There was a good crowd of dock-workers in the bar, but there were also a great many men wearing khaki, and Sean grumbled, 'There must be something about the military life that drives a man to drink. We'll be run off our feet at this rate.'

Kathie pouted. 'Why shouldn't Our Brave Boys wet their whistles if they feel like it? It's no more than they deserve. If it was my pub, I'd give 'em drinks on the house – I couldn't refuse them anything.' Then she broke off, saying in a different tone, 'Look who's here!'

Sean followed her gaze, and saw she was staring at a young soldier who had just walked in. He was tall and broad-built, with a kitbag over his shoulder, and the badge of the Lancers on his peaked cap.

'My God!' he exclaimed: 'If it isn't Con!'

Connor swung his bag to the floor. 'I'll not be staying long – just a couple of nights. I've a weekend's leave before they pack me off on a troopship to foreign parts.'

'Isn't that marvellous?' Kathie's face lit up. 'Excuse me for saying so, but I never saw you look so well. That uniform really suits you, doesn't it, Sean?'

'Think so?' Sean was determined not to be impressed. 'What's the meaning of it, eh? I thought you were up in Liverpool, learning to be a prizefighter.'

'Ah, that can wait. I've better things to do just now . . . For a start, you can pull us a pint, for I've a mouth on me like sandpaper. Will you take one with me? And you too, Miss Simes?'

'Don't mind if I do, I'm sure. A sweet sherry, please. What'll your Mum and Dad say, when they see you looking so handsome?'

'Will you stop flattering the man?' Sean protested. 'Can't you see you're embarrassing him?'

'Devil a bit of it.' Connor slapped a ten-shilling note on top of the bar. 'It's the uniform that does the trick. You should try it yourself, my boy, it'd work wonders for you.'

Sean opened his mouth to make a crushing retort, then shut it again. He could not forget the way Kathie's eyes had gleamed at the sight of Connor. Pulling the beer-handle, he said defensively, 'I'd like nothing better myself, only I can't leave Mam and Da with no one to run the pub, now can I?'

'Gammon!' Connor took the foaming tankard from him. 'You could find someone to come and manage this place if you look around. Come on now, take the King's shilling, why don't you? Join the 21st Lancers – I'll put in a good word for you . . . We'll go over to France together, and show the Huns a thing or two! What do you say, Miss Simes? D'you think Sean ought to volunteer?'

'Oh, Sean, I'd be ever so proud of you.' She raised her glass of sherry and her lips parted, moist and quivering. 'Bottoms up!'

Sean felt a thrill of excitement – a sudden urge to escape from the plodding routine of the pub and the daily domestic round at Meadow Lane. He had visions of generous, accommodating women flinging themselves at his feet – French mademoiselles and Belgian beauties, plying him with wine. He never thought of his wife at all.

'Well, why shouldn't I?' he declared, as they clinked glasses. 'Here's to us – the O'Dell boys, off to war! Damn it all to hell – why not?'

·—16—·

'Won't be long now,' said Sean. He swallowed, and ran his finger round the inside of his stiff collar, which seemed to be tighter than usual.

'I'm wishing I hadn't worn my best suit,' he complained. 'Seems a waste of time, dressing up smart to go and join the Army.'

'Not at all,' his mother reproved him. 'You want to look your best; you'll be a credit to us.'

It had all happened so quickly. Sean had gone to the Recruiting Office and put his name down for the 21st Lancers, explaining that he wanted to follow his brother to France. Now, little more than a week later, he was waiting with three or four new recruits on the Underground Railway platform at Whitechapel.

They had to report near Sloane Square, where they would be picked up by an Army lorry which would take them to Tidworth Barracks in Wiltshire. After a few weeks of basic training, Sean would be sent across the Channel, to join Connor on active service.

Ruth and Mary had come to see him off; the other recruits all had wives, sweethearts or parents with them, and they stood about in little groups on the gritty, windswept platform, talking in low voices and looking uncomfortable.

'Anyhow, it won't be for long,' Sean announced breezily. 'Home for Christmas, they say.'

Hardly anyone really believed that now, but people still repeated the phrase, hoping that if they said it often enough it might come true.

'God willing,' said Mary. Then she looked back along the railway lines, hearing the rumble of an approaching train. 'Here it comes now – you haven't lost your ticket?'

'No, Mam.' He showed her the printed travel warrant he

had been given, and picked up his suitcase. 'Well, this is it, then.'

He kissed his mother, then turned to kiss Ruth – a swift, obligatory peck, like a schoolboy saying goodbye before going off to school.

She felt his lips on her cheek, and then the train pulled up, its wheels screaming on the rails, and Sean stepped into the carriage. She raised a hand in a meaningless gesture, wishing him a good journey. Putting on a bright smile, she tried to make herself feel the warmth of love, the sweet sadness of parting – but in truth, she felt nothing at all.

A few hours later, Ruth made her way to Silmour Street. The shop windows had been replaced, but the blinds were down and there were no lights in the upper storey. Hoping that Ernest and Rosie had not gone out for the evening, Ruth rang the bell.

After some time she heard footsteps, and then Rosie's voice said warily: 'Who is it?'

'Me – Ruth. Open the door, will you? It's freezing out here!'

She heard the rattle of a chain, and two bolts were drawn back, top and bottom, then the door opened and Rosie said, 'Sorry to keep you waiting, but we don't take any chances now – and I'm on my own tonight. Come on in.'

They went through the shop and up the stairs. Rosie took Ruth into a room which had originally been used to store photographic equipment, but now did duty as a sitting-room as well. A dim light came through the curtained windows, and Ruth asked, 'Were you sitting in the dark?'

'I generally do, when Ernest's out. If people saw me up here, and realised I was by myself, there's no knowing what they might do. You heard how our windows got smashed?'

'Yes, it must have been awful. How can people be so cruel?'

Rosie lit the gas-lamp, and the friendly glow of light seemed to drive her dark fears away, at least for the moment.

'Let's not think about that,' she said. 'There hasn't been any trouble since then, thank God. How are you? How's Sean?'

Ruth told her that Sean had gone to join the Army, and

Rosie hastened to explain that Ernest too had volunteered, only to be rejected by the Medical Board.

'You'll miss Sean dreadfully, won't you?' she asked.

Ruth said, 'Yes, of course,' and suffered a pang of guilt. She could never admit to anyone – not even to Rosie – that what she really felt was relief.

Changing the subject, she continued, 'Mrs O'Dell came with me to see him off. I told her I was coming here tonight, and she sent her love. She says she wishes you'd come and see her one day. She still misses you, especially now that the boys have gone.'

Rosie's face clouded. 'I know. I miss her, too . . . but it's so difficult. Perhaps one day, but not yet.'

'Soon, then, because she worries about you. When I told her you were living here with Ernest, she was rather shocked! Of course I explained there was nothing like *that* going on. I said Ernest wasn't that sort of man.' Then she stopped short, for Rosie was smiling – a secret smile, filled with quiet joy.

'Ernest's a surprising person,' Rosie said.

Ruth guessed at once. 'You mean it *is* like that? Ernest – and you?'

Rosie began to laugh. Torn between shyness and excitement, she opened her heart to Ruth. 'You won't breathe a word, will you? Oh, it's so wonderful to be able to talk about it. I've had to keep it to myself for weeks.'

'I didn't know you felt like that about each other. You certainly managed to hide it very well.'

'I suppose I knew from the start how he felt about me, when I first went to live in his parents' home. And he's such a lovely man, the more I got to know him, the more I fell in love. Then, the night I moved in here, it just sort of happened . . .' She was blushing now, and she put her hands up to her cheeks and laughed again.

'Are you planning to get married?' Ruth asked kindly.

'Oh, I'd like nothing better. I'd marry him tomorrow if I could, but he hasn't said anything yet. I'm sure we shall – in time.'

'And what do Mr and Mrs Kleiber think about all this?'

'Goodness, they don't know! At least, I expect they probably guess there's something going on, but they pretend there isn't. Well, that's not surprising since they've got enough troubles of their own. I mean, being German, and everything.'

At that moment, in the front parlour of the Kleibers' house, Aaron was saying to his son, 'We are German, and we are Jewish – what else can we expect? Of course the people hate us. We must try to bear it with patience, that is all.'

Ernest ran his hand through his curling black hair. 'How can you resign yourself to it?' he demanded. 'It's criminal, the way these idiots behave. It should not be allowed!'

A few patriotic residents of Poplar, fired with warlike enthusiasm, had painted hideous slogans on the front wall of this house, calling upon the public to boycott the 'Huns and Yids' . . . Since then, orders at the tailoring shop had fallen away almost entirely. Customers were taking their trade elsewhere, for fear of being branded as 'Friends of Germany'.

Every morning when Ruth went to work at the Kleibers, she expected them to send her home, for there was little sewing to be done. Sarah still came in for a few hours every afternoon, while three-month-old Benjamin took his nap and Grand-mama Miriam kept an eye on him, but there was not enough work to keep them both occupied, and Ruth knew that this state of affairs could not continue much longer.

The situation resolved itself unexpectedly.

One evening, when Ruth went in to the Watermen, she found Patrick and his wife engaged in a gloomy discussion.

'Don't I tell you, they're as rare as hens' teeth!' Patrick was saying crossly. 'All the young men are gone off to fight and the ones that are left behind aren't worth tuppence.'

Mary explained to Ruth, 'We're having no luck in finding a manager for the pub. All the able-bodied lads are in the army, and the only ones who offered have been boys not long out of school.'

'Or else they're nearly as old as meself,' Patrick chimed in.

'And what's wrong with that?' Ruth wanted to know.

'If they've reached my age without getting a pub of their own, there must be something wrong with them. When you ask for references, they generally give you a sideways look.

253

They've either been dipping their fingers in the till, or else they've been drinking the profits!'

Kathie Simes, although not directly involved in the conversation, was standing in the doorway, taking in every word. Now she piped up: 'Is it the sort of work a woman could handle, Mr O'Dell?'

Patrick looked doubtful, but Mary answered promptly. 'Certainly it is. There's many a decent widow-woman of our acquaintance who took over licensed premises after their husbands passed on, God rest 'em – and they mostly made a very good job of it, too. Isn't that right, Patrick?'

'True enough,' Patrick admitted. 'You'll be thinking of Dolly Madigan at the Angel, I dare say.'

Kathie Simes didn't wait for him to finish. Preening herself a little and flashing a bright smile, she said, 'How about me having a shot at it, then? I pick things up very quick, though I says it as shouldn't, and I don't believe you've had any fault to find with my work since I've been here?'

Patrick and Mary looked rather taken aback.

'Not faults as such, no,' said Patrick. 'But, well, it maybe calls for someone more *settled* in life, as you might say . . .'

'A married woman, perhaps?' Mary suggested. 'After all, if we trained you to do the job, Kathie, and you were to get wed to some fine upstanding young feller who'd carry you off to another town entirely, we'd be left high and dry, wouldn't we?'

'I've no intention of marrying just yet,' began Kathie.

'But you might do it, all the same,' said Ruth, joining in the discussion for the first time. 'In any case, I don't think we need trouble you with the problem, Kathie – because it strikes me I might take on the duties myself.'

'*You?*' They all stared at her.

'Certainly.' Ruth smiled at the O'Dells. 'If you've no objection?'

Patrick's face cleared, as if the sun had just come out. 'Now isn't that a regular brainwave?' he exclaimed. 'Sure, we can teach you the tricks of the trade, can't we, Mary? And you're the obvious person to step into our boy's shoes – keeping them warm for him till he comes home again, as you might say.'

Mary came over and embraced Ruth. 'I can't think of anyone better.'

Kathie Simes tossed her red curls, saying, 'I should have realised that you'd be wanting to keep it in the family.'

'Won't we just?' Patrick took Ruth's hand, shaking it heartily. 'It beats me why I never thought of it before.'

So it was fixed up, there and then. Next morning, Ruth went to see Mr and Mrs Kleiber, explaining that she would have to give up her job at the workshop at the end of the week. They agreed that this was a very sensible arrangement, and wished her well in her new position.

After that, Ruth began to spend every spare minute at the Watermen with Patrick, learning the mysteries of the licensing laws – of putting in the brewery order, ensuring that the cellar was neither overstocked with beer nor allowed to run dry, how to change over a barrel, the workings of the pumps and filters, the book-keeping and the sales figures and the daily 'float' and the monthly profit-margin – and the thousand and one other pitfalls that could beset a publican.

'Of course, we shall still be here in charge,' Mary assured her. 'And we shall have to remain responsible to the brewery, for the place is still in our name – but there's no denying we're not as young as we used to be, and it will be a great relief to have you here sharing the burden.'

Ruth had not realised quite how heavy that burden was until she took it on. She discovered that a publican's life began early in the morning, and did not finish until very late at night. True, there were those precious hours between the morning and the evening openings, when if she was very lucky she might snatch a brief rest – but as a rule there was all the bookwork waiting to be done, and this was her only chance to catch up with it.

Sometimes she wondered if she should give up the flat at Meadow Lane and move into Sean's room over the pub, which would save her the journey back and forth – but in the end she hung on to her own place, feeling she must retain that much independence at least. She needed to know that she still had a certain amount of private life, however limited, even though this meant travelling back to a cheerless, empty flat every night.

It also meant that she had to fit in her own housework on top

255

of everything else; so on those blessed days when there was no book-keeping to be done, she used to trudge back to Meadow Lane in the afternoon to put in a couple of hours of sweeping and dusting and washing before returning to the pub for her evening duties.

One Friday at the end of November, the journey seemed longer than ever, for it was pouring with rain – a nasty, freezing rain that ran down the back of her neck and seeped through her clothes. By the time she reached the flat, she was feeling very sorry for herself, and when she climbed wearily up the stairs and saw a shadowy figure perched on the top step, she burst out angrily, 'What do you want? If you're selling something, you're wasting your time. Go away and stop bothering me!'

'Please, Auntie Ruth, I don't want nothing,' said a croaky voice.

She rubbed the raindrops from her eyes and saw that the uninvited visitor was her nephew Thomas, Ebenezer's twelve-year-old son.

'Tommy! I'm sorry, I didn't recognise you. Come in, and I'll light the lamp.' The little flat was not very welcoming, but she had laid the fire in the grate at breakfast-time, and now she put a match to it. 'It'll soon burn up. Take off that coat, you look wet through,' she said.

The boy's hair was plastered to his head. She found a clean towel and he dried his face and hands, shivering, while they waited for the little kitchen-range to give out some warmth.

'Had you been waiting long?' she asked. 'What's the matter? Is there some trouble at home?'

'Oh, no. Anyhow, we don't live at home now,' said the boy. 'We're staying with Aunt Emily.'

He explained that after his father had gone into the Army, his mother decided she couldn't face living alone and so had moved in with Aunt Emily and young Maudie, taking Thomas with her.

Ruth opened the kitchen cupboard and found a slab of cake. Slicing it up, she offered it to her nephew, saying, 'Could you help me finish this? It'll only get stale and be wasted otherwise.'

'Ooh, thanks!' He took a piece, and munched hungrily.

'But you still haven't told me what you came for,' she reminded him.

'Aunt Emily sent me,' he said, through a mouthful of cake. 'She'll be pleased if you can come round to tea and see us. She says how about next Sunday afternoon?'

Sunday afternoon was a convenient time for Ruth to go visiting, since the pub didn't re-open until seven in the evening. When she arrived at the little corner-shop, she felt a genuine glow of pleasure. It was kind of Aunt Emily to think of her, and offer such a friendly invitation.

In the parlour at the back of the shop, Aunt Emily welcomed her with a quick, uncertain kiss. Florrie followed her example, looking even more nervous, and apologising.

'Oh, dear, I meant to have the table laid all ready for you – but Emily and me got talking and the time just flew by, didn't it, dear?'

Arnold's wife sat on the floor with Tommy, a draughtboard spread out between them. She looked up under her long lashes, saying, 'How do you do? We can't stop now – we're nearly at the end of our game, aren't we, Tommy?' She looked younger than ever. Sitting on her heels, wearing a pinafore dress and with that childish plait over her shoulder, Maudie didn't appear to be very much older than Tommy.

Aunt Emily set out a plate of bread-and-butter, another of jam tarts, a jar of potted meat and a dish of plum jam, while Florrie filled the teapot and brought it to the table.

'There!' exclaimed Tommy triumphantly, and made a zig-zag move across the board, taking half a dozen of Maudie's pieces in a single sweep. 'I won!'

'You're too quick for me,' Maudie laughed. 'I'm always the loser.'

'Now put your game away, and come and sit down. Tea's all ready,' Aunt Emily told them, as if they were both children. 'Tommy, as you're the only man present, you must say Grace.'

They all bowed their heads, while Tommy rattled through the words as fast as possible. For a while, the ladies exchanged polite conversation. Ruth asked after Ebenezer and Arnold, and Florrie said that Eb wrote to her once a month. A shade smugly, Emily broke in, saying that Arnie was a very good boy.

'He writes once a week regular as clockwork, doesn't he, Maudie?'

'Oh, yes. It's not his fault if the post is held up – sometimes we get two or three letters come all at once.'

Florrie wanted to know if Ruth's husband wrote to her very often, and she heard herself saying without any hesitation, 'Not very often' – which was not exactly a lie. She could not admit that Sean had not, as yet, sent her any letters at all.

Then she noticed Emily and Florrie were exchanging meaning looks. Her aunt smoothed her hair with fluttering fingers, and tentatively, 'While we're on the subject, my dear, I happened to hear from one of our customers in the shop that since your husband's gone away, you've taken his place at the public-house. Is that right?'

'Yes, I have,' said Ruth, wondering where this might be leading.

'I'm sure it's good of you to try and help them while he's in the Army. It must be very difficult, of course, and we don't mean to criticise, but . . .' Emily began fidgeting with her bead necklace. 'But . . . your dear father was saying to me only the other day, it's not the kind of employment we would wish for a member of the family. Selling alcoholic beverages, that is.'

The glow of pleasure Ruth had felt earlier now cooled abruptly. 'Is that why you asked me here today, just to pass on his message?' she asked quietly. 'Well, perhaps you could give my father a message from *me*. Tell him he's got a nerve, passing judgement on me and what I do. Tell him I'm not ashamed of my job – I'm glad to say I work hard, and I earn my own living. Tell him, from me, that I don't make money out of bullying and slave-driving and last of all, tell him that in future I'd be very grateful if he would mind his own damn business!'

Emily gave a little cry, and the thread of her necklace snapped, scattering beads in all directions. Giggling, Maudie and Tommy got down on all fours, scrabbling to pick them up, while the table rocked and the milk-jug overturned.

'Oh, dear,' said Florrie faintly.

·——17——·

'Nice bit of whiting, lady?' The fishmonger raised his straw hat in a mocking salute, but Ruth shook her head.

'No, thanks – not today. I just want something for breakfast tomorrow, and whiting might go off before then in this weather. I'd better have a kipper instead – that'll keep.'

As the old song said, it was very, very warm for May. The month had surprised everyone, masquerading as high summer and coming in with a heatwave. Already, the leaves were green on the trees and tulips and wallflowers brightened the window-boxes outside some of the gaunt, grey houses.

'One kipper or two? Make you a special price for a pair, lady?' the fishmonger suggested.

'Just one, thanks.'

'Don't your old man like kippers?' The man gave Ruth a cheeky wink as he wrapped the fish in a sheet of newspaper. 'He don't know what's good for him – tell him it'll make his hair curl!'

'He likes kippers all right, but I don't think he gets many where he is now, across the Channel.'

At once, the saucy smile was replaced by serious concern. Everyone looked sympathetic and respectful when they heard that her husband was serving in France. Ruth felt ashamed, because she didn't really miss Sean at all – she hardly ever thought of him, these days.

For six months now she had been managing the Watermen, and the job seemed to be working out pretty well. Of course, she couldn't have done it without Patrick and Mary to guide her – but then they couldn't have managed without her, either. They seemed to have aged a good deal, last winter. Ruth knew how much they were missing their two sons – and their daughter. Still, they put on a brave face every night when they welcomed the customers, and they prayed that the war would soon come to an end.

The Official Bulletins referred optimistically to 'successful onslaughts against the enemy' and a 'Big Push' that was always just about to begin – but there were other, unhappier stories in circulation.

Wounded men were invalided home, bringing terrible tales of mismanagement and incompetence at the highest level – and news of a horrifying death-toll. There were no great victories out there. The British and the French were doing their best to keep the Germans at bay, but one side would advance a few hundred yards, at enormous cost to life and limb – and a few days later the tide of war would turn the other way, and the tiny patch of churned-up earth would be recaptured . . . It seemed to be a drawn game, which nobody would ever win.

As Ruth dawdled through the market, such thoughts were driven from her mind, for she saw a familiar face in the crowd – familiar, and much loved.

Mother and daughter met on the pavement, their arms outstretched, and hugged one another in the narrow space between a poulterer's stall and an ironmonger's barrow. And for that brief moment they were alone in the world.

'Fancy meeting you round here!' Ruth exclaimed, burying her face in the familiar scent of soap and fuller's earth, and the sweetness of her mother's softly-wrinkled cheeks. 'Have you got time to drop in for a cup of tea? Ah, come on, say yes. I haven't seen you for ages!'

'No. It's very nice of you, but I'd better not.' The sparkle faded from Louisa's eyes.

'You're thinking of him, aren't you?' said Ruth. 'Father wouldn't like it – right?'

Louisa pursed her lips. 'Let's not get started on *that* again – we don't want another argument, do we?'

'Of course we don't. Well, if you won't come and visit me, I'm going to walk part of the way home with you. I'm not letting you go that easily!' Ruth linked her arm through her mother's. 'I want to hear all your news.'

They strolled along together, into the maze of buildings that skirted Jubilee Wharf. Away from the busy market, the streets were almost deserted and they were able to talk quietly.

260

'I'm glad I ran into you,' Louisa continued. 'To be perfectly frank, I was rather hoping I might find you out shopping. I wanted a word with you, Ruth.'

Ruth sighed. 'If he's sent you with another message to tell me I must give up my job at the pub, you're wasting your breath.'

'It's nothing to do with that. Nobody sent me . . . and it's no concern of mine what job you do. When you moved into that public-house, it was only natural you'd finish up working there – I could see it coming. No, this is about Gloria.'

'Gloria?' Ruth frowned. 'What about her?'

'Did you know she was ill?'

'No, I didn't – how would I know? I haven't seen any of the family for months. What's the matter with her?'

'She's not at all well. It's something internal.' Louisa's face seemed to close down, like a blind being lowered at a window. There were certain things she could not bring herself to discuss, even with her own daughter. 'Women's ailments, you know . . . she nearly died. She had to have an operation, and then they found out it was worse than they thought. They say she's very bad. She's got to be operated on again, seemingly, and they don't know how it will turn out.'

'I'm so sorry.' Ruth did not know what to say. 'Have you been to see her? Where is she?'

'She's at the Infirmary, I believe. I haven't been there myself, none of us have.'

'What? I don't understand.'

Through the railings at the end of the street, the sunlight was blazing on the waters of the dock, and Louisa screwed up her eyes against the dazzle. 'Your father says we mustn't. She's brought shame upon the family by her conduct, you see – going with men, living in sin. She brought her misfortunes on herself, and she's no longer one of us, that's what he says.'

'And you agree with him?' Ruth stared at her mother.

'He's the head of the family. He must decide what's right – what he thinks is right – for all of us.'

'He won't even allow Aunt Emily to visit her own daughter?' Ruth threw back her head, looking up into the infinite blue of a cloudless sky. 'Do you think that's right? Tell me honestly – is that really what you think?'

261

Her eyes still fixed on the shining water, Louisa answered in a low voice, 'I think somebody should go and see her. I thought perhaps you might.'

'Of course I will. I'll go tomorrow afternoon.'

The Infirmary was very old-fashioned; it had not changed much since it was built fifty years earlier. The Women's Medical Ward had a high, raftered ceiling, and long narrow windows down the length of one wall, which let in very little light because they faced an identical wall only a few yards away. The lofty roof gave the ward a solemn, ecclesiastic air; perhaps that was why patients and visitors alike seemed to be overawed, talking only in whispers.

Ruth's attention was caught by a movement under the snow-white counterpane, as Gloria stirred in her bed and woke from her sleep.

'Hello.' She looked up at Ruth without any expression in her face. 'It's you . . .'

'Hello, Glory,' said Ruth. 'I thought I'd come and see how you're getting on.'

'I'm not getting on,' said Gloria flatly. 'I'm getting worse, if you really want to know.' She had lost a lot of weight. There were mauve shadows under her eyes, and hollows beneath her cheekbones. Her hair, once bright blonde and fashionably curled, now straggled across the pillow, lank and lifeless.

'Mum told me you'd had an operation,' Ruth continued. 'You're bound to feel bad for a while, but I'm sure you'll soon be a lot better.'

'Not me.' Gloria shook her head slightly, adding, 'I've got to go down for another operation – the first one didn't do the trick. I don't suppose I'll get through the next one, but I don't really care. Anything's better than lying here like this. Did you say your Mum told me you I was ill? Auntie Lou?'

'Yes, I saw her yesterday. I'd no idea – I'd have come before if I'd known.'

'Thanks. Nobody else has been near me. Not even my own Ma.'

'No, well, they're a funny lot, aren't they?' Ruth tried to

speak lightly. 'They get silly ideas in their heads sometimes.'
She held up a bunch of lilac she had bought at the market. 'I
brought you these – they smell nice, don't they? Shall I see if I
can find a vase to put them in?'

'If you like.' Gloria sniffed the flowers, then turned her head
away. 'Makes a change from the stink of this place, anyhow.'
She frowned as she noticed the sound of a hubbub in the street
outside. 'What's that row going on out there? I can hear a
band . . .'

Ruth began to explain about an anti-German demonstration, and Gloria nodded.

'Oh, yes, I heard about that. The Germans sank one of our
ships the other day, didn't they?'

'I believe so. Not a warship – the *Lusitania*; it was a
passenger-liner, torpedoed by a submarine.'

Gloria sighed. 'We had a clergyman come round this
morning, and a lot of old girls singing hymns. He said we must
pray for the souls of the men and women who'd been drowned
– more than a thousand people, he said, but I didn't bother. I
just wished I'd been on the boat and gone down with them,
then it would all be over by now. No more aches and pains.'

'I'm sorry.' Ruth took her hand. 'You've had a rotten time,
haven't you?'

'Oh, well, I s'pose it was my own fault, really. I let people
take advantage – I should have had more sense. There were
these men – men I trusted – and they let me down. When
things go wrong, they don't want to know you any more. They
all turned against me when I was no good to them . . . just like
my bloody family.'

Suddenly she squeezed Ruth's hand. 'I don't mean you,
Ruthie, you're all right . . . but then you're like me – you went
off on your own, too. We're the odd ones out in the family, eh,
you and me.'

They went on talking quietly for a while, and Gloria seemed
to cheer up a little. Quite soon, her eyelids began to droop and
Ruth saw that the effort of talking had exhausted her. She
stood up to go.

'I'll come and see you again, very soon. I promise.'

'If I'm still here,' said Gloria.

For a moment, Ruth thought she meant that she might be moved to another ward. 'Oh, where are you going?'

Gloria managed a tired smile. 'God knows,' she said. 'And He's not telling. We'll just have to wait and see, won't we?'

The protest march outside had been carefully controlled by the police, and passed off without causing any serious trouble – but that was by no means the end of the matter.

The people of the East End would not leave it at that; anti-German feeling was running high, and their anger flared up in little outbreaks of violence here and there. A pastrycook from Cologne had his shop-windows smashed, and his store of flour scattered from an upper floor. One slogan was chanted endlessly: *'Get the Huns out – Huns out – Huns out . . .'*

Second-generation immigrants, who had been granted British citizenship years ago and in many cases encouraged their sons to join the armed forces and fight the enemy, began to take advertisements in the press, declaring their loyalty to their adopted country – but this made not the slightest difference to the outraged mob. If a man had a German name, he was not to be trusted. Even that lovable and popular dog, the dachshund, was anathema to the patriotic Britisher and had to be sworn at, kicked and driven off the streets.

By the end of the week, these pent-up feelings found expression in an open riot.

Rosie was out delivering some photographs to a customer but she had not been gone long when Ernest heard the side-door open and close.

'Where are you?' Rosie called out.

'I'm just starting work in the dark-room!' he replied.

'Can you leave it, please? This is very urgent!' she said – and he heard a note of panic in her voice.

Quickly, he put his work aside, and opened the door. He saw that she was out of breath. 'What's happened?' he demanded.

'I ran all the way back. We've got to pull down the blinds – they're on the rampage again. Those lunatics are breaking in and looting people's houses, and they're heading this way. Ernest, I'm frightened.'

He thought fast. 'Putting down the blinds isn't going to stop them. I'd better try and board up the windows, and while I'm doing that, you can make a start by carrying all the expensive equipment downstairs. We can lock it up in the cellar.'

Swiftly, they put the plan into action, and half an hour later the job was done. Then Ernest said, 'It still seems quiet enough out there. Who told you about them looting the houses? How did you know they're heading this way?'

'A postman in Millwall warned me. He says they're all over the place. Whitechapel's got the worst of it – Limehouse and Poplar, too. They're bound to make their way down here soon.' She broke off, for he was no longer listening. In three strides he crossed the shop, grabbing his hat and coat from the peg behind the door.

'Where are you going?' she asked.

'Home, of course. Why didn't you tell me before? You never said they were at Poplar. I have to make sure my parents are safe!'

She followed him into the street. 'But what about me? You can't leave me here all by myself!'

'Lock the door after me, and bolt it. Don't let anyone else in till I get back – understand? Stay out of sight, and keep quiet. I'll be as quick as I can.'

He did not make straight for Poplar High Street, but avoided the main roads, using the side streets and weaving to and fro; he kept up a brisk pace, walking at top speed and often breaking into a run. Even so, it took him twenty-five minutes to reach his parents' house – and when he turned the corner into their street, he saw that he was too late.

The roadway outside the house was blocked by a crowd of people, some of them shouting and booing, others laughing and chanting, *'Huns out – out – out. . . !'*

It was worse than he had imagined. The windows on the first floor were wide open, and there were strangers up there, leaning out and yelling to the crowd below, 'Stand back! Mind your heads!'

Somehow the people on the pavement managed to press back, leaving a space – and a few seconds later a mirror in a heavy gilt frame was dropped from an open window, smashing on the paving-stones.

There was a shriek, whether of fear or of triumph, Ernest could not tell. The mob were incapable of rational thought by now. He knew that mirror well: it had been in the family as long as he could remember. Originally from Frankfurt, where it had been given to his parents as a wedding-present, it had travelled with them since them and was always to be found in a place of honour, above the parlour fireplace.

'Seven years' bad luck!' roared a fat joker in the crowd, and several women squealed with laughter.

Ernest felt sick with fear and helplessness. There was nothing he could do, but he knew he must do something – he could not stand by and watch as they wrecked his family home. He began to make his way towards the front door, pushing through the crowd and muttering, 'Excuse me. Let me pass, please. Excuse me . . .'

'Watch out – something else is coming down!' called a girl, pointing up at the windows.

A gasp of amazement arose from the onlookers, for now the men above were lifting a fumed-oak sideboard over the window-sill – a sideboard, Ernest remembered, which contained his mother's best china.

'You stop that!' he shouted at the top of his voice. 'Stop it at once, do you hear?'

Everyone turned and stared at him. Oddly enough, he did not feel afraid – he was too angry for that.

'Who d'you think you are?' asked somebody, and another voice chimed in: 'That's their son. He's another of the dirty Huns . . .'

'Grab 'im – collar 'im – chuck 'im out!'

Furious shouts came from all sides, and a dozen hands clutched him. Ernest was no fighter, but he would not go under without putting up a struggle. Blindly, he lashed out with both fists, and had the satisfaction of hitting one man in the eye, and giving another a backhand swipe across the jaw that rattled his teeth. With a howl of fury, the crowd fell upon him and he thought he would be torn to pieces but at that moment, through the din, he heard a whistle blowing – then another, as if in reply – and a voice yelled: 'Look out – it's the bleedin' rozzers!'

266

A dozen police constables broke through, their batons raised, and though the crowd put up a token resistance, the outcome was never in any doubt. The law-abiding citizens of Poplar fell back, abashed, as the police moved in and surrounded Ernest.

Trying to speak clearly and calmly, he explained that his parents were inside the house which had been besieged and entered by the wreckers. He led the way in through the open front door, and found that the invaders had already slipped out by the back yard.

His mother and father had taken refuge at the top of the house, and were sitting huddled together on their bed, their arms around one another.

The Sergeant spoke quietly to Ernest. 'Tell them to get their coats on, and pack a bag for them. We're going to take them back to the station with us – they can spend the night there.'

'You can't arrest them – they have done nothing wrong!' began Ernest. 'They are innocent people!'

'Never mind that, we're taking them into custody for their own protection,' said the Sergeant. 'Explain that to them, will you?'

Ernest went over to his parents. They looked up at him with huge, frightened eyes, and seemed to be numb with shock. He tried to tell them what was happening, but did not know what to say. In the end, he heard himself stammering, 'It's going to be all right, Papa. Everything will be all right. They didn't get the sideboard – there's nothing to worry about, Mama. They haven't broken your good china . . .'

Less than a mile away, Ruth left Meadow Lane to walk to the pub, ready for opening-time. She had been scrubbing her kitchen floor during the afternoon, and after that she had snatched forty winks in the armchair, so she had no idea what had been going on.

On her way out of the Lane, she heard a harsh voice raised in a melancholy dirge:

Only a Jew – but the insults I remember . . .
Only a Jew – but why not a Christian too?
There's the same sun shining o'er us,

267

And the same world lies before us—
So why should they insult a man who's
Only a Jew. . . ?

When she walked out under the brick archway she saw him there, the blind beggar, tapping with his stick and holding out a tin cup, the black glasses shielding his eyes.

She paused, about to look in her purse for some small change, and then another voice broke in: 'I bin looking for you.'

Ruth whirled round, and saw her cousin Saul standing close beside her, at the pavement's edge.

'You startled me,' she gasped, and suddenly felt dizzy, as if she were in a dream. For time had rolled back: she seemed to be outside the grocery shop once more, on a misty November morning, eighteen months earlier . . . She remembered the street-singer passing by that day, just before her meeting with Saul, when he invited her to live at Cyclops Wharf.

'I didn't have no proper address for you,' Saul mumbled. 'Aunt Emily told me you lived round here somewhere – that's why I come looking. And here you are.'

'Yes. Just a minute, I must give that man something,' began Ruth, opening her purse, but when she turned and looked back, the blind beggar had disappeared and the street was empty.

'Save your money, he don't deserve it anyhow,' Saul remarked sourly. 'Listen, I want to ask you – is it right Gloria's been took ill? That's what I heard, but Aunt Emily wouldn't say no more about it. All she wants to talk about is that other girl – what's her name? Arnold's missus, skinny little thing she used to be.'

'Her name's Maudie. What do you mean, "she used to be"?'

He grinned. 'She ain't skinny no more. In the family way, she is. The baby's due next month and Aunt Emily can't talk about nothing else. I only wanted to ask her about Gloria. Can you tell me where she is?'

Ruth smiled. 'I can do better than that. I'm going to see her tomorrow – why don't you come with me? She doesn't get many visitors.'

*

When Ernest returned home some hours later, Rosie came to unlock the door and let him in. Although she was relieved to see him, by now she did not know whether she loved or hated him.

'I've been worried sick!' she burst out. 'You said you'd be back as quick as you could – do you know what time it is? You don't care a damn about me, do you? Just so long as your mother and father are all right, that's all that matters to you!'

He put his arms round her, and kissed her, but said nothing. Then he moved away, taking care to lock the side-door, and walked slowly up the stairs. Rosie followed him, mystified by his silence, and the strange, set look on his face.

'They *are* all right – aren't they?' she asked.

He dropped into a chair, completely worn out. 'They're alive, if that's what you mean,' he said at last. 'They're being held at the police station overnight – to protect them, the Sergeant said.'

He told her the story as best he could, in disconnected fragments. He was so exhausted, he sometimes forgot where he was and reverted to his native tongue, using German and English phrases jumbled together, so that Rosie found it hard to follow him.

'But at least they're safe, aren't they?' she persisted. 'That's the main thing.'

'Safe?' he repeated. 'You call it safe – *im gefangnis wohnen?*'

'I don't understand.'

'I'm sorry, I cannot think clearly.' He tried again. 'You call it safe, to live in prison?'

'I thought they were just staying at the police station for tonight? They'll let them go home tomorrow, surely?'

Ernest shook his head. 'I don't think so,' he said. 'Tomorrow I have to pack up all their possessions and put everything into store. The British Government have decided that it is not in the national interest that men and women of German origin should be permitted to live here in freedom. All enemy aliens are to be interned for the duration of the war.'

'Interned – what's that?'

269

'Sent into a prison camp. For my parents, it will be like living in the ghetto once more, only much, much worse. They do not know this yet. I have to break the news to them tomorrow.'

'You mean they're being sent to jail? That can't be right! They're not criminals.'

'They are the enemy of Britain – and so am I. That is the one crumb of comfort I can give them. I have to go, too.'

His face was so white, Rosie thought he was going to faint. She gripped his hands, saying fiercely, 'No, Ernest. It's not true – it can't be true!'

Making a great effort, he tried to talk about it calmly and sensibly. 'Perhaps it will not be as bad as it sounds. At least we shall be with our own people. Sarah and her child will be there, too – and Mr Vogel – and many other old friends.'

Clinging to him, Rosie burst into tears, pleading, 'Let me come with you! Where are they taking you?'

'I don't know that. Some of us are being sent to a disused workhouse at Islington, some to a camp in Essex – but there are so many Germans, and so few places. We may have to go far away – there is somewhere in the Midlands, I believe. Of course you will not be allowed to come with me.'

'No! Don't say that,' she begged, with tears streaming down her cheeks.

He patted her hand. 'I was afraid that this might happen – thank God you still have your freedom. We must both be strong and patient, and wait until the war is over. Will you wait for me, my love?'

That night, they lay awake in each other's arms, unable to sleep. Early next morning Ernest made out a long, methodical list of all the things that had to be done. Some of them he could do himself, others he had to ask Rosie to do on his behalf. She was to close the photographic shop and pack up everything, sending it into store along with the Kleibers' furniture.

When the moment of parting came, they said very little. Rosie was not crying now; she had no tears left. She promised she would wait for him until they were together again, however long that might be. Then they kissed for the last time, and Ernest walked away without looking back . . . She did not know if she would ever see him again.

In Poplar, kindly neighbours helped Sarah to pack up. She had the consolation that she would not be among strangers, for the authorities had promised her that she and Benjamin would be sent to the same camp as the Kleiber family. The little boy would have an uncle, a grandmama and a grandpapa to care for him . . . and, of course, a great-grandfather.

For Sarah, that was the most difficult thing of all. Old Mr Vogel accepted the move stoically. He had been shifted from place to place all his life, and was quite used to it – but he was also very puzzled. He knew that there was a war in Europe – that Great Britain and Germany were now enemies – but he could not understand why the authorities should wish to intern foreign immigrants.

'They call this the land of liberty, is that not so?' he kept asking Sarah. 'America has no quarrel with Germany, so why is President Wilson treating us like this?'

Nursing her baby, Sarah bent her head and pretended not to hear. How could she confess to her grandfather that she had been lying to him, all these years?

·—18—·

When Ruth took Saul into the Women's Ward at the Infirmary, he looked very uncomfortable and hung back in the doorway.

'I dare say she won't want to see me,' he said. 'I think I'd best go home. It's you she wants to talk to, not me.'

'Don't be silly. You must say hello to Gloria now you're here,' said Ruth, dragging him after her. 'You've got to give her those chocolates.'

Unhappily, Saul shuffled up the aisle between the beds, keeping his eyes fixed to the floor. A lifelong bachelor, he never felt at ease when surrounded by women.

They found Gloria lying back against a heap of pillows, looking thinner and very weak. Ruth hastened to explain. 'Saul came to see me, because he'd heard you weren't well, so I said he ought to come and visit you. Isn't that right, Saul?'

He nodded dumbly, and sank on to one of the wooden stools beside the bed, crouching down and trying to make himself as small as possible.

'That's nice,' said Gloria faintly. 'Makes a change to see a new face.'

'And he's brought you a little present.' Ruth nudged Saul with her elbow, neglecting to say that she had bullied him into paying for the box of chocolates. 'Go on then – give them to her.'

Without a word, he placed the chocolates on the end of the bed, while Ruth produced a bunch of grapes and some oranges from her shopping-bag.

Gloria seemed pleased. 'Ta – I'll have some later. Could you put them in my cupboard? I daren't reach that far, or I might pull out my stitches.'

'Have you had another operation, then?' asked Ruth.

'Yes. And I'm still here – that was a big surprise to everybody. They say I'm making a good recovery, but I don't

272

know – I still feel bloody awful. The nurses said I was on the operating tables for ages. I shouldn't think I've got any insides left. Still, I suppose it's better out than in, as the saying goes.'

By now, Saul was brick red and wriggling with embarrassment, so Ruth said briskly, 'Well, I'm glad it was a success. Have they said when they're going to let you out?'

'No, they never tell you things like that. Anyhow, I'm in no hurry. I don't suppose Ma's going to welcome me back with open arms after this, is she?'

On the other side of the ward, an elderly woman with one arm in a sling was weeping quietly, and Ruth lowered her voice. 'That poor soul sounds very miserable. What's the matter with her arm?'

'Broke in three places. I don't know much about it, 'cos she can't hardly speak English, on account of she's German . . . Didn't you read about it in the paper? She ran a little tobacconist's shop in Limehouse, and she got knocked down when they broke in. Terrible, really. When she's well enough to go out, she'll be sent to prison. They're all going to be put inside, till the war's over.'

Ruth had heard some talk about the internment law, but she thought it only applied to immigrants who had been stirring up trouble; she had no idea that all Germans were being taken into custody.

'But that means the Kleibers will be interned!' she exclaimed. 'And Sarah, and Ernest. I should have gone to see them this week, but we've been run off our feet at the pub and I haven't had a minute.'

Suddenly she thought of Rosie, and stood up. 'Gloria, I'm ever so sorry but I've got to go. I just remembered – you know Rosie O'Dell, who used to be at the Watermen? I think she may be in serious trouble. I must go and see her. You do understand, don't you? You've got Saul to talk to – I'll come back another day.'

And she set off down the ward, almost at a run. Gloria watched her go, remarking, 'She's in a rush, and no mistake.' Turning her attention to Saul, she enquired, 'Well, and what have you got to say for yourself?'

Saul thought for a long time and cleared his throat, then he

273

opened and shut his mouth a couple of times, and finally mumbled, 'I'm not much of a one for talking.'

'No,' Gloria sighed. 'That's what I thought. Never mind, we'll just have to sit and look at one another, won't we?'

When Ruth arrived at Silmour Street, Rosie let her in, taking her through the empty shop and up to the bedroom, where a suitcase lay open on the bed.

'You don't mind if I carry on doing this?' she asked, and continued to fold her dresses and underclothes, putting them into the case. 'But I'm leaving here very soon – you only just caught me.'

'You weren't going away without telling me?' Ruth protested.

'Everything's happened so fast lately, I didn't have time to go round saying goodbye to people,' said Rosie. 'I suppose you know Ernest's gone? The whole family's been sent away.'

'I didn't know, till someone explained about the new law. I'm ever so sorry – where have they gone? I suppose you're moving, so as to be nearer Ernest?'

Rosie threw her a sidelong glance. 'No, I'm not doing that. I don't even know where he is – he could be miles away by now. Besides, I've no money. I've got to earn my living somehow.'

She spoke rapidly, in a curiously toneless voice, but Ruth could sense the deep unhappiness and confusion raging within her.

'What do you mean?' she asked. 'What are you going to do?'

'I'm going up West. I've always fancied working in one of those big department stores. They have hostels for the staff, so I won't have to worry about finding a place to live.' She rattled off this information like a child repeating the multiplication tables, without any expression at all.

'Oh, you mustn't! You don't know anybody in that part of London,' Ruth protested. 'Stay here on the Island, where your friends are. Why don't you come back to the pub?'

Rosie froze for an instant, her hands arrested in mid-air. 'No, I'll not do that.' She went on folding and packing her clothes. 'I'll never go back there.'

'Why not? Your mother misses you terribly – she'd love to have you at home again.'

274

Rosie lifted her chin, and her eyes glittered. 'If you mean Mary O'Dell, you're making a mistake. My mother is Mary O'Dell's sister . . . My mother is the woman who never wanted a daughter – she gave me away as soon as I was born – and my father is the man who helped her do it. I shall never forgive them for that.'

Ruth tried to argue with her. 'We all miss you, we all want you to come home, and I'd be very glad of your help in the pub, so you'd still be earning your own living.'

'You're wasting your breath,' Rosie broke in sharply, 'because I've got fixed up already. I'm moving into the hostel tonight, just behind High Holborn. I start work in the Fashion Department tomorrow morning.'

'But what about Ernest? How will he feel, when he hears that you—'

Rosie slammed down the lid of the suitcase, and turned on her furiously. 'Don't talk to me about Ernest! They've taken him away from me – I don't even know where he is. I don't know how long this hellish war is going on and I don't know if I'll ever see him again! And don't look so reproachful – it's all right for you, you've got a husband. It's different for me, I'm on my own now – I've got to make a new life for myself . . . If you want to give me a hand to carry my luggage to the bus, I'll be much obliged. If not, you can go back to the pub – you can go to hell for all I care! I don't need you, Ruth O'Dell. I don't need anyone, do you understand that?'

Ruth realised that Rosie was on the edge of a total breakdown – emotional, physical and mental – and she could do nothing to help her. Nothing, except to offer her love and sympathy.

'I'm sorry,' she said again, and took Rosie in her arms. 'Of course I understand. And of course I'll help you with the luggage.'

Sunday afternoons were Ruth's only spare time nowadays. She felt badly about not visiting Gloria, but oddly enough, Saul seemed quite happy to go by himself.

This Sunday, Ruth had to go to Greenwich. When she

pulled the bell at the tall, elegant house, a maid in a black dress and white apron opened the door.

'Good afternoon,' said Ruth. 'Is Mrs Marriner at home?'

'What name shall I say?' asked the girl.

'Tell her Mrs Ruth O'Dell would like to see her.'

But before she had finished speaking, Moira appeared, looking astonished and calling over her shoulder, 'Henry! It's Ruth. Come in, my dear, what a nice surprise.'

She led Ruth into the sitting-room, where Henry Marriner reclined upon a chaise-longue with his feet up, studying a racing paper. Hastily, he scrambled to his feet and tucked the newspaper behind a cushion, aware that it was hardly suitable reading-matter for the Sabbath, then advanced with out-stretched hand.

'Mrs O'Dell – charming, charming. I was only saying to Moira the other day, why do we never see anything of your family now?'

'We're always so busy at the Watermen, we hardly ever get out,' Ruth apologised.

'Didn't I tell you, Henry?' Moira chimed in quickly. 'As long as this dreadful war drags on, no one has time to be sociable any more.'

'But you're all well, I hope?' Mr Marriner pursued. 'Mary and Patrick and the three children?'

'As far as I know they're all well,' Ruth answered, 'but I don't have any recent news of the boys – they're both serving in France.'

'Ah, yes, good lads. And the girl – Rosie, isn't it? You haven't brought her with you?'

'No, I came by myself,' said Ruth, refusing to be drawn into this particular topic. 'It's such a lovely afternoon, I thought I must get some fresh air and walk on the grass and look at the trees. So I came to visit Greenwich Park, and as I was passing the end of your road, I felt it would be rude of me not to call in and enquire after you both. In fact, I wonder if you might care to join me on my walk, Mrs Marriner?'

'What a good idea,' said Moira. 'Henry, we won't interrupt your peaceful Sunday. I'll bring Ruth back for tea at four o'clock.'

'Good heavens, I can't let two lovely ladies wander about in the Park without an escort,' said Henry gallantly. 'I'll come with you, the exercise will do me good.'

So they all set out together, and strolled up the long grassy sweep of Greenwich Hill towards the Observatory. At first they exchanged polite conversation, but as the hill grew steeper, they became a little breathless.

'Oh, dear – it's almost too warm to be comfortable,' said Moira. 'I do wish I'd brought my parasol. Henry, would you be a dear and fetch it for me?'

'What?' He mopped his glistening brow. 'You mean, go all the way home and back again?'

'Yes, dear. You'll find it in the umbrella-stand in the hall. It won't take you more than ten or fifteen minutes. Ruth and I will wait here for you, won't we, Ruth?'

Henry Marriner set off unwillingly. His wife watched him go, and as soon as he was out of earshot she turned back to Ruth. 'Now then,' she said. 'You wanted to talk to me on our own – I could see that, right away. It's Rosie, isn't it? What's happened to her?'

They sat down on a park bench, and Ruth told her the whole story of Rosie and Ernest – their efforts to set up the photographic shop, and Rosie's sudden departure after the shock of the Kleibers' internment.

'Where do you say she's gone? Which department store is it?'

'She didn't say.'

'You should have asked!' said Moira sharply, then apologised. 'I'm sorry, I didn't mean that. I'm very grateful to you for coming to see me. I've heard nothing from the family, since – well, you know about that, but she shouldn't be on her own in London. I must try to find her.'

'I don't think you should. It would be difficult to trace her, and even if you did she wouldn't thank you for it.'

Moira averted her face, as if warding off a blow. 'She still hates me – so much?'

'She's in a very sensitive frame of mind. She's put up barriers – against Ernest – against the O'Dells, who are very

277

worried about her – and against you. She won't let herself be hurt any more.'

They sat in silence for some time. Above them, the birds were singing among the leaves and on the green slope, children ran and shouted and laughed, watched by fond parents.

'So there's nothing I can do,' said Moira at last.

'Not now. Perhaps, in time. But not now.'

'I see.' Moira looked down the path and waved. At the foot of the hill, Mr Marriner was beginning the long ascent, carrying a bright pink parasol. 'Here comes Henry. Thank you for telling me all this. Can I ask you to do me another favour?'

'What is it?'

'I'm sure Rosie will get in touch with you again one of these days. When she does – if there's ever anything she needs, anything I can do to help her, will you please let me know? You mustn't tell her, of course. It will be a secret between us . . . Will you promise me that?'

'I promise,' said Ruth.

Then they stood up, wearing polite, social smiles, and walked down the path to meet Mr Marriner.

A fortnight later, Ruth had to carry out another errand.

She was going to buy some pickles and made a special detour across the Island, to call at the shop in Millwall Road. Before she went in, she glanced at the cramped window-display. It had not changed much since she used to work there, and she could have sworn those were the same tins of fancy biscuits, gathering dust, but then something new caught her eye. It was a hand-lettered notice, stuck in the middle of the window, saying simply: *It's a Boy!*

She hurried inside, and found Aunt Emily behind the counter. Wreathed in smiles, her aunt kissed her on the cheek and said, 'Ruth, dear! How good of you to come. You've heard our glad tidings?'

'I hadn't heard anything, but I've just seen the notice. It's true, then? Maudie's had her baby?'

'Yes, last week, such a sweet little boy – six pounds, two

ounces. He's to be christened Trevor Luke Judge – Luke after my dear husband. Isn't that nice?'

'I'm so happy for you. Does Arnold know yet?'

'Oh, my dear – that's the best part of all! Poor Maudie hadn't been at all well – in fact, the doctor was quite worried. She's never been robust, you know, and he said she was anaemic. That's why we had to send a telegram to Arnie, and his Colonel gave him compassionate leave, to come home and see Maudie – wasn't that kind of him? It was touch and go for a few days, but in the end she was blessed with such a bonny baby and Arnie was here, all the time. It was like a miracle!'

Half-laughing, half-tearful, Emily dabbed her eyes with a lace handkerchief, gasping, 'You must come in and see them all, they'll be so pleased. I'll just put the *Closed* sign on the door for a few minutes.'

'Well, thank you, but before we do that,' Ruth took Emily's arm, 'there's something I want to tell you . . . about Gloria.'

The smile on Emily's face vanished as if a light had gone out. 'Gloria! What about her? It's not bad news?'

'Not at all. I've been to see her several times at the Infirmary. You know she had to have a second operation?'

Emily shrank away, unable to meet Ruth's eye, whispering, 'I don't know anything about it. I don't want to know.'

'Please listen. I promise it's good news. The second operation was successful, and she's getting a little stronger every day. Very soon now, they'll be discharging her but she has nowhere to go. That's why I came to ask you – could she come back here?'

Emily ran her fingertips over her face, touching her cheeks, her eyelids, her quivering lips . . . 'Oh, no, I don't think so. No, it's impossible. You mustn't ask me that.'

'But why not? She's going to need plenty of rest when she comes out. You could look after her.'

'No, I really couldn't – your father wouldn't like it.'

Anger flared up in Ruth. 'My father has nothing to do with it! Gloria is your daughter – this is her home!'

'Marcus would be so angry. He's very cross with me already, because I've let the accounts get into such a muddle. No, I'm sorry – please don't say any more about it. You must come and see my dear little grandson.'

'Yes, but just let me explain!'

'No!' Emily turned her back, leading the way to the kitchen. 'I won't hear another word. I only want to think about happy things. Please don't mention Gloria again – we never talk about her now.'

Ruth had to follow her, furious and frustrated – there was nothing else she could do.

Though the sight of the happy family was welcoming and cheerful, it underlined the fact that Gloria was now an outcast, and Ruth had to force herself to smile. 'Hello, Maudie, Arnold – congratulations!' she said.

Aunt Florrie fussed in the background, warming a saucepan of milk for the baby's bottle, while Maudie herself, more wide-eyed than ever, sat on an armchair with her feet up on a low stool, looking as if she could not quite believe what had happened to her.

In a Moses-basket on the table, the tiny baby clucked and cooed, while the proud father, in his uniform, stood polishing his spectacles. Young Tommy hung over the crib, fascinated by the youngest member of the family. When it held out a groping, starfish hand, Tommy offered his finger, and the little fist closed around it.

'I hope your hands are clean.' Arnold frowned slightly. 'Germs, you know.'

'It's all right, Uncle Arn,' said Tommy. 'I just had a wash, didn't I Mum?'

Florine took the baby's bottle to Maudie, asking, 'Would you like to give it to him, dear?'

'I don't mind,' began Maudie, but Tommy jumped in quickly, 'Can I do it, please?'

'If you want to,' Maudie told him, and Florrie smiled. 'Tommy's so good with his little cousin – isn't that nice?'

Emily murmured in Ruth's ear, 'Such a pity Maudie can't manage to nurse Baby herself, but well, she hasn't really got the proper *development* . . .'

Arnold came up to talk to Ruth, and enquired how she was getting on at the public-house.

'We're doing quite well, thanks,' she replied. 'You must drop in and see us one of these days.'

280

'I don't think so.' Arnold breathed on his glasses, and gave them a final polish. 'As you know, I do not indulge in alcohol. If I ever had any doubts on that score, I've seen enough cases of drunkenness in France to convince me. Besides, I shan't be here much longer. I have to report back to my Unit the day after tomorrow.'

Emily sighed. 'Oh dear, I can't bear to think of you going away again. I shall miss you dreadfully, Arnie . . . and so will Maudie, won't you, dear?'

'Yes, ever so,' said Maudie, but she only had eyes for the baby in Tommy's arms. 'Let me have him when he's finished his bottle, Tommy. I'd like to hold him.'

'Oh, Arnie, I meant to ask,' Emily recalled. 'Before you go away, I wonder if you could take a look at my account-book? Marcus went through it the other day, and he got so impatient with me because I couldn't see where I'd gone wrong. Perhaps you could explain it to me?'

'Certainly, Mother.' Arnold replaced the spectacles on his nose. Even in khaki, he still looked more like a clerk than a fighting man. 'No time like the present – I'll go through the accounts right away.'

Ruth looked round the contented family group – and thought of Gloria.

When she got back to the Watermen, a surprise awaited her.

As soon as she opened the side door, Mary O'Dell hurried to meet her, saying under her breath, 'Ruth, dear – such news! He asked me not to tell you, for he says he wants to see your face when you walk in, but I was afraid it might be too much of a shock for you, seeing him there like that . . .'

'Him?' Ruth saw that her mother-in-law was radiant with happiness. 'You don't mean—?'

Then she heard a familiar shout of laughter from the back room, and Mary nodded joyfully. 'Yes, it's Sean. But you mustn't worry – he says it's nothing serious.'

Ruth did not wait to hear any more. She rushed into the kitchen and found her husband there: he was sitting in the best chair, red-faced and grinning from ear to ear . . . and both his hands were swathed in bandages.

'Ruth, my darling girl, come and give us a big kiss!' he exclaimed. 'Only don't touch my hands, because they're still as sore as hell.'

She stared at him, hardly able to believe her eyes. 'What's happened to you?' she asked.

'Shrapnel wounds. Nothing serious, don't worry. They promise me the scars will soon heal up.'

He held out his arms as she walked towards him, then pulled her to him in a bear-like hug, holding her between his forearms. She put her mouth to his, and he kissed her – a long, moist kiss – and she tasted the beer in his mouth.

'Now I know I'm home again,' he said with satisfaction, when he let her go.

'Tell me about it,' she said, looking at the fearsome bandages.

'There's not a lot to tell. A shell exploded just a few yards from our trench. I was just pulling myself up to look out over the parapet when it went off – I had my hands above the edge, d'you see? It's God's mercy it was no worse. Another second, and the shrapnel would have caught me full in the face. And it was a blessing I copped it on both hands, as well. If I'd only injured the one, they'd have sent me to base-hospital for a day or two, then put me on light duties and posted me back into the front line. But seeing I'm helpless as a baby with both hands out of action, they decided it was a "Blighty one", and packed me off home on sick-leave till the wounds heal up. Aren't I the lucky feller?' He put up his face to kiss her again, nuzzling her ear.

The O'Dells stood looking on, delighted at their son's return and thankful his injuries were no worse. Then Mary tugged at her husband's arm, saying, 'Come along with you, Patrick. You and I are going to be very busy this evening working in the bar, so we can give Ruth a night off.'

'So we will, but there's no hurry,' Patrick objected. 'It's not opening-time yet – we can stay a while longer, and have a good old crack.'

Mary threw up her hands. 'Was there ever such a thick

lummox of a man? Don't you see they want to be alone? Have a bit of tact, do!'

Chuckling, Patrick allowed himself to be led away, leaving the young couple together. Sean smiled at Ruth.

'That's good of them. They say they'll manage without you tonight, so we can have some time together. God, it's been so long!'

She felt a sudden surge of affection for him. This was the Sean she remembered – the laughing, carefree man who had swept her off her feet. The man she had loved . . .

'Much too long,' she agreed, looking into his soft blue eyes.

'You're the best wife in the whole wide world,' he murmured fondly, 'and I don't deserve you, that's a fact. I know I haven't always treated you too well in the past, but—'

She stopped his mouth with another kiss, and whispered, 'Never mind the past, that's over and done with. You're here now – that's what matters.'

'No, hear me out.' For a moment, his face was serious. 'I want to tell you I'm sorry. I was an eejut, fooling around with other women when I had you, my darling, but things will be different from now on, you'll see. We can begin all over again. We'll make a fresh start.'

'Of course we shall. A fresh start.'

Having got his speech off his chest, Sean's mood changed again, and he added with a grin, 'Now then, d'you mind passing me the glass of beer that's on the table? If you hold it steady, I can take it between my fists – and I bet you I won't spill a drop.'

They made a game of it. She handed him the half-empty glass and he gripped it clumsily, but managed to lift it to his lips, draining it in one long gulp. Laughing, he pulled her on to his knee, and they made their plans for the evening.

'Mam's going to give us a bite of supper. Afterwards, I said I'd stay in the bar for an hour or so, to meet all me old mates – all our regulars. But why don't you slip away home and make yourself ready for bed?' He winked at her. 'I thought we should have an early night . . . Oh, I almost forgot – I've a little present for you. If you put your hand in my coat pocket, you'll find a package there but be careful, for it's breakable.'

The package contained a large bottle of French perfume. She took out the stopper and sniffed it – the heavy scent of jasmine overwhelmed her.

'Mmm, it's gorgeous,' she enthused. 'It must have cost you a fortune!'

'Not at all, I picked it up for next to nothing. By the time I come home, I'll expect to find you lying in bed waiting for me, smelling like a flower-garden. My very own flower-garden.'

After supper, Ruth went home. She took out her best nightdress, put clean sheets on the bed and washed herself all over, standing in the tin bath in front of the kitchen sink. Afterwards, she dabbed perfume on her wrists and behind her ears then, shivering a little at her own daring, put some between her breasts and on the inside of her thighs.

She put on her nightdress and spent a long time brushing her hair, letting it fall loosely over her shoulders, the way Sean liked it. When it was soft and shining, she climbed into bed and lay there, waiting for him . . .

She must have dozed off, for when she woke the bedroom was in darkness, and she heard the slam of the front door and the clatter of boots on the linoleum. Sean flung open the bedroom door, and announced, 'I'm back! Sorry I'm a bit late –the fellers were so pleased to see me they all had to buy me a drink. And they laughed themselves to pieces, watching me try and lift the beer-mug without spilling any! They offered to help me, and took it in turns to pour it down my gullet. I dare say you can smell it on my shirt – they wasted a lot of good beer . . .'

He lurched over and sat heavily on the bed. The springs groaned beneath him, as he explained, 'You'll have to undress me, my darling. I can't manage it for myself.'

Ruth unfastened his buttons, pulling off his jacket and then his shirt. She unbuckled his belt and removed his boots, then pulled off his trousers, while he rolled around on the bed, enjoying this enforced intimacy. When she had stripped off his underclothes and his socks, he lay there naked, unable to stop laughing.

'You're a good girl, so you are,' he gasped, between fits of giggles. 'You're very good to a poor helpless feller . . . but

284

you're going to find I'm not so damn helpless as you think!'
Suddenly, he rolled on top of her.

As he could not use his hands, he did not even try to caress
her; there were no embraces, no kisses, no loving endear-
ments. Now he was aroused, he wanted immediate satisfaction.

She did her best to gratify him. She remembered his
promises – 'Things will be different from now on, we'll make a
fresh start' – but all she could think of was their honeymoon
night, when he had taken possession of her, crudely and
selfishly. It was less painful this time, but it was still an act of
violence, not of love.

As soon as he was satisfied, he pulled away from her and
turned over. He belched, sighed contentedly and within minutes
was snoring. Ruth lay awake for a long while, thinking about the
'fresh start'. It had been no different at all; it would never be any
different. The smell of stale beer, mingled with the overpowering
scent of jasmine, made her feel sick. Silently, she began to cry and
fell asleep at last, with the tears still wet upon her cheeks.

The following evening, Arnold Judge went to call upon his
uncle at the Rope Walk.

'Come in, Arnold,' said Louisa. 'It's very good of you to
come and see us. Marcus, we have a visitor! Arnold's here.'

Marcus Judge, sitting at the kitchen table, looked up at his
nephew under bushy eyebrows.

'You're welcome,' he said. 'I was about to read a short
passage from the scriptures. Will you sit with us and listen to
the word of God?'

'I'm afraid I can't do that,' said Arnold stiffly.

Marcus' eyes narrowed. 'And why is that?' he asked.

'I can't stay long. I have to leave early in the morning, and I
mustn't be late. I wouldn't have called in like this tonight,
but—'

'We're very glad you did. Do sit down for a minute,' urged
Louisa. 'Can I get you a cup of tea? A slice of cake?'

'Nothing, thank you. As I was saying, I wouldn't have come
but felt it was my duty to do so. A very painful duty.'

'I don't understand you,' began Marcus then stopped, as Arnold produced a book with a red cover from inside his coat. 'What is that?'

'I'd have thought you might recognise it – you've seen it often enough. It's the accounts from my mother's shop.' Something in his tone made Louisa look more closely at him. Arnold's face was pale but determined as he sat down facing his uncle. 'I think you should put away the Bible,' he added. 'We've got business matters to discuss.'

Marcus rose to his feet. 'How dare you give me orders? If you are insolent, I will not listen to you!'

'I'm not insolent – I'm only concerned with the truth.' As he turned the pages of the book, Arnold's knuckles were white. 'And you *will* listen to me.'

'Arnold, whatever's the matter?' Louisa tried to put a stop to this ugly scene. She had no idea what her nephew was talking about, but she knew that he was threatening her husband – and that was unthinkable.

'I'm sorry, Aunt Lou.' Arnold would not look at her. 'I wish I could have spared you this, but you have to know. Your sister has suffered a grave injustice, and she must be protected.'

Breathing hard, Marcus sank back into his chair. 'I believe you are suffering some kind of brainstorm, and you don't know what you are saying. That is why I have not turned you out of my house already but I must warn you, if you continue these wild accusations . . .'

'What accusations? What is it all about?' Louisa looked from one man to the other. 'Has something happened to Emily?'

'She's been tricked out of her money – out of everything she ever had,' said Arnold, still looking steadily at his uncle. 'She asked me to go through the accounts because she couldn't understand what was wrong. When I looked at the books, I understood very well. You took advantage of my mother's ignorance of business – you have swindled her.'

'Hold your tongue!' roared Marcus Judge. 'I could have the law on you for slander – wicked falsehoods!'

'The facts are in this book and they speak for themselves.' Marcus tried to snatch it from his hands, but Arnold held it out of reach. 'You have transferred my mother's business into your own name. You have tricked her into signing away everything – the shop, the stock, the goodwill: everything she owned belongs to you now.'

In the silence, the ticking of the clock on the mantelpiece seemed unnaturally loud. Then Louisa asked, in a whisper, 'Marcus – is this true?'

He took time before replying, then smoothed his beard carefully, and said, 'I did not want to trouble you, as I know how concerned you are for your sister, but it was clear from the start that she was incapable of running a business. It lost money steadily, year by year. Over and over again I had to pay in some of my own money, to reduce her debts. I did not lend her money – that would have been foolish, for she had no hope of repaying it. Instead I made a fair and just arrangement. Each time I provided her with additional capital, I took a small share of the business. Gradually, my share became larger – and now the shop belongs to me. It is as simple as that.'

'You never told my mother that was what you were doing!'

'She would not have understood it. I did it out of consideration for her, because of our family connection. You need not worry – I shall not turn her out. She may continue to live there during her lifetime, although I may soon have to look about for someone else to manage the shop. I'm afraid it is quite beyond her now.'

'You had no right to do such a thing!' said Arnold. 'There are laws to protect people like my mother! If she can't understand what you have done, I must act on her behalf. I'm going back to France in the morning, but I shall write to my solicitor, asking him to commence proceedings against you . . . I thought I should give you due notice of that.'

He stood up, slipping the book inside his coat once more. 'I have the facts and figures here in black and white. It will be an open-and-shut case.' As he was leaving the room, he turned to say, 'I'm sorry if I've upset you, Aunt Lou. Don't trouble to come to the door – I can see myself out.'

When he had gone, Louisa asked her husband, 'Could he take you to court for this?'

Marcus shrugged. 'He could try, but a competent lawyer would make mincemeat of him. Once we get Emily into the witness-box, any jury will see she's incapable of managing her own affairs. As I say, I managed the business for her – it was in her own interests. Without me, she would have been bankrupt years ago. I did it for her sake, Louisa, you must see that!'

'Yes, I see.' Louisa went over to him, putting her hand on his shoulder. 'And for my sake you will have to put things right for Emily. We've never had a lawsuit in the family before: you can't let that happen.'

'It won't happen, take my word for it. The boy is young, stupid and headstrong. He'll think better of it when he cools down. I tell you, he will never sue me – it will not happen.'

Then he opened the family Bible, and his voice was like the tolling of a great bell. 'Let us now seek enlightenment, as we hearken unto the word of God.'

As it turned out, Marcus Judge was both right and wrong. He was wrong in one respect, for Arnold had no intention of going back on his decision. At the earliest possible moment, he wrote a long letter to his solicitor, sending him a parcel that contained the account-book as evidence.

But Marcus was right – unexpectedly right – when he said that Arnold would never sue.

When the telegram arrived a month later, Emily Judge opened it with trembling fingers: the sight of the envelope made her heart beat faster. Slowly, she unfolded the message, and read: *WAR OFFICE, LONDON: Deeply regret to inform you that Pte A. Judge, Essex Regt., was killed in action: Friday, August 13th, 1915 . . . No further details.*

It was a very bad time for the Judge family and a cruel blow for the young widow, who had not spent more than a dozen days and nights with her husband since their wedding. For that reason, perhaps, married life had never seemed entirely real to Maudie, and she recovered from the shock fairly soon.

For Emily Judge, it was far worse. Already distraught after the scandal of Gloria's disgrace and the recent crisis over her own mismanagement of the shop, this new tragedy nearly destroyed her.

Everyone rallied round, and she was especially grateful to have Florrie in the house as a permanent shoulder to cry upon. When she was living under Ebenezer's domination, Florrie had always felt herself to be an abject failure but in her new role as Emily's friend and comforter, she gained a little strength and confidence. When he was not at school, Tommy volunteered to help in the shop, running errands and delivering groceries, and he was still fascinated by baby Trevor, helping Maudie to bath him and change him and take him out for airings in the perambulator.

Ruth, too, came round to the corner-shop whenever she had a spare moment. There was nothing she could say to console Aunt Emily for the loss of her son, but she tried to help in other ways, by serving a customer when there was no one else free to do so, making cups of tea or cutting sandwiches when Emily was too upset or Florrie too disorganised to notice that it was time for a meal, and generally making herself useful.

As the weeks passed, Emily began to recover. She received a message of sympathy from Buckingham Palace, signed on behalf of Their Majesties by their Private Secretary, and this did a great deal to support her through her ordeal. She carried the letter about with her until it became creased and tattered, and then Ruth had the bright idea of getting it framed. From that day, it hung above the counter so that Emily could show it proudly to everyone who came into the shop.

It almost made up to her for the absence of a funeral. That seemed to worry Emily more than anything else. For the first time, there had been a death in the family which could not be honoured in the traditional way. There was no coffin, no ritual laying-out of the body, no wreaths, no horse-drawn carriages draped in purple and black, no slow procession of mourners to the cemetery.

'It's not *right*,' she kept saying unhappily. 'What will people think? It isn't right at all . . .'

Instead, there was a memorial service at the Emmanuel Chapel conducted by the Reverend Mr Evans, in the course of which Marcus Judge delivered a short address, thanking Almighty God for Arnold's brief but glorious life, and extolling his virtues. Arnold Judge would, he reminded the congregation, be a sad loss to the community.

Inevitably, during a time of such grief, the question of Arnold's proposed law-suit was temporarily forgotten, but some weeks later Louisa Judge brought the subject up.

It was a Sunday afternoon. She and Marcus had returned from morning service at the Chapel, where he had read two passages from the Scriptures in splendid and sonorous tones, and they had sat down to their usual Sunday dinner of roast beef and Yorkshire pudding, followed by one of Louisa's best apple pies.

Bowing his head, Marcus thanked the Lord for what they had received and they both said, 'Amen.' Then he stood up, according to his usual custom, to retire to his bedroom for an hour's rest.

'Before you go up,' Louisa began, 'I'd like to talk to you about Emily.'

Marcus looked surprised. 'What about Emily? I thought she seemed a little easier in her mind when we spoke to her this morning after the service. She's beginning to settle down at last, don't you think so?'

'I hope she is, but I wasn't thinking of that.' Louisa hesitated, then started again. 'We must talk about the shop . . . and the law-suit.'

290

'There is nothing to talk about.' Marcus frowned. 'Since Arnold is unhappily no longer with us, the matter is closed.'

'No, it isn't, not quite. On Friday evening while you were out rent-collecting, Emily came round to see me. She'd just had a letter from Arnie's solicitor, and she couldn't understand it. He'd written to ask her if she wanted him to act on her behalf in the law-suit. Of course, it was the first she'd heard about it.'

Slowly, Marcus sat down again. 'What did you tell her?' he asked heavily.

'I said there'd been a difference of opinion between you and Arnold. I told her you both wanted to do what was best for her – and for the shop – and I explained that you'd taken the business out of her hands, to try and make a go of it, and that Arnold hadn't altogether approved.'

Marcus broke in angrily. 'You should have said nothing at all! You should have left me to deal with Emily. It's no concern of yours!'

'Yes, Marcus, I know you like to keep your business matters to yourself – that's what caused all this trouble in the first place, not telling people things . . . Besides, Emily is my sister. When she asked me what it all meant, I had to tell her, didn't I?'

After a moment, Marcus said in a steely voice, 'Very well, so you told her. And what did she have to say about that?'

'She seemed quite relieved at the idea of you taking over the business. Well, she's always been worried about that side of it. She likes serving in the shop, but she's got no head for figures.'

'My point exactly!' Marcus pounced upon this with satisfaction. 'That's why I took charge of the business, and that's why I have to put a manager into the shop.'

'Yes, but that won't really solve the problem, will it?'

He knitted his brows. 'I don't follow you. If Emily is not going to raise any objection, there is no problem.'

'I'm afraid there is. Emily doesn't quite understand, you see. She still thinks of the shop as belonging to her – it would break her heart if you took it away from her now. Don't you think she's suffered enough lately?'

Marcus looked at his wife incredulously. He wasn't accustomed to being spoken to in this way. 'What are you saying?' he demanded.

'Well, you've always told me that whenever we have a problem, we must pray to the Lord for guidance. So this morning, during the service, I asked God to help me . . . and He did.'

'What do you mean?'

'He told me what we ought to do. He said, if Emily isn't capable of running the shop by herself, it's up to us to do it for her. I can go and work there whenever she needs me, and you can do the book-keeping and the ordering and the accounts, that sort of thing. Then we shan't need any strangers coming in and taking it over. Between us, we can keep Emily's shop going.'

'But I—'

'Just a minute, dear, I haven't quite finished,' said Louisa. 'What I'm trying to say is, I'm sure Emily will be very happy about that. She can write to that solicitor and tell him there's no need for any law-suits after all.' Then she gulped, for she was beginning to run out of breath. 'That's what God told me, Marcus.'

After a very long silence, Marcus rose slowly to his feet. 'I see,' he said. 'You'll explain that to your sister, will you? Very well, I shall go up and have my rest now.'

Moving rather more slowly than usual, he went up the stairs. When he had gone, Louisa looked up at the ceiling, and said quietly, 'Thank you, God.'

Then she cleared the table, and started the washing-up.

Soon after this, Ruth was on her way to the Infirmary to see Gloria. Knowing that her cousin was making a good recovery at last, Ruth expected to hear she would be discharged from hospital any day now. The problem of finding accommodation for her was becoming urgent. If the worst came to the worst, she would have to invite her to stay at Meadow Lane – but that was not a satisfactory solution. There was only one bedroom, and one double bed; if Sean were to come home again unexpectedly on a short leave, he would not be pleased to find Gloria installed there.

Turning over the possibilities in her mind, Ruth walked the

length of the ward and stopped at Gloria's bed, then saw with dismay that it was Gloria's bed no longer. An old lady lay there, fast asleep. Ruth looked round, wondering whether Gloria had been moved to another bed, but she was nowhere to be seen. She went quickly to the Ward Sister's office, and enquired after her cousin, only to be told that Miss Judge had been discharged earlier in the week.

'But where did she go?' Ruth wanted to know.

'I couldn't tell you, I'm sure, I wasn't on duty myself at the time.'

'Didn't she leave an address?'

'Not to my knowledge. As I say, I wasn't here so I can't help you.'

'If you could just look up her records?'

'I can't stop now, I'm very busy. If you make an application in writing to the Almoner, I expect you'll be given the details. Excuse me!' And the Sister flounced off, her starched apron crackling with impatience.

Ruth was alarmed. If Gloria had nowhere else to go, she might have sought help from one of those men who had let her down when she was taken ill. By now, anything could have happened to her. As she walked back towards the Island, she happened to see an omnibus going to West Ferry Road. Impulsively, she jumped on. The bus would take her to Cyclops Wharf – she knew Saul had been visiting Gloria regularly, and her cousin might have told him where she planned to go.

As it was a Sunday afternoon, the ship-chandlers was shut. Ruth hammered on the door, hoping that Saul would be in and peered through the dusty windows, but there was no sign of life. The place looked more untidy and neglected than ever. She was about to give up and go home when there were sounds of someone moving about inside, and she called out: 'Saul! It's me, Ruth!'

She heard him stumping down the rickety staircase, then the bolts were drawn and the door creaked open. 'Well? What do you want?' he asked grudgingly.

'I'm sorry to disturb you, but I've just been to the Infirmary and Gloria isn't there any longer. They wouldn't tell me where she's gone – I thought you might know.'

'Course I know . . . she's upstairs.'

'You mean she's staying here?'

'That's right, so you don't have to worry.' He seemed as if he were about to shut the door in Ruth's face, but she stopped him.

'Could I see her?' she asked.

He scowled uncertainly. 'You want to come in?'

'If you wouldn't mind. Just to make sure she's all right.'

'Course she's all right! I'm looking after her, 'cos she didn't have nowhere to go.'

'That's very good of you, but I'd still like to say hello. I won't stay long.'

Reluctantly, he stood aside to let her in. Ruth found herself looking at the spot at the foot of the staircase where she had discovered Uncle Matthew's body after his fall. She shivered as she stepped over it.

'I put her in the old Dad's room. I done it up nice,' Saul explained, as he followed her up the stairs.

Remembering the filthy state it had been in when her uncle was alive, Ruth's heart sank. When she reached the third floor and walked in, however, she was pleasantly surprised. It was very bare, but Saul had done his best to clean it up – a broom and a scrubbing-brush had done wonders. Late afternoon sunlight shone through one window that had not been boarded up, and on the table there was a bunch of michaelmas daisies in a jam jar. Gloria was sitting up in bed, a knitted jacket over her night-dress, smiling at Ruth.

'Fancy seeing you!' she exclaimed. 'Quite a surprise for you too, I dare say?'

'It's good to see you looking so much better,' Ruth told her. 'You've got a spot of colour back in your cheeks.'

'Have I? I started feeling better the minute I got out of that hell-hole . . . I didn't have a notion where I was going, but then Saul said why didn't I come here for a while, so I thought –well, why not?'

'I'm very glad. But you've still got to stay in bed, have you?'

'Not really. I get up in the morning and do the shopping and the cooking and all that – only Saul likes me to take a little rest in the afternoon, to build up my strength.'

'I'm going to take real good care of her,' Saul explained, 'because she ain't got nobody else to do it.'

'It's nice for both of us. Saul's been on his own a long time,' said Gloria. 'We can keep each other company.'

'I'm glad things have worked out so well,' said Ruth.

'Yeah, except Ma would have a pink fit if she knew so I'd be glad if you'd keep it to yourself, eh?'

Ruth was smiling as she walked home. They were such an ill-assorted couple, she wondered how long they would stay together. She could not imagine Gloria being content to live in that ramshackle old house indefinitely, with no one but Saul to talk to. Still, in some odd way they seemed to suit one another, and the most unlikely people sometimes settled down happily enough. Then she thought of Sean, and her smile faded. When they first met and fell in love, they had been blind to the fact that they had so little in common. Now the first attraction had worn off, Ruth saw their marriage with different eyes and asked herself what there was to keep them together.

A week later, she found a possible answer to that question.

Dear Sean, she wrote. *I have some news which I hope will cheer you up. Last month I felt a bit under the weather. I thought I was probably just over-tired, but I went to the doctor anyhow, and he gave me some iron-pills and a bottle of tonic, and I thought no more about it. Since then, I've been as right as rain, but this month the same thing happened – or didn't happen, if you see what I mean – so I had to go to the surgery again, and now the doctor tells me I'm going to have a baby.*

She put down her pen, gazing into space. It seemed all wrong that the night of Sean's homecoming and their loveless union should have resulted in such a miracle, but God moved in a mysterious way. Perhaps the child within her would be a joy to them both, and create a new bond between them. Perhaps, after all, this would be the new beginning that Sean had promised.

Picking up her pen, she resumed: *The doctor says the baby will be due in April. It would be wonderful if you were able to get compassionate leave then, like poor Arnold did – but of course Maudie was not at all well, whereas I am in very good health. Please write and tell me that you are as pleased as I am.*

She went on to give him some other items of family news, mentioning that Gloria was now living at Cyclops Wharf, and she passed on loving messages from his mother and father. Feeling generous, she even added that Kathie Simes sent her good wishes. One thing she could not put into words: she could not express the depth of her happiness. If she were to be absolutely honest, she would have to write, *For the first time in my life, I feel that I shall never be lonely again* . . . But how could she say such a thing to her husband?

At first sight, the landscape appeared to be completely deserted – an endless sea of grey mud, the colour of death. The shell-holes looked like moon-craters: only the splintered remains of a tree-stump and a shattered row of palings, skittled by an explosion, showed that there had ever been any life here.

The distant sound of artillery-fire died away. For a while there was silence, and then – incredibly, in the midst of such desolation – a bird started to sing.

Then a rifle-shot, which might have come from any direction, and a sudden whirr of wings as the bird flew away. Down in a dug-out, a man's voice began to intone lugubriously to the tune of an old hymn:

> *We are but little Tommies meek,*
> *We only earn eight bob a week.*

Other men took up the refrain. Although he was not familiar with the original Church of England hymn, Sean too joined in the sing-song.

> *The more we work, the more we may,*
> *It makes no different to our pay.*

As the last ironic *Amen* died away, another voice broke in. Less than fifty yards away, across the stretch of mud called No-Man's-Land, a German soldier called out, 'Hey! You – Tommies – good song!'

The front-line troops were not supposed to communicate

296

with the enemy, but after long periods of inactivity, any event that broke the monotony was welcome. Sean yelled back, 'Thanks, mate!'

After a moment, the German called again: 'Where you come from, Tommy?'

Cautiously, Sean raised his head, so that his eyes were level with the top of the parapet. 'London!' he replied.

'London very good! Last year I am working in London.' Now Sean could just see the man's head, above a line of sandbags. 'I am waiter, in Soho!'

With great care, Sean pressed a bullet into his rifle, sliding home the bolt. 'You speak good English – tell us some more!' he shouted, lining up the target between the fore-sight and the back-sight.

'In Charlotte Street, I have wife and two children!' called the German, cheerfully.

Sean began to squeeze the trigger, and then – 'Keep your bloody head down, or you'll have a widow and two orphans!' roared another voice, just behind Sean's head.

Sean jumped, the rifle kicked and a harmless bullet whizzed away into mid-air. He turned furiously. 'What the hell did you do that for?' he began, and then recognised his brother standing in the trench behind him. 'Jesus Christ, what are you doing here? I thought you were back at HQ.'

'So I was, till this morning,' said Connor. 'They posted half a dozen of us out here as a relief platoon, to make up the numbers.'

The two brothers settled themselves at the bottom of the dug-out, their backs against a wall of muddy clay.

'Some people have all the flaming luck,' grumbled Sean. 'How is it you get to stay back at base all the time, while poor buggers like me are stuck in the line for weeks on end?'

'I've been picked for the regimental Boxing Championships, with special training all day and every day – weight-lifting, skipping and road-running.' Connor gave one of his rare, crooked grins. 'It's true we get given extra rations, but in every other way it's a dog's life. You can't call your soul your own.'

'Jammy bastard.' Sean dug into his pocket for a tin of tobacco. 'What's so special about being able to punch a feller's head in?'

'Good for the morale of the Regiment, they say,' Connor told him. 'If the 21st Lancers win the Cup, they think it'll encourage our brave boys to go out and cross the Rhine! Anyhow, don't blame me – I never asked to be selected for the damn team, did I?'

Sean rolled a cigarette, cupping it in his hands as he struck the match, so that no spark should be seen from the German trenches. After a couple of draws, he offered it to his brother.

'No, thanks, bad for my wind,' Connor told him. 'By the by, I've got something for you – I brought it from HQ.' Slipping a hand inside his tunic, he pulled out an envelope addressed to Sean in Ruth's handwriting.

'Is that all? I thought you were going to give us a food-parcel.' Sean glanced at the letter without enthusiasm, and was about to stuff it into his pocket when Connor said, 'Aren't you going to read it?'

'I suppose I may as well.' Sean tore open the envelope and began to skim through the contents, then his face creased into a smile and he added, 'Will you listen to her? She says she's going to have a kid: *The doctor says the baby will be due in April. It would be wonderful if you were able to get compassionate leave then* . . . What d'you think of that?'

'Congratulations,' said Connor quietly.

'No, I meant what do you think my chances are? Maybe I could wangle something if I tell the CO the poor girl's at death's door. It'd be worth trying for a few days in Blighty.'

Connor glared at him. 'Don't be a fool! What are you trying to do, wish bad luck on Ruth and the child?'

'Ah, that's just superstitious rubbish, but I tell you what I *will* do. Tonight when we come off-duty, I'll take you down to a little estaminet I found in the village, less than a mile away. Half the roof was took off by a German shell, but it's still doing business. It's run by this old Froggie woman, so cracked about the British she never lets you pay for anything. We'll have a real party, so we will, to drink the baby's health . . . I tell you, Con, you'll not have to stick your hand in your pocket all bloody night!'

Some time before midnight, Connor dragged his brother out of the little wine-shop, half-guiding him, half-carrying him back to the trenches. Then, as Sean lay on his bunk in a drunken stupor, Connor wrote a short letter to Ruth on one of the regulation letter-forms.

He could not say much, for all outgoing mail had to be read and passed by the field-censors – and in any case there was not much he could have told her. But he finished: *Sean asked me to write and congratulate you, for he's not much of a fist at letter-writing, and begs to be excused – but I can tell you he's the proudest man in the British Army this day . . . He says to tell you he loves you with all his heart, and wishes you well – you and the baby – and he looks forward to seeing you both before too long. Your affectionate brother-in-law, Connor O'Dell.*

The year rolled on, and November 1915 came to the Isle of Dogs under a sky as muddy and grey as the battlefield itself.

Within Gloria's bedroom, however, everything was warm and cosy. She had hung some bright pink curtains at the window, almost matching the pink cushions on her bed, and had persuaded Saul to put up some shelves and move in an old cupboard to take her clothes. She had painted the woodwork in cheerful primary colours, and had even cajoled Saul into buying an oil-stove. At night, it threw circles of orange light on to the ceiling.

Gloria's bedroom had become the centre of the house, and in the evenings Saul would sit by her bed, enjoying the warmth, the pink and orange glow – the soft outline of Gloria's body, her laughter, her perfume, her femininity . . . Though he was always close beside her, devouring her with his eyes, he never touched her and she wondered why that was. When she first came out of hospital she had not wanted any man's hand upon her, but as the weeks passed she began to feel a need for some masculine excitement.

Saul could not be described as a handsome man, but he was big and powerful, with a rugged strength that attracted her – and she was curious to know what secret desires he might have. At the end of one peaceful evening together, when he stood up to go to his own room she caught his hand and pulled him towards her, putting up her face to be kissed.

He gave her a chaste kiss on the brow; she returned it, full on the lips. He drew back his head, not displeased, but asking warily, 'What did you do that for?'

'No special reason,' she told him. 'Just a good-night kiss.'

He mulled this over for a moment and nodded, satisfied with her answer. 'Good night then,' he said, and went off to his own bed, where he lay awake for a long while, thinking hard.

The next night he came to her room again. She knew he had something on his mind from the way he kept staring at her and starting to speak, then frowning and looking away. At last she challenged him. 'Was there something you wanted to ask me?'

He chewed his lip, unable to reply.

'Never mind,' she continued softly. 'I think I can guess.'

Smiling, she turned back the blankets, inviting him into her bed. He seemed quite taken aback, and for a moment she was afraid she had made a mistake but then he came and sat on the bed, taking her hand in his.

'I want to ask you if you'd like for to do – something special,' he mumbled.

'Tell me what you want,' she whispered.

He looked into her eyes, and then surprised her by saying deliberately, 'I want for you to marry me . . . if you'd like to.'

She stared up at him, hardly able to believe what she heard. 'You really mean that?'

'I got a bit of money put by, that's why I did say you could live here. Now I know you're a good girl, Glory – and I wants you to be my wife,' he said, with the same stiff formality. 'What d'you say to that?'

A thousand thoughts ran through her head. She had never imagined that Cyclops Wharf would be anything but a temporary resting-place, but now Saul had put the question to her, she began to see all kinds of advantages to it. She had nowhere else to live and she was afraid to go back on the old game. Even if she had chosen to do so, she wasn't sure who would have her. In a few years she would be thirty, and she had seen too many young women reduced to walking the streets – women burned out by poverty and disease, old before their time – and she could not face that.

Saul had been kind to her, kinder than any other man she

had known. And she could feel the old, familiar thrill of physical magnetism . . . Now, as she took him in her arms, her body responded to his, and she heard herself saying, 'Yes, Saul, I'll marry you. I'll do whatever you want.'

Their love-making was slow and difficult. He was very inexperienced and Gloria realised that she would have to teach him a great deal, but there would be all the time in the world for that.

The next morning, they went to make enquiries at the Registrar's Office, and a few days later Ruth received a letter from Gloria. It was misspelled and untidy, with lots of blots and crossings-out, but the contents were plain enough: the pleasure of Mrs Ruth O'Dell's company was requested at their wedding, on the last Saturday in November.

The rain poured all day, and never let up for a minute.

Ruth was the only witness. She stood by, listening to the Registrar's automatic recitation of the marriage ceremony, and watching the raindrops chase one another down the window-panes. She remembered her own wedding-day, and could not help comparing this brisk, businesslike arrangement with the solemn ritual at St Anthony's Church. She and Sean had received the blessing of Almighty God, and now she felt the new life within her growing day by day and knew that she had been blessed indeed.

When they left the office, huddling together under an umbrella, Gloria said ruefully, 'Happy is the bride the sun shines on . . .'

Ruth had brought a little bag of confetti to throw over them, but the scraps of coloured paper stuck soggily together, landing in a lump on Saul's shoulder.

Sloshing through the puddles, they went back to the Watermen, where Ruth had provided a meal of cold meat and salad and some sparkling wine. Patrick and Mary joined her in a toast to the happy couple. There was no question of their happiness. Saul gazed open-mouthed at Gloria, dazed by his good fortune, and she smiled back at him fondly. They seemed completely wrapped up in one another.

Ruth felt a touch of envy, wishing that she and Sean were in love like that, then she remembered Maudie and reproached herself for her selfishness. Sean was alive and well, and would be coming home to her one of these days. Soon they would have their child, and then the three of them would begin a new life together. Maudie had a beautiful baby son already, but she would never know the happiness of a full family life.

That night, Maudie sat up in bed, nursing her beautiful baby son and wishing she were dead. Little Trevor was five months old and going through a difficult time. Purple in the face, he flung himself about in paroxysms of pain and rage. Maudie did everything she could to console him, but he refused to be pacified. She dipped his comforter in gripe-water and put it in his mouth, but he spat it out ferociously. She rocked him in her arms, crooning a lullaby, but he drowned her voice with his yells and fought off sleep with grim determination.

'Oh, for goodness sake shut up!' she exclaimed at last.

He would not shut up: he looked at her with hatred, and Maudie was in despair. Exhausted and hopeless, she began to cry too. The tears ran down her cheeks, and she couldn't find her handkerchief.

Then the bedroom door swung open, and Tommy Judge appeared. 'Want me to take him for a bit?'

Gratefully, she handed her son over and Tommy perched on the end of the bed, dandling the baby on his knee and pulling faces to distract him. The tiny boy gazed at him in astonishment, and forgot to cry.

'Did he wake you up?' Maudie asked. 'I'm ever so sorry. I was trying to get him off again, but he wouldn't stop.'

'That's all right.' Tommy wriggled his eyebrows, and the baby gurgled in approval.

'I only hope he didn't disturb your Mum and your Aunt Emily,' Maudie continued.

'Not much fear of that. They don't hear him so loud, down below.'

Florrie and Emily shared the main bedroom on the first floor, while Tommy and Maudie had two attic rooms, side by side at the top of the house.

'They will thump him on the back to get his wind up, and that only makes him worse. I keep telling them it's colic, but they don't listen.'

'Poor old Trev.' Tommy introduced the comforter again. Taken by surprise, the baby accepted it and a blissful silence followed. 'He'll drop off soon now, you'll see.'

'You are good with him.' Maudie dried her eyes with the back of her hand, beginning to relax.

'You been crying too?' Tommy asked.

'Just a bit. Silly, wasn't it?'

'You ain't got stomach-ache as well, have you?'

'I'm just tired, I expect, and a bit miserable. I know he's a lovely baby, but I do get fed up with him sometimes.'

'It ain't his fault, though.' Tommy lowered his voice, but the baby's eyelids were drooping. 'What did I tell you? He's sleepy now.' Moving slowly and cautiously, he put the baby back into the cot then laid a blanket over him. 'There . . . let's hope he stays quiet till breakfast-time,' he said, and moved towards the door.

'Don't go,' said Maudie, in a small voice.

'Why, what's up?'

'I'm wide awake now. Stay and talk for a bit, eh?'

He smiled at her. 'Want me to rock you on my knee, and all?'

'Sit down for a minute.' She patted a space on the bed beside her.

'Well, I dunno . . .' He hesitated, a little bashful. 'I'm not dressed proper.' Tommy was growing so fast his mother could not provide him with nightshirts that fitted him, so now he slept in his undervest and an old pair of drawers.

'I'm not dressed either,' said Maudie. 'Come on – sit by me.'

Tommy obeyed, adding, 'You're still missing Arnie – is that it?'

'Perhaps, I don't know. I don't really think about him very often.' She hung her head. 'That's a dreadful thing to say, isn't it?'

'You can say anything you like, I don't care. Besides, you didn't know him all that long, did you?'

'Not very long.' Another tear trickled down her nose, and she fumbled under her pillow. 'Oh, why am I so stupid? I've lost my handkerchief.'

'Here.' Tommy pulled up his vest, using the edge of it to wipe her face.

It was still warm from his body, and it carried a faint smell of him. Maudie held it against her cheek for a moment – his naked chest looked unexpectedly broad and muscular. When she let go of the vest, he covered himself up.

'What were you really crying for?' he asked gently.

'I get lonely sometimes. Now Arnie's gone, there's nobody. I don't suppose I'll ever meet anybody else. I haven't got any friends,' she said.

'You got me,' he said. 'I'm your friend, ain't I?'

'Course you are – my very best friend. But you're still a boy.'

'I'll be fourteen soon, and I'm big for my age, everybody says so.'

'I know, but . . . I need somebody to look after me,' she faltered.

'I'll look after you,' he said. 'What do you want?'

His freckled face was very close to hers, and she could feel his breath upon her cheek. Opening her arms to him, she whispered: 'Hold me . . .'

Slowly, he did so. After a moment, they slipped back on to the pillows, and curled up together. At last they fell asleep in each other's arms.

Less than a mile away, Gloria and Saul lay awake, drowsily contented.

'Well, then?' Gloria asked, fondling him. 'How does it feel to be a married man?'

'Good . . . very good,' said Saul, with a grunt of pleasure. 'You know how to do things . . . things what I like.'

'You're not so dusty yourself,' she said, digging him in the ribs.

'Tell me something.' He raised himself on one elbow, looking down at her. In the warm, reflected light from the stove, her skin looked soft and ripe like a peach. 'You bin with other men, aincher? Lots of men.'

'Don't ask me about that.' She turned her head away. 'That's over and done with – I don't want to think of that no more.'

'But I want to know – were they good when they did it? Better than me?'

'Don't be so soft! You're very good, and getting better all the time, so stop asking silly questions. There's no other men now, only you.'

'Am I getting better?' He flopped down beside her. 'I'm glad of that.'

'You're daft, you are.' She stretched out like a cat, rubbing herself against his body, then a thought crossed her mind. 'Now it's your turn to tell me something,' she said.

'Tell you what?'

'Why did you ask me to marry you? If going to bed was what you wanted, you know I'd have done that anyhow. Why did you want to get married?'

'I suppose it was to make it – you know – all right in the law.'

Touched, she rolled over, facing him. 'You mean, for my sake? That's nice. I really appreciate that.'

'Not only for you. I was thinking about the baby, too. He's got to have a birth certificate.'

She stared blankly. 'What baby? What are you on about now?'

'You know, when we start a family, like. That's what I want most – it's what I always wanted: a boy, to grow up and take over the shop when I gets old. My own son.'

Her eyes shone, large and lustrous in the soft glow, as she asked, 'Is that why you married me? To start a family?'

'That's right. Ain't that why people do get married? To have babies?'

Very slowly, she shook her head. 'You never said. I didn't know that was what you wanted. It's no good, Saul, I can't do that for you. That's what they did, when they operated on me – I can't have babies now.'

His happiness died before her eyes, extinguished like a candle-flame. She had given him a precious gift, and now she had taken that gift away for ever.

'I'm sorry,' she said brokenly. 'I'm so sorry.'

· ——20—— ·

'What a day!' Ruth sank into a chair. 'I'll be glad when it's over.'

She had been on the go ever since she arrived at the pub. For one thing, it was their delivery day. When the brewery dray arrived, the new barrels had to be rolled down into the cellar and the old empties taken away. That always caused an upheaval but today had been worse than usual, for when the new barrels were connected to the pumps, one of them seized up and refused to function.

Then Ruth had to send for the handy-man, and he proceeded to take the pump to pieces in order to find the blockage, which involved removing some of the floorboards in the public bar, and dismantling part of the counter. That took up most of the afternoon, so instead of going home for a couple of hours and putting her feet up, Ruth had to remain on duty to supervise the work and tidy up afterwards.

'You ought to have gone off to have a rest,' Mary O'Dell told her. 'I'm sure we could have managed perfectly well on our own.'

'I wanted to be here to make sure everything was all right for this evening,' Ruth explained. 'Anyhow, there's only a few hours to go now, then I'll get back to my bed for a good night's sleep. I'll be fine by tomorrow morning, don't you worry.'

She wouldn't admit it, but she found that as the months dragged on she was getting tired more quickly. The baby was due in the middle of April and now, in mid-March, she was ticking the days off on the calendar.

'That's as may be, but you should be taking things easy now,' Mary fretted. 'Patrick and me will be looking after everything once the little stranger arrives, and we've got Kathie Simes here to give us a hand – she's not a bad worker.'

'She's an even better talker.' Ruth shut her eyes. 'I think we

306

should be looking around for temporary bar-staff, just for a few weeks while I'm in bed upstairs, doing nothing to help.'

It had been agreed that when her time came, Ruth would move back into the pub. The O'Dells flatly refused to let her stay at Meadow Lane on her own. As a rule, babies were delivered at home – by a midwife or a doctor, if the parents could afford to pay for expert help, or by an experienced friend or neighbour if they could not. If there were any serious medical complications, a woman could be admitted to the Infirmary or sent to the London Hospital in the Whitechapel Road. Otherwise, the expectant mother gave birth in her own bed and remained in that bed for two or three weeks afterwards.

Patrick came into the back-kitchen. 'It's just on opening-time. Will I go round and unlock the doors?'

'That's all right, I'll do it.' Ruth struggled to her feet. She could not get used to the extra weight she had to carry, nor the clumsiness of her movements and this was one of those days when the baby within her was being particularly restless, kicking and wriggling energetically.

The pub was unusually busy for a Wednesday, and by the middle of the evening the bars were crowded but in spite of the incessant chatter and the tinkling piano, there was no mistak-ing the wail of the sirens outside.

'There goes the warning!' exclaimed Kathie Simes. 'The Zeps are here again!'

Patrick O'Dell made an announcement. 'Any customers wishing to go home should leave now, if you please. Anyone who cares to stay is requested to move down to the cellars until the raid is over.'

Without undue haste, he and Mary began to close the bars, emptying the tills and locking up, while Ruth opened the door at the top of the cellar stairs and Kathie went down first to light the lamps.

'I hate them nasty sirens,' Mary confided to Ruth. 'They sound like a lot of banshees keening . . . Why can't they send the police round on bicycles, blowing their whistles, like they used to?'

Now the air-raids were more frequent, the precautions had

become more efficient. At the first note of the sirens, cellars and basements opened up as shelters and the streets were cleared of traffic. At the Watermen, a makeshift bar was set up underground so the customers who chose to remain on the premises could go on drinking until the all-clear sounded.

Ruth waited until the last man and woman had taken refuge below, and was about to follow them down when a sudden explosion made her jump. It was so unexpected, and so deafening, she stumbled and missed her footing on the top step. She tried to clutch the banister but her hand slipped and she slid down the whole flight on her back, landing in a heap on the cellar floor.

'Dear God!' Mary O'Dell was at her side in a moment, dropping to her knees. 'Are you all right?'

'Yes, I think so.' Cautiously, Ruth moved her arms and legs. 'No bones broken . . . I just feel a bit bruised and battered.' Other people gathered round, helping her into a chair. 'That big bang made me jump. Was it a bomb?' she asked.

'Not at all. That'll be the big anti-aircraft gun they've set up at Blackwall Point. It makes more noise than all their bombs put together,' Patrick told her. 'Are you sure you're all right now? You don't think maybe we should send for a doctor?'

'No, I'll be fine. Just let me get my breath back,' Ruth told him. 'It was my own silly fault – I should have been more careful.'

'Fetch her a sup of brandy,' Mary told her husband, and Patrick went across to the improvised bar where Kathie was serving drinks.

Up above, they heard a series of thunderclaps as the big gun fired again and again. When it stopped another sound began, a roaring noise like an express-train approaching.

'There's your Zeppelin now,' said Patrick, returning with a tot of brandy. 'Right overhead, by the sound of it.' Some of the women in the cellar were becoming hysterical, and one burst into tears, but Patrick took charge of the situation, calling out, 'Come on, my friends, we won't let them get us down! How about a real old sing-song?'

He launched into a spirited rendition of *The Londonderry Air*, and one by one the customers joined in: 'Oh, Danny-boy! The

308

pipes, the pipes are calling . . .' Soon the cellar was filled with music, drowning out the sounds of warfare, and the frightened women began to calm down.

Sitting beside Ruth, Mary saw her grimace with pain, and asked immediately, 'What's wrong? Is it your back?'

'No!' Ruth gasped, for the sharpness of the spasm had taken her breath away. 'It's not that, but I think perhaps the baby got shaken up. I think it could be starting . . .'

'What will we do, for pity's sake?' Mary looked helplessly around the crowded cellar. 'You can't stay here, we must get you into bed.'

'I can get upstairs,' said Ruth. 'I'll go into Sean's room.'

Moving very slowly, she managed to stand up as Patrick came over to see what was happening. When Mary explained, he called out urgently, 'Kathie! Leave what you're at, and come here this minute.'

He gave them their instructions; Mary would put Ruth to bed upstairs, while he stayed in the cellar to attend to the customers. Meanwhile, Kathie had to go out and fetch a doctor.

'Me? Go out in the middle of an air-raid?' the girl protested.

'Yes. Run to Dr Mackay, he's the nearest, and if he's not there stop the first policeman you find and ask him to telephone for help. Tell him it's an emergency!'

By the time Mary got Ruth into bed, the pains were coming at regular intervals. At first they had hoped it might be only a false alarm, but there was no mistaking this slow, steady rhythm.

'Don't go upsetting yourself, my love. I'll be here with you all the while, and if nobody else comes, I'll help with the baby myself,' said Mary, trying to sound more confident than she felt. 'Haven't I had two great bouncing boys of my own? To be sure, there's nothing to it at all.'

The air-raid rumbled on. Each time there was a lull, they hoped it might be over but then a sudden explosion would rock the house again. Kathie returned, pale and breathless, saying she couldn't find the doctor but that she'd talked to a policeman, and he'd promised to send a midwife.

'Let's hope she gets here soon.' Ruth spoke through gritted

teeth, gripping Mary's hand. 'And I hope to God the baby will be all right. It's much too soon – I still had four weeks to go.'

The midwife arrived, and upon hearing that the baby would be premature, asked if there was a tin bath in the house. Mary produced an old zinc tub from the wash-house at the back, and the midwife asked for hot-water bottles – or hot bricks wrapped in flannel.

'We must make sure the baby is kept warm,' she explained. 'Being early, it will be very sensitive to cold.'

They stoked up the kitchen fire, filling three stone hot-water bottles, and heating four loose bricks from the yard. On top of these, they lined the tub with cushions, making a cosy nest for the baby.

By now the contractions were deep and very frequent. Mary began to pray under her breath, and Ruth tried to repeat the words with her: *'Holy Mary, mother of God, pray for us sinners now, and in the hour of our death . . .'*

Another big explosion set the gas-brackets on the wall dancing, and grotesque shadows leaped across the ceiling.

'Hail, Holy Queen, mother of mercy – hail our light, our sweetness and our hope . . .'

Two floors below, the community-singing continued. Patrick had worked through all the tunes he could think of, from *Ten Green Bottles* to *Mademoiselle from Armentières*, and now he went back to the beginning: 'Oh, Danny-boy! The pipes, the pipes are calling, From glen to glen, and down the mountain-side . . .'

Ruth tried not to fight the pain, but to float with it, meeting it like a swimmer as the waves ebbed and flowed. She looked up into Mary's face, and saw Sean's lips moving soundlessly, and Connor's eyes gazing down at her with love. The gunfire and the singing and the prayers became jumbled together. She made one more great effort and at last, high and clear above all these sounds, she heard the cry of a new-born child.

He was as skinny and wiry as a baby monkey, and he weighed under five and a half pounds, but he was full of life. Ruth took one look at him, and said to herself, 'Thank God, he's going to be all right.'

He had a will of his own, for when the midwife had cleaned

him up and wrapped him in a clean pillow-case (for there were
no baby-clothes ready) she laid him in the zinc tub, in his warm
nest, and he shouted with rage at this indignity. He wanted to
go back where he had come from; he wanted his mother.

'Do you think it would be safe?' Mary asked uncertainly.

'He seems to be pretty strong,' the midwife decided. 'I dare
say he'll be warm enough, close to his Ma.'

So they gave him back to Ruth. She smiled down at her son,
and knew a moment of absolute joy.

'Have you a name for him?' the midwife asked, entering up
her notes.

'Of course,' said Ruth confidently. 'His name's Daniel.
Danny-boy . . .'

After that the sirens began to sound the all-clear and she
closed her eyes, falling peacefully asleep with her baby in her
arms.

Next morning, Patrick sent off a telegram to France on Ruth's
behalf, congratulating Sean on the birth of Master Daniel
Patrick O'Dell, born at ten minutes past midnight, on
Thursday, 16 March 1916.

A week later a parcel arrived by way of the War Office. When
she opened it, Ruth found a picture-postcard of a stork
carrying a baby in a bundle, and a single French word:
Félicitations! On the back, Sean had scrawled a brief message:
Well done! See you soon, love, S. And there were two little gifts
for mother and baby; a brooch worked in silver filigree for
Ruth, and a woolly rabbit for Daniel.

Ruth was astonished. She had not expected these tokens of
Sean's affection. She tried to imagine him shopping for them
in some little French village, struggling with the problems of
the language and the unfamiliar currency, and she felt a great
surge of love for her husband. It was true then, this was to be a
new beginning after all.

Mary asked, 'What do you suppose he means by *See you soon*?
Do you think he'll get leave in time for the christening?'

She and Patrick had gone to tell Father Riley the good news,
and they had arranged for the baby to be baptised on the first

Sunday in April. Surely, Mary said, the Army would grant Sean compassionate leave on such a special occasion? But the weeks passed with no further word from France, and their hopes gradually faded.

The christening was complicated by the Judge family's anti-Catholic sentiments. Ruth would have liked her mother to be present, and sent her an invitation, but got no response. She also sent one to Aunt Emily and another to her sister-in-law Florrie; they did not reply in writing but called at the Watermen instead, to pay their respects and satisfy their curiosity. Neither of these ladies had ever crossed the threshold of a public-house before and they held themselves very stiffly, perhaps afraid of some unspeakable contamination, as they picked their way up the stairs to Ruth's bedroom.

'Good afternoon, dear,' said Aunt Emily, her fingers darting as tremulously as ever to adjust her hat and her tippet and the little black velvet ribbon round her throat. 'We're so sorry we can't accept your invitation to the christening but we felt we should bring some little presents for the baby, and we wanted to see how you're getting on.'

'Yes, how are you getting on?' Florrie peered over Emily's shoulder, echoing her words.

'We're both very well, thank you.' Ruth had been feeding Daniel, and he was sleepily full of milk. He opened one eye and lifted a lazy hand, but took no other notice of the visitors.

'What a dear little chap. We heard he was premature – so worrying for you. Early babies can be very delicate,' Emily said.

'Not this one. He drinks like a fish and roars like a lion,' said Ruth proudly. 'And he's putting on a little weight every day.'

'There's a clever boy. Just like my Tommy – he never gave me a minute's anxiety,' Florrie chimed in, handing over a package wrapped in tissue-paper. 'This is a little jacket I knitted when Tommy was born. I kept it all this time, because I couldn't bear to part with it.'

The white wool had yellowed over the last fourteen years, but it was a kind thought and Ruth was very touched. Aunt Emily had brought another family heirloom: a baby's rattle, in coral and silver.

'It was given to my late husband when he was born – and

then poor Arnie had it when he was little.' She sniffed, and dabbed her nose with her handkerchief. 'I was intending to pass it on to Trevor, but Maudie didn't seem to appreciate it so I thought you might like it instead.'

'That's very good of you,' said Ruth. 'We're really grateful, aren't we, Danny-boy?' But Danny-boy was already fast asleep, and she continued, 'How did you manage to get away in the middle of the day? Is Maudie looking after the shop now?'

'Oh, no. She's always too busy with little Trevor and anyway, she's such a dreamer, I never dare leave her in charge,' fussed Emily. 'But your dear mother's been helping me out recently. She's been so good, hasn't she, Florrie? Your father sees to the book-keeping now, and the ordering. I don't know what I've done to deserve it all.'

'Mum's working in the shop? I thought Father didn't approve of that.'

'He's changed a good deal lately. I think he's mellowing as he grows older – people do, you know.'

'But not mellow enough to let Mum come to Daniel's christening,' said Ruth dryly. 'I suppose Father put his foot down when he saw your invitation, as well?'

'Well, to be honest, I didn't show it to him. There's no use asking for trouble, is there?'

'Oh, couldn't you both sneak out and come to the church? Or at least pop round here afterwards for a slice of cake and a cup of tea. I do wish you would.'

Emily and Florrie exchanged glances.

'I don't think so, thank you very much,' said Emily uncomfortably. 'The thing is, a little bird told me you'd already invited Saul and Gloria, is that right? I'm afraid I haven't any wish to meet Gloria now, not after the way she's been carrying on.'

'Why ever not? Didn't you know she's married to Saul? I went to their wedding,' Ruth began.

'A wedding in a registry-office.' Emily drew down the corners of her mouth. 'I don't know how you could bring yourself to encourage her, I don't really. And they say she was living in sin with that dreadful man for months before that, so the whole thing was nothing but a mockery.'

'God is not mocked,' said Florrie, popping up over Emily's shoulder again.

'No, I don't think He is,' said Ruth. 'But I'm sorry you feel like that about it, because I'm very happy for Glory and Saul, and I'm looking forward to seeing them next Sunday.'

The christening went off very smoothly. Danny did not care for the holy water that trickled over his forehead, but when Father Riley put a few grains of salt on his lips, he investigated them with the tip of his tongue and continued to lick his lips happily throughout the rest of the ceremony.

Saul and Gloria stayed at the back of the church. Saul looked awkward and uncomfortable in a rusty black suit that Ruth had last seen him wearing on the day of his father's funeral, and Gloria had dressed up for the occasion in a broad-brimmed hat with an ostrich-feather, and a long feather-boa in a matching colour wound around her neck, but despite her finery, her smile was a little remote.

At the reception in the Watermen afterwards, Ruth threaded her way through the guests to speak to them both, pressing them to take another glass of wine or another piece of cake, but they still seemed ill-at-ease.

'No, thanks.' Gloria smiled a little too brightly. 'We've got to be getting back, haven't we, Saul? But thanks for inviting us. We do wish you all the best – you and the nipper.'

'That's right,' growled Saul. 'Good luck to both of you. We'll be pushing off now.'

Ruth knew that something had upset them. 'I hope you don't feel hurt because I didn't ask you to be godparents? I would have, but it's difficult with you not being Catholics.'

'Oh, yes, we know that,' Gloria hastened to assure her. 'We're neither of us churchy sort of people anyhow, are we Saul?'

'No, we couldn't have done that. It wouldn't be right,' agreed Saul, backing away. 'Come on, Glory, time to go home.'

Ruth watched them go, still feeling she had offended them in some way, but not knowing how.

As they walked back to Cyclops Wharf, Gloria said quietly, 'I know how you're feeling, wishing it could have been us with our own kid. I let you down, didn't I?'

'Not your fault. But why should Ruth be able to have a son and not us? It don't seem fair somehow.'

They walked on down the long road that wound around Jubilee Wharf, their footsteps echoing between high grey walls on either side; and they said no more.

On Monday afternoon, Ruth told Patrick and Mary that she was going to take Danny out for an hour or two. They looked rather anxious, and Patrick said, 'Are you sure that's wise? It's not three weeks since the little feller was born. Don't you think it might be as well to wait a few more days?'

'I'm sure we'll be fine,' said Ruth. 'We went to church yesterday without coming to any harm. Danny's fighting fit, and I'm fed up with sitting about all day long doing nothing.'

Reluctantly, they let her go. Ruth had bought a second-hand pram and she was determined to give her son his first airing. She had already decided where she would take him.

It was a fine, bright day, with a southerly wind whipping up the water in the docks, making it sparkle like cut-glass. As Ruth walked along, a gang of stevedores working on one of the timber-ships recognised her from the Watermen and called out a cheery greeting. She waved back, but did not stop; she couldn't wait to get to the little grocery shop.

She left the pram outside on the pavement and carried her son indoors. Her mother, busily slicing bacon, looked up and surprise and delight chased across her face as she exclaimed: 'Ruth! You've brought him with you?'

'Of course.' She offered her the child. 'He had to come and meet his Grandma.'

Louisa took him in her arms, her eyes bright with unshed tears. 'He's a fine boy,' she said, with a catch in her voice. 'Emily tells me you've called him Daniel . . . a fine name, too.'

'Daniel Patrick O'Dell,' said Ruth. 'Patrick, after his grandfather. I mean, his other grandfather.'

'I know.' The happiness in Louisa's eyes dimmed a little, and for the first time since she had left home Ruth felt a twinge of disloyalty.

315

'I'm sorry,' she said in a different tone, 'but it meant such a lot to Mr and Mrs O'Dell, being their first grandchild.'

'That's all right, I do understand,' said Louisa, then added gently, 'Even though he's not my first grandchild, he means a lot to me as well. Thank you for letting me see him.'

'Aunt Emily said you were helping out in the shop now, so I decided to risk it. Father isn't here, is he?'

'Oh, no, he never comes here in the daytime. He's so busy at the Wharf now. With the men going into service, he has to work twice as hard.'

At the beginning of the year, the Government had finally given way to public pressure and passed a bill enforcing conscription; although dockers on essential work were exempted, most of the able-bodied young men had volunteered to fight, so the ranks of the Brotherhood were seriously depleted. Only middle-aged men or youths fresh from school were available as dock-labour.

'It's a dreadful worry for your father,' Louisa continued. 'He's finding it hard to get the boats unloaded and turned round as fast as they used to; all the responsibility's on his shoulders. I keep telling him he mustn't drive himself so hard, but you know what he's like.'

'Yes, I know what he's like,' said Ruth shortly. 'This war's made life hard for everyone, not just Father.'

Louisa changed the subject. 'Just look at Daniel, I do believe he's smiling at me. I know they say tiny babies don't really smile, and it's only the wind, but I still think you can tell the difference sometimes. You must be so proud of him – won't you take him into the kitchen? I'm sure Emily and Florrie would like to see him again, and Maudie's in there with Trevor.'

It was fascinating to compare the two babies. They were both dark-eyed and dark-haired, for Daniel had been born with a fine, silky fuzz, but there the resemblance ended. At ten months old, Trevor was a round, placid dumpling, a lethargic giant beside Daniel, who was so spare and energetic.

'He's very nice,' said Maudie politely, admiring the tiny baby. 'Isn't it funny? I can't remember Trevor looking as small as that, can you, Tommy?'

Tommy was sitting at the kitchen-table wrestling with sums in his homework book, and he glanced across, saying, 'Trev was always a big boy.'

'It must run in the family,' Ruth told him. 'You seem more grown-up every time I see you, Tommy. You're quite a young man now.'

'Yes, I'll be out of school next year,' he said, and grinned at Maudie. 'No more rotten old homework then, thank goodness!'

'What are you going to do when you leave school?' Ruth asked.

'Go to work at the docks. Grandfather says he'll take me on.'

Ruth's face changed. 'You don't have to do that, you know. I mean, just because it's in the family.'

'But I want to!' Tommy told her. 'It's a good job. I can do a year or so at the Wharf, and after that I'll go as a soldier when I'm old enough . . . if the war's still on.'

The women all began to talk at once, saying that the war could not possibly last that long, and Florrie protested tearfully, 'I couldn't bear to see you go into the Army. All that killing and wounding – it doesn't bear thinking about.'

Late that night, when they had all gone up to bed, Maudie crept across the attic landing and pushed open the door of Tommy's room. 'Are you still awake?' she whispered.

'Yes, I was just thinking about you,' he said. 'Shut the door quietly, then they won't hear us.'

Over the past few months they had fallen into the habit of meeting like this, late at night, when Emily and Florrie were asleep. Originally it had been a simple need for company; then, during the worst part of the winter, they had curled up together to keep warm. At first they had shared Maudie's bed, but then they went into Tommy's room, for fear of waking the baby. If they fell asleep it did not matter, for they woke early in the mornings and were invariably up and about before the older women came downstairs.

Their childish friendship had matured into something stronger, and by now they were devoted to one another. Emily and Florrie were aware of their deep affection, and found it very gratifying. They said it was so charming to see how well the two young people got along together.

Tonight when Maudie climbed into Tommy's bed, he knew immediately that something was wrong. 'What's the matter?' he asked.

'You know what you said this afternoon, about going in the Army? You didn't really mean that, did you?'

'Why not? My Dad's in the Army, and Uncle Josh, so why shouldn't I join up too?'

'I'd hate it if you went away. Besides, I keep remembering, you know – Arnold. Suppose anything happened to you. Suppose you were to get . . .' She broke off, unable to finish the sentence.

'Don't be daft, you don't have to worry about me,' Tommy said stoutly. 'Anyhow, it won't be for a long while yet, so don't go making yourself miserable. Here, I heard a good joke today. Listen to this, it'll make you laugh.'

'I don't feel like laughing,' she said.

'I bet I can make you laugh, all the same.'

'Bet you can't.' Challenged, he did not waste time on jokes but began to tickle her instead. She giggled helplessly. 'Stop it! That's not fair – you know I'm ticklish!'

'Yes, but you like it really – you know you do!'

'Stop it, Tommy, they'll hear us!' she gasped, in fits of laughter.

He took no notice, but as she tried to wriggle away from his tormenting fingers, he reared up, kneeling over her and pinning her down. As they struggled together, her nightdress slipped from her shoulders, and in a glimmer of moonlight from the dormer window he saw her breasts.

'Stop, please stop!' she pleaded. 'I'm half undressed.'

This time he obeyed her, but remained where he was, staring down at her nakedness and breathing hard. 'I never seen you like that before,' he said at last. 'Let me see you, undressed, all over. Let me see what you look like – down there.'

Maudie was breathing faster too, light-headed from so much laughter, and she suddenly retorted: 'I'll show you what I look like, if you show me yours . . .'

Tommy was very excited, but he drew back, embarrassed. 'No, I mustn't,' he began.

'I'll help you,' she whispered. Her small, soft hands lifted his undervest and pulled it over his head. He made no move to stop her, but stayed quite still as she eased his drawers down his thighs. For a long moment, they gazed at one another in silence then, tenderly and shyly, they began to explore the mystery of their bodies.

Tonight there was no difference in age between them. They were neither adults nor children, they were just Maudie and Tommy together, two people – becoming one person. When it was over, and they lay side by side with their arms and legs entwined, Tommy drifted off to sleep, his face against Maudie's breasts. She lay awake for a while, stroking his hair, still in an ecstasy of pleasure and fulfilment.

She knew she had done something very wrong, yet how could it be wrong, when it made them both so happy? She knew that the world would call her wicked and say she had committed a sin, but she did not feel sinful at all. She could not make sense of those words – wrong, wicked, sinful – they meant nothing to her now. She only knew she loved Tommy, and he loved her – and she didn't care about anything else.

On Tuesday evening, Gloria was waiting for Saul to come home. What could have happened to the man? He had promised he would get back in time for tea – six o'clock at the latest, he'd said, and here it was nearly ten. She had made a hot-pot from a shin of beef, with some onions, carrots and potatoes. It had been simmering on top of the range for hours. The meat would have turned to rags by now, floating in a thick vegetable soup, but that didn't matter. All that mattered was Saul – where could he have got to?

Soon after she came to live at Cyclops Wharf, he had told her of his profitable sideline as a resurrection man. She did not like it, but merely commented, 'If that's what you've got to do to make a living, you'd better get on with it. Only don't tell me any more. Pull them out of the river if you have to and take them straight to the police, but don't ever bring them into this house, that's all.'

Perhaps that was what was keeping him so late tonight. Her

skin crawled at the thought of it. Perhaps he had found a floating body and was at the police station this very minute, handing it over and collecting his remuneration. On the other hand, it might not be that at all. Time and again he had told her how many men fell into the river each week – strong men, men who could swim, men who could fend for themselves. One false step in the darkness, then a bang on the head from a floating baulk of timber, or the stone wall of the dock . . . There were not many who survived the cruel, treacherous waters of the Thames.

She began to feel frightened. If anything had happened to Saul, what would become of her? Where would she find another man to take her in, to support her and cherish her as Saul had done? At ten o'clock, when she heard the shop door closing downstairs, she did not know whether to be thankful or furious.

'What time do you call this?' she demanded, as he walked into the kitchen. 'Your supper's spoiled – I've been worried sick!' Then she broke off, for he had a strange look on his face and was giving her a sly, secret smile.

'I've had a bit of luck,' he said. 'I got something to show you, down in the shop. Come and see what I've found.'

'What are you talking about?' she asked fearfully, as he beckoned her to him. 'What have you found?'

'Treasure,' he said, and now his smile was triumphant.

She shrank back from him. 'If it's a drowned man, I don't want to know about it. I don't want to see it.'

'Don't be afeared, it ain't a deader,' he told her. 'It's a surprise for you. You'll like it.' He held his hand out. Slowly and fearfully she went to him. He took her by the arm, leading her down the creaking wooden stairs.

Down below, in a patch of lamplight, she saw a bundle on top of the shop counter, a bundle that might have been a bag of old clothes. But it had not been dragged from the river, for there was no puddle of water around it. Reassured, she moved closer then stopped, frozen with horror, for the bundle moved slightly.

'It's alive!' she exclaimed.

'Alive and kicking,' he said. 'Come and look.'

She allowed Saul to take her still closer. He unfastened the wrappings – an old blanket and a torn piece of flannelette – and she gave a cry of amazement as a foot appeared, a small foot and a chubby leg. Saul pulled aside the flannelette, and Gloria saw a baby's face looking up at her.

'It's a boy,' Saul told her. 'I found him on the mud-flats at low tide. Some woman must've abandoned him, God forgive her.'

'Wasn't there any name? A note pinned to the blanket?'

'Nothing. I was going to take him to the police, but then I thought, what if I do? They'll only send him to the orphanage. What this kid needs is a proper home, a Mum and a Dad to love him and look after him.'

She stared at her husband. 'You and me?'

'What's wrong with you and me?' he asked. 'Like you said, I'm not much of a one for God and churchifying and all that, but if you ask me, this baby's been sent to us. I reckon as how we're meant to keep him and raise him as our own. I reckon it's like an answer to prayer.'

·——21——·

The air was warm and soft with the smell of freshly-ironed clothes. For Ruth, Sunday afternoon was the best time of the week. After the Watermen closed in the afternoon, she was free to do whatever she wanted until they re-opened at seven. Six months after Daniel's birth, she was still living above the pub. It was convenient to have the baby close at hand when she was working in the bar, and Mary was always happy to keep an eye on her grandson.

Now, while Danny slept off his midday feed, Ruth finished some ironing and folded it ready to put away. Mary came into the back-kitchen, and asked immediately, 'You're never thinking of moving back with him to Meadow Lane?'

'No, why?'

'I see you're sorting that washing into two different piles. I thought maybe you were going to take one lot back to your own flat?'

'Oh, no. I'm just making up a bundle of baby-clothes to take round to my cousin Gloria. Danny's got more than he needs since everyone's been so generous, and I believe Gloria's having a hard time to look after her own baby.'

'What's that? Are you telling me Gloria and Saul Judge have a baby now?' Mary was astonished. 'Heavens above, I didn't even know she was in the family way.'

Briefly, Ruth explained the situation. When Saul found the child abandoned on the mud-flats, they applied to adopt it, and were given permission to bring it up as their own. As Ruth picked up the sleeping Daniel, she concluded: 'Seeing that the rain's holding off, I thought I'd call round and visit them this afternoon.'

'Imagine! To think of them two rearing a child in that ramshackle old place.' Mary shook her head disapprovingly. 'It doesn't seem right at all.'

'Oh, Cyclops Wharf isn't so bad. Gloria's brightened it up a good deal since she moved in. And they're both so happy about the baby – it's made all the difference in the world.'

'Let's hope you're right. I can't picture that young woman bringing up an infant,' said Mary darkly; there had never been any love lost between her and Gloria. 'Is it a boy or a girl?'

'A boy.' Ruth paused, then added, 'I was thinking just the other day, I've known four babies born in the last couple of years. There was Sarah Kleiber's Benjamin, Maudie Judge's Trevor, our Danny, and now Gloria's baby – and they've all been boys . . . isn't that strange?'

Mary said quietly, 'Not so very strange, perhaps. When you think of the number of young men out in France now, getting themselves killed, it seems like the good Lord above is trying to right the balance.'

Ruth managed to transfer Daniel to his pram without waking him, and began to put on her hat and coat.

'Have they given the child a name yet?' Mary wanted to know.

'Yes. They've called him Matthew, after Saul's father,' said Ruth, fixing her hat in place with two long pins. 'Matt for short. Of course, nobody can tell exactly when he was born, but he seems to be more or less the same age as Danny.'

As Ruth opened the back door to wheel the pram out, Patrick came in from the yard, where he had been stacking crates of empty bottles.

'Where are you off to?' he asked.

'A little trip across the Island to visit my cousins at Cyclops Wharf,' Ruth told him.

He frowned. 'Do you think you should?'

'Why not? Danny needs a breath of fresh air, and if it should start to rain, I can put the hood up. He won't come to any harm.'

'I wasn't thinking of the weather,' said Patrick uncomfortably. 'Suppose there should be an air-raid while you're out?'

'Oh, I'm sure there won't be any raids this afternoon,' Ruth said lightly.

'You can't be sure of anything these days. Didn't you hear, the old Black Swan in the Bow Road had a bomb land on top of it last night. Wiped out altogether, it was. Totally destroyed.'

'Well, if there's a warning, I'll take Danny into a shelter till the all-clear. You mustn't worry about us.'

'I can't help worrying. I knew the landlord of the Black Swan and his wife. Fine, decent people they were, God rest them. It's terrible to think – one minute they were safe and sound, and the next . . .' His hands were shaking, and he stuffed them into his pockets.

'Then you must try not to think of it,' Mary advised him. 'Aren't you going up for your afternoon nap?'

'I suppose so, though I doubt I'll be able to close my eyes.' He shuffled across the room, and they heard him making his way slowly up the stairs.

Mary turned to Ruth defensively. 'He's not afraid for himself, you understand. It's for you and Danny – for all of us. He gets so tired, nowadays. He tries to do so much, it's wearing him out.'

'I know. I wish I could find another man to help with the heavy work, but that's pretty well impossible.'

'And if you could, he'd not thank you for it. He doesn't like to admit he's getting old, none of us do. You have to make allowances.'

When Corporal Ebenezer Judge awoke at dawn, he could not at first remember where he was, but then it all came back to him in a rush. The Battalion had made a strategic withdrawal from the front line, that thin, straggly line along the banks of the Somme which had proved too costly to maintain. The remnants of the Battalion had fallen back, taking up defensive positions among the farmlands and villages of Picardy. Ebenezer's platoon were now bivouacked under canvas in the remains of an apple orchard, though Eb himself had commandeered a small barn as his billet. Built of sturdy brick, with a steeply-tiled roof, it kept out the wind and the rain better than any khaki bell-tent.

Roused, Eb pulled himself up on his right elbow and listened for the sound that had woken him. Could it have been a rumble of thunder? No, when it came again he recognised the sound at once. German howitzers . . . Another artillery attack

324

had begun. All this went through his head within a few seconds, but then he realised that something else was happening: something inexplicable, and more alarming.

He was finding it hard to breathe – he was almost suffocating.

There was only one grimy window in the barn, and that did not open. Before he settled down for the night, he had made sure the door was fastened and bolted securely. It must be very stuffy in here to give him this sensation of breathlessness. He needed some air – quickly.

As he scrambled out of the blankets and the paillasse he tried to take some deep breaths, filling his lungs, and then he noticed a peculiar smell, like rotting hay or sour fruit. It must have been something the farmer had stored in the barn, though it was puzzling that he had not been aware of it last night.

Dragging back the bolts, he swung the heavy door wide open – and stood transfixed. There were men of his platoon lying sprawled in the long grass, men who had collapsed as they tried to leave their tents – men crawling – men coughing – men choking . . . and the grass was no longer green, but black.

One look at the horrific scene was enough. He recalled a lecture he had attended on chemical warfare. There was something called phosgene which smelled of musty hay or green apples. The grass, the orchard, the men of his platoon were all being destroyed by a poison-gas attack.

Some of his comrades were already dead or dying. Others, half-alive, saw him in the doorway and tried to call for help, holding out their hands to him, dragging themselves laboriously through the blackened grass. Without a moment's hesitation, Ebenezer Judge stepped back and slammed the door shut, ramming the bolts home; then he soaked his towel in the water-jug and put it over his face, shielding his eyes, his nose and mouth.

He would be safer in the barn than outside in the orchard with those poor wrecks. The gas was much less strong in here – if he sat very still, trying to breathe as little as possible, he might be all right.

A faint banging at the door startled him, then the noise of fingernails scrabbling at the wood, trying to wrench the door open. He heard a horrible sound, something between a cry for help and a gut-rending, retching cough – a sound that was barely human.

Eb did not move, or attempt to reply. He knew he must concentrate on his own survival. Sweating with fear, he tried to remember the words of a prayer, pleading for deliverance, and almost immediately, his prayer was answered.

There was a blinding flash and an explosion so loud, it made his ears ring. He was aware of more light, a patch of grey sky suddenly revealed above his head, and a shower of bricks and brick-dust, falling tiles and rubble, as the shell blew the roof apart. Then he slipped back into darkness and knew no more.

When he came to, he did not know how long he had been lying there unconscious. He was not in pain; he felt nothing at all. Around him, there was silence, but it was not a total silence for he could hear the faint ticking of a clock – a homely, reassuring sound – and he realised that he was not under a heap of debris in a derelict barn. He was lying on a mattress between cool, clean sheets, with his head resting on a soft pillow.

'Thank God,' he thought. 'Oh, thank God – I've been dreaming again. It was a bad nightmare, but now it's over. I was asleep, and now I'm awake, but where am I?' Puzzled, he opened his eyes.

There was a single light, dimmed by a blue shade, in the middle of the ceiling and he could just make out the face of a big clock on the wall opposite his bed. Twenty past three – it must be the middle of the night. Still only half-awake, he tried to sit up, and automatically leaned on his right elbow.

That was when he remembered.

In one shattering instant of revelation, as the pain exploded within him and he slumped sideways, half in and half out of the bed, he knew he could never again lean upon his right arm, for his right arm had been amputated just above the elbow.

The pretty VAD on night-duty, who had been writing up her notes at a desk in the middle of the ward under the blue-shaded light, heard him cry out and hurried to his bedside.

'You're all right, Corporal. You'll be all right,' she whispered, as she helped him to settle back against the pillows, and he began to choke, gasping for air to fill his ruined lungs.

326

'Bad dream.' He heaved out the words between spasms. 'Nightmare.' She wiped the sweat off his forehead, and waited until he became a little calmer. 'Only it wasn't a nightmare,' he managed to say at last, when he had recovered his breath. 'It was true. All of it – true.'

On Monday afternoon, while the pub was shut, Ruth took Danny out in his pram again. They did not have such a long journey this time, skirting Jubilee Wharf and the Rope Walk and making for the corner grocery.

Looking through the shop window, Ruth was surprised to see Maudie behind the counter. She left the pram out on the pavement and carried Danny inside, saying, 'Hello! I didn't know you were working in the shop these days.'

'I don't as a rule, only Mrs Judge and Aunt Florrie have got things to sort out, so I said I wouldn't mind. As long as Trev's asleep he won't be any bother, and when Tom gets home I expect he'll look after him.'

Trevor was stuffed into a high-chair beside her, fast asleep, his head lolling and his plump cheeks smeared with chocolate. Secure in Ruth's arms, Danny looked down at his second cousin in a lordly way, but showed no desire to be reunited with him.

'So my mother isn't here today?' Ruth asked.

'No, she does her washing Mondays.'

'Of course, I should have realised.' Ruth sighed. She had been looking forward to seeing her mother, but of course Monday had always been washing-day, as far back as she could remember. 'Well, perhaps I should go in and have a word with Aunt Emily, if she's not too busy?'

Maudie lowered her voice. 'They're in a bit of a state,' she said confidentially. 'Aunt Florrie's had a letter from Tom's Dad.'

Ruth took Danny into the back room, where Emily and Florrie were seated at the table with cups of tea.

'Ruth dear!' Emily looked up, rather flustered. 'There now, how nice of you to call in— Florrie, fetch down another cup and saucer from the dresser and pour Ruth some tea, will you? There's still plenty left in the pot.'

Ruth pulled up another chair and joined them. Danny sat on her lap, watching everything that went on with a grave, unblinking stare.

When Florrie passed her a cup of slightly stewed tea, Ruth thanked her, then added, 'Maudie tells me you've heard from Eb. That's nice.'

Florrie's lips trembled. Ruth realised she had been crying, and was still on the verge of tears.

'Is something wrong?' she asked. 'It's not bad news?'

Florrie nodded, unable to speak, and passed her a crumpled sheet of lined paper, written almost illegibly in violet indelible pencil.

'Poor Ebenezer,' said Emily.

Ruth smoothed out the letter and read: *Dear Florrie, Please excuse writing, as I am trying to use my left hand which does not come natural to me. You will see from above address I am in the Military Hospital at Brentwood. I was badly wounded in a dawn raid on our lines, more than a month ago now, and have been sent home to recover as far as poss before receiving my papers of discharge . . .*

'Discharge?' Ruth looked up eagerly. 'He's going to get out of the Army?'

Emily gave her a warning look. 'It's not exactly good news, dear. You'd better read the rest of it.'

The letter continued: *On account of having been badly gassed, and having lost my right hand and most of my right arm, so His Majesty does not require my services any longer. If the journey to Brentwood is not too difficult, I would like to see you and the boy, but if not the MO says I will be fit enough to be discharged within a week or two, and then I shall be coming home. I will try to write again when I know the date for certain. With best wishes to all, Yours affct., Ebenezer.*

Slowly, Ruth put down the letter. 'I'm so sorry,' she said at last. 'What a dreadful thing to happen.'

Florrie blew her nose, and spoke in a high tremulous voice. 'Emily says he'll learn to use his left hand, but he doesn't say much about the other thing – being gassed, and all that, so we don't know how bad he is.'

328

'They do say you never recover from it, not properly,' chimed in Emily. 'He may never be fit to work again.'

'I'll look after him,' said Florrie, wiping her eyes. 'The boy and me, we'll make a good home for him and do whatever has to be done.'

She broke off as Maudie came into the room, hand in hand with Tom. He had just got home from school, and still had his cap on. 'What's happened?' he asked. 'Maudie says Dad's been wounded – is it true?'

'Take your cap off, there's a good boy,' said Emily. 'And I hope you wiped your feet. We don't want you tramping mud all over the floor with your boots, do we?'

'Sorry, Auntie.' Impatiently, he snatched off his cap then turned back to his mother. 'What is it, Mum? What's going on?'

Florrie tried to tell him as well as she could, but her voice betrayed her. She broke down again before she could explain completely, and Emily came to her rescue.

'The doctor says your father will be home in a few weeks, so we shall all have to help get the house clean and tidy for him, and give him a hero's welcome.'

'The house? You mean – he's going back to our house?'

'Of course he is. Where else could he go?'

'But we're living here now . . .' The words died on Tom's lips.

'Don't be silly, Tommy.' Florrie took a deep breath. 'That was only while your Dad was in the Army. Now he's coming back to us, we can all live at home again, won't that be nice?'

'Mum, I asked you not to call me Tommy!' He lifted his head, trying to make himself as tall as possible. 'I think I ought to stay here, with Aunt Emily and Maudie and little Trev. They need a man in the house to look after them.'

Emily and Florrie smiled indulgently, and Emily said, 'That's very kind of you, dear, but you have to go to your own home now, with your family. That's where you belong.'

Tom Judge turned his head and looked helplessly at Maudie; the anguish in his face was reflected in hers – but neither of them spoke. There was nothing they could possibly say.

329

· ——22—— ·

'The end of the world . . . that's what it is.'

On the last Sunday in October 1916, Ruth had gone to visit her brother Ebenezer's house for the first time since she had walked out of the Judge family. In four years, she had never had any wish to visit Eb, for she knew that she would not be welcome there, but today was different. Now he had been discharged from the Army at last and sent home from hospital, wounded and severely disabled, she felt she had to see him and make some attempt at a reconciliation.

Knowing that it would not be an easy meeting, she had left Daniel with her mother-in-law. Unencumbered by the perambulator, she was walking quickly through the darkening streets as the wintry sun set and the light thickened, when a high-pitched voice arrested her – a woman's voice, hoarse with fear. 'Look! Look at that! The world is coming to an end.'

At the corner of Jubilee Street, a little group of people stood gazing at the sky, awed and alarmed.

Ruth looked up to see what they were staring at – and gasped. In the western sky, a strange cloud formation glowed in the last rays of the sun – an extraordinary mass of cumulus, shaped like a gigantic cross.

One of the bystanders was the blind ballad-singer, whom Ruth had often seen wandering through the streets, and he was asking urgently: 'What is it? What can you see?'

'Clouds, in the west – like a crucifix,' she told him. 'Like a huge cross, made of opals.'

As soon as the words left her mouth, she scolded herself for such thoughtlessness. How could a blind man know what an opal looked like? But he was no longer listening. Throwing back his head, he began to intone a passage from St Matthew's gospel: *'And then shall appear the sign of the Son of Man in the heavens – and then shall all the tribes of the earth mourn . . .'*

'I said so,' the woman repeated hysterically. 'The end of the world!'

'No.' Ruth tried to calm her. 'It's only clouds, that's all. There's nothing to be afraid of.' But as she walked on down Jubilee Street to the house where Eb and Florrie lived, the little group was still standing there, watching the sky.

Tom opened the front door, saying flatly, 'Oh, it's you. Come in.'

'How are you, Tom?' she asked, walking into the tiny hallway.

'I'm all right, I s'pose,' he replied in the same dull tone, but she could not help noticing that he looked pale and thin. 'Dad's in the bedroom – Mum's sitting with him. You'd better go up.'

She mounted the steep, narrow staircase to the front room on the first floor and found Florrie sitting by the bedside, knitting. In the bed was a man whom she scarcely recognised. If she had seen him in the street, she would have passed him without a second look, unless she had paused to wonder how such a sick man could be up and about.

Eb was leaning against a pile of pillows, reading a daily newspaper. He looked up as Ruth entered and stared at her, his face gaunt and haggard, his cheeks sunken, his eyes feverishly bright. He held the paper in his left hand, for the right sleeve of his nightshirt hung limp and empty at his side. Opening his mouth, he forced out the syllables with an effort. 'So, it's Ruth,' he said, and his voice was a breathless thread of sound.

'Hello, Eb,' said Ruth. She kissed Florrie, then held out her hand to her brother. He let the newspaper fall, the pages slithering over the counterpane and on to the floor.

'Other hand,' he directed impatiently. 'Shake – left hand – now.'

She changed hands quickly; his palm felt dry and flaky. 'I'm very sorry,' she said simply.

'What for?' He tried to speak, choked slightly, then began again. 'What – you got to be – sorry for?'

'I'm sorry to see you like this,' she answered. 'But I'm glad you're home again.'

'He's getting better all the time,' piped up Florrie. 'Of

331

course he gets tired, as talking takes it out of him, but he gets up for an hour or so each day. The doctor says he'll soon be well enough to go over to Emily's.'

'To visit Aunt Emily? That's nice.'

'Not visiting, working!' Eb corrected her irritably. 'Father says – best thing all round. Mind the shop – manage the business.'

Ruth was bewildered. 'You're going to manage the grocery shop?'

'Isn't it wonderful how things work out?' Florrie was determined to look on the bright side. 'After all, that shop's been a burden to poor Emily for a long time now. It was Mr Judge's idea – Eb's going to learn the ropes, and take it over gradually.'

'Doesn't Aunt Emily mind?' Ruth asked.

'I think she's relieved. It's time she handed over to someone younger. She'll still live over the shop, of course, with Maudie and little Trev, but she can take things easy now. It'll all be for the best in the long run.'

'All for the best.' Eb's face twisted into the caricature of a smile. 'Mud and blood – Flanders fields – gassed – amputated. All for the best.'

His heavy eyelids drooped, and Ruth wondered what images he was seeing in his mind's eye. Searching for another topic of conversation, she told them about the unusual cloud formation, and the people who regarded it as an omen.

'End of the world?' Eb spoke without opening his eyes. 'That's not to come – already here – seen it myself.' His voice was fainter than ever, and Ruth had to strain her ears to hear him. 'Time of tribulation. Abomination of desolation. Seen it – own eyes . . .'

Silence fell, broken only by the rattle of Eb's breathing; then Ruth said, 'Well, like I say, I'm glad you're home again. And I'm sure you'll do very well at the shop. You were always a good organiser.'

He opened his eyes at that. 'I'll manage,' he said. 'Not much of a job, though, for a man. Never thought I'd end up – shopkeeper . . .'

'I never thought I'd finish up managing a public-house,' said Ruth lightly.

'Different altogether. You chose your way of life . . . I've no choice.'

'Yes, well, if there's anything I can do.' She was determined to remain on good terms with her brother. 'I mean, if you need any help?'

He would not accept her offer of friendship. 'Don't bother, I'll manage,' he repeated shortly. 'You go your way – I'll go mine. Needn't trouble yourself coming here again.'

So that was that. She had done her best; she would not make that mistake a second time.

As the year ran its course, she kept to her own part of the Island and did not try to see her family. With the approach of Christmas, the Watermen was busier than ever and she had no time to think of anything else, until one morning she met her mother in the street market and insisted on taking her back to the pub for a cup of tea and a chat.

'I suppose you came this way because the fish is so much fresher?' she teased her.

Louisa took little Daniel on her lap, saying firmly, 'None of your nonsense! I came to see my grandson – and you. It's been a long while, Ruth.'

'Yes. Last time I came over, Eb made it pretty clear I wasn't welcome.'

'Oh, don't pay any attention. Eb's like that with everybody. The bad time he had in France has left him very bitter – you can't wonder at it.'

Ruth shook her head. 'Eb's always been the same with me, you know we never got on. How's he settling in at the shop?'

'He's making a go of it. Whatever you think of Eb, you must admit he's got a head for business. Emily's so soft-hearted, she was always letting customers have things on tick, running up bills they could never pay. Eb's put a stop to all that.'

'I'm sure he has,' said Ruth dryly. 'But how is he in himself? In his health, I mean?'

'He manages very well, considering. It's amazing how he's got used to being left-handed. Of course, his lungs will never be cured, but Florrie takes good care of him. In a way, I think she's happier now than she was before. Looking after him has given her something to be proud of.'

Ruth had put out a plate of digestives, and now Louisa dipped the edge of a biscuit in her tea to soften it, then offered it to Daniel, who gurgled with delight.

'Mum! You'll spoil him!' exclaimed Ruth. 'You never let us do that when we were little.'

'Of course not – I made sure my children were properly brought up, but it's different with grandchildren,' said Louisa, her eyes twinkling. 'He's a lovely boy, aren't you, Danny? He's got his father's looks . . . Have you heard from him lately?'

'Yes, I have. I got some good news only the other day. They're giving him some leave, so he'll be home for Christmas. Sean will be able to see his son at last.'

The first time Sean saw Daniel, the little boy was in his cot, fast asleep.

'He's bigger than I thought. Handsome little devil, isn't he?' Sean stooped to get a closer look, and his shadow fell across the child's face; Daniel frowned and stirred in his sleep. 'Will I pick him up?'

'Wait till he's awake. If you disturb him now, we'll never get him off again,' Ruth advised him.

'Ah, who cares? I want to talk to him! He's my boy, damn it – I've been waiting a long time for this.'

Disregarding Ruth, Sean pulled back the cot-blankets and picked Danny up. Ruth tried to be patient; he had just got back after a long, difficult journey – and he had kept himself warm with frequent nips of brandy, smuggled through from France. He was not exactly drunk, but he was certainly not sober.

'Thanks for the presents you sent us,' Ruth said. 'The filigree brooch and the woolly rabbit.'

'Oh, is that what they were? I didn't have much chance to go hunting round shops, so I gave Con the money and asked him to see to it.'

'Oh, I see. Well, thank you anyway.' She made a move to take Danny from him, but Sean lifted the child high out of her reach.

Daniel awoke to find himself in mid-air, held by clumsy, unfamiliar hands, a stranger's face only inches from his own

334

and the rank smell of brandy on a stranger's breath. He struggled, and began to cry.

'Hey, now! What sort of a welcome d'you call that? Don't you know me, Danny-boy? I'm your Da, so I am! Aren't you going to say hello?'

Once more Ruth tried to take him. 'Better let me have him.'

'Leave us alone, woman, he's got to learn to know me!' As Daniel continued to howl, Sean said crossly, 'Can't he do anything but cry?'

'He's only nine months old – be gentle with him.'

'Sure I'll be gentle! We're going to play games, my son. Come and sit on my lap – ride a cock-horsie!' Sean sat on the edge of the bed, dandling the baby on his lap. Daniel went on crying, reaching out for his mother.

'He's fretful because he woke up suddenly. Let me put him down and try to get him off again. He'll be fine in the morning, after a night's rest.'

Rebuffed and sulky, Sean handed the child over. 'Very well, have it your own way. I'm pretty tired meself after the travelling – what d'you say we have an early night?'

While Ruth was settling Danny back in his cot, Sean began to get undressed, flinging his boots, khaki tunic, khaki breeches and shirt to the four corners of the room. Ruth felt the baby flinch at every thud and crash as Sean got ready for bed, but she said nothing.

They had not slept together for nearly eighteen months, and Ruth was hoping that their first night together would be a happy one. Instead, it was a disaster. Sean's love-making was as crude and selfish as ever and to make matters worse, Daniel could not settle down again. Each time Sean was about to reach his climax of relief and satisfaction, Danny woke and started to yell. Each time, Sean cursed, while Ruth apologised and scrambled out of bed, pulling her nightdress around her, trying to calm the child.

Eventually Sean lost the desire to make love, and the ability to do so. Furious and frustrated, he demanded: 'Doesn't that bloody kid ever shut up?'

Resisting the temptation to say, 'I told you so,' Ruth answered, 'I'd better sit and nurse him till he goes off. You

335

have a rest, Sean. I'll come back to bed presently.' By the time Daniel had calmed down and fallen asleep, Sean himself was dead to the world, and snoring.

The next day, the brewery dray arrived with the new delivery and Ruth was kept busy. Sean had volunteered to help out in the public bar and she hardly saw him all the morning, until the afternoon closing-time, when she went to tell him his dinner was ready.

She found Patrick on his own in the public, locking the front door, and saying, 'Sean's gone down to the cellar. Kathie said she had some trouble changing over to a new barrel, so Sean offered to fix it.'

When Ruth went down the cellar steps, holding the hand-rail very firmly, she heard smothered giggles and a moment later found Sean holding up a sprig of mistletoe in one hand, his other arm round Kathie's waist as he snatched a kiss.

When he saw Ruth, he grinned sheepishly and said, 'Old-established custom. Compliments of the season and all that . . .'

Kathie tucked her blouse back into her waistband and straightened her collar, adding, 'Merry Christmas, Mrs O'Dell.'

'And a Happy New Year to you too,' said Ruth. 'Your dinner's on the table, Sean, don't let it get cold.' As she went back up the stairs, she thought,

'He'll never change. I was a fool to think he might . . . and the worst of it is, I don't even care any more.'

Oddly enough, things were easier after that.

The Watermen closed at three o'clock on Christmas Day, then the O'Dells had a traditional Christmas dinner. After-wards, Patrick and Mary went up to their room for a rest.

Left alone together in the back kitchen, Sean sat in his shirtsleeves, a glass of beer in his hand, while at the other side of the fire Ruth darned his socks. They were the very picture of a happily married couple. Now that she had given up hoping for a fairy-tale romance, she no longer felt unhappy. When she and Sean finally made love, it meant no more to her than a brief moment of frenzy, but they were not arguing any more. It could have been far worse, she decided.

'Do you ever think of me, when I'm off in France?' he asked lazily, watching the darning-needle plying to and fro.

'Of course. I try to imagine what it must be like for you, out there.'

'How would you know what it's like?' He took a long swig of his beer. 'They don't print the truth in the newspapers over here, that's for sure.'

'Perhaps not, but we do get some idea. Last July I read about the great battle of the Somme; that was what they called the Big Push, wasn't it? They said it was a glorious victory.'

'That's a load of rubbish.' Sean drained the last drops and wiped the foam from his lips. 'If you're really interested, it was a bloody massacre. The War Office tells you nothing but lies. D'you know, in one single day of that glorious victory, we lost sixty thousand lads? The fighting went on right up to November, and I heard tell there's been more than a million men lost, all told – French and English . . . It's nothing but a slaughter-house.'

Ruth put aside her darning, deeply shocked, not only by these terrible facts but by the casual, matter-of-fact tone in which Sean referred to them.

'I'm sorry,' she said at last, realising how feeble the words must sound to him. 'I had no idea.'

'Of course not. They don't print things like that in your newspapers.'

'But it can't go on like that, surely? What's going to happen? How will it all end?'

'Maybe it will never end. I reckon they've reached a kind of deadlock; there'll be no victory in this war. It will go on for ever, or until there's no men left on either side.'

There was a long moment of silence, and then Ruth asked: 'How is Connor getting on? You don't say much about him – is he all right?'

Sean uttered a mirthless bark of laughter. 'My big brother's all right, never you fear! He's not out in France, with the shells bursting around him. He's safe and sound in Blighty. You'd best not mention it to the old folks, 'cos it might hurt their feelings, but Con's been over here for weeks now.'

Ruth stared at him incredulously. 'Here? What do you mean?'

Sean explained ironically. 'Seemingly he's such a first-class sportsman, they can't risk losing him to a stray bullet – the Battalion Boxing Champion is much too valuable for that. They sent him home to England, so he can go round giving demonstrations of his great skill. It's part of the recruiting drive, encouraging the youngsters to join up the minute they're old enough.'

'But they've got conscription now, they don't need volunteers.'

'The rate they're killing men off out there, they need everybody they can muster, believe you me. Haven't you seen the posters? – *Your Country Needs You!* They'll not stop till every last man and boy is in uniform; that's why our Con is doing his bit for the nation, touring round with a boxing show, just like the old days.'

After another silence, Ruth asked, 'But if he's in England, why hasn't he been to see us?'

'Search me! Maybe he's up north, or maybe he's found livelier company elsewhere. How should I know?'

A sudden rage boiled up in Ruth, and she burst out, 'We're his family! He can't treat us like that – I never heard such a thing! Christmas Day, and he can't be bothered to come and see his Mum and Dad, or to see his own nephew. How *dare* he?'

'Ask me another. Anyhow, it's not worth getting upset about.' Sean stood up. 'Con always was a law unto himself, you know that. I think I'll go and get meself another glass of beer.'

Soon after New Year's Day, 1917, Sean went back to France and life at the Watermen returned to normal.

It was bitterly cold that winter, and there was a shortage of coal. The O'Dells tried to economise as best they could, but they had to keep the kitchen range going to heat the water and the oven, so they put bricks at the back of the grates in the

338

public and the saloon, and only kept very small fires burning there.

'Put on another lump, there's a good girl,' one of the customers pleaded with Ruth. 'I've been outside on the Wharf all afternoon, and I'm perished through to me bones.'

'Just one knob of coal, then, I can't spare any more.'

She was about to pick up the tongs when she felt an extraordinary vibration that seemed to come up from the foundations, rocking the entire house. At the same instant a voice outside yelled: 'Come and look – look at the sky!'

Then came the explosion – a colossal bang, followed by a mighty rushing sound. Ruth thought the whole building was going to fall apart. Windows shattered and fell inwards, doors slammed, and from the street a dozen voices cried out in terror amid the crash of tiles falling to the pavement.

'My God, what was that?'

Most of the customers ran outside without stopping to think but Ruth's first thought was for Daniel, whom she had left in the kitchen, being bathed in front of the fire by Mary O'Dell.

She ran to make sure they were safe, and found Mary clutching the naked child to her breast. They were both unhurt, but her mother-in-law was white as a sheet. Patrick, nearer the window, had cut his hand on some flying glass and was holding his fingers outstretched, watching the blood dripping on to the floor, and saying stupidly, 'I've hurt me hand. I've cut meself.'

Ruth flung one of Danny's bath-towels at him, but he seemed too dazed to understand what it was for, so she wrapped the towel round his hand, saying, 'It's nothing, only a scratch. Nothing to worry about.'

Then she took Danny from his grandmother and finished drying him, wrapping him up in another warm towel.

'Do you think we should go down to the cellar?' asked Mary. She too seemed quite stunned by what had happened. 'It must be one of them Zeppelins – they'll maybe drop another bomb.'

'There was no air-raid warning,' said Ruth. 'I don't believe it was a bomb.'

Daniel appeared to be more surprised than frightened, so

she threw a blanket round him, holding him very close, and followed the customers out into the street.

Every house had suffered some damage from the blast. Hardly a window was left unbroken, and there were gaping holes where tiles had fallen from the roofs, and some doors and windows had been blown out of their frames, hanging drunkenly askew. It was nearly seven o'clock, and at this time of year it should have been dark, but over the rooftops, towards the east, the sky was an amazing spectacle – all the colours of the rainbow, from indigo, blue and green through yellow to deepest crimson.

Ruth remembered the clouds shaped like a cross that she had seen a few months earlier, and wondered, could this really be the end of the world? Was this the way it would happen?

As she watched, the swirling colours faded and settled into a continuous glow of red and orange, the colours of flame. The crowd in the street stared up, their dazed faces reflecting the unearthly light. Ruth heard someone say, 'Must be the worst fire ever. Worse than the Great Fire of London.'

Eventually, as they realised nothing more was going to happen, people moved on and the long business of clearing up began. The night was filled with the sound of tinkling glass being swept up, and the staccato rhythm of hammering as temporary shutters were nailed over empty window-frames.

Inside the Watermen, Ruth, Mary and Kathie did their best to make the place habitable. A lot of tumblers and beer-mugs had fallen from the shelves at the moment of the explosion, and Kathie had dropped a full bottle of whisky, but they had been spared any serious damage. Ruth found a piece of chalk and scrawled across the front door: *Open As Usual – Wide Open!*

One by one, the customers drifted back, ordering large drinks and lifting their glasses in shaking hands. 'What was it?' they asked each other. 'Was it a bomb? Was it sabotage?'

Gradually, during the evening, the news came through. It was not easy to sort out wild rumours from hard facts, but it seemed that the explosion had occurred in a factory at Silvertown, a couple of miles away, across a double loop of the river. The Brunner-Mond plant, manufacturing caustic soda, had been instructed to adapt their refinery to the production of TNT – high explosive, to make munitions.

340

From the start, a great many people had raised objections; it was dangerous work under any circumstances, and doubly dangerous when such a process was carried out in the middle of a densely-populated area, close to a busy wharf and surrounded by other factories – a soap works, a sugar refinery, a flour-mill. When the melting-pot exploded, a mass of blinding white flame had gushed out – flame that seemed to possess a life of its own – a terrifying mass of pure energy, suddenly released, engulfing the entire neighbourhood.

During the hours that followed, the Islanders heard the sound of alarm-bells ringing as ambulances and fire-engines made their way to the scene of the disaster. Later, they saw little groups of people stumbling along the streets like sleep-walkers. Some were pushing prams or barrows laden with whatever they had salvaged from their wrecked houses, and others carried nothing at all, and did not know where they were going. One man, his clothes grey with dust and his face covered in dried blood, kept calling out every few yards, 'Janey? Jane, where are you? Janey, can you hear me?'

Towards the end of the evening, a police constable came into the pub, checking to see if they had any casualties.

'We're all right,' Ruth told him. 'Except my father-in-law still seems to be very shocked. He cut his hand on some broken glass – nothing else – but now he can't seem to understand what's happened. We've put him to bed, so perhaps he'll be all right tomorrow. I expect you could do with a drink, Constable?'

'I won't say no. I've been on the go ever since it happened.' The policeman took off his helmet and mopped his brow. 'It's been a shock for everybody, I reckon. Terrible tales we're getting back from Silvertown. It'll be a long time before they know how many are dead, or missing, or wounded. There's not a building left standing within a quarter-mile of the factory. Nothing left but rubble and twisted metal, they say.'

Ruth remembered Eb's words: '*The abomination of desolation* . . .' For the first time, she began to have some inkling of what they meant.

'And of course the effect of the blast covered a much wider

341

area – well, you know that already. All I can say is, you can think yourselves lucky you got off so light.'

The following afternoon, Ruth had finished cleaning up the mess and was glueing a sheet of plywood in the gaping kitchen window. Mary, who had just taken a cup of tea up to her husband, came downstairs and Ruth asked her, 'How's he feeling now?'

'A little better, I think, though he still doesn't seem to take in what's going on. It's as if he'd suddenly become very old, and very tired, all in a moment.'

As it was the middle of the afternoon, the pub was shut so they looked at each other in surprise when they heard the side-door open and shut, followed by footsteps along the passage.

'Who's there?' Mary called out. 'What do you want?'

'Hello, Mam,' said Connor, framed in the doorway. 'Hello, Ruth.'

He looked very smart in his uniform and Ruth felt her heart leap, as if the blood were suddenly racing more quickly through her veins.

'Con! I don't believe it! Oh, thank God.' Mary dissolved into tears of happiness, flinging her arms around him.

'I heard the news of the explosion last night. I was up in Coventry, but I managed to get leave at short notice and caught the first train I could this morning,' he said. 'I had to make sure you were all right.'

'I'm fine now,' Mary told him, trying to dash the foolish tears from her eyes. 'And it'll do your Da a power of good to see you. He'll be a new man, so he will. Come up and surprise him!' Halfway to the stairs she stopped, saying, 'Wait now – it might be too much for him, the state he's in. Maybe I'd best go first and break it to him gentle. Stay here below till I call you, son.'

She went on alone, and Con came back into the kitchen, frowning. 'What's wrong with the old man?' he asked.

'He's not been well. The raids were getting him down and now this, on top of everything else.' Ruth gestured at the boarded-up window. 'But I'm sure he'll be fine in a day or two.'

Connor came closer, then caught his breath as he saw

Daniel asleep in the cot by the fire. 'So this is my nephew,' he said softly.

'Yes, that's Daniel, taking his after-dinner nap.'

'He's a great wee man, and no mistake. I've been wondering for months how he'd look, but he's even better than I imagined.'

'If you were so interested, I'm surprised you didn't come to see for yourself,' said Ruth, turning away to get on with her work.

Con lifted his chin. 'Is it my imagination, or is the weather in here colder than outside?'

Ruth shrugged. 'Did you expect a warm welcome, when you couldn't even look in on us at Christmas? Don't bother to lie – Sean told me you were in England.'

'I wasn't intending to lie to you.' Connor gripped her wrist, pulling her to face him. 'Don't you know me better than that?'

Taken off-guard, Ruth let go of the glue-brush, which splattered on to the linoleum. 'Now look what you've made me do!' she exclaimed. 'I'll have to wipe that up before it dries.'

She fetched a rag and dropped to her knees, scrubbing at the smear of glue. Connor sat on the floor beside her and said awkwardly, 'I wanted to come home – I wanted it more than I can say, only I couldn't bring myself to do it.'

Concentrating on her task, she would not look at him. 'You were having a good time, I expect, wherever you were.'

'Did Sean tell you why they sent me back to England?'

'He said you were giving boxing demonstrations for the recruiting campaign, is that right?'

'So you do know. Can't you understand – I was too ashamed to show my face here.'

Now she turned to him, and found herself looking directly into those dark green eyes. 'Ashamed?' she repeated.

'All the other lads are still over in France, living under the threat of death each day while I'm on a cushy number in Blighty, having the best of everything. I heard how your brother got his discharge, and your cousin was killed in action. Nearly every family on the Island has lost a son or a brother or a nephew by now. What would they think of me, if I'd come sailing in without a scratch on me? I tell you, I couldn't face it.'

343

She had been looking into his eyes so deeply, she felt she would drown in them. With an effort, she stood up, carefully replacing the glue-brush in the gallipot. 'I see . . . I didn't realise.'

'Of course not, why should you?'

'But you're home now, that's the main thing.'

'I had to come. I had to make sure you were safe. I mean, Mam and Da – you and the boy . . .'

When she turned her head, he saw that she was smiling. 'We're fine,' she said. 'Don't stay away so long another time.'

His face creased into one of his rare, lop-sided grins. 'I won't. And that's a promise.'

He broke off as Mary bustled into the room, saying, 'I've told your Da, and he's like a dog with two tails! Come away upstairs and see for yourself.'

Con nodded to Ruth, then turned and followed his mother out of the room.

·——23——·

When the summer of 1917 came to the Island, it brought little relief.

The June weather was sultry, threatening storms, but though the nights were shorter there was no respite from air-attack, for the nightly Zeppelins had been followed by hit-and-run raids from small swift aeroplanes during the hours of daylight.

It was nearly midsummer, and when the sun rose over Cyclops Wharf, another child was crying.

In their sagging double bed on the third floor, Saul rolled over and groaned to Gloria, 'Can't you give him something to quieten him? How about some sugar-water?'

'It's not sugar-water he's crying for. He's hungry.'

'He's not the only one,' growled Saul. 'I'm hungry, you're hungry – we're all hungry.'

Gloria turned on him. 'Is that my fault? You told me once you had some money put by – what's happened to to that, I'd like to know?'

'Gone, all of it. We bin spendin' money faster'n I ever dreamed . . .' Then, as Matt cried again, Saul snapped impatiently, 'Ain't you going to do nothing for that kid?'

Wearily, she heaved herself out of bed and went into the adjoining room, returning a moment later with Matt in her arms. He was nearly eighteen months old now and big for his age, but his cheeks were sallow, and his long arms and legs were sadly thin. He was not crying with rage or grief or boredom; he was keeping up a plaintive demand for food. When Gloria took him into bed with her, he responded to the comfort and warmth of her body, reducing his complaint to a whimper.

'You think I'm a rotten housewife, don't you?' she asked Saul. ''Cos I can't make the money go as far as it used to. But

345

the prices in the shops are going up all the time. If you want meat, or butter, or eggs come to that, you've got to pay a small fortune. That is, when you can get them at all.'

'I'm not blaming you, Glory.' Saul punched his pillow savagely. 'We've got precious little money coming into the shop. I never knew trade so slow.'

She tried to console him. 'It's the same for everybody.'

'Don't talk daft. Look at Ruth – she's sitting pretty in that public-house, and Eb's doing all right for himself at the grocer's shop, by all accounts. They manage to keep the money coming in, so why can't we?'

'Ssh! Not so loud.' Gloria was stroking the child's head. 'He's dozing off at last.'

When Saul spoke again, his voice was quiet but determined. 'So it's up to me, then. All right, girl – I'm going out today, to make some money. I don't know how, but I'll not come back empty-handed. We'll have a decent supper tonight, you and me and the nipper. Just you wait and see.'

In Jubilee Street, old Bessie put the pea-shooter to her lips and directed a stream of split peas at an upper window. It was the first time the knocker-up had included Ebenezer Judge's house on her rounds, since Eb went into the Army. Now there was another member of the family needing an early-morning call.

Almost before the peas finished rattling against the window-pane, Tom Judge pushed up the sash and called out, 'All right, Bessie – thanks!'

He had been lying awake since four, tossing and turning in his bed: today was to be the first day of his new life. Impatiently, he finished dressing and ran downstairs. His mother was cutting sandwiches for his mid-day snack – doorsteps of bread, with slabs of cheese between them. He threw her a 'Good morning.'

Florrie said: 'Sit down and have your breakfast before it gets cold, there's a good boy.'

'I'm not hungry, Mum.'

'Do as you're told, dear, you can't go to work without some

food inside you. Besides, you'll get there too early if you set off now. The gates don't open till six.'

She had made him some porridge; he did not care for it at the best of times and today it stuck in his throat. Though he would never admit it, Tom was feeling rather sick, and very scared.

Florrie chattered on. 'It's very good of the Headmaster to let you off school before the end of term. I dare say he gave you special treatment on account of Dad being poorly.'

Now he was fifteen, Tom was old enough to start work. The authorities might have made him stay at school until the holidays, but Tom Judge was to be released early.

'I think Grandad wrote a letter to the school, saying he needs more help on the Wharf,' said Tom. 'Dad told me they have trouble finding enough men for all the shifts.'

'Yes, of course, it's important work,' agreed Florrie. 'Without the dockers unloading food off the boats, we'd very likely starve to death. Run up and say goodbye to Dad before you leave. He'd like to see you, on your first morning.' Ebenezer enjoyed the luxury of a lie-in until seven these days; he did not have to open the shop until eight.

Stuffing his packet of sandwiches in his jacket pocket, Tom went up to his parents' room. Sitting up in bed, Ebenezer held out his left hand. 'Behave yourself, boy,' he wheezed. 'Do as you're told, don't answer back and keep out of trouble.'

'I'll try, Dad.' Tom felt uncomfortable and tried to withdraw his hand. 'I'd better be going now. I don't want to be late on my first day.'

'Plenty of time – call you in last – swear you in before you start.'

Tom made his way through the empty streets, conscious of the cloth cap pressing down on his ears – it had been passed on to him by his father, and was two sizes too big – and wondered what was about to happen to him. Other boys at school with fathers or elder brothers working as stevedores, had dropped dark hints about cruel ceremonies, secret rituals, even threats of torture . . .

When he reached the gates, he found a small crowd already there. Some of them were boys about his own age, but the rest were men in their late thirties or forties. There was not one man there between the ages of seventeen and thirty.

At six o'clock a whistle blew, and the old iron gates squealed and swung open. The little crowd pressed forward as Marcus Judge appeared at the top of the steps outside the Wharf-master's Office. Another man, whom Tom did not know, pulled numbers from a bag and called them out. One by one, the men went forward to take their places on the working teams. When the numbers had all been called, Tom was the only one left. In these days of labour-shortage, there were jobs for everybody.

Marcus saw him standing there and descended the steps, lifting a beckoning finger. 'Come with me,' he commanded.

'Yes, Grandad,' began Tom dutifully.

His grandfather flashed a stern look from beneath beetling brows. 'When we are at work, you will address me as "sir", like the rest,' he said. 'You will receive no special treatment here, you understand?'

'Yes, sir.'

He led Tom along a narrow alley between the office buildings, and they entered a small, shadowy room. It was dark inside for there were no windows, just a grimy fanlight over the door.

'You will wait here,' said Marcus, and left the boy standing there while he went through a second door into an inner room.

Tom waited, a leaden lump of fear at the pit of his stomach. It was worse than being sent to the Headmaster at school, when you had done something wrong. He tried to remind himself that he was not a schoolboy now; he was a young man, setting out in the world – but he could not quite believe it. Straining his ears, he could hear a low mutter of voices beyond the inner door.

After some moments, it opened slowly, and a man said to him, 'Take off your cap. You may enter.'

Tom pulled his father's cap from his head and obeyed.

There was a semi-circular table facing him. Behind it sat nine men, and at the centre, in the place of honour, was Marcus Judge, who looked up and said, 'Come forward.' His voice seemed to rumble like distant thunder. 'What is your name?'

348

'Tom, Grandad. I mean, Tom, sir. I mean, Tom Judge.'

'Thomas Judge . . . do you wish to become a member of our Brotherhood?'

'Yes, sir.'

'Are you prepared to abide by the Rules and Regulations of our Guild?'

'Yes, sir.' Tom found that he was turning the cloth cap round and round in his hands; the coarse material was already damp with sweat.

'Are you prepared to swear an oath of silence, vowing never to repeat to any other person anything you may learn within our Brotherhood?'

'Yes, sir.'

'Very well.' Marcus snapped his fingers. 'Give him the book.'

The man who had admitted him put a book into Tom's hands, a Bible, so big and so heavy he nearly dropped it in his nervousness. The man drew in his breath sharply, then began, 'You will repeat after me: I, Thomas Judge . . .'

'I, Thomas Judge . . .'

'Do hereby solemnly swear . . .'

'Do hereby solemnly swear . . .'

'To obey all commands given to me by those in authority over me . . .'

The voice droned on for several minutes. Tom faltered once or twice as he recited the unfamiliar words, but he managed to get through the ritual without breaking down. At last they reached the closing phrases: '. . . And if I should ever break these solemn promises, I shall be duly punished for my misdeeds, and in the last resort expelled from this Guild and cast out into darkness, never again to be received within the Brotherhood. All this I swear by Almighty God . . . Amen.'

The Bible was taken away, and another man came towards him, saying sternly, 'Thomas Judge – hold out your hands.'

Tom did as he was told. With memories of school and echoes of Chapel in his head, he did not know if he was to receive a caning or a prayer-book. Instead he found himself holding two metal objects: a brass tally with a number on it and a curved, double spike with a wooden handle.

'Accept this tally – accept this claw – as the tools of your trade and the symbols of your membership. You have been admitted to our Guild; you may now go to work.'

Someone patted him on the back and turned him round to face the door. Dazed and breathless with relief, he stumbled out into the fresh air . . . Now he was one of the Brotherhood.

A few hours later, Ruth was coming back from the shops, wheeling Danny in his pram, when she heard the sirens begin to wail. The slow ascending moan made her uneasy, and she quickened her pace. Of course it might be just a false alarm – they happened often enough nowadays – but she could not take any chances while she had Danny with her. She still had some shopping left to do, for the local bakers had sold out of bread and that meant going all the way to the little bakery in Cubitt Town, but she could not risk that now.

Briskly, she began to head for home. A policeman on a bicycle swept past her, calling out, 'Take cover! Take cover, if you please – there's a raid on!'

'I know,' she said. 'I'm on my way home.'

The noise of the anti-aircraft guns made her jump – that meant the aeroplanes must be very near. She could see the Watermen now, safe and welcoming at the far end of the street: she had to get there as quickly as possible. Picking Danny up, she abandoned the pram and the shopping, and began to run.

Overhead, she saw puffs of white smoke and high above them, some small black specks moving across the sky. For a second she thought they were a flock of birds, but then she realised they were German aeroplanes – ten, fifteen – so many, she could not count them. She lowered her head and did not stop running until she reached the pub.

Down in the cellar, Mary had her rosary in her hands and her lips were moving while Kathie tried to persuade Patrick to drink a cup of tea. 'Go on, have a sip. It'll buck you up.'

They all looked up as Ruth came down the steps with Danny in her arms, and Mary exclaimed, 'Praise be! I was worried to pieces, wondering where you both were.'

'I was nearly home when the aeroplanes came over. I just left

350

the shopping in the pram and made a run for it . . . I can go back for them later.'

Patrick looked bewildered. He was becoming rather deaf, and found it hard to follow everything that was being said. 'What is it? What's happening?' he wanted to know.

'Just another warning,' Ruth told him, raising her voice. 'I don't suppose it'll come to anything.'

That was when the bombs began to fall. First one, then two in quick succession, and then another one – the loudest and nearest of all.

'What was that?' Patrick was starting to shake again. 'Are they bombing us now?'

'No, no,' Ruth lied to him. 'That's our own guns you can hear, keeping the Germans away.'

Kathie began to contradict her. 'They weren't guns. I heard the whistle of bombs coming down!'

Quickly, Ruth shut her up. 'The guns often make that kind of noise – it's nothing.'

Mary was silent, and when Ruth glanced at her, she saw that there were tears running down her cheeks. She turned her head so that her husband should not see her crying and whispered, 'I'm sorry, I can't help it. I've tried to have faith and trust in the Lord. I try to be brave, I do really . . . but I don't know how much longer we can carry on like this.'

At lunchtime, after the raiders had departed, the news began to come through. Some customers told Ruth that it had been one of the worst daylight raids yet, with bombs falling in the City of London, demolishing shops and office buildings and a bank at Bishopsgate.

'One of them sounded much nearer than that,' said Ruth.

'That's right. When I came through Poplar, there were roads closed and barriers up,' said another man. 'According to what I heard, the Huns dropped a bomb on a school in Upper North Street while the kids were at their lessons . . .'

All that day, the rumours ran like wildfire through the Island; tales of terrible casualties – of demolished buildings and slaughtered children – but no one knew anything for certain.

*

351

When the whistle blew again, Tom Judge was free to go home. Some of his workmates invited him to go with them, for they knew a place behind the warehouses where you could play pitch-and-toss for pennies without getting caught. Tom made his excuses. He couldn't stop – he was in a hurry.

'Running all the way home to tell tales to your Mum?' jeered one of the older boys. 'Telling her how her little darling got roughed up?'

Pretending not to hear, Tom set off quickly. He had a long way to go. He was not going home yet, and in any case, he would not tell anyone what had happened to him today.

When they stopped work for the midday break, Tom had settled down to eat his sandwiches, but he was not left to enjoy them in peace. He was soon surrounded by the other lads, who dragged him off to a deserted spot behind the coalyards and put him through their own initiation ceremony. They set on him and pummelled him, they daubed him with engine-grease and rolled him in the coaldust, and when they tired of that, they ducked him in a water-tank and left him to clamber out, soaked to the skin.

'Now you've been baptised as a member of the Brother-hood!' they told him.

It was meant as harmless fun; they had all been through the same thing, the day they joined the Guild. When Tom went back to work, still dripping, some of the older men grinned and the foreman asked how he got so wet.

'I fell in some water, sir,' answered Tom.

'Then you'd better look where you're going in future. As long as you keep working hard, you'll dry out soon enough.' And they all roared with laughter. No, Tom was not going to tell anyone about that.

Instead of returning to Jubilee Street he headed south towards the Island Gardens. He knew Maudie would be waiting for him – and there she was, under the trees, with Trevor in the push-chair. When Tom left the corner shop, they had made a pact. Every day since then, when it was fine, Maudie had come out with her small son for a walk in the Gardens and Tom had met them there after school. Today, she told Aunt Emily that the weather was too hot and muggy, and that she would take her walk after tea instead.

'You won't stay out too long, will you dear?' Emily asked anxiously. 'Don't forget – it's nearly Trevor's bedtime.'

'I won't stay out long,' said Maudie.

She could never stay very long. Their meetings were precious, for they were all she had now – but they were always brief.

As they strolled beneath the trees, Maudie said, 'Did you hear the bombs this morning? We went down into the shelter.'

'We didn't. The foreman told us we'd got to carry on working.'

'Somebody said they bombed one of the schools, and I kept thinking thank goodness you weren't at school any more. I'd have been worried sick all day wondering if you were all right.'

He smiled at her, and she slipped her arm through his, then wrinkled up her nose. 'Ugh, your coat's ever so damp,' she complained.

'Yeah, I got wet – but I'm near dry now. The job's a bit messy.'

'It sounds awful. I kept thinking about you – what was it like?'

'Bits of it were all right. I just kept telling myself: "This is better than school. I'm earning my living – this is a real job!" ' He took a deep breath and continued, 'I'm going to save up as much as I can, and then in a year or so, I'll be old enough to marry you. I've got it all worked out. We're going to find somewhere to live, Maudie – a home of our own, for you and me and Trev.'

She stopped and looked at him. 'You really mean that? You really want to marry me?'

'Course I do. There'll never be anyone else, only you.'

She longed to throw her arms round him, but somebody might be watching. They walked on along the path until they reached the gardener's shed, then strolled round it, and for a moment they were screened from view.

Only Trevor watched them, wide-eyed, as they clung together, kissing each other again and again – hungrily, desperately.

*

353

That evening, soon after the pub opened its doors, Ruth met Mary at the foot of the stairs. She had just been up to settle Danny for the night, and Mary enquired, 'Did he go off easy? I thought I heard him shouting once or twice.'

'He was a bit over-tired, I think. Anyway, he's out like a light now, so I'll take over the saloon, shall I?'

'Thanks. I'll go and sit with the old feller for a while, to keep him company.'

As they passed one another in the hallway, they heard the side-door opening – someone was coming in from the street. Ruth did not have to turn her head and look, she knew at once who it was.

'Con!' Mary was delighted to see her son, but she couldn't help scolding him. 'Why will you never tell us you're coming home, so we can make things ready for you?' Then her voice changed, and she gasped, 'Mother of God, whatever's happened to you?'

Ruth whirled round and saw Connor silhouetted against the evening sunlight, almost filling the narrow passage. Swaying slightly, he put a hand to the wall, steadying himself.

As he took a step towards them, she saw what Mary meant. His uniform was torn, covered in mud and dust, his face was grey with fatigue and there was a cut above his right eye. She felt suddenly angry, and turned on him indignantly.

'I can guess what's happened. You've been fighting, haven't you?'

His lips twisted into the ghost of a grin as he replied, 'You might say that. Is there any hot water? I need to clean up.'

He made a move toward the kitchen, but Mary stopped him. 'Don't go in there! If your Da saw you like that, it'd be the finish of him. Go up to your room. Ruth, fetch a jug of hot water, would you? And you'd best make his bed up while you're about it. I'll go back to keep an eye on the saloon till you're done.'

Con put down the kitbag he had been carrying on his shoulder. 'I've got a change of uniform here. All I want is a wash and brush-up, and get me head down for an hour or two, then I'll be fine.'

When Ruth went into his bedroom with the water-jug, she

354

found him stretched out on the bed, and a strange feeling swept over her. She had been through all this before . . . Then it all came flooding back: the first night she met Connor – the first time she had entered this room, after he had been beaten up. Nothing had changed.

'Just look at you!' she said bitterly. 'Getting dirt all over the counterpane. You couldn't even be bothered to take your boots off, could you? I suppose you'd been drinking.'

'Not a drop has passed me lips – honest to God.' With an effort, he pulled himself upright and began to unlace his boots.

'Is that so?' she retorted. 'Then how did you get yourself in such a state? What were you fighting about?'

'About six hours,' he said, mocking her questions.

'What do you mean? You can't have been in a fight for six hours!'

'Please, miss, it wasn't my fault. It was them other fellers started it,' he protested, in a parody of a whining schoolboy.

She frowned. 'Are you quite sure you haven't been drinking?'

Slowly, laboriously, he began to unfasten the brass buttons of his tunic. 'As heaven is my witness! It was the Germans began it – them and their bombers,' he continued, and Ruth realised that his slurred tone and clumsy movements were due to immense exhaustion. 'I'd just left the railway station this morning, and I was making my way here when the raiders came over. I was close to Upper North Street when the bomb fell.' He pulled his shirt over his head and she saw dark patches of blood staining the khaki, and then the jagged wound in his shoulder . . .

'You got hit by shrapnel! You've been hurt!'

'Nothing of the sort. It's only a bit of a cut – I'm right as rain.'

'How can you say that?' She took charge of the situation. 'Stay there and don't move while I go to the medicine cupboard. I'm going to clean that up before it turns septic.'

A few minutes later, she set to work. Connor sat on the edge of the bed, stripped to the waist, while she washed him with warm, soapy water and dried him with a soft towel. Then she applied the iodine, saying, 'This will sting for a while, but it can't be helped.'

She expected him to wince or curse, but he did not react in any way. He sat watching her as she finished the job, putting a piece of lint over the cut, and strapping it up with sticking-plaster.

'How does that feel?' she asked, when it was done.

'A whole lot better. You missed your vocation, Nurse,' he teased her. 'You'd have been another Florence Nightingale!'

'Don't talk nonsense. Now go and sit in that chair while I make up your bed. Oh, and you'd better finish undressing. That uniform will need washing and mending before it's fit to wear again.'

He stood up and faced the wall, unbuttoning his trousers. She turned her back on him, busying herself with clean sheets, blankets and pillowcases. Over her shoulder, she asked, 'Aren't you going to tell me what happened? You said you weren't hurt, but . . .'

'I wasn't. I'd not a scratch on me, but there was a whole crowd of folk running toward the place where the bomb landed. It had fallen on a school . . . I could hear the kids crying out, calling for help, so I went along with the rest to see what I could do. You never saw anything like it.'

She braced herself. 'Were there – many hurt?'

'Eighteen children killed outright. Twenty or thirty injured at the last count . . . They were the ones we got out of the wreckage.'

'You helped to rescue them?'

'We did the best we could. The trouble was, there were parts of the building left standing, but they were so shaky, you could see they'd come down any minute. There was an old galvanised iron roof hanging over the debris, with kids trapped underneath . . . I managed to get my back under it, to hold it up for a while until they dragged those kids out. When they were all safe, I let it fall, and – well, that must have been when I cut meself. We went on as long as we could, digging away the rubble, still searching.'

Ruth closed her eyes. 'I thought you'd been fighting.'

'So we were – all of us, fighting to save the kids. It took a hell of a time, that's why I'm feeling a bit done up . . .'

His voice wavered slightly. Turning, she saw that he was

leaning against the wall. An underlying pallor made his bronzed skin look greenish.

'The bed's all ready,' she said gently. 'Come and lie down.' He was almost naked, wearing nothing but a pair of underpants, but she felt no embarrassment as she helped him into bed. 'I'll bring you a hot drink, and then you can have a good rest,' she told him.

'Thanks, Ruth,' he said, lying back against the pillows. 'You're a pal.'

She smoothed back a lock of hair from his forehead. 'Last time you came home, you told me you felt ashamed to be safe in England. You don't have to be ashamed any more. Today, you were in the right place at the right time.'

Connor shook his head. 'Don't say that. I finally made up my mind – I asked to be released from duty over here, and sent into the front line. That's why I was on my way home, to see you all. I'm going back to France tomorrow.'

Ebenezer pulled out his pocket-watch and glanced at it; it would soon be time to shut the shop. He slipped down from his high stool behind the counter, about to call young Maudie in to put up the shutters. This was one of the jobs he could not do by himself, and he resented having to depend on the girl for help.

At that moment, the shop-bell pinged and the street door opened. He sighed, moving back to the stool. Trade had been slow today – he couldn't afford to turn away a last customer.

Then he saw who the customer was, and pursed his lips. 'Evening, Saul,' he wheezed. 'Don't often see you – these parts.'

'That's right.' Saul was looking along the shelves, filled with tins and jars. 'I'll help myself, shall I? Save you the trouble.'

Eb perched on the stool, watching him. Saul was carrying an old canvas bag, and now he began to fill it: a tin of corned beef, another of beans, a jar of pickled pork and a jar of plums . . . packets of sugar, of biscuits, of custard-powder.

'Pushing the boat out?' commented Eb curiously. 'Special occasion?'

'Feeding my family, that's all. Oh, and I want half a pound of that cheese, if you'd be so good.'

Ebenezer drew the cheese-wire through the cheddar, cutting off a neat slice, then wrapped the paper round it. He enjoyed showing off his dexterity with one hand. 'That all?' he enquired. 'Right – just tot up the bill.'

'No need for that,' Saul told him. 'I'm not paying.'

Eb looked at him, unable to believe his ears. 'What's that?' he said at last. 'Not – paying?'

'I've got no cash on me. I thought as how you might like to pay the bill for me, out of the kindness of your heart.'

Eb began to struggle for breath. 'If this is – some joke . . .'

'No joke, Ebenezer. I'm pushed for money, see, but you've got plenty. I reckon you owe me a little favour, don't you?' Saul gave a knowing leer, tapping the side of his nose. 'Remember Izzy Kleiber? All those years ago?'

Eb gripped the edge of the counter. 'Don't know – what you mean.'

'You and Josh asked me to do a little job for you. Now times is hard, I need some help in return. You wouldn't like it if the coppers was to come round asking questions, eh?'

'All forgotten. Dead and buried – long since.' Eb could hardly find enough breath to push the words out. 'Police satisfied – accident.'

'Ah, but what if I was to tell them it's been on my conscience all this while? What if I told 'em you and Josh was mixed up in it?'

'No proof – your word – against mine.'

'Oh, no, there's proof enough.' Regretfully, Saul shook his head. 'Remember the tally and the claw what you took from Izzy's pockets? You gave 'em back to me, along of his other belongings.' Unable to speak, Eb could only nod his head. 'I kept back the tally and claw. I've still got 'em put by, somewhere safe. I took good care – never handled 'em without me gloves on, holding 'em by the edges. They've still got your fingerprints all over 'em.'

For a moment he thought Ebenezer would choke. He opened and shut his mouth like a fish, heaving and gulping for air.

'Of course, I won't say nothing to nobody, not as long as you and me stay good friends, Ebenezer. That's why I thought

358

you'd like to pay for the groceries. And while you're about it, a few quid out of the till wouldn't come amiss, neither.'

It was beginning to get dark by the time Saul got back to Cyclops Wharf. Gloria waited in the kitchen with Matt cradled in her arms, fast asleep. 'Any luck?' she asked in a low, hopeless whisper.

By way of reply, Saul tipped the shopping bag out on to the table. The sudden clatter of tins and jars disturbed the child, who whimpered fretfully.

'Don't cry, my son!' exclaimed Saul. 'There's nothing to cry about. Your Ma's going to make us a fine supper tonight . . . and if there's anything I've forgotten, Glory, you can run out and buy it for yourself.' As a final gesture, he pulled a handful of pound-notes from his pocket and slapped them down in front of her, saying triumphantly, 'And there's more where that came from, much more!'

·——24——·

'What's the good of a pub with no beer?'

It was a fair question, and Ruth sighed sympathetically. 'I know – we're waiting for the brewery to deliver the new barrels,' she explained. 'Till then, we've no mild and no bitter, but we've still got some stout. Or we've plenty of cider?'

The customer pulled a face. 'No blooming fear. Give us a whisky, and make it a double.'

'I'm sorry – singles only,' Ruth apologised again. 'We're trying to make our stocks last as long as we can.'

She was glad when it was three o'clock and she could close the pub. Trying to keep the customers happy was becoming more and more difficult nowadays.

When she returned to the back kitchen and sat down to Sunday dinner, Mary O'Dell said to her, 'I've made us an Irish stew. Well, it's as near to Irish stew as I could manage. The shop had run out of pearl barley, so I tried to make do with porridge oats instead, which is why it looks peculiar. But I could only get scrag-end of mutton, so it had to be stew or nothing.'

Patrick did not join them at the table. These days, he would not leave his favourite chair in the chimney-corner, and preferred a tray on his lap. He complained that this was the only way he could keep himself warm – he'd never known such a cold winter. It was only October, and the winter had not even begun yet, but they did not argue with him.

It felt like winter all the time now.

With the war in its fourth year, the weather never seemed to improve. The spring and summer of 1918 had been bleak and grey, and the morale of the British people was at its lowest ebb.

'Do you know what I heard this morning?' said Mary, making conversation. 'Mrs Rafferty tells me there's a notice up in the Post Office, saying it's forbidden to send Christmas

360

puddings to the men out in France. Whatever next? Why shouldn't they have their puddings, the same as ever?'

Little Daniel, seated in his high chair next to his mother, immediately lost interest in the stew and banged his spoon on his plate, urging hopefully, 'Pudding! Pudding!' At two-and-a-half years old, Daniel had a sweet tooth and a hearty appetite.

'Presently, my darling,' his grandmother told him. 'Eat up your dinner like a good boy, and Gran will give you some apple-pie. There's still a couple of helpings left over from yesterday.'

'Danny can have my share,' said Ruth. 'I won't stay for pudding – I promised I'd be at the church hall by half-past.'

When she was not on duty at the pub, Ruth gave up her spare time to the Union of Catholic Mothers, who were involved in voluntary war-work at the Parish Hall. At the moment there was a demand for more bandages, and the good ladies of St Anthony's met regularly, cutting out and rolling bandages, packing and despatching them to the military hospitals.

'You'll wear yourself out, so you will,' Mary scolded Ruth. 'You should take a rest from it now and then, *and* you need fattening up. You're thin as a rake – isn't she, Patrick?'

'What's that?' Vaguely, the old man looked up from his bowl of stew, trying to catch the drift of the conversation. 'I wish you wouldn't mumble, woman. What are you saying?'

'Oh, never mind!' Mary called across to her husband. 'It's nothing important.'

It was true, Ruth had lost some weight, but then most people were losing weight this year. It wasn't only beer and whisky that were in short supply; food rationing had been in force since February for butter and margarine and butchers' meat – and tea was added to the ration-card in August.

'Like I was saying,' Mary went on, 'they're banning Christmas puddings for our brave boys. They say we're not to waste time and money posting them, when the Army cooks will make them for the troops anyhow. I'd just like to see any Army cook turn out a pudding as good as mine!'

'Look on the bright side,' suggested Ruth. 'You never know – the war might be over by Christmas, and they'll all come home.'

'They said that four years ago,' said Mary grimly. She leaned across the table and lowered her voice. 'The poor old fellow asked me this morning how much longer this war was going on – I didn't know what to tell him.'

'Lloyd George says the prospects of victory have never been as bright as they are now.' Ruth had read that somewhere. 'He says all we've got to do is "Hold fast"!'

'And what's that supposed to mean? We've got precious little left to hold on to, if you ask me!' Mary pushed her plate away. 'I can't eat any more. Those porridge oats were a mistake – it's like eating dinner and breakfast rolled into one.'

Since he became Prime Minister, Mr Lloyd George had done all he could to revive the nation's flagging spirits, but without much success. The lists of casualties published in the newspapers grew longer day by day, and despite occasional reports of major victories and advances on the Western Front, the prospect of peace seemed as remote as ever. That was why Ruth devoted her spare time to war-work. At least it gave her the feeling that she was doing something to help, however small her contribution.

As she walked down the road towards the Parish Hall, a voice hailed her: 'Ruthie, coo-ee! Wait for me!'

Looking round, she saw Gloria hurrying after her and waited until her cousin caught up.

'I guessed I'd find you here. Still rolling bandages, are you?' asked Gloria. 'Would you like me to come and give you a hand?'

Ruth was surprised. 'You'd be more than welcome, but you're not a member of the Mothers' Union or the Legion of Mary. You're not even a Catholic.'

'Oh, my!' Gloria tossed her head. 'I never realised you had to be an RC – don't they let us heathens do war-work?'

Ruth laughed. 'Of course you can! I only wondered, why aren't you helping at the Emmanuel Chapel? They're busy making bandages, too. In fact, we've got a sort of unofficial competition to see which of us can turn out the most.'

'That's why I'm offering to come and work for your lot,' said Glory, with a wicked smile. 'If you win, that'll be one in the eye for the high-and-mighty old cats at Emmanuel!'

Ruth led the way into St Anthony's Hall, and they found places at one of the long trestle tables. The room was full of women, all hard at work, and the air was shrill with the sound of their chatter.

'Between you and me, I think we're bound to win,' Ruth said confidently, 'because the chapel-goers never work on the Sabbath – but our lot don't bother about that!'

Gloria unfastened her outdoor coat and hung it over the back of her chair, revealing a very striking dress of royal blue velveteen with the latest princess neckline and marabou trimming.

'Goodness, don't you look smart!' exclaimed Ruth. 'That's new, isn't it?'

'Yes, Saul bought it for me the other day as a little present. Suits me, doesn't it?' It was certainly becoming, and showed off Glory's ample bust to advantage. Ruth made a mental note that her cousin, at least, had not been losing weight recently.

'Very stylish,' she said. 'What have you done with Saul this afternoon? And young Matt?'

'Saul's gone out in the wherry, plying for trade,' Gloria explained, 'and he's taken the boy along with him. Matt's never so happy as when he's out in the boat.'

'Aren't you afraid he might fall overboard?' Ruth asked, as she prepared to start on the next lot of bandages.

'Oh, he's been used to the river ever since he could crawl. Saul says he's a proper water-baby. Now then, show me what I've got to do.'

'It's very simple.' Ruth instructed her quickly. 'Cut the cloth into long three-inch strips, like this, then roll them up and finish them off with a piece of tape at the end, that's all.'

As they settled down to work, she added, 'I didn't know Saul had gone back to ferrying again.'

'Yes, and I'm glad he did. Well, you know trade had fallen off badly in the shop, and he enjoys working outside. He's getting lots of passengers, too. In fact, he's bringing home more money than ever, these days. It seems like we've struck lucky at last.'

*

The clock on the mantelpiece chimed the half-hour, and Aunt Emily choked back a yawn, hiding her mouth behind a fluttering hand. 'Gracious me, half-past nine already! I think I must go up to bed, if you'll both excuse me – I'm quite sleepy. And I expect you'll be wanting to get along home, Tom. I know you have to make an early start in the morning, seeing it's Monday tomorrow.'

'Yes, Aunt Emily.' Tommy lifted his teacup, adding, 'I've still got half a cup to finish. I won't swallow it all at once – I might give myself hiccups.'

'I can see him out,' suggested Maudie, almost eagerly.

'Oh, very well, dear. You will be careful to lock up afterwards, won't you? Don't forget the bolts – top *and* bottom.'

'I won't forget.'

Emily Judge said good-night to them both, and went upstairs. Tom and Maudie only hesitated for a moment before they fell into each other's arms – touching, stroking, caressing and kissing one another. He let his tea get cold; they did not talk, for they had used up all their small-talk during the evening, counting the hours until they would be alone together. Now, at last, the waiting was over. Maudie took Tom through the darkened shop and opened the street door, calling loudly: 'Good night, Tom, it was nice to see you! Will you come round again next Sunday?'

'Thanks, I'd like to. Good night!' he called back.

Then she shut the door and bolted it carefully. Without a word, they went back to the kitchen and turned out the gas-lamps; in silence they climbed the stairs, tiptoeing past Emily's door then on, up to the top floor. Trevor did not share Maudie's attic bedroom now. He was a big boy and had acquired a room of his own – Tom's old room. Maudie went in to take a look at her son and returned a few moments later, whispering, 'He's fast asleep.' Then she smiled: 'You didn't waste any time!'

Tom was already undressed and in her bed. She took her clothes off quickly and slipped in beside him. Once again, there was no need for words. Slowly at first, then more impatiently, they made love, giving and receiving joy. It was always the same, yet it was always different. They knew each

364

other's bodies so well by now, but still there was always some new revelation, something astonishing and wonderful.

At last it was over, and they lay curled up together, breathless and contented.

'You mustn't go to sleep,' she warned him.

'I won't. Just give me a minute, then I'll get dressed.'

'I wish you didn't have to go.'

'So do I. One day, I won't. One day we'll be together all the time.'

She propped her chin on her hand, looking down at his body in the faint light from the window; his beautiful, muscular body – gentle as a boy, yet as strong as a man.

'What will your Dad say when you get home?' she asked. 'Will he tell you off for being so late?'

'I'll just say we got talking, and I didn't notice the time.' Tom stretched out luxuriously. 'I wish he'd give me a key of my own, though. I told him, if I had a key he wouldn't need to sit up –but it was no good. He likes to know what time I come in.'

'He wants to know what you've been up to!' said Maudie, and they both giggled.

Tom gave her one more kiss – one more loving embrace – then got out of bed. Maudie pulled on her nightdress; she would have to creep downstairs silently, to let him out and lock the shop door after him. When Tom was ready, they went downstairs. Softly, she opened the door. They exchanged one last, lingering kiss and then she watched him slip away into the dark. Now she would have a whole week to wait, until next Sunday evening.

Tom made his way home as quickly as possible. It wasn't very far, and he reached Jubilee Street in a few minutes. Standing at the front door about to lift the knocker he paused, hearing a man's voice raised in anger. He knew that voice: deep, penetrating, merciless . . . What was his grandfather doing here at this time of night? And what was he angry about? He could not catch all the words, but odd phrases reached him: 'Serious discrepancy . . . Carelessness . . . Dishonesty . . .'

Then came his father's voice, strangled by chronic breathlessness. Tom could not understand what he was saying, only that his father was in some sort of trouble. Scared, he felt tempted to run away and come back later when the fuss was over, but he sensed that his father needed help, and he felt a curious loyalty towards him.

Ebenezer Judge had never shown much affection for his son, and Tom had never felt any great love for his father, but he had a grudging admiration for him. In time of war, he had gone to defend his country; he had narrowly escaped death and suffered a crippling disability that could never be cured.

Boldly, Tom banged the door-knocker and the voices stopped. He heard his grandfather say, 'Stay where you are, I shall see who it is.'

When he opened the door, Marcus Judge raised his bushy eyebrows. 'Thomas! Still out, at this time of night? I thought you were in bed.'

'No, sir.'

'Where have you been?'

'I went to supper with Aunt Emily and Maudie.'

'You should not have stayed so late. Do you realise what the time is? Very well, you'd better come in.'

He led the way into the parlour. Ebenezer, looking pale and drawn, sat at the table with some account books open in front of him – the accounts, Tom realised, of the grocery shop.

'Is there something wrong, Dad?' he asked.

'No – course not – go to bed.'

'But if there's some trouble . . .'

'You heard your father – go to bed at once!' Marcus repeated. 'You have to be at the Wharf at six o'clock. If you are late, you will be turned away.'

Bravely, Tom held his ground. 'I won't be late, Grandad – sir – but I want to know what's happened.'

'There is a small discrepancy in the accounts: I felt I should bring it to your father's attention. However, it is no concern of yours. Go up to your room. I will see you in the morning.'

Tom looked at his father, who would not meet his eye, but mumbled, 'Do as you're told. Run along now.'

Reluctantly, Tom muttered a good-night and left the room. Halfway up the stairs he stopped, consumed by curiosity, then crept back and sat listening, feeling like a spy.

366

'I'm surprised you let the boy stay out so late,' Marcus was saying, in the same accusing tone.

'Harmless – family evening – Emily and her daughter-in-law . . .'

'You should have told me – it might have been very awkward. I have no wish for our discussion to become common knowledge, that's why I came round at this hour, trusting that your wife and son would be safely out of the way. This is a serious matter, Ebenezer, extremely serious.'

'Yes, Father – I know . . .' He choked on the words. 'I'm – sorry.'

'Is that all you can say? Two hundred and forty-five pounds not accounted for! Two hundred and forty-five pounds missing from the cash takings during the past nine months, and you tell me that you are *sorry*?' The old man's voice was like a whiplash. Tom could imagine his father wincing under its sting.

'I really am – sorry.' His voice was agonised. 'My fault –can't explain it.'

'But I demand an explanation: where has the money gone?'

'Can't tell you. Must be – error – arithmetic.'

'I find that hard to believe. You have an excellent brain. When you were the Treasurer of the Brotherhood, your book-keeping was meticulous.' Tom heard the drag of his father's laboured breathing, but no words emerged. Marcus continued: 'Is it possible that you have been tempted to put the money to your own use?'

He spoke quietly, but with deadly precision, and Eb gasped, 'No! Never that. Never think such a—'

He could not go on. The old man waited for a moment, giving him time to pull himself together, then resumed in a tone that was slightly less harsh, 'I believe you are speaking the truth – I hope you are – but it does not answer my question. If you did not steal that money, what has become of it?'

'Go through books – check everything – trace the money – I promise.'

There was a tense pause, and then Marcus said, 'Very well, be sure that you do. I shall expect a full explanation in due course. Now you should go to bed, you are looking far from well. Good night. I shall see myself out.'

The interview was over. The front door opened and closed, then Tom heard another sound, horribly like a sob. It was unthinkable that his father – a grown man – could be reduced to tears, and yet . . . Slowly, he walked downstairs and into the parlour. Ebenezer was still at the table, his hand over his eyes. Startled, he looked up, pulling out a handkerchief and blowing his nose.

'Damned catarrh,' he whispered, then turned on his son angrily. 'What are you doing? Thought I told you – bed.'

Tom looked at the account-books, with their columns of spidery figures. 'I heard what you and Grandad were saying. It is a mistake, isn't it?'

'Eavesdropping on me. How dare you?' Suddenly Eb's blustering manner collapsed and he said faintly, 'Don't believe – your father – a thief?'

'No, Dad. But you never make mistakes about money. What went wrong?'

Eb looked at him for a long moment, and when he spoke at last his words came out slowly and deliberately. 'Perhaps – it was stolen.'

'Stolen? But who could—' Tom stopped short. There was nobody but Aunt Emily and Maudie living at the shop and surely neither of them could have done such a thing? Instantly, he reproached himself for considering such a thought, even for a second. 'You mean, someone broke in? A burglar?'

'Yes, someone from outside!' Suddenly Ebenezer was panting with relief. 'Needn't be burglary, though. Sometimes –have to leave shop – few minutes. Time for sneak-thief – walk in – rifle the till. Yes, that's the answer – knew it all along.'

'But you should have told Grandad. Why didn't you say so?'

'Still my fault. Not as sharp as I was – can't move as quick. My responsibility – replace money somehow. Be on guard from now on.' He put out his left hand, and gripped Tom's arm. 'Thanks, son. Stand by your Dad, eh?'

'Course I will. I'll help you any way I can, you know that.'

'Good boy. Our secret . . . No need to tell your mother.'

November arrived, wet and foggy, bringing an influenza

epidemic which spread through south-east England, and did not spare the Island. Patrick O'Dell was one of the first to be struck down.

'How is he now?' asked Ruth, when she came back from shopping.

'Very feverish. I've given him a whisky-toddy and some more aspirin, in hopes he may sweat it out.' Mary O'Dell had been up half the night with the old man, trying to make him comfortable, but he still had a high temperature, a sore throat and a hacking cough.

'I tried to get some lemons for him from the greengrocer, but there were none to be had. I thought a drink of hot lemon might help his throat.'

'It might, but I think he prefers the whisky!' said Mary. 'Did you bring some fish for our dinner?'

'They'd nothing left but an old piece of cod that smelled as if it was on the turn so I decided not to risk it.'

'No fish? On a Friday?' exclaimed Mary in dismay. As good practising Catholics, the O'Dells abstained from meat on Fridays.

'We've still got some eggs left and a bit of mousestrap,' said Ruth. 'If I grate it, it might stretch to a cheese omelette.' Taking her hat off she added, 'The market was buzzing with rumours. Three different people told me they'd heard it on good authority that the Kaiser was about to surrender. They say the German troops are laying down their arms and giving themselves up.'

Mary crossed herself. 'Dear God, let it be true.'

On Saturday, Patrick seemed a little better but now it was Mary's turn to feel shivery. Ruth tried to persuade her to go to bed with a hot-water bottle, but she refused point-blank. 'I'll be fine, and I certainly won't leave you and Kathie to run this house by yourselves! Two bars open, with nobody but a couple of girls to mind them – it wouldn't be safe. Suppose the customers was to get out of hand?'

However, the customers showed no signs of getting out of hand; they were all as miserable as the weather. No more had been heard about the German surrender and there was a general mood of hopelessness. Every time the saloon door

369

swung open, a swirling white mist came in off the river like a thick wet blanket.

From her post behind the bar, Ruth looked up. This particular newcomer was a tall, well-set-up man in khaki with a sergeant's stripes on his sleeve. He asked if there was any bitter, and she was able to tell him, 'You're in luck. We got a new supply only two days ago. Pint or half?'

'Make it a pint please, miss.'

As she pulled the beer-handle she asked, 'Home on leave, are you?'

'In a manner of speaking. I was one of the lucky ones – I only came out of hospital yesterday, after three operations. Had part of me insides shot away. I won't go into details, as it's not a subject for mixed company. Still, they patched me up pretty well. I'll be going back to France in a week or two.'

She tried to think of something encouraging to say.

'You never know, perhaps it won't be long now. Everyone's talking about the Germans surrendering.'

'Don't you believe it! The Boches will never give in; they've too much pride for that. They're like machines – they'll go on chucking shells over and firing machine-guns as long as there's one man left to pull a trigger.'

After that, it came as a surprise when, on her way to Mass on Sunday morning, Ruth saw the latest news-bulletin in the Post Office window: *On our right, Fourth and Third Armies are advancing along the Sambre towards the Belgian frontier, meeting little organised resistance . . . The German Chancellor announced that the Kaiser and his son have decided to renounce the throne . . . No other news of importance to hand.*

When she got home she couldn't wait to tell Mary, for surely this must be the beginning of the end, but Mary shook her head, refusing to take comfort. Weighed down by gloom and influenza, she snapped: 'Don't you go clutching at straws! You can't trust them Germans – it might just be another of their cunning tricks.'

As it turned out, Ruth's optimism was amply justified. The following afternoon, she sat down and wrote a letter to her husband.

Monday, November 11th, 1918

Dear Sean,

    It's not often I write you a letter at the beginning of the week, but this is a special occasion, isn't it? It's been a very exciting day for all of us here at home, but I'm sure it must be even more wonderful for you.

    The day began with a thick grey fog, which made everything dark and depressing – but we didn't stay depressed for long. We heard the first news about the signing of the Armistice soon after eleven am. At once all work stopped, and it turned into an unofficial public holiday. The schools broke up, and all the children were sent home. Everyone I saw was wild with excitement, and people started putting out flags. I managed to find some Union Jacks in the attic. Goodness knows how long they'd been up there – your Mam said they must have been left over from Mafeking – so we've made the front of the pub look very festive.

    The church bells were rung at St Anthony's, of course, and the other churches, too. You could hear them all over the Island. The boats on the river sounded their hooters. Tomorrow will be another holiday – they're busy organising parties for the children. Your mother and father are both suffering from influenza, but the news was the best medicine they could have had, and they're looking better already.

    I wonder when you will be coming home. I suppose we must be patient for a little longer, but I hope we may be together again very soon. I know things have not always gone well between us, but today I feel this is a chance to bury the past and begin again. I will try to be a good wife to you, my darling. We have so much to be thankful for. Daniel is very well – he escaped the influenza, thank goodness. I told him I was writing to you, and he sends you a kiss – and so do I. God bless you, my dear, until we meet again. With all my love, Ruth.

Monday had been unbelievably exciting, but Tuesday was just as extraordinary in its own way.

The mood of celebration seemed likely to continue indefinitely. From early morning, the streets were crowded with merrymakers. People wandered about, arm in arm, wearing red, white and blue rosettes or waving flags. Several of them had squeakers or tin-whistles to add to the hubbub, and once again the church bells pealed.

The Islanders were determined that the whole day should be one continuous party. At St Anthony's Hall, the bandages had been put aside and the trestle tables were laid out with plates of sandwiches, jellies and iced buns for the children, paper hats and balloons. In the streets, people collected wood for a bonfire and when night fell, the revellers joined hands, singing and dancing round the flames.

Watching from the open doorway of the Watermen, Ruth saw old Bessie the knocker-up standing at the corner of the street, a minute Union Jack in one hand and a bottle of beer in the other. She was alternately raising the flag and taking a nip from the bottle.

'I shan't have to do me early-morning round tomorrow – nobody's going to be fit to go to work!' she told Ruth, waving the flag again. 'So I decided this must be my duty instead – and I always does me duty.'

A musician strolled among the happy crowds, playing an accordion. There were no wartime songs tonight – no more *Tipperary* or *Pack Up Your Troubles*. Instead, there were tunes from the good old days – memories of love and romance – *The Honeysuckle and the Bee* and *The Lily of Laguna*.

In the flickering light from the bonfire, Ruth thought she saw Tom and Maudie dancing, her head upon his shoulder, but they disappeared into the crowd and before she could take a second look, she had to step aside in order to let a customer enter the saloon.

He was wearing an Army uniform – but it was not a uniform she knew. Although the United States had joined in the war against Germany eighteen months earlier, American soldiers were not an everyday sight in East London.

'I'll take a scotch, if I may,' the stranger said. Then, as he studied her more closely, 'It is Mrs O'Dell, isn't it?'

'That's right.' Suddenly she recognised him. The last time they had met, he had not been in khaki. 'Of course – you came to see my brother-in-law. It's Mr Cassidy, is that right? Mr Leopold Cassidy?'

'Right on the button, ma'am – except it's Major Cassidy now. Though not for much longer, I sincerely hope.' He paid for his drink, then raised his glass. 'Here's to you and your

372

family. I'm over in London for a few days on military business, and I thought I'd take the opportunity to look you up. I don't suppose Connor is here as well, joining in the celebrations?'

'No, he's still over in France, with my husband.'

'I thought as much. That's the reason I brought this along.' Slipping a hand into an inside pocket of his smartly-tailored jacket, he took out an envelope. 'I've written Connor a letter, as this seems like a good time for us to get together again. I'm offering the boy another contract; as soon as this ballyhoo is over, I'll be off to the States and I want to take him along. I have plans for Connor O'Dell – he could have a big, big future.'

'In boxing, you mean?'

'I sure do. I was all set to take him over there before, but the war kinda delayed things. Now there's nothing to stop him, and believe me, that boy's really going places . . . I'd be grateful if you'd see he gets my letter.'

'Do you want me to send it on to him in France?'

'No need for that, ma'am. I guess he'll be released from duty any time now. When he gets home, you can give it to him. Just tell him to be sure and get in touch with me right away.'

'Very well.' She wasn't altogether sure that she trusted Major Cassidy. He was very charming and polite, but perhaps a little too good to be true. However, she put the letter behind the kitchen clock, and then forgot about it.

It was very late on Tuesday evening before she finally got to bed and on Wednesday morning, when she came down to start making the breakfast, she found another letter waiting for her. It was on War Office stationery, and it had come from France –but it was not Sean's handwriting on the envelope.

Tearing it open, she began to read – then put out a hand to steady herself, clutching the arm of a chair. As she read on, she sank slowly into Patrick's armchair by the fireside. The letter had been written by Sean's Commanding Officer, following up a telegram – a telegram that she had never received.

November 8th, 1918

Dear Madam:
  It is with deep regret that I write to you now, but I must express my personal condolences over the loss of your husband on November 4th.

373

All the officers, NCOs and Other Ranks wish to express their sympathy with you in your bereavement. Sean O'Dell was a first-class soldier, and will be much missed by all who knew him.

His death was a tragic accident. On his way back to Base Camp with the rest of his platoon, he was riding in the back of a lorry when the tailboard gave way. He fell on to the road, and was immediately crushed beneath the wheels of the following vehicle. He had been talking and laughing with his companions only a few moments before, and death must have been mercifully instantaneous.

Your husband was given a first-class funeral with full military honours, and a cross was erected in his memory. He gave his life for his country no less than if he had died in battle. His personal effects will, of course, be forwarded to you as soon as possible . . .

Unable to take it all in, Ruth began to re-read the letter. *The loss of your husband on November 4th . . .* When she had written her last note to Sean – when she had written to him about a new beginning for their marriage – he had already been dead for a week.

· ——25—— ·

Everybody had been very kind.

Ruth kept repeating those words, telling herself the same thing again and again. Everyone had tried to make things as easy as possible for her.

On Sunday, when she and Mary came out of church after early Mass, several members of the congregation nodded and smiled – gentle, sympathetic smiles. The O'Dell ladies returned their smiles, but did not stop to speak to anyone.

During the past weeks, they had talked about Sean's death so many times, there was nothing left to say. Holding themselves very upright in their mourning black, they walked home to the Watermen; Ruth was wheeling the push-chair and Mary looked down at Danny, saying fondly, 'You were very good in church, my lad. I'm proud of you.'

'He enjoys the hymn-singing,' said Ruth, 'but I was glad when he dozed off during the sermon. Do you remember the way he howled, all through—' She did not complete the sentence. She had been about to say, 'All through the eulogy at Sean's Requiem Mass' – but that was something they did not discuss either. In any case, her mother-in-law knew what she meant.

'I remember,' said Mary quietly.

There was nothing to be gained by talking about it. Sean's death had been tragic and unnecessary, but now he was at rest and they had to let him go. For the first few days, Ruth had suffered agonising grief. Ever since she left home, her life had revolved around Sean. It had not been a perfect marriage by any means – how many marriages could claim to be that – but she had hoped and prayed that they would settle down to an amicable, understanding partnership in the end. Sean was no saint, but his death had left a gaping void at the centre of her life.

375

The first shock was replaced by a sense of loss and of regret, of time wasted that might have been better spent, of love wasted that could have been so much happier for both of them. Worst of all, she felt empty and useless; her life seemed to be devoid of purpose. She thanked God for Daniel. He was a great blessing, and she devoted all her care and affection upon him . . . and Mary O'Dell was a tower of strength.

Sustained by her faith, Mary had found new reserves of courage and patience at the time when she needed them most. Now, as they reached the pub, she said to Ruth, 'I'll just go and see how the old feller's getting on.'

Sean's death had hit Patrick hardest of all. When they broke the news, he seemed to shrink before their eyes, unable to bear this new misery. Since then he had taken to his bed, and remained there. Somehow Mary discovered the energy she needed to nurse him. Supporting her husband in his grief, she managed to conquer her own.

'We must be thankful that the war is over at last, and look forward to Connor coming home,' she said that evening, sitting by the fireside with Ruth. 'It won't be much longer now, will it?'

That was when Ruth remembered the letter tucked away behind the kitchen clock, but she said nothing. How could she tell Mary that when her eldest son returned from the war, he would soon be off again – to America?

On Saturday morning, Ebenezer was at his usual place, perched on the high stool behind the grocery counter, when Saul walked into the shop. Eb looked up at him with hatred, which he made no attempt to conceal.

'Go away!' He spat out the words, between gulps for breath. 'You're not wanted here – leave me alone.'

Saul saw the hatred in his eyes but he saw fear there, too, and that made him feel strong. 'Don't be so hasty,' he said. 'You'n me's got to have another talk.'

'Nothing to say. I told you – I've finished. Father's on to it. Not another penny.' At moments of anxiety, Eb's amputated arm ached horribly. He could almost imagine the limb was still there, tormenting him, and although it was only the ghost of an arm, the pain was as real as ever. 'Get out,' he groaned. 'I'm not well.'

'I won't stay long,' said Saul. 'Give me what I come for, and I'll leave you in peace.'

'I tell you, I *can't*!'

'Up to you, my friend. D'you want me to turn in the evidence?'

'You wouldn't dare!'

'Think so? I mean what I say.' Saul turned, as if he were about to leave. 'But if that's the way you want it . . .'

As he put his hand on the door, Eb managed to dredge up a last appeal: 'Wait. Come back!' Stretching across to the till, he took out a five-pound note, panting, 'Take it and go. Last you'll get – from me.'

Saul's lips curled with satisfaction, showing yellow teeth. 'Ta,' he said. 'Glad you come to your senses . . . I'll see you.' Pocketing the note, he turned to go and at the same moment, Tom entered the shop. Saul threw him a curt acknowledgment and walked out.

Seeing the sweat on Ebenezer's forehead, Tom asked quickly, 'What's wrong, Dad? What did Uncle Saul want?'

'Nothing. Don't call him that. Not your uncle . . .' Fumbling for a handkerchief, Eb mopped his face. 'What you doing here?'

'It's Saturday. I'm on a half-day – don't have to report for work till after dinner so I thought I'd drop in. Is Maudie in the kitchen?'

'Good morning, Tommy. Maudie's just putting her coat on.' Emerging from the back room, Aunt Emily answered his question. 'We're going out shopping – perhaps you'd like to come with us?'

'I don't mind,' said Tom. He would have preferred to stay with Maudie, but he could hardly say so. 'I was going to ask if she felt like a walk.'

'Oh, good. You'll be able to carry our shopping baskets.' Emily opened her purse and continued, 'I'll need some change, Ebenezer. I've got nothing smaller than a pound note, and some of those costermongers in the market can be quite rude if you don't have the right money. I'll just take a pound's worth of silver.'

Before Eb could stop her, she opened the till and began to count out a handful of coins. Then she stopped and asked, 'Why, where's that five-pound note gone? There was one in here first thing. I put in the float from the cash-box like I always do – a five, and five ones. What's become of it?'

'I – took it out.' Eb could hardly speak. 'Making up money. Pay in to the bank presently.'

Emily stared at him. 'But today's Saturday. The bank's shut.'

'Ah, yes. Forgot that.' He broke off with relief as Maudie came through with Trevor. 'Off out, are you? See you later.'

Maudie greeted Tom eagerly as Emily explained, 'He's coming to help us with the shopping – isn't that nice?'

As they were about to set out, Tom said abruptly, 'You go on, I'll catch you up. I just remembered, I've got to talk to Dad about something.'

Puzzled, the others went off without him. Tom shut the door carefully, then turned the *Open* sign round to read *Closed*.

'What you doing?' Eb asked uneasily.

'I don't want anybody coming in.' Tom clenched his fists: this was the hardest thing he had ever had to say to anyone. 'You weren't telling the truth then, were you? About the five-pound note?'

'What d'you mean?' Feebly, Eb tried to bluster but it was hopeless.

'I knew as soon as I came in that something had happened. Uncle Saul took that fiver, didn't he? I saw him through the door, putting something in his pocket – and he hadn't bought anything, so it wasn't change.'

Eb clutched at the counter, his mouth gaping, his face leaden.

'I suppose it was him all along,' Tom went on. 'He's been coming in here, pinching money – but why did you let him? Why didn't you tell Grandad? Or the police?'

His father heaved a deep, shuddering breath, then said hoarsely: 'You're old enough to know the truth. Years ago, a man was drowned – terrible accident. Member of the Brotherhood.'

*

378

A fortnight later, Connor came home.

When he walked into the back kitchen, Mary did not exclaim with delight or shed tears of joy. For a long time she held him tightly, and then asked, 'Are you really home for good, son?'

'Not quite. They can't let us all go at once.' He began to unbuckle his khaki webbing, shrugging out of his haversack, pulling off his great-coat. 'But I've three weeks' leave. I don't have to go back till the tenth of January – you'll be sick of the sight of me by then.'

Then he saw Ruth, standing in the scullery, her sleeves rolled up and an apron tied round her waist. 'It's good to see you,' he told her. 'I'm sorry – I couldn't write. I didn't know what to say.'

She nodded, trying to smile. She had a sudden, irrational longing to throw her arms about him as Mary had done. 'I'm well, thank you,' she said.

'I'm glad of that.' He turned back to his mother. 'And how's the old man?'

Mary hunched her shoulders. 'What can I tell you? He's not left his bed this past month. He took it terrible hard, Con.'

'Will I go up to him? Or do you want to warn him that I'm here?'

'It's better so. Wait here, I'll not be long.'

Left alone, Ruth and Connor threw sidelong glances at one another and she began to take off her apron, saying, 'Kettle's on. I'll make some tea when it boils.'

'Thanks.' Connor pulled out a chair. 'Come and sit down. I've something I was told to give you . . . I hope it won't upset you.'

'I don't understand.' Taking the chair he offered her she looked up at him, mystified. 'Something to give me?'

'Sean's things. All that he had, when . . .'

Connor placed a brown-paper package on the table, fastened with red string and sealing-wax. Her fingers trembled, and he had to help her open it; then he tipped the contents on to the tablecloth. There wasn't much there. Sean's wedding-ring, his fountain-pen, his purse – containing a few English coppers and half-a-dozen French francs – a water-proof bag which held a piece of soap, his shaving-brush and

379

razor, together with a few of her own letters, sent during the last weeks of the war, and lastly, a patent gun-metal cigarette-lighter.

'There was a packet of fags too, but I thought you wouldn't want those so I gave them to his pals.'

'I see. Thank you.'

He put his hand on her shoulder for a moment, then withdrew it again, saying, 'I'm very sorry.'

'Yes. We were all sorry.' Determined not to break down, she dared not look at him. Suddenly she thought of Major Cassidy's letter, and stood up to fetch it from the mantelpiece. 'I've something for you, as well.'

She explained how it had arrived, and he opened the letter. He was still reading it when Mary returned, and he glanced up, saying, 'Ruth just gave me Cassidy's letter – I suppose you'd call it a contract. He's offering me a hell of a lot of money.'

Ruth cut in quickly, 'I didn't tell your mother. I thought you should explain it yourself.'

'Oh, I see, sorry. Well, Mam – I've been offered a tour of America. Cassidy wants to promote me as a possible champion. It's a big opportunity for me.'

Mary's face was quite blank as she said, 'That sounds very good. When does he want you to go?'

'As soon as I'm demobilised, whenever that may be. Don't worry, I shan't desert you altogether. I'll come home as often as I can. Maybe I'll send over a couple of boat tickets, so you and Da can sail across and visit me there.'

Mary shook her head. 'I don't think your Da would enjoy travelling. Why don't you go up to him? He's waiting to see you.' Then her eye fell on the little collection of objects scattered over the tablecloth, and her face changed. 'I'm sorry, son. I can't take in your good news all at once; there's been so much happening just lately.'

Connor folded the letter and put it back in its envelope, replacing it behind the clock. 'It won't happen yet, anyhow,' he said. 'It could be months, even. There's no hurry.'

When he left the room, Mary said softly, 'Mother of God, what an old fool I am. Here I've been all this while, expecting him to come home and take on the pub, once he was out of the

Army. He's got his own life to live – I should have realised that.'

Ruth frowned. 'What do you mean?'

'You don't suppose the Brewery will let us stay here for ever, do you, with the old feller the way he is – and I'm no spring chicken meself! They'll be wanting someone younger to manage this place, and I can't blame them. I had hoped Connor might want to take it over, but I wouldn't wish to stand in his way.'

Then the kettle started to boil, and Ruth was glad of an excuse to escape into the scullery and fetch the cups, her head whirling with new, unwelcome thoughts.

On the Monday before Christmas, Ruth was hanging up decorations in the saloon when Kathie Simes came in from the public, saying, 'Can you spare a minute? There's a chap here asking for you.'

With paper-chains festooned around her neck and a bunch of holly pricking her fingers, Ruth snapped impatiently, 'If it's a traveller trying to sell us something, you can tell him—'

'Forgive me. I am not trying to sell anything.'

A thin-faced young man followed Kathie into the bar, holding out both hands and saying, 'How are you, Ruth? A Merry Christmas to you.'

His accent was foreign, yet very familiar. For a split second Ruth did not know him – he looked so much older, so tired and worn, and yet . . .

'Ernest!' she exclaimed, and turned to Kathie. 'It's all right, Mr Kleiber and I are old friends. Do sit down, Ernest – can I get you a drink? Would you like something to eat?'

'I thank you, no!' Smiling, he lifted a hand in protest. 'If I eat too much, I get sick. I should not interrupt you at a busy time, but I had to see you as soon as possible.'

'Of course. I haven't heard any news of you since – how long is it?' They sat side by side on the wooden settle. He had changed so much, she found herself staring at him, and looked away.

'Yes, I was interned as an Enemy Alien soon after the war

381

began. I was sent with my parents to a camp on the Isle of Man . . . It might as well have been on another planet.'

'It must have been dreadful. How are your parents? I hope they are well?'

Ernest continued to smile, but his eyes were shadowed with pain. 'My mother became very ill with heart trouble, and she died in 1916. My father is alive, thank God, but he is very much changed. He forgets things – sometimes he forgets Mama is no longer living and sometimes he does not know me . . . But I have brought him home, and Sarah also.'

'Sarah was in the camp with you? And her grandfather?'

'Mr Vogel did not survive the first winter.' Ernest shook his head. 'He was very old, and he passed away in his sleep. Right to the end, he still believed that he was in America. I do not think he was unhappy – and he was so proud of his great-grandson.'

'Benjamin! He must be a big boy now. I was with Sarah the day he was born.'

'I remember, and now he is nearly four and a half – a fine boy.'

'And now you are free at last.' Ruth took Ernest's hands in her own. 'I am so happy for you. Please give Sarah my love – where is she now?'

'She is living with us, at Poplar. The old house needs some work done. It was shut up all the time we were away, but suffered no real damage – just a little damp, through broken windows and missing tiles.'

'I'll come and visit you very soon, if I may.'

'Please do.' Ernest gripped her hands more tightly. 'I have so many things to ask you, but there is one question more urgent than all the rest. Where is Rosie?'

Ruth stared at him, and felt a sudden chill. 'I was going to ask the same question. You mean you haven't seen her?'

'No.' Ernest was no longer smiling. 'But you must know where she is?'

Ruth shook her head. 'When you went away, I tried to persuade her to come home to us, but it was no good. She wouldn't have anything to do with her family. Didn't you write to each other?'

'She never wrote. I sent letters to the address in Silmour Street – the photographic shop – but they were returned marked *Gone Away*. Didn't she tell you where she was going?'

'It was all so long ago.' Ruth struggled to remember. 'She said she was getting a job as a salesgirl in one of the big department stores up west. She was going to live in at a staff hostel. I told her to send me a postcard as soon as she was settled, but I never heard from her.'

For a moment Ernest was silent. Then he said firmly, 'Very well. We shall find her, you and I.'

'But I don't know where to start looking! I don't even know the name of the shop.'

'Then we shall try them all. Will you help me, Ruth?'

She could see how desperate he was, and her heart went out to him as she answered, 'I wish I could, but I can't promise. It might take a long time.'

'That doesn't matter. I have all the time in the world,' he said.

'Yes, but I haven't. I don't even know how long I shall be staying here. I may have to move quite soon.'

He frowned, as if she were creating unnecessary obstacles. 'Move? Where to? Why?'

As simply as possible, she explained the situation, telling him about Sean's death and Mr O'Dell's illness. If the Brewery decided to put in a new landlord, she would have to leave the pub.

'I see. I am very sorry – I have been wrapped up in my own problems. Please forgive me.' He rose to his feet. 'I must not intrude upon you any longer. I hope things work out well for you.'

'Thank you. I shall come and see you, anyway. I hope you find Rosie very soon.'

'Oh, yes. I shall find her, however long it takes. Somehow I will find her – and then I will marry her.'

After Ernest had gone, Connor walked in from the public bar, saying casually, 'Want me to lend a hand with the decorations?'

'I'd be very grateful. I haven't got very far before I was interrupted. Could you make a start on the picture-frames?'

She gave him a bunch of holly, adding, 'I thought you'd gone out for a walk. Have you been back long?'

'Long enough,' he said.

On Christmas Eve, Tom went to have supper with Aunt Emily and Maudie. When the meal was over, he produced three small packages wrapped in coloured paper.

'These are for tomorrow,' he said. 'One for each of you, and one for Trev – only don't expect too much. I got a pop-gun for His Lordship; I thought he might like it.'

'Oh, dear. I hope it doesn't make too much noise,' said Emily. 'I don't like bangs.'

'No, it only shoots corks – it's not loud. I thought you might put it in his stocking tonight.'

'Can we open ours now?' Maudie asked, her eyes dancing. Without waiting for an answer, she tore off the wrappings and took out a pendant on a chain – a ruby-red heart, set in brilliants.

'It's not proper jewellery,' Tom confessed. 'I couldn't afford any more, on account of I'm saving up.'

'I know.' Maudie gave him a swift, private smile. 'I think it's beautiful. I'll wear it always.'

Aunt Emily opened her present, and found a patchwork kettle-holder inside.

'I got it from the missionary sale-of-work at the Chapel,' explained Tom. 'It seemed to be the right thing as you're always making us pots of tea.'

'Thank you, Tommy, that's very thoughtful.' Emily glanced from the kettle-holder to the heart-shaped pendant, but made no further comment.

They began to talk about Christmas Day. As head of the family, Marcus Judge was keeping up an annual tradition and had invited them all to tea at the Rope Walk.

'But it's a pity we shan't all be there,' Tommy added thoughtfully.

'You mean poor Arnie? Yes, we shall miss him, won't we?' Emily sighed. 'At a time like this, we can't help remembering the dear departed.'

384

'I wasn't thinking of that so much. There's some still alive who won't be there either,' Tom pointed out. 'Like Uncle Josh.'

'Yes, such a shame he can't be with us, but never mind. I expect he'll come home on leave very soon.'

'And there's Aunt Ruth, too. Grandad never asks her.'

Emily pursed her lips. 'No, well – you know there's been a rift between Ruth and her parents. It's very sad.'

'I think Grandma still sees her sometimes, though.'

'I believe she does. I'm glad they keep in touch, but of course your Grandfather wouldn't approve. He has very strong principles.'

'Do you have strong principles too, Auntie?' asked Tom innocently. 'I was just thinking – you never see Gloria now, do you?'

Emily became rather flustered, fidgeting with the kettle-holder. 'I'm sorry to say that Gloria behaved in a way I really can't forgive,' she said primly. 'Going off like that – marrying that shocking man.'

'But Christmas is a time when you're supposed to forgive people, isn't it?' Tom pursued. 'Wouldn't it be nice if Gloria came round to see you? She could bring her little boy – Maudie and Trev would like that.'

'That's a lovely idea!' Maudie chimed in. 'It would be wonderful to see them. Oh, do say yes!'

Emily was racked with indecision. Secretly, she longed to see Gloria again but she did not want to incur Marcus' displeasure. 'I don't know,' she said, her fingertips flicking her lace collar, dabbing at stray wisps of hair, touching her trembling lips. 'It's true, we should try to be charitable to those who have gone astray, but . . .'

'If Grandma still sees Ruth, why shouldn't you see Gloria?' Tom urged.

'Yes, why shouldn't I?' Suddenly Emily clasped her hands together. 'You're right, it's my duty to offer her an olive-branch – tea, and a slice of fruit-cake. I'll send her an invitation!'

'No need for that. I'll call in and tell her first thing tomorrow,' said Tom. 'I'll ask her to come round for tea on Boxing Day, and bring the little 'un – how about that?'

He was delighted that his aunt had agreed to the idea. The first part of his plan had gone without a hitch, but the second stage would be more difficult.

At the Watermen, the back-room was silent except for the ticking of the clock and the occasional crunch of coals settling in the grate.

'It doesn't seem like Christmas Day, somehow,' said Ruth.

Connor was on the opposite side of the fireplace, seated in the armchair that had been his father's favourite for so many years. They had hoped Mary might persuade Patrick to come downstairs for Christmas dinner, but he refused to leave his bed. In the end, she took up a plate of roast chicken and bread-sauce on a tray, and sat with him while he picked at it, then returned to join her son and daughter-in-law for the rest of the meal downstairs. Now, at the end of the day, she had gone up to bed and they sat alone.

'It's certainly been quiet,' Connor agreed, 'but that's no bad thing.'

'Oh, yes. It wouldn't have seemed right, this year, to have a crowd of people in.'

After a moment, Connor went on, 'I realise this must be harder for you than anyone. I mean – the first Christmas since – well, you know what I'm trying to say.'

She broke in quickly. 'It's the same for all of us. It's your parents I feel sorry for.'

'So do I.' Connor stood up, stretching his arms and legs. 'There was something I meant to say to them, only I never got round to it. It might have cheered them a little, but I could never find the right moment.'

'Oh? What was that?'

He did not reply immediately, but took the letter from behind the clock. Ruth thought he was about to re-read it. Instead, he tore it into small pieces, dropping them into the fire. They flared up and turned to ash in a moment.

'I won't be needing to reply to it now,' he said.

Ruth stared at him. 'What are you saying?'

'I decided to write to the Brewery instead. I'm going to ask if I can take over the pub from the old man.'

'But it was such a wonderful opportunity, training for the World Championship.'

'It was nothing but a silly notion. I've forgotten it already.' Then he chuckled. 'It may be Boxing Day tomorrow, but my boxing days are over . . . I'm going to hang up my gloves and become a publican instead.'

'But *why*?'

'Why not? *A publican and a sinner* – isn't that what the Good book calls it? So you see I'm halfway qualified already . . .' Then his smile faded, and he added gently, 'The other night, when that feller Kleiber came to see you, I couldn't help hearing what you said and it set me thinking. I never realised things were that bad. I never thought of you all having to pack up and move out of the place.'

Ruth rose to her feet. For a moment they stood face to face, gilded by the firelight glow. 'Go upstairs and tell them now,' she said softly. 'Knock at their door and say you've some news for them. I don't think they'll be asleep yet, and they'll sleep all the sounder when they've heard what you have to say.'

After one day's holiday, the dockers went back to work on the 26th of December. Tom put in a full shift, finishing at five o'clock. Night had fallen when he came through the dockyard gates, and fog was eddying round the street-lamps. He was not going home yet; it was time to carry out the second part of his plan.

When he reached Cyclops Wharf, the ship-chandlers was in darkness. He knocked at the door and when there was no response, knocked again, calling out: 'Anyone at home?'

His heart sank. He had made sure that Gloria and the child would be safely out of the way, but it never occurred to him that Saul might have gone out as well.

Then, with relief, he heard shuffling footsteps inside and Saul's voice saying, 'Who's there?'

'It's me, Tom Judge!' he shouted back.

387

After a moment, the door was unlocked and Saul stood there in his shirt and trousers, saying crossly, 'What d'you want?'

'I've got something to say to you,' said Tom. 'It's about my Dad.'

Saul hesitated, then let him in. 'You'd better come up.' When they reached the second-floor kitchen, Saul did not invite Tom to sit down but demanded: 'What's this all about then?'

Tom took a deep breath. This was his chance to set things right: he must not make a mess of it.

'Dad told me about what happened the night Israel Kleiber died,' he said.

Saul sucked at his teeth, considering this, then grunted, 'Oh, he did, did he? Told you it was just an accident, I dare say?'

'Of course it was an accident. Oh, I know it was very wrong what they did – I'm not making excuses for them.' He did not have to admit that the horror of his father's story still haunted his sleep, giving him a recurring nightmare. 'It was wicked, and they deserved to be punished for it.'

'So?' Saul scratched his chin. 'What are you driving at, boy?'

'I think my Dad's been punished enough. You know how he is – he was nearly killed in France. His lungs were poisoned and he's lost an arm.'

'Izzy Kleiber's lungs was full of water, and he lost his life,' retorted Saul. 'I've no sympathy for the men who finished him off.'

'You didn't say that when they asked you to help them. Dad told me – you hid the body, you helped them cover up the crime and they paid you for your trouble. You were in it as deep as anyone.'

'That's a lie! I never knew what they was up to till the man was dead. By then it was too late to save him, so I just – I tried to patch things up, best I could.'

'But that's a crime, too.' Tom held his ground. 'You're as guilty as the rest of them. You daren't go to the police, and you know it.'

'Shut your row! I'm not listening to this!'

'You've got to listen. You've got to stop torturing my Dad.

He can't afford to give you any more money – you must leave him alone. I want you to hand over those things you took – the tally and the claw. Give them back to me and I'll get rid of them, then there'll be a proper end to it.'

Saul uttered a yelp of laughter. 'Think a lot of yourself, don't you? What right have you to come round here, telling me what to do?'

'I'm asking you to have pity on him. Please, give them back.'

'You must be off your head, expecting me to fall for that soft-soap.' Contemptuously, Saul turned away. 'Now get out, and don't show your face here again.'

Tom was breathing faster now, and his heart thumped as he said, 'It's no good, I'm not leaving without them. Gloria will be home soon. She'll want to know why I'm here – what are you going to tell her?'

'*Get out!*' Goaded, Saul lost his temper, rounding on the boy in a sudden fury. 'Get out this minute, or by God you'll be sorry.'

'What are you going to do?' Tom lifted his chin. 'I dare say I'm as strong as you are.'

He was well-built for his age, but Saul was a head taller and Tom stepped back as the older man lunged towards him. Expecting a blow, he brought his arms up to ward it off but Saul took him by surprise, making a grab for his throat.

'Get out, d'you hear me? Before I choke the life out of you . . .'

It was meant as a threat, but when the boy began to struggle he redoubled the pressure on his windpipe. Tom threshed about wildly, clutching at Saul's wrists. Already the blood was rushing to his head and he could feel himself growing dizzy.

Desperately, he fumbled in his pockets, hoping to find a weapon of some sort – something he might use to defend himself – and his fingers closed around a wooden handle. Of course – he had come straight from work, and he was still carrying his claw with him.

'I'll kill you for this!' Saul yelled, and Tom could feel the man's hot, sour breath on his face. 'Kill you! *Kill you!*' And then his eyes opened wide in amazement, and his voice twisted into a scream of pain – and his hands loosened their grip at last.

For a moment, Tom did not realise what had happened. Gasping for air, he staggered back, supporting himself against the kitchen table. He watched as Saul slipped sideways, clawing at the curved steel hooks, driven deep between his ribs. But his strength was running out already, and the blood was running too – dribbling obscenely through the matted hair on his chest, soaking through his shirt, turning it crimson . . .

Only when he fell heavily on the floor, with his eyes staring and the death rattle in his throat, did Tom understand that he had killed him.

Less than a mile away, the Watermen had just opened for business and Ruth was polishing glasses in the saloon.

Connor walked in and glanced round. The holly and paper-chains, the leaping flames in the hearth, the *Merry Christmas* spelled out in glittering tinsel above the bar – all these looked warm and welcoming, but so far there were no customers.

'Think we'll do much business tonight?' he asked.

'Sure to. Give them a few minutes – they'll soon start rolling in,' Ruth told him.

'I certainly hope so.'

She smiled at him. 'I suppose you're taking a special interest, now you're to be our new landlord?'

He looked away uncomfortably. 'There's still some doubt as to that,' he said. 'The Brewery might not take me on.'

'Of course they will! They'd be mad not to.'

He moved away, putting another log on the fire. 'I've been meaning to have a word with you about it,' he said, over his shoulder. 'Seemingly, it's not quite as simple as I thought.'

'Why not?'

He knelt down, busying himself with the fire-irons, sweeping up ashes in the grate, playing for time. 'When I told Mam and Da last night I was going to apply for it, they said there could be a problem,' he mumbled. 'You see, it's not a job for a single man. The Brewery like to have a married couple running a pub.'

'Oh yes, I see. I suppose that's true.' Ruth was at a loss. 'Does this mean you've changed your mind?'

'Not a bit of it. But what it *does* mean . . .' He straightened up, turning towards her. Perhaps it was the heat from the fire that coloured his face. 'I don't know how to say this but, I was thinking – if you're still interested in working here, and if I'm to apply to be the new landlord . . . There's only one answer, so far as I can see.'

He came towards her, his cheeks a dull red. 'Maybe it's too soon to be saying this to you, but . . . well, what I mean is . . . How would it be if I was to ask you to marry me?'

Then the door swung open, and the first customers of the evening came jostling in.

Tom ran down the rickety staircase two at a time, desperate to get out of the house.

During the past few months he had begun to feel so much older, like a grown man, with a job, a future, a girl he loved and planned to marry . . . Now, in a single moment, all that had collapsed and he was a child again.

Sobbing with fear, tripping over his feet, he stumbled down the last few steps and nearly fell. Rushing to the front door, he tugged at the handle, and found that it was locked. He could not think what to do. His brain refused to work – it had been frozen at the moment of Saul's death. Frantically, he rattled the door, beating upon it with his fists. He had to get out, to get away!

Then he saw that the key was in the lock. Saul must have turned it when they went upstairs, to make sure they were not interrupted. Tom threw open the door and tumbled into the street. The key was still in his hand and on a sudden impulse, he locked the door again and dropped the key down a drain. It was as if he had to seal up the house, to conceal the crime and hold off discovery as long as possible.

He took to his heels, and began to run.

The patchy fog was thickening now, and the occasional street-lamps were veiled in hazy circles. Racing along the street, Tom's footsteps set up clattering echoes between the high walls, but the sound of his heartbeats were louder still and more terrifying. He could feel the blood pulsing through his veins – and he remembered the blood streaming over Saul's chest as he lay dying.

He had killed a man. They would hang him if they caught him . . . he had to hide somewhere.

In his haste, he nearly collided with a stone bollard at the end of a narrow alley. It was the short cut through to Jubilee Street

– he had come home from school this way a thousand times, leap-frogging over that bollard. Now he stopped, clutching the damp grey stone.

He could not go home. That was the first place the police would come looking for him. His Mum and Dad could not protect him from the law; he had to go somewhere else. He thought of Maudie, and yearned to be within the safety of her bed, hidden and protected . . . but that was impossible now.

He swerved away, changing direction. Without any clear idea where he was going, he found himself running towards the Wharf, as if he were on his way to work. Then he heard a ship's hooter, muffled by fog, and he knew what he had to do.

A giant freighter was moored alongside the harbour wall and a seaman stood at the foot of the gangway, checking a list in his hands. He glanced up impatiently as Tom stepped out of the mist.

'What time d'you call this?' he demanded angrily. 'You were due here half an hour since.'

Tom tried to speak, but he had no breath left. His chest heaved, and the seaman saw the tear-stains on his face.

'Here, what's up with you?' he said, and took a closer look at him. 'Hang on – you're not on our list, are you?'

Tom shook his head, and managed to blurt out, 'Take me with you.'

'What the hell?' The man frowned. 'Who are you?'

'That don't matter. Just take me along. I got to get away.'

'Trouble, eh?' The seaman looked him up and down. 'No luggage, eh? No papers either, I don't suppose. How old are you, boy?'

Tom lied. 'Seventeen, sir.'

'Been at sea before, have you?'

'No, sir, but I'm quick to learn. I'll do anything you say.'

The man stared at him for some time, then made up his mind. 'You've struck lucky, boy.' He folded up his list, stuffing it into his pocket. 'We're a man short – and we can't wait any longer or we'll miss the tide. Get aboard – we'll talk later.'

Tom ran up the gangplank, and the seaman cupped his hand to his mouth, shouting, 'All present and correct, sir!'

From somewhere high overhead, a voice called down, 'Make ready to cast off, fore and aft!'

Clanking and juddering, a windlass turned on deck and the anchor-chain emerged from black water, scattering spray like diamonds as it was hauled in. Later, when the big ship was heading slowly toward the open sea, Tom stood at the stern, looking back at the misty lights that fell away into the darkness.

He had no home, any more. He could never go home again.

Gloria wrapped little Matt tightly inside her coat, and said to him, 'Your Dad must've gone to sleep. Let's try again.' She hammered on the shop door, calling, 'Saul! Wake up – we're back!'

There was no sound within the old building. Shivering a little, she blamed herself. Why hadn't she thought to take the key with her when she went out to tea? But Saul had said he wouldn't go out this evening – she was sure he would be here to let her in. Where could he have got to? She knocked at the door, calling his name again.

A window in the adjoining house rattled up, and the woman next door hailed her. 'What's up, dearie? Can't you make your husband hear?'

'No. I didn't take a key, and he must've gone out. We'll be catching our death at this rate, me and Matt.'

The child stirred in her arms, and gave a little moan. Gloria shivered again, but it was not the clammy fog that chilled her. She knew that there was something wrong – horribly wrong.

'He's not gone out,' said her neighbour. 'I saw him an hour or two ago, when he came down to let the lad into the shop.'

'Which lad? What do you mean?'

'Your nephew, or whatever he is – young Tommy. I heard him call out, and your husband came down and let him in; then, twenty minutes after, the boy came rushing out like he'd been packed off with a flea in his ear! I saw him running up the street as if the hounds of hell was after him.'

'But Saul didn't go with him?'

'Oh, no, just the boy. Your man's still inside. I should give him another shout.'

Gloria obeyed, calling so loudly that little Matt was frightened and began to cry. But even while she shouted his name, Gloria knew that Saul could not hear her.

'Something wrong, ma'am?'

A sudden flash of light played across the door. Gloria turned, and was dazzled by the beam of a bull's-eye lantern. The local police constable was on his nightly rounds.

'It's my husband. I know he's in, but I can't make him hear,' Gloria explained. 'I went out without a key. I've been calling and calling – I'm afraid he's ill.'

The constable took a turn at knocking and shouting, but without success. At last he said, 'Do you want me to break in?'

Gloria nodded, dumbly. He asked her to stand back, then took a run at the door, putting his shoulder to the lock. It gave way easily and they went inside.

There was a light on the second-floor landing, and Gloria called up the stairs in sudden desperation, 'Saul – it's me!' There was no sound except Matt's cries, muffled under Gloria's coat.

'I'll just see what's going on,' said the policeman. 'You stay down here, ma'am, till I call you.'

He mounted the staircase. Glory waited for a moment then, unable to bear the suspense any longer, hurried up after him.

When she entered the kitchen, the constable tried to stop her, but it was too late. She had already seen her husband's body – his white face and glassy eyes – the crimson stain upon his shirt – the wooden handle of the claw that pierced his heart.

At closing-time, the last customers were leaving the Watermen.

Connor stood at the door, easing them into the street in a manner that was both firm and friendly. 'Good night, Joe. Good night, Lily – sweet dreams! Good night, Henry, Bert. Good night. Good night.'

He closed the door and bolted it. When he turned round, Ruth was standing behind the bar watching him and he said, 'I thought this evening was never going to end. I feel as if I'd been holding my breath all night.'

She gave a shaky laugh. 'Connor, you shouldn't have—'

'I know it! I was over-hasty. I picked the wrong moment, didn't I?'

Automatically, she began to clear dirty glasses from the counter. 'You were worried about the pub, I realised that. You want to make sure the Brewery will agree to your offer.'

'For God's sake, it's not only that!' he burst out.

'It isn't?' She looked up quickly. 'What else, then?'

'I don't know how to tell you this. Maybe I shouldn't be saying it all now, when you're still grieving for Sean. Oh, I'm well aware I can never take his place, but I'll do my best to be a good husband to you, Ruth . . . if you'll give me the chance.'

Before she could reply, there was a knocking at the street door.

'Bloody hell!' Connor exclaimed furiously. 'Are we never to have a minute's peace?' He went to the door, shouting, 'Can't you see the pub's shut? Get off to your own home, will you?'

'Open this door, if you please,' said a deep, penetrating voice. 'I wish to speak to my daughter.'

Connor recognised the voice at once. Even after all this time, the hairs at the back of his neck stirred a little, and he looked over at Ruth. 'Will I let him in?' he asked.

She did not hesitate, but lifted the counter-flap, stepping into the middle of the room with her head held high. 'Please do,' she said.

Connor pulled the bolts, and Marcus Judge walked in.

His coat-collar was turned up against the cold, and a black muffler was knotted about his throat. He wore a broad-brimmed hat of black felt which he swept off, acknowledging Ruth – and he looked more like an Old Testament prophet than ever.

He threw a swift glance at the unfamiliar surroundings, his nostrils flaring at the smell of alcohol and tobacco. Ignoring Connor, he addressed himself to Ruth. 'This evening I learned that your husband met his death recently in France. We must mourn his passing, as we mourn the death of all those loyal Englishmen who gave their lives for this country, but I cannot feel any regret that your marriage is at an end. I never made any secret of my views upon that subject, I think?'

'No, Father, you did not.'

Ruth looked at him steadily, refusing to be intimidated, as he continued, 'Let us give thanks unto the Lord, that in His infinite wisdom, He has freed you from the consequences of your folly. In your blind selfishness, you turned against your own kith and kin. You went in search of false gods, and followed the Roman idolaters . . .'

When Ruth tried to interrupt, he swept aside her protest, his beard bristling and his eyes shining with self-righteous fire. 'Do not despair, my child! As proof of the Almighty's everlasting forgiveness, I have come to tell you that I am prepared to overlook your sin and shame, and to let bygones be bygones. I am ready to take you back into the fold, like a lost sheep that has gone astray, to welcome you into the loving arms of your family – yes, and your child with you.'

It was a powerful oration, delivered with all Marcus' skill as a lay-preacher. When the glasses on the shelf stopped vibrating, Ruth said politely, 'Thank you, Father. It's a generous offer, but I've made other plans.'

He glared at her. 'What do you mean, other plans?'

'I am going to be married again. I should like to introduce you to my future husband – Connor O'Dell.'

She held out her hand, and Connor stepped forward, saying, 'No need for introductions, Ruth. Mr Judge and I met long ago.'

Marcus Judge refused to look at him. Drawing himself up, he turned on his heel and walked out of the pub without another word, and Ruth fell into Connor's arms, laughing and crying at the same time.

She had discovered the truth: a truth she had never dared to face until now. She realised that she had always loved Connor O'Dell.

At their first meeting, she had been thrown into a strange turmoil. Ever since then, she had been pulled this way and that by conflicting emotions – fear, excitement, anger, affection and trust – and at the heart of all these things was the strong, overpowering magnetism that had drawn her to him again and again. In his arms at last, she knew she had found what she had always wanted.

His lips were close to hers, and his sea-green eyes looked deep into her own as he said huskily, 'You're certainly full of surprises . . . D'you think maybe we should go upstairs and tell the old folk our good news?'

The O'Dells were delighted by the announcement of Connor's engagement to Ruth, but their rejoicing was touched with sadness.

They still mourned the loss of Sean, and a suitable time had to elapse before Ruth could decently re-marry. After some discussion with Father Riley, it was decided that the wedding should not take place until six months after the death of her first husband, and a date was fixed for the beginning of May.

There was sadness, too, at Connor's departure when he returned to his regiment, awaiting his discharge from the Army. This was especially difficult for Ruth; it seemed that she had no sooner accepted him than she had to say goodbye to him again. When she went to see him off on the troop-train at Victoria Station, she felt he was still a stranger to her.

He kissed her once, formally, before stepping into the railway-carriage. She knew he was trying to pay respect to her status as a widow, and she appreciated that, but when the train steamed out she walked slowly back along the platform, feeling lost and very lonely.

And inevitably, the events at Cyclops Wharf overshadowed everything.

As soon as Ruth heard that Saul was dead, she hurried over to see Gloria and found that the ship-chandlers had closed and was about to be put up for sale.

It was a mercy that, on the very evening Saul died, Gloria and Emily had been reconciled.

At that time, when she had nowhere else to go, Gloria returned to her mother and moved back to her old room over the corner shop. Slowly, she came to terms with her situation. Slowly, the horror of Saul's death would fade, and she would begin to re-build her life. Upon the sale of the property, she would come into a little money, and she was determined to bring Matt up to be a credit to the family.

She found an unexpected ally in Maudie. Despite the difference in their ages, the two women had a great deal in common. Both of them were tragically widowed and both had a small son to care for. There was one real difference between them. Although Glory often talked of Saul, harking back to their life together, Maudie hardly ever referred to Arnold. Clearly, she was suffering intense grief, and Gloria decided it must be the kind of grief that lay too deep for words.

For several weeks Maudie remained in a state of shock. Only Ruth had some inkling of her true feelings, but when she tried to express her sympathy Maudie turned away, changing the subject. It was something she could not bring herself to talk about.

There was never any doubt that Tom had been responsible for Saul's death. He was seen running away from the scene of the crime, and his claw – the tool of his trade – was used as the weapon.

The police hunted him without success. A description of Thomas Judge was circulated throughout East London, and then further afield – but the boy was never found, and eventually the search was called off.

One evening, when Emily and Maudie were washing up the tea-things, Emily glanced at the pendant round the girl's neck, and frowned. 'It might be as well not to wear that any more, dear. It's hardly suitable, is it?'

'What do you mean?'

'The pendant he gave you. Oh, I know you never realised, but I couldn't help noticing – that young man was getting too fond of you, Maudie. In some ways, it may be a blessing in disguise he's gone. If I were you, I'd put that away – throw it in the dustbin. It's not worth anything.'

Maudie bent her head, staring at the soapy water in the sink. When she spoke, her voice was so low, Emily could hardly hear her.

'It's worth a lot to me . . . I told him I'd wear it always – I can't ever break my promise.'

*

Gradually, the British Army were brought home from overseas, returning to civilian life.

Joshua Judge came back, to the great joy of his wife and children, but there was no general celebration within the family, still recovering from Saul's death and Tom's disappearance.

Marcus shook his hand and told him that the Brotherhood would be proud to take him back into their ranks as soon as he chose to resume his duties at the Wharf.

When Josh went round to Jubilee Street to visit his brother, both men were taken aback, each thinking how much the other had changed.

Josh looked down at Ebenezer, twisted up in his chair, crippled in mind and body – and did not know what to say. Eb looked up at Joshua and felt a sudden surge of bitterness. How dare his brother come back from the war, hale and hearty, without a scratch on him?

As they shook hands, Eb caught a whiff of alcohol on Josh's breath. 'You've been drinking,' he gasped. 'Reek of the barroom. Father will have something to say about that!'

'What Father don't know won't hurt him.' Josh spread himself out on the sofa. 'Yes, I took to beer, out in France. It was the only thing that kept us going. Don't worry – I'll suck peppermints when Father's about.'

'He'll find out, all the same. He finds out most things.' Painfully, with long pauses for breath, Eb told his brother the story of Saul's blackmail – and Josh's florid complexion turned muddy.

'The bastard,' he said at last. 'Well, at least it's over. He can't do us any more harm where he's gone!' Unbuttoning his waistcoat, he scratched his paunch. 'Sorry to hear about young Tommy, though. Bad business, that.'

'You were the lucky one,' snarled Eb. 'Well out of it. It cost me my son, that did, and most of my savings too, covering up for the pair of us. I reckon you should see me right – out of your discharge gratuity.'

'Well, now, I don't know so much about that,' began Josh uneasily.

'I do!' There was bile in Eb's mouth as he panted, 'Unless you want – Father to find out – how Israel Kleiber died?'

400

'You wouldn't tell him!' Joshua's jaw sagged.

'Wouldn't I?' It was a long while since Eb had tasted power, and he was going to relish it. 'Just you try me!'

'Seems strange not to be in uniform,' said Connor. He had come home, too, wearing his own clothes for the first time in over four years.

'It's like the end of a bad dream,' Ruth told him.

He walked towards her, and she thought he was about to put his arms round her, but then he changed his mind, taking her hands instead.

'It's good to be back,' he told her, kissing her lightly on the cheek.

'Yes. You'll be wanting to take over the reins here now, I dare say? I'll go through the books with you whenever you like.'

'I'm in no hurry. You know the job ten times better than me. I'd just as soon take over gradually.'

In any case, Patrick and Mary were to remain in charge, nominally, until the wedding-day so, for a few more weeks, life went on much as before.

One bright April morning in 1919, Connor took a step-ladder into the street to clean the front windows. Ruth brought him out a mug of coffee to lighten his labours, and as she handed it up to him, she saw a familiar figure crossing the road. It was familiar, but so much older . . . Louisa Judge's hair was quite white now, and her shoulders were bent, as if she had carried the burden of her family's troubles for too many years.

'Ruth, I must talk to you,' she began.

'I'm so glad to see you, Mum.' Ruth hugged her, then took her into the empty saloon bar. 'I've been hoping you might call in. I want you to meet my fiancé – I suppose Father told you?'

'Not directly. He was very angry when he came home that night, but I heard about it in a roundabout way through the neighbours gossiping.'

'I'm sorry. I should have written and told you myself.'

'It wouldn't have done any good. He'd only have torn up the letter.'

Connor abandoned his window-cleaning, following them indoors. Ruth introduced them, and they shook hands.

Louisa looked at him, and for a moment the lines of anxiety on her face softened into a smile. 'I remember you,' she said. 'You came to our house once, when you were on the coal-cart.'

'I did so, ma'am,' Connor agreed. 'I was anxious for your daughter then – and now I hope to take good care of her.'

'I believe you will,' said Louisa. Then her brief smile faded as she turned back to Ruth. 'I'm sorry to trouble you with my problems, but I didn't know who else I could turn to. I'm so worried about your father. He's been acting very strangely lately.'

'How do you mean, strangely?' Ruth chose her words carefully, trying to spare her mother's feelings. 'He's never been an easy man – we both know that.'

'He's a difficult man, I've never denied it, but now . . . He had to work so hard all through the war, and so many terrible things have happened. I'm afraid he's not quite in his right mind.'

Ruth saw that she was trembling and tried to help her into a chair, but the old lady refused. 'No thank you, dear. I mustn't stay long . . . but I had to tell you. He's become so vindictive against his own family. You remember the big Bible at home?'

Ruth nodded. The family Bible had been at the centre of her childhood: as long as she could remember, she and her brothers had been forced to swear oaths of loyalty or truthfulness upon its heavy black covers – and she knew that it was used for the same purpose at meetings of the Brotherhood.

'Well, he's going to take it to a meeting tomorrow night. He says there are certain members of the family who have disgraced us and he is going to strike their names out of the book for ever.'

Ruth stared at her mother, lost for words. There were half a dozen generations of Judges recorded upon the fly-leaves of that Bible; every time a new child was born, its name and date of birth were solemnly entered. Year by year, the list grew longer. When someone died, the date of death was added – but no name had ever been removed from the family archives.

'I tried to talk to him. I tried to make him see it wasn't right,

402

but he wouldn't listen.' Ruth saw tears shining in her mother's eyes. As she went on talking, they brimmed over, trickling down her wrinkled cheeks. 'That Bible is precious to me – to all of us – because the family is precious. What he's going to do is wrong, terribly wrong, only I can't make him see it. Isn't there anything we can do to stop him, before it's too late?'

The gas-jets hissed in the wall-brackets, as Marcus Judge rose to his feet and announced, 'It is with much pleasure that I welcome back our Brother Joshua into the Inner Circle of this Guild.'

An approving murmur ran round the table. Joshua, red-faced and jovial, grinned modestly from his place at his father's right hand.

'It gives me particular pleasure to see him here tonight, taking his rightful place among us, for he has passed close to the gates of Hell, and in God's boundless mercy he was spared. I need hardly say that I take a special pride in him, since he is my son – and he has proved himself in every way to be a worthy member of our Brotherhood – a valiant soldier, bearing the Cross.'

A little spatter of applause broke out, but Marcus raised his hand, and they fell silent.

'Joshua's return is one of the reasons that I summoned you here tonight, but I am sorry to tell you – there is another, unhappier reason.'

The men around the semi-circular table shuffled uneasily.

'Not all the members of my family have been worthy of praise. There have even been certain members of this Brotherhood who have brought sin and shame upon us all.'

He paused, then lowered his voice. Although it sank to a low rumble, every syllable was crystal-clear. 'I must tell you now that word has reached me, by way of a cargo-ship newly arrived from the United States of America, that a certain Brother of our Guild has begun a new life out there. That young man committed a vile crime before he left us, and that is why his name must be struck out of this Bible, to ensure that we tear him from our hearts and minds evermore.'

403

Marcus took up his pen, and dipped it into a small bottle of Indian ink. 'There are three names which must be removed – three sinners to be cast into eternal darkness, for the wages of sin is death everlasting. I hereby blot out the name of my grandson, Thomas Judge, of my nephew, Saul Judge and of my daughter, Ruth Judge – who are no longer worthy to be members of this—'

Then the door burst open. Suddenly there was a blaze of evening sunlight and a gust of fresh air that ruffled the papers on the table and fluttered the pages of the Bible.

'Put down your pen,' said Connor.

Marcus stood as if turned to stone, completely at a loss, as Connor crossed the room in four long strides.

'And don't touch the book,' he added.

Some of the Inner Circle gasped and muttered. Others protested, starting to rise, but Connor threw a warning glance around the table and they slumped back.

'Some of you here might remember me,' he said pleasantly. 'The name's Connor O'Dell, and I've been here before – but this time I'm not wearing a hood and my hands aren't tied. I don't have any weapon to defend myself, either, but I've got a pair of fists that serve me pretty well.'

Before Marcus could stop him, he picked up the Bible, adding: 'This is what I came for – nothing else.'

At Marcus' side, Joshua struggled to his feet, leaning across the table to make a grab for the book. Connor's response was like lightning. Cradling the Bible along his left forearm, he brought his right fist up from nowhere, and Joshua's chair overturned as he went sprawling across the floor.

'How dare you!' began Marcus, in a voice of thunder.

'It's not too difficult,' retorted Connor, 'but then I don't try to play God with other people. You can't wipe these names out, Mr Judge. This isn't a book of death – it's a book of life.'

Taking the Bible with him, he walked out into the golden evening.

The wedding took place on the first Saturday in May.

As Mr and Mrs Connor O'Dell were to take up their duties

as landlord and landlady of the Watermen immediately, there was to be no honeymoon.

The ceremony had gone off without a hitch, followed in the afternoon by the wedding breakfast, which was attended by a small number of close friends and family. At opening time, the pub welcomed customers as usual, and Connor and Ruth worked happily all the evening, side by side in the saloon bar.

It was nearly midnight by the time they had cleared away and tidied up, ready for the morning. Ruth led the way upstairs, walking into Connor's room, which now contained a double bed.

She sat at the dressing-table and began to unpin her hair, letting it fall loosely round her shoulders. In the mirror, she saw Connor standing uncertainly in the doorway.

'What's the matter?' she asked. 'Did we forget something?'

'Oh, no.' He took a step into the room, saying quietly, 'I just thought I'd come in and say good night.'

She turned, looking at him in bewilderment. 'What do you mean?'

'I don't want to embarrass you.' He spoke carefully, as if he were testing every word. 'I know it's still too soon – that's why I thought I should sleep in the spare room. No need for Mam and Da to know about it,' he added quickly. 'I wake at the crack of dawn – I'll be up and about before they're stirring.'

Ruth looked away, and came face to face with her own reflection in the glass. She was a widow of twenty-four, no longer the fresh young girl she had been when they first met.

'So that's it,' she said at last. 'I understand now. You had to have a wife in order to get the pub. Well, that makes good sense.'

'So it does.' He nodded a couple of times. 'But I'll not bother you with – anything else. Not till you feel – comfortable with me.'

'I'm comfortable enough,' she said wearily. 'I'm sure we'll get along very well. I've always – liked you. You know that.'

'That's a lie!' Stung, he contradicted her. 'For a while there, you hated my guts. You made that clear enough!'

'I never did!'

'You only threw a word to me now and then, like you'd throw

405

a bone to a dog, because you were in love with Sean and you had to be civil to his brother!'

'Not at all! It was you detested me, from the word go. The night we met, you told me to go to Hell.'

'I never said any such thing!'

'As good as!' She sprang up, suddenly furious. 'You wouldn't stay two minutes in the same room with me. You ran out of the house as soon as you could, and went off on your travels. You couldn't stand the sight of me!'

'I couldn't stand to see you in his arms!' The confession spilled out of him before he could stop himself. 'I was in love with you before you ever married my brother, so what else could I do?'

He took a deep breath, then added gruffly. 'Well, now you know. I didn't mean to tell you – and I won't go on pestering you, I promise you that. Goodnight, Ruth.'

He was walking out of the room when she called his name. 'Connor . . . will you come back, please?'

She began to unbutton her blouse. He stood and watched her, transfixed.

'I've loved you from that very first evening, only I didn't know it,' she said softly. 'And you can pester me whenever you want to.'

Slowly, he came back into the room, closing the door behind him, gazing at her as she continued to undress. When she was naked, she turned and held out her arms to him. He picked her up as if she were a child, and carried her to the bed.

The ways of love were gentle and tender. The movements of love came so easily, they might have been created for one another. The rhythms of love were deep and strong, overpowering them with passion, revealing a world that they had never known . . .

And at last the words of love came, as a blessing upon their marriage.

'I love you,' he said.

'I love you,' she said.